PRAISE FOR
CROAK

"Go ahead and die laughing, knowing that the safe transport of your mortal soul will be the summer job of a sweetheart teen with godlike power and discipline problems. A lot of books make me wish I could live within their pages, but I wouldn't mind dying in this one." —Adam Rex, author of *Fat Vampire*

"Creepy and hilarious." —*VOYA,* 4Q, 5P

"Funny and fresh. . . . Fantasy fans who like their tales gritty and filled with irreverent humor will be eager for the follow-up." —*Kirkus Reviews*

"The morbid subject matter is kept in check by entertaining characters, clever twists, and a sly, self-aware sense of humor." —*Publishers Weekly*

"Damico nicely balances the grim subject matter with a heavy dose of humor. . . . An intricate and imaginative construction of the afterlife that is as amusing as it is unique." —*The Bulletin*

"Teens looking for something new will find this scythe-swinging debut novel to die for. . . . [A] wacky, highly entertaining new series." —*Booklist*

"Creative details, sarcastic humor, and quick-witted dialogue makes *Croak* rise above other stories of its type." —*SLJ*

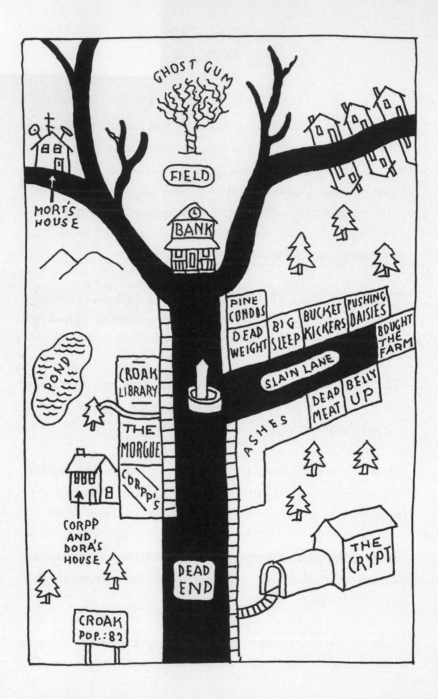

SCORCH

GINA DAMICO

G RAPHIA

Houghton Mifflin Harcourt
Boston New York

Graphia and the Graphia logo are trademarks of
Houghton Mifflin Harcourt Publishing Company.

www.hmhco.com

Text set in Garamond Premier Pro

Library of Congress Cataloging-in-Publication Data
Damico, Gina.
Scorch / by Gina Damico.
p. cm.
Summary: Sixteen-year-old grim reaper Lex Bartleby tries to redeem herself among
her fellow Grims by finding a renegade reaper who is indiscriminately damning souls.
ISBN 978-0-547-62457-0 (pbk.)
[1. Death—Fiction. 2. Future life—Fiction. 3. Humorous stories.] I. Title.
PZ7.D1838Sco 2012
[Fic]—dc23
2012014799

Manufactured in the United States of America
DOC 10 9 8 7 6 5 4 3
4500479904

To Will, who added an exclamation point.

ACKNOWLEDGMENTS

I must once again give much love to my agent, Tina Wexler, who is not only an inspiration, cheerleader, and all-around great person, but who also gets very angry and threatens to disown me when bad stuff happens to my characters, which just goes to show how much she cares. And much love to my editor, Julie Tibbott, as well, for her continued awesomeness and advice on how to make a better book, and also for not disowning me when I threw hot apple cider at her.

Thank you to the team at Houghton Mifflin Harcourt: Jenny Groves, Carol Chu, Jen LaBracio, Peter Bohan, Mary Huot, Sarah Sherman, and Maxine Bartow. You all deserve a ticker-tape parade, and I will get right on that as soon as I figure out how to rent out Fifth Avenue.

Thanks to my family, for their continued love and support, and to my extended family, for the polite yet baffled smiles they give me when I tell them what my books are about. Also to my friends, whose generous understanding that I couldn't *possibly* come to your party, I have a *book* to write . . . is much appreciated.

I'd also like to give a shout-out to the faculty of my high school, CBA, especially Eugene Moretti and Bob Caraher. Thank you so much for inspiring creativity among those of us who ran screaming from baseballs and other deadly athletic projectiles.

To the awesomesauce YA community, especially all you tireless bloggers and librarians out there — keep doing what you're doing! Don't stop believin'! Save a horse, ride a cowboy! And so forth. Plus a very special thanks to the Apocalypsies, an outstanding group of debut authors I forgot to thank in my first book, which I do believe is a federal crime and should land me in prison. They are wonderful writers and even more wonderful people, and their support has been invaluable. You should read all of their books.

More heaping thanks to Melissa Carubia, John Fraley, Brendan Mulhern, and Dave Green for their musical devilry, and to *MST3K,* ABC's old TGIF lineup, mayonnaise, and that cool website that can map out distances between random places, without which an entire chapter of this book would not exist.

To Will, the ole husband, for not only being generally amazing but also for making our house livable and putting up curtains and topping our Christmas tree with a sombrero, all while his useless wife does nothing but type and stare off into space and leave dirty mugs all over the place.

And finally, thanks once again to you, dear readers, for picking up this book. It was quite brave of you, seeing as how the pages are coated with POISON. Enjoy!

SCORCH

Carl Scutner wondered, for a brief moment, what it would feel like to punt his wife off a cliff.

"Would you shut up in there?" he yelled from the sofa. Between the noisy construction crew down the street, the whimpers coming from the dog cage that sat in the corner, and the pots and pans his wife was banging around in the kitchen, the baseball game on television had become nearly inaudible. "Jesus Christ, I can't hear myself think!"

Lydia appeared at the kitchen doorway. "Like there's anything worth hearing in that so-called brain of yours."

"Woman, I swear to God..."

"Here." She handed him a fresh beer and sat on the edge of a hideous orange chair, its matted fabric dingy and stained. "Cubs losing?"

Carl let out a belch. "As usual."

Lydia looked down. Crumpled fast food wrappers littered the floor. A glob of ketchup had leaked onto the carpet. As the construction noises down the street grew louder, so too did the whimpers from the cage. She glanced at the telephone, then couldn't stop staring at it. Her breaths became shallow.

"They haven't called, Carl."

He took a drag from his cigarette. "They'll call."

"You always say that. You're not always right."

"Lydia. They'll call."

"They better," she said, wringing her hands. "I don't want to do *that* again."

"It's up to them, not us. You know that."

Lydia picked through her mousy hair with a trembling hand. She shot a resentful glance at her husband and his ever-expanding beer gut, then sniffed the air. "It smells like shit in here."

"It *is* shit."

Lydia looked at the dog cage, into the big brown eyes staring back at her. "Maybe we should let him out for a little while."

"Are you kidding me? The last one got halfway down the driveway before I caught him." He took a swig of beer. "You're getting sloppy."

"I'm just — " She stopped and looked around. "Did you hear that?"

"Hear what?"

She listened. "I thought maybe — the back door — "

"Alarm system's on." He stubbed out his cigarette on the arm of the sofa. "Would you knock it off? You should be used to this by now."

Unnerved, Lydia grabbed his empty beer bottle and walked into the kitchen. "At least let me feed the poor thing."

Carl gestured at the bowl of kibble on the floor. "He's fine. Too fat as he is, if you ask me."

Four things happened next.

The construction crew grew louder, so Carl grabbed the remote and turned up the volume as high as it could go. This just so happened to coincide with a home run, which prompted Carl to let loose with a torrent of obscenities.

And so, as the living room erupted into a sustained cacophony, Carl never heard the bottle shatter on the kitchen floor. He never heard his wife's tortured screams. And he certainly never heard the intruder enter the living room; in fact, he didn't even realize she was there until she was right in front of him, her eyes peeking out from beneath a black hood, her nose almost touching his.

"Hello, Mr. Scutner," she said, extending a thin, pale finger. "Goodbye, Mr. Scutner."

||||||

"I'm sorry you had to see that," she said a few moments later, opening the door to the dog cage. "Are you okay?"

The little boy inside nodded his head, his eyes blurred with tears. She took his hand and led him across the living room, careful not to let him get too close to the scorching remains of his captors.

"I have to go now," she said, grabbing a phone and dialing 911. "But I need you to be brave and do one thing for me." She handed him the phone. "Just tell them who you are and that you're at fifty-one Forest Drive. Then go sit out on the front steps. Can you do that?"

He wiped his nose and nodded.

"Good boy. And don't tell anyone I was here." She smiled and raised something that looked like a knife. "It'll be our little secret."

||||||

The news reports that aired later that night were confusing, to say the least. A married couple by the name of Carl and Lydia Scutner were found dead in their home, victims of an apparent murder-suicide. All evidence pointed to the fact that they were the suspects the police had been hunting for a while now, the monsters responsible for kidnapping and holding for ransom at least a dozen children from the suburbs of Chicago over the past six months. Small, fresh mounds of dirt in the backyard indicated that a few of those children had never been returned.

No cameras were allowed inside the house. Too gruesome, the police said.

The little boy was clearly still in shock. The descriptions he gave of what had happened — the Scutners bursting into flames almost instantly, without burning a single other item in the house, only to self-extinguish a few minutes later — were too ridiculous to be taken seriously. The police smiled politely at his tales and ruffled his hair, while his parents were so overcome with relief that they barely listened to a word he said. And the media, clearly of the opinion that children should be seen and not heard, were perfectly content to snap photo after photo of the adorable tear-stained lad, yanking the microphone out of his face the moment he started to embarrass them with talk of spontaneous magical fires.

No one listened to him. And it was about that time that the child realized why the girl had told him to remain silent: because no one would have believed him anyway.

Who would have believed that his savior was merely a teenage girl wearing jeans and a plain black hoodie? Who would have

believed that she simply appeared inside the house, set the Scutners ablaze with nothing more than a jab of her finger, and then
disappeared just as quickly?

No one.

And so he kept the little secret.

2

"Looks like Zara's at it again," the old bat's voice crackled.

Lex ignored this jolly piece of news and stared out the car window at the blurring foliage of the Adirondacks. The leaves were just beginning to change — a few splotches of yellow, a speckle or two of red. Though a chill had settled in the air, she had opened her window far wider than just a crack, and neither the loud gusts of wind nor the occasional chattering of teeth issuing forth from the passengers stuffed into the tiny back seat had prompted her to close it.

"Keep it down, Pandora," Lex's uncle replied into his Cuff, the staticky, ether-infused communications device around his wrist. "I've got rookies in the car. Don't freak them out any sooner than we have to."

"But this is getting ridiculous!" the voice rasped back through the Cuff. "First those mail bombers in Houston, then that rapist in Nebraska. Now kidnappers in Chicago! Ever since that little snake found herself a new scythe, she's been going hog-wild!" There was a pause. "I guess we should count our lucky stars she hasn't come after us."

"Count our lucky stars? She found a scythe, Dora. Which means she also found an ally."

"Which means," Pandora added, "that once again, we're screwed eight ways from Sunday."

They exchanged a few more words before hanging up. Uncle

Mort glanced at Lex's twitching eye, then turned his attention back to the road and absent-mindedly ran his finger up and down the scar across his face. "You okay?"

This was precisely the forty-third time since they had left her parents' house in Queens that Uncle Mort had asked her this. Lex had been keeping track.

"I don't know, are *you* okay?" she shot back, also for the forty-third time.

After her twin sister's funeral in New York City, Lex and Uncle Mort had gotten back in his cheddar yellow '74 Gremlin and taken off on a road trip to fetch the rookies. And ever since they left, Lex had turned into such a jittery pile of nerves that she'd chewed through no less than fifty packs of gum. The constant supply of truck-stop coffees probably wasn't helping, either.

She just couldn't turn off her brain. It toiled and hummed like a factory, ceaselessly churning out worries and concerns and the dreaded what-ifs. It never quit — not when they stopped for food, not when they'd gained two new passengers, not even when she slept. Or didn't sleep, in her case. Most nights she just stared at the dingy hotel ceilings and picked at her long, dark hair, replaying what had happened, worrying about her sister, wondering what would happen now that they were almost back in Croak.

In the car, she began compulsively flicking the cheap plastic lighter decorated with a skull and crossbones that Uncle Mort had bought her at a truck stop somewhere in Ohio. She was thankful that they were together, at least; Uncle Mort could be a pain sometimes, but in the way she imagined an older brother would be — annoying, but protective. And with the added benefit of being a total badass.

He ran a hand through his black, electrocution-style hair, then shot her another concerned look and leaned over. "Do you need to stop?" he said in a quieter voice, in a tone that suggested he wasn't talking about urinary demands.

"No." Lex shrank in her seat a little. "I . . . discharged back in Buffalo."

"Good girl. Should only be another hour or so, okay?"

Lex sank farther into her standard-issue, thermoregulated black hoodie and pulled the hood over her head. The thought of having to discharge — even the ugliness of the word itself — made her feel so *diseased*. Fittingly, a hospital flew by her window just then, its stark concrete façade mocking her copious dysfunctions.

She thought back to where she'd been nearly three months earlier: on her way to Croak for the first time with a rap sheet so long and terrible that her fed-up parents had decided to send her away for the summer to live with her uncle, in the hopes that he'd straighten her out. Of course, they'd had no idea that his idea of straightening her out meant informing her that she was a Grim and proceeding to give her a crash course on how to reap mortal souls. Not exactly the kind of thing one can describe in a pamphlet.

It had started out so well, though. For the first time in years, Lex made friends; hell, she even snagged a boyfriend. And true, she didn't agree with everything the Grimsphere stood for — letting murderers go free without punishment was at the top of her list, and she'd had more than a few urges to deliver her own idea of justice — but overall, it was turning out to be the best summer of her life.

Until it all turned into a steaming pile of crap. The abnormal abilities that at first had turned her into the best Killer in Croak soon morphed into something much more sinister: the ability to Damn souls, a foul, unspeakable act that resulted in everlasting torment. And before she could even figure this out for herself, Zara — a fellow Junior, a Grim-in-training — jumped right in to twist it to her own advantage. Not only did Zara murder almost a hundred people under the radar all summer long, but she also devised a way to Cull Lex's Damning ability for herself.

She did this by using Lex's twin sister, Cordy, as bait.

And Lex had fallen for it.

That wave of nausea arose yet again. Lex bent over to pick through the bag at her feet, her sister's old backpack. In it sat a few clothes and Cordy's old stuffed octopus, Captain Wiggles, along with two items Uncle Mort had invented just for Lex: a Lifeglass — an hourglass-shaped device that stored and recorded all her memories — and a Spark, a flickering glass bulb that measured her life force. The Spark he'd made for Cordy was in there too, although it was just a bright, glowing ball now —

Lex gulped another breath, sat back up, and closed her eyes. *This drive will be over soon,* she told herself. *You'll be home.*

Because despite everything that had happened, Croak *was* still her home, and she loved it. The quaint streets, the rolling hills, the complete and utter lack of a Starbucks — all the things that she'd initially hated about the small town, she now missed with a burning passion. Being a Grim, traveling through the mind-numbing space that was the ether, Killing targets, delivering their souls to the Afterlife — it was what she was born to do, and Croak was where she belonged.

It was the citizens in it that were the problem. Very soon she'd have to face the townspeople, whom she hadn't seen since Uncle

Mort had whisked her out of town two weeks earlier. What could she possibly say to everyone? They must hate her for letting Zara escape with the ability to Damn whomever she wanted, wherever she wanted.

Still, she'd get to go back to the job she loved. She'd get to see Driggs and be kept up until two in the morning by his incessant drumming. She'd get to see her friends.

Friends that she'd be putting in danger. And it wasn't as if things were going back to the way they were. She'd have to be on her guard at all times. She'd have to control her vengeful urges even more vigilantly now. She'd have to find Zara and stop her.

And she'd have to see Cordy.

Lex anxiously shoved the lighter into her pocket. She couldn't avoid her sister forever. Cordy was waiting for her, just on the other side of the great hereafter, and by now had undoubtedly learned that she was dead because her dumbass sister had been too stupid to realize she was being manipulated. Lex didn't know what to expect. A cold, unloving stare? The silent treatment? The angriest bitch slap of all time?

Lex grabbed the handle and cranked the window down as far as it could go. She stuck her head out into the frigid air, letting the wind sting at her face, futilely hoping to numb her thoughts.

|||||||

Her friends were waiting for her, sitting atop the fountain at the center of town. They were hard to miss; Ferbus's orange hair stood out like a traffic cone, and Elysia's blond ponytail caught the sun as she climbed up onto the fountain's ledge to get a better look at the car — though she was so short, it didn't make much of a difference. Ferbus stood too, rolling up the newspaper he'd been reading. And Driggs —

Driggs was lying on the ledge, staring at the sky. At the sound of the engine, his head flopped to the side and followed the car as it made its way down Dead End. He barely moved.

Lex rolled up her window with shaking hands. By the time the car came to a stop in front of the fountain, her body felt as if it was about to snap apart at the seams.

Uncle Mort glanced at the welcoming committee, then back at Lex. "You ready for this, kiddo?"

"Do I have a choice?"

He gave her a sympathetic smile as she clambered out of the car. "That's the spirit."

"Lex!" Elysia squealed, jumping to embrace her in an epic bear hug. "Oh my God, we missed you so much! Ow!" Ferbus had pinched her. "What?"

"Let her breathe," he said as Elysia detached herself. "Hi, Lex."

Lex couldn't even muster a response. Elysia's contagious zeal usually had a way of making terrible things seem not so terrible after all, but it wasn't working this time. Lex wrung her clammy hands, her anxiety heightened by this deluge of undeserved love. Didn't they know what she'd done? Didn't they realize how much danger they were in by even being in the same zip code as her? She didn't even want to *look* at Driggs . . .

Of course, she had to. There he was, just as she had left him, her imperfectly adorable partner with that messy coffee-colored hair, those mismatched eyes — one brown, one blue. Her brain spun into overdrive. Did he even care that she was back? He was looking at her with an unreadable expression. Was it a sneer? Was he mad?

Her face was doing that weird twitching thing again, so she looked away. The last thing she wanted was for Driggs to realize that he was now in a relationship with a spastic robot. He inched to her side, wordlessly hooked his pinkie finger through hers, and gave it a squeeze.

But he didn't say anything.

Uncle Mort exited the car, frowning. "Ferb, Lys, what are you doing here?"

Elysia threw a nervous glance at the library. "We didn't really have a choice."

"But you know the drill—you're not supposed to meet your new partners until training."

A muffled burst of sound came from within the library. Someone peeked out from behind the blinds, then disappeared as soon as the Juniors looked over.

"What are they like?" Elysia said. She squinted at the two-door, where the rookies were trying desperately to free themselves from the back seat.

"Dumb, right?" said Ferbus. "Scared? Liable to get us in even more trouble than we're already in?" He shot a bitter glance at the library.

"Go easy on them, okay?" Uncle Mort said, following Ferbus's gaze with a hint of suspicion. Ferbus and Elysia had spent the past year guarding the Afterlife, but now that rookies were arriving, it was their job to train them as Killers and Cullers—much to Elysia's delight and Ferbus's dismay.

"I'll try," said Ferbus. "But I anticipate suckitude."

"Um, hello?" A trapped voice came from the car.

Uncle Mort sighed. "Fine. Introductions today means more time for training tomorrow. Give me a minute to pry them out of there." He walked back to the car and started to wrestle down the tricky front seats. He'd confided in Lex that some of the towns-people thought he was nuts for bringing new kids into a such an unstable and dangerous environment, but firm believer in the Junior Grim program that he was, he had summed up his reply with one rude flip of a finger.

Elysia leaned in to Lex. "I still can't believe he let you go with him."

Ferbus let out a snort. "What's so hard to believe? The man would let her blow up the moon if she wanted to. And she prob-ably does."

Lex narrowed her eyes, but was still too rattled to think of a good comeback. And Driggs didn't even jump to her defense. Odd.

It didn't matter, as Elysia could always be counted on to fill a silence. "But Mort's never taken *anyone* with him on his annual trip to fetch the rookies. No Juniors, no Seniors, not even anyone who's retired. Was it cool, Lex?"

"Of course it was cool," Ferbus said. "I remember when he got me — just picked me up, like I had called for a taxi." He glared at Elysia. "Imagine my disappointment when we fetched *you* next."

"Shut up, Ferb."

Uncle Mort let out a triumphant yell as he finally collapsed the front seat. The Juniors' eyes flew to the car.

First to bound out of it was a boy with dirty-blond hair and a seemingly unlimited cache of pent-up energy. His gaze darted about maniacally, not settling on anything for more than a sec-ond or two. Though he stood not much taller than Elysia, a set of sturdy muscles sliding beneath his skin suggested a hidden, tena-cious strength. And a flicker of jumpiness seemed to compel his every motion, as if he might run off to scamper up the nearest tree at any given moment. Indeed, everything about him — the quick movements, his nimble hands, the way he even seemed to be sniffing the air — led to the overall impression of a peppy little squirrel.

His counterpart, on the other hand, resembled less a rodent than a large, flightless bird. A lanky girl of Indian descent, she slipped out of the car in total silence and hardly moved, the very portrait of someone who had recently been blindsided by a particularly cruel blitz of puberty. The kid was all angles; she didn't seem to know how to stand or what to do with her limbs or how best to hide her knobby knees. Poker-straight black hair hung down to her waist, and a curtain of thick bangs nearly covered her eyes, though not completely. Massive, round, and wavering somewhere between blue and green, they popped so radiantly against the darkness of her skin that her stare seemed electrified.

Eventually she settled into a dejected stance, hugging a book to her chest and rocking nervously from side to side. "I got a two-for-one deal," Uncle Mort told the Juniors. "Foster kids from the same family. Can you believe it?"

"Where are we?" the boy said. "Is this the town? Who are they?" He began to hop from foot to foot. "What are we doing here? Aren't you going to tell us? Didn't he say he was going to tell us?" he asked the girl, who didn't move.

"Good Lord, kid," Uncle Mort said over his questions. "No more sodas for you."

"I only had three!"

"Like they made a difference," Uncle Mort told the Juniors under his breath. "Intrinsically buoyant, that one."

Ferbus stared in wonder. "He's like a bag of microwave popcorn."

Driggs finally spoke, his voice equally amazed. "But popcorn tends to stop popping after a couple minutes. He's . . . still going."

"Are we in the Adirondacks? Where are we staying? Do we need money? How—"

"Zip it, jumping bean." Uncle Mort took the boy by the shoulders to still him. "All will be explained shortly. For now, meet Ferbus, Elysia, and Driggs."

The boy nodded at each of them. "Hi. Hi. Hi."

"Kids, meet the new rookies." He prodded the boy. "Go ahead, introduce yourselves."

"I'm Pip," he said with a little wave. "And this is Bang. Because she's originally from Bangalore, India. And—"

"No need to say where you're from," said Uncle Mort. "You're earthlings, that's all that matters."

Ferbus studied the odd pair. "You sure about that?"

The girl unfolded her arms, tossed her book to the ground, and directed a flurry of frantic hand gestures at Pip, who followed them with an intense stare. When she finished, she dropped her hands to her sides and looked at Uncle Mort.

He stared back, uncomprehending. "What did she say?" he asked Pip.

Pip had stopped bouncing around. He looked hurt. "She said that you promised they would be nice to us."

"What's wrong with her?" Ferbus said. "She deaf?"

"Nothing's wrong with her!" Pip said. "She can hear perfectly fine. She just doesn't talk."

"But that's not—" Elysia looked confused. "I learned some

sign language when I was a kid, and whatever all that was — that's not sign language."

Pip looked at her blankly. "It's *our* sign language."

Bang inched closer to him. He grabbed her hand and backed up a little. "You're not going to be mean about this, are you?" he asked. "Because high school back home was hard enough for us, and if you're going to be the same as those jerks — "

"No, of course we're not!" Elysia cried. "I'm so sorry. We're all sorry." She elbowed Ferbus in the ribs.

"Right." Fergus coughed. "Sorry."

"Different is good here," said Driggs. "We've all got weird things. The weirder, the better."

Pip's face slowly softened back into a grin. Almost imperceptibly, Bang's did too.

"You guys ready for a walk?" Uncle Mort asked them.

"A walk where?" asked Pip. "Why are we here? Where is everyone? What — "

"Silence." Uncle Mort clamped a hand over Pip's mouth. "Actually, that's not a bad question," he said to the Juniors. "Where *is* everyone?"

They exchanged anxious glances.

Driggs cleared his throat. "You're not going to like this."

3

"Change of plans."

His anger barely contained, Uncle Mort removed his hand from Pip's mouth and almost flung him to the ground. "Take your new partners to the Crypt and get them settled in their rooms," he said, popping the trunk and handing the rookies' backpacks to Ferbus and Elysia. "I'll be back to talk to them a little later. Got it?"

"Okay," Elysia said, sensing the danger in disobeying. She threw a last wave at Lex, then put her arms around the rookies' shoulders and began walking them toward their dorm.

Uncle Mort waited until they were out of earshot before turning back to Driggs. "What do you mean, a secret meeting?"

"Norwood and Heloise pulled all off-duty Seniors — and even a bunch that were *on* duty — into the library and locked the doors." He unhooked his hand from Lex's and removed a small video camera from his pocket. "I ran home and grabbed this, then we snuck in for the first few minutes. I shot what I could before they kicked us out."

Uncle Mort pressed play. The picture was shaky and the sound muffled, as if the camera had been stuffed underneath Driggs's shirt. It finally focused on Norwood, the director of Ether Traffic Control. He stood at a podium in the same authoritative stance he took in the hub at the Bank, where he and the other Etceteras controlled the scything activities of all the Grims out in the Field.

His wife and codirector, Heloise, posed behind him, as severe and batlike as always, a smug look plastered across her face.

"I'll make this brief," Norwood said in his typical gruff voice, his sharp yellow eyes scanning the crowd. "We want to leave enough time to take care of those two." He pointed at the closed door of the supply closet.

The spidery proprietress of Ashes, Croak's fanciest restaurant, raised a finger. "Does Morrrrrt know you're dooooing thisssss?"

"Of course he does," Norwood said, dismissing the question with a wave of his hand. "Now, as you've no doubt read in the paper, Zara has gotten her hands on another scythe, which means that she can once again Crash — that is, scythe at will to a location of her own choosing without it being programmed by the Etceteras. She's been hopping all over the country, ten victims so far."

"So she could Crash here and Damn us too!" someone else jumped in. "With one little swipe of a scythe!"

"Exactly." Norwood swept a hand through his curly brown-with-gray-streaks hair. "Now, I'll admit it looks bad. But if there's anything positive to be gained from this situation, it's the confirmation that Juniors are *not to be trusted*." He pounded his fist on the podium. "They're combative, impulsive, and above all, insubordinate. Who knows what sort of conspiratorial junk Mort has been filling their heads with? Especially that niece of his."

This ignited the crowd. One young woman stood up and put her hands on her hips, looking as if she'd just walked off the set of a movie about bitchy sorority girls. "I heard she *gave* Zara her power!"

"Me too!" another voice shouted. It belonged to Trumbull, the town butcher and Zara's former boss. His lack of supervision had given Zara the free time and seclusion to carry out her attacks, embarrassing him thoroughly in the process. No doubt he was seeking to repair the damage done to his already seedy reputation. "I heard Lex is even worse than Zara!"

"Well, it's no wonder!" yelled another. "Don't you know who she is?"

"Mort never should have brought her here!"

"Do you think she's the Last?"

"She very well could be." Norwood spoke at a normal volume, but the people quieted down to listen to him. "You're right, she's just as bad as Zara. And she shouldn't be here. None of them should. But Mort insists they stay, so for the time being, we're stuck with them."

"Well, maybe we shouldn't be stuck with Mort anymore," Trumbull said.

A hint of a smile rippled beneath Norwood's lips. "Maybe not."

As the crowd talked among themselves, Heloise gave her husband's hand a squeeze. She briefly scanned the room, her expression smug until she spotted the camera. "What are you —"

The video froze. "That's when they kicked us out," Driggs said.

Lex's hands had grown clammy. "Everyone hates me," she said. "I knew they would."

Driggs swallowed, but still wouldn't look at her.

"He pointed at the supply closet at the beginning, said he was going to 'take care' of something," said Uncle Mort. "What was he talking about?"

As an answer to that very question, Norwood burst out of the library and walked briskly toward the fountain, his bony white hands clamped on the shoulders of Kloo and Ayjay.

Lex had wondered why the two oldest Juniors hadn't come out to greet her along with the others, but the possibility that they might be locked in a supply closet hadn't really crossed her mind. A visibly troubled Kloo played with one of her many braids, her chocolate brown skin glistening in the heat, while Ayjay nervously adjusted the eye patch that hid the injury he'd sustained in Zara's attack over the summer.

"Hello, Mort," Norwood said with a disappointed sneer as the townspeople crowded out behind him. They swarmed toward the fountain, putting as much distance as they could between themselves and Lex, staring at her as if she were a many-legged, poisonous bug.

"Norwood," Uncle Mort answered, a calculating smile on his face. "What's shakin'?"

"I thought I'd get a jump on the initiation vote while you were off on your little vacation," Norwood replied. "Why wait?"

Uncle Mort kept the smile on his face, but when he spoke, his voice was tight. "You know that's *my* responsibility."

"Oh, you've got too much on your plate as it is. Think of this as a favor. No need to thank me."

"No," Uncle Mort said, holding his gaze. "No need at all."

He started to say something else, but Norwood had already climbed onto the fountain ledge, yanking Ayjay and Kloo up with him.

"What's going on?" Driggs asked Uncle Mort.

"Standard induction into the Senior population. After the vote, they'll put their hands on the obelisk and get sworn in. You guys should leave, Juniors aren't supposed to see this," Uncle Mort said without conviction, clearly too distracted to care.

"Induction involves a vote?" Driggs asked. "I thought Juniors were automatically promoted to Seniors once they put in their five years and turn twenty-one."

"They are. Asking for the Seniors' approval is just a formality. You know, speak now or forever hold your peace."

"People of Croak!" Norwood shouted with a trace of annoyance. "Kloo and Ayjay stand before us as candidates for the Senior Grim population. Should they pass the town vote, they must solemnly swear to uphold all rights, responsibilities, and duties entrusted to them as Senior Grims, to Kill and Cull souls to the best of their ability and with the utmost objectivity, and to at all times adhere to the Grimsphere Terms of Execution and all that is implied therein."

His eyes narrowed. "Furthermore, they will become privy to all affairs of the Senior Grim population. Their words and deeds will be a reflection on all of us, the citizenry of Croak. They'll have the same rights as we do whether they're qualified or not, regardless of any past transgressions or personal associations with Juniors of the more treasonous persuasion," he finished, throwing a sour glance at Ayjay's eye patch.

Uncle Mort's hands had tightened into fists. "He's going off script."

Norwood turned to the crowd. "And so I turn to you, Seniors of Croak, with one simple question: Is there anyone present who objects to this?"

A short, meaty arm shot up at once. Trumbull wanted to make damn sure everyone saw him.

Soon another hand was raised. And another. One by one they popped up — some hesitant, some firm — until roughly three-quarters of the town had their hands in the air, waving their disapproval at the shocked, hurt pair of Kloo and Ayjay.

Norwood looked at his wife, who, as a final touch, raised her own hand with a flourish. "That's a majority," he said with a false tone of regret. "Sorry, kids. Maybe next year."

Incensed, Uncle Mort pushed through the crowd and climbed atop the fountain, facing the people. "What are you *doing*? You know these two are good kids!"

"We don't know that," said the sorority girl toward the front. "We thought Zara was a good kid too, and look what happened with her. And with your niece!"

"Well, the niece was bad from the start," Trumbull grumbled, shooting Lex a harsh look.

Uncle Mort didn't take the bait. "They've put in their time," he said, focused. "And all that work. You *know* they're qualified. They have every right to be Seniors, same as you do."

"But the people have already voted, Mort," said Norwood with an innocent look. "What are you going to do, overturn their decision? You think you know better than your lowly subjects?"

Uncle Mort glared at him, then at the crowd. He seemed to be thinking.

"Two months," he said, nostrils flaring. "We'll do another vote in two months. Kloo and Ayjay will take on Senior shifts until then to prove that they're worthy of the title." He jumped off the fountain. "Though I'm no longer sure that certain Seniors present are worthy enough themselves," he said under his breath as he pushed through the crowd, returning to Lex and Driggs.

The townspeople looked to Norwood for guidance. He had the look of someone who'd just tasted something rancid. "Back to work," he said curtly. The crowd dispersed while Kloo and Ayjay climbed down from the fountain, looking crushed. Pandora and Corpp, the elderly couple who, respectively, owned the town's diner and bar, gently escorted them through the plaza to where Uncle Mort, Lex, and Driggs stood.

"Slap my sassafras!" Pandora squawked, watching Norwood with a look of extreme distaste. "Who does he think he is?"

Corpp hugged Kloo and Ayjay around the shoulders. "Are you all right?"

Ayjay scowled harder. "No."

"What did we do wrong?" Kloo asked, close to tears. "We have flawless records! Don't we?"

"Yes, you do," Uncle Mort said. "This isn't your fault, Kloo. Or yours, Ayjay. You got that?"

"And why Norwood?" Kloo went on, not hearing him. "I thought *you* were always the one to induct Seniors."

"I was. I *am*." He suppressed a growl. "Listen, guys, I'm sorry. I know you've been looking forward to this for years, and the fact that it didn't go as planned — let's just say I will look into it. Carefully."

Corpp and Pandora took one look at the seething mayor and took the hint. "Come on," Corpp said to Kloo and Ayjay, steering them toward his bar. "Let's get some Yoricks in you."

The miserable still-Juniors nodded an assent as they left. "Oh, hey —" Kloo turned around with a pained smile. "Welcome back, Lex. We missed you."

Lex jumped at the sound of her name. "Thanks," she said, her eye twitching again. "I missed you too."

Ayjay kept his eye on her as they walked away. "Is she all right?" he not so subtly asked Kloo.

"Shhh!" she hissed, adding, "I don't know."

Uncle Mort, Driggs, and Lex stood in silence. It wasn't until Lex's lip started bleeding from her picking at it that she realized they were staring.

"You're not all right," said Uncle Mort.

Lex blotted the blood with her sleeve. "Ahviouthly."

Uncle Mort watched her for a moment more, then turned to Driggs. "I think you better take her. Now."

"What about Norwood?"

"I'll deal with him. I want Lex back to normal. Things are changing fast, and I need all of you at full capacity. Distraught, fidgety teenagers are the last thing we need right now." He turned to Lex and took her by the shoulders. "Lex, I know these past couple of weeks have been hard, but it's time to snap out of it. You chose this, remember? You chose to come back here and deal with it. I know it sounds callous, but you need to sane up and turn back into a functional human being. Otherwise I can't let you stay."

Lex started picking her lip again.

Uncle Mort straightened up with a sigh and pointed at the Bank, Croak's official command center. "Go."

Lex began to feel even more nervous as they walked to the Bank, though she couldn't tell why. Maybe it was the fact that the whole way there, Driggs didn't say a word to her.

"Welcome back, Lex!" Kilda yelled as they entered. Lex blinked at the ever-jubilant director of tourism/public relations specialist/postmaster. "We've missed you terribly! It just hasn't been the same without you! And be sure to stop by the desk sometime, I've got some new potpourri!"

"Some things never change," Driggs said, dragging Lex down

the hallway. She looked at the clouded windows of the hub
— where Norwood and Heloise were no doubt toasting to their
devious success — then at the stairs she soon found herself as-
cending. Pangs of nausea stung with every step. Something was
making her feel frantic and sick, but her brain was spinning out
like a car on ice, unable to gain traction on whatever the Big
Dreaded Thing was —

"Wait!" she yelled at the top of the stairs.

"What?" Driggs said, his face worried. "What's wrong?"

Lex's mind snapped into focus. She looked at the door. "I
know what you're doing. I know why we're here."

Driggs softened. "You have to do this. You *want* to do this."

"I know. But — " She took a deep breath. "Oh, shit. Shit."

He took her hand. "Come on."

The office on the second floor of the Bank had changed very
little since Lex last saw it. The desk, the gigantic vault door that
led to the Afterlife, the potted plant — all were the same. The
only difference was a new security keypad fixed next to the door
to the Lair, where thousands of black widow spiders produced
both the silken Vessels used to transport the souls of the dead and
Amnesia, a venom that made tourists forget they'd ever stumbled
into Croak.

There was one other difference, Lex noticed: a change in per-
sonnel. Sitting at the desk was a Senior Grim whom Lex had seen
around town but never formally met — a young guy with expensive-looking clothes, slicked-back hair, a pair of sunglasses atop
his head, and an artfully placed patch of facial hair beneath his
lower lip. "Well, look who's here," he said in a mocking tone. "The
little revolutionary."

"Knock it off, Snodgrass," Driggs said. "Let us in."

"Not by the hair of my chinny-chin-chin," he sang in an infuriating voice. "No unauthorized entry, remember?"

Driggs moved closer. "We *are* authorized."

"By?"

"Mort, who else?"

Snodgrass flashed a smarmy grin. "Not sure that's enough, bro."

Driggs narrowed his eyes at him and leaned in to Lex. She could have listened to what he was whispering — that when Ferbus and Elysia had been fired from their respective posts, they had been replaced by first-rate douchebags — but she barely registered a thing he said. All she could think about was who was behind that vault.

Driggs eventually fell silent and stared at Snodgrass, who by then had gone back to inspecting his eyebrows in the reflection of the computer screen. "Fine then, *bro*," Driggs murmured, his lips barely moving. "Plan B it is."

Driggs grabbed the sunglasses from Snodgrass's head and hurled them out the door and down the stairs. Snodgrass jumped up to chase them, but by the time he realized his mistake — by the time Driggs had grabbed the computer keyboard and entered the code — it was too late. The vault had swung open.

"Go!" Driggs shouted to Lex. Her body obeyed, propelling her into the fluffy white Afterlife and shutting the door behind her. Her mind, however, was in a panic. She shut her eyes tight, terrified at the prospect of seeing Cordy hurt, betrayed, miserable, dead —

A minute passed in silence. Lex opened one eye, then the other.

Nothing.

She was standing in the atrium, the neutral mingling space for both the living and the dead. Other than the usual gaggle of deceased presidents — along with some poor sap Senior Grim in the middle of them all, trying to keep them in line — the place was empty.

Then a faint, sustained whoop began to issue forth from the Void, the bright area in the distance that was off-limits to the living. It grew louder and closer, kicking up so much fluff that Lex couldn't see what it was until it came to a stop in front of her.

Cordy blew her hair out of her eyes and beamed. "Hi, turd-face."

Lex nearly had an aneurysm. She pounced at her sister with a savage lunge, so intense was her need to bury her head in Cordy's frizzy hair. But the closer she got, the farther away Cordy retreated. It was as if they were being repelled from each other, like opposing magnets.

"We can't touch," said Cordy with a crooked smile. "Kind of a bummer, I know."

Lex had forgotten this. Her outstretched arms fell limply to her side. She could do nothing but stare into her sister's eyes, trying to discern what possible reason there could be for the joy and warmth she found there. Didn't Cordy know what had happened? Didn't she know that Lex was responsible? Didn't she know she was *dead*?

"You can stop making that face," Cordy said. "I'm fine."

"You're *fine*?" Lex sputtered. "Cordy, don't you get it? You're dead! Deceased! Your body is rotting in a grave in Maple Grove Cemetery, all because of me!"

"I'm aware of the situation," Cordy said. "Seriously, Lex, it's no big deal."

"It is a big deal. It is a very big deal."

"Only to the living."

"But you're — " Lex choked on the words. "You're gone."

"I'm not gone. I'm right here. And so are you, and I can see my dear freakypants sister whenever I want. That's a lot more than most other souls can say."

Lex studied her. "Wait a sec. You're happy in here?"

The expression on Cordy's face confirmed this. "Not gonna lie, Lex. It's pretty bitchin'."

"So I've been worried sick about you this whole time, picturing you miserable and wrecked and plotting my excruciating demise, and you're telling me this has all been a summer cruise?"

"Yeah. Sorry." Cordy looked guilty for a second, then smiled. "I can't even begin to explain it, Lex. Do you know how many roller coasters I've built since I got here? Four!" Her face was glowing. "Not sketched, not made out of Tinkertoys, but built, life-size! No — bigger!"

"But — "

"And Gramma and Grampa are in there!" she went on. "Nana and Pop-Pop too! Do you know what they did when they saw me?"

"Gave you butterscotch candy?"

"Yes! And the places you can go, the people that are here — it's unreal. Just unreal."

Lex looked at Cordy's face, its exhilaration such a stark contrast to the ponderous dread of the town outside. Lex smirked sadly. "Maybe I should off myself right now and come join you."

Cordy frowned. "Why?"

"Well," said Lex, "it's no picnic over here in the land of the living. The whole town hates me, Mom and Dad probably despise me, there's an angry, murderous bitch tearing up the country, I've got *your* death to avenge, and no one's offering *me* any hard candy."

"Yeah, but — "

"Seriously, Cordy, if the Afterlife is so amazing, what's the point of staying here on this stupid, miserable planet?"

A flicker of sadness flew through Cordy's eyes. "Because it's life," she said softly. "I mean, it *is* amazing here, but I still miss things."

"Like what? What could you possibly miss?"

"Like — " Cordy thought for a moment and sighed. "Like our room. I tried to reconstruct it here, but it's just not the same. Plus, you're not in it, so why bother?"

Lex softened. "Oh."

"Ice cream's different too. The consistency is wrong." Cordy bit her lip. "I miss Mom and Dad. The way Mom would put those silly 'Made with love' notes in our lunches, the way Dad honked the horn in the school parking lot extra embarrassingly whenever the football team ran by." She let out a small laugh. "Other things, too. Sneezing. The smell of gasoline. That blurry feeling between being asleep and being awake. The way you can hold your hands at just the right angle in the shower so that it looks like beams of water are shooting out from your fingertips like a superhero." She looked at Lex. "None of it's the same. I'll never get any of that back."

Lex's chest tightened. "You'd still have it if it weren't for me."

"Lex, stop. If you say that this was your fault one more time, I'm going to make President McKinley kick your ass on two non-consecutive occasions."

"But—"

"I mean it, enough with the guilt. Life was—" She twisted her mouth, thinking. "Life was like that time we went to that little hole-in-the-wall dessert place on the Lower East Side and we got that peanut butter and banana cheesecake that was so good it made our taste buds stand up and sing the 'Hallelujah' chorus."

"The place that closed a week later?"

"Yes! Remember how we went to a dozen more after that, even the supposed best places in the city, but they were always only second best? So there was nothing we could do but savor the graham-crackery-crust memory and move on." She gestured at the Void. "That's all I can do—savor the memory of life and move on. But *you* can still scarf the good stuff. So do it for as long as you can."

Lex felt exhausted. "Fine. I won't throw myself under a bus. But what about you?"

"What *about* me? I'll be okay in here. The Afterlife may be second-best cheesecake, but it's still cheesecake."

"But aren't you mad? I mean—" She gestured weakly at their surroundings. "This is great and all, but Zara killed you. She *killed* you. Aren't you pissed?"

Cordy's eyes darkened briefly. "Yes."

"Good. For a minute there, I thought you were gunning for sainthood."

Cordy shook her head. "I hate her for what she did to me—and even more, for what she did to you—but it's hard to be full of rage here. Trust me, I've tried. But then I just go build a roller coaster or something." She shrugged. "I guess there's just a lot more here to distract you from being sad."

"Yeah. Until the novelty wears off and you realize she trapped you here for eternity before you even got a chance to live."

"Still cheesecake, Lex."

Lex gave up. Cordy was happy, more or less — and wasn't that all Lex had wanted in the first place? For the first time in days, her heart unclogged itself from her throat and slid back to its rightful place in her chest.

"Okay," she said, her voice now situated in a more natural octave. "So what else have you been up to besides building vomit comets and choking down butterscotch?"

"Looking for a boy," Cordy said with a sly grin. "Shouldn't take much longer, either — this place is a buffet of hotness. John Steinbeck? Stone-cold fox."

Lex laughed. Just then the vault door swung open to reveal a harried-looking Driggs. He stumbled in and made an attempt to smooth his hair. "Good, you found each other."

"Have you guys met?" asked Lex.

Driggs shook his head. "Not yet. Mort wanted us to wait until you reunited first." He waved to Cordy. "Hi, I'm Driggs."

"Damn, boy. You're even cuter up close." Cordy looked him up and down hungrily. "Got any dead brothers in here?"

Lex made a face. "Cordy, ew."

"Doesn't hurt to ask!" She peered at Driggs. "Now tell me, what are your intentions with my sister?"

Driggs became flustered. "Um, I don't know. To love her . . . and, uh . . . honor . . . protect . . ."

Lex went red. "Driggs, shut up."

"Awkward." Cordy beamed. "Love it."

"We have to go," Driggs said in an unnecessarily loud voice.

"Yeah, you do," said the approaching Senior who had been wrangling the presidents. He had straight bleached-blond hair that swept over his face, leather pants, and a nose ring through his septum, all of which made him look like a bull that got lost on the way to a punk rock concert. He too had an air of douchebaggery, though his face looked slightly kinder than Snodgrass's. "You're not supposed to be here."

Driggs glared at him. "So we keep hearing."

"Sounded like you were torturing Snodgrass."

"Come on, Lazlo. I messed up his hair."

"Precisely."

Driggs rolled his eyes. "Lex, say goodbye."

Lex looked at Cordy. Now that she'd seen her and knew she was all right, she didn't want to leave. "I'll be back, okay?"

"I know you will." Cordy grinned. "Good luck with the angry mob."

"Thanks."

"Later, Cordy," Driggs said. "Nice to finally meet you."

"Nice meeting you too." She looked at Lazlo's alluringly long eyelashes. "And you as well. Don't be a stranger."

"You're embarrassing yourself!" Lex yelled as Driggs dragged her out.

"Don't care!" Cordy shouted back.

||||||

The walk back to Uncle Mort's house was strange. Lex yammered on about how relieved she was to see Cordy, but Driggs just nodded and remained silent. With the exception of that weird and seemingly automated "love and honor" nonsense, he'd been all business since she'd arrived. He just seemed so distant, so distracted. The longer they walked, the tighter Lex's stomach got. Maybe he didn't like her anymore. Maybe he wasn't crazy about dating the girl who'd really shit the bed on the whole not-demolishing-the-Grimsphere thing.

It wasn't until they approached the house that he finally said something. The door was wide open, and shouts were coming from within.

He looked at her. "That's probably bad."

4

Three pairs of furious eyes watched them as they entered. Uncle Mort, Norwood, and Heloise stood facing one another in a triangle, their scythes drawn.

"Oh, good," Heloise said, her mouth forming into a thin line. "The peanut gallery's here."

"Kids, go up to the roof," Uncle Mort said, his voice tense. "We're just talking."

Lex's gaze jumped back and forth between Heloise's ruby red scythe and Norwood's bright yellow sulfur scythe. "Doesn't look like you're just talking."

"Lex. Go."

One look at his face confirmed that he wasn't kidding around. Lex and Driggs backed out the door, the codirectors watching their every step.

They made a beeline for the ladder and climbed up to their typical hangout spot. Once atop the roof, they stayed silent for a minute or two, straining to hear what was being said beneath them, but all they could make out was a series of intense yet inaudible murmurings.

And Driggs still wasn't talking.

Lex looked at him, really looked at him for the first time since she had gotten back, focusing especially on his weird eyes. She loved the way the moon reflected off the blue one more than the brown. It made him look like he was constantly winking.

She took a deep breath. Maybe he was mad at her, maybe not. Either way, he deserved to know the full story. He deserved to know what he was getting into with her.

"I have to tell you something."

"Shoot," he said in a flat voice.

She swallowed. "Ever since that day I tried to Damn Zara, I've sort of . . . changed. A little."

His face remained the same.

She bit at her lips, too humiliated for words. "Whatever it is that causes the Damning that I can do — it sort of builds up now, like an electrical charge. Sometimes it comes when I get too mad, sometimes it just pops up out of nowhere."

Driggs's eyebrow was now slightly raised. Lex knew she was babbling, but she kept going, directing the rest of her spiel to his ratty high-top Chuck Taylors. "So every few days I have to, like, discharge. That's the only word I can come up with for it. Release the Damning energy that gets pent up, so that I don't accidentally Damn someone."

Driggs was getting squirmy. "Release?" he asked. "How?"

Lex's face burned red. This was so humiliating. "By Damning things, setting them on fire. It doesn't even hurt or burn my hands anymore," she said, holding up her unblistered fingers. "Just stupid things, like a box of cereal. Or a newspaper. Nothing living, if I can help it. Except once when we were on the road, it got really bad and we had to pull over, and I did it to a run-over skunk — it was dead already, I think, but — "

"Okay, stop."

Lex's mouth went dry. This was it. The breaking point. She was too bizarre, too gross. He was going to dump her right here and now, and there was nothing she could do about it but sit there and look pathetic and try not to blow a snot bubble when she started crying.

"Here's the thing," he said, his face strained. "It's just that I've been treading carefully around you and this whole Cordy thing all day, just like Mort told me to. And I had to make sure you saw her and were okay with it and got home safe — again, just like Mort told me to. And as much as I'd love to continue exploring the existential implications of Damning roadkill, the truth is" — he plunged his hands into his hair until it stuck up even more than usual — "you've been back here in my presence for two agonizing hours now, and if we don't properly make out soon, I'm going to hurl myself off the roof."

Lex blinked.

Then Driggs smushed his lips into hers so quickly that she had to grab the gutter to keep from falling.

After that (many, many minutes after that), everything came spilling out. All the fears and regrets that had been festering in the back of Lex's mind, all the anger toward Zara and the helplessness Lex felt at the thought of trying to stop her. She told him about the funeral and the subsequent rookie trip, about the shocked yet jubilant looks on the rookies' faces as Uncle Mort swooped in to rescue them from their miserable lives. Driggs filled her in on what had been going on since she left, including the most recent headlines in *The Obituary* regarding Zara and the special teams that had been dispatched to track her down.

Whenever they ran out of things to talk about, they kissed some more.

Until an especially loud shout from below snapped them out of it. They paused, rubbing at their raw lips. "Mort is so pissed,"

Driggs said after straining to hear more of the conversation. He took out a handful of the Oreos he always kept with him and offered one to Lex.

"Can you blame him?" Lex said, taking a bite. "Norwood and Heloise are trying to convince the townspeople that he's some kind of a tyrant. When did they grow the balls to call a meeting without him?"

"I know. I mean, Mort's got a better head on his shoulders than anyone here. That's why he's the mayor and has been for years — because he's just so damn good at it. And no one's ever complained or demanded a change or even said a word against him. But now . . ." He exhaled with a puff.

"How *has* he been the mayor for so long?" Lex asked. "He's so young, he must have been elected when he was — "

"Twenty-three. Youngest mayor ever."

"Wow."

"Well, you're only allowed to run for public office if you're under thirty-five. The Grimsphere government places a really heavy value on youth and its drive, its fresh ideas. That's why the whole Junior program was created in the first place."

Lex frowned. "There weren't always Juniors?"

"Nope, it only started about thirty years ago. Before that, Grims just came full-on into the Grimsphere as Seniors at the age of twenty-one. Norwood and Heloise were some of the last of those, I think. They never got to be Juniors, which is probably why they hate us so much."

"Or because they're getting older and more obsolete," Lex said. "I mean, let's face it, I've got more power in my little finger than they've ever had in their whole bodies. And so does

Zara. They feel threatened, so they're trying to gain some ground back."

"Yeah, but crossing Mort is the wrong way to do it."

Lex shifted. "Hey, what was that thing someone yelled out about me — that I could be the Last? What does that mean?"

He rolled his eyes. "It means people are getting panicky and ridiculous. It's just some lame-ass legend — the Last is supposed to be this single, powerful Grim who triggers a massive shift in the natural laws of the world and ends up destroying the Grimsphere. The Last Grim."

Lex stifled a laugh. "Destroy the Grimsphere? I don't even have my driver's license."

"Exactly. Those Seniors are out of their tree."

Three seconds of silence followed, which was way too much time to go without making out, so they dove right back into each other's faces. But after a minute or so, Lex pushed him away. "Stop."

"Why?" He looked horrified. "What's wrong?"

"Nothing —"

"Was it that thing I did with my tongue?"

"Um, no. Your tongue and its many talents are perfect. Keep up the good work." She reached into her pocket and pulled out a crumpled-up scrap of paper. "I never got a chance to tell you about this before I left. After Zara killed —" She swallowed. "When Uncle Mort was addressing the townspeople and I was alone in the library, I started looking through the Grotton section, and this was written in one of the books at the bottom of the page."

Driggs took it from her, his face questioning as he read.

IF REDEMPTION IS THAT WHICH YOU PRIZE,
DO NOT BELIEVE ALL OF THESE LIES.
THE KEY TO THE DEAD AWAITS OVERHEAD —
ALL YOU NEED DO IS OPEN YOUR EYES.
— BONE, THE SICK SCYTHE BANDIT

Driggs looked up. "I've never heard of anyone named Bone."

"Me neither. But it's the same handwriting as — " She listened to one of Norwood's shouts, then lowered her voice. "Every book in the Grotton section has the same thing written in it. They all say 'wrong book.'"

Driggs's eyes widened. "What?"

"I think Zara took whatever was the *right* book, because there was an empty space at the end of the — "

"No, that's not it," said Driggs. "'Wrong book' isn't an instruction. It's a title."

"What?"

"The Wrong Book," he said excitedly. "According to legend, it's the ultimate authority on all the horrible things Grotton did, all the mysteries of the universe that he stumbled upon and exploited for personal gain. Supposedly he wrote it himself, sort of as an instruction manual for anyone who might want to wreak havoc the way he did."

A flutter of nerves swept through Lex. "Where is it now?"

"No one knows. Supposedly it was locked away somewhere safe centuries ago, but everyone who knew where is long dead."

"Locked away," Lex said slowly. "With a key?"

They both looked at the note again.

Driggs gave her a dubious look. "You're not seriously suggesting that this note is going to lead us to a key that'll unlock the Wrong Book, are you? Because that would make you sound like an insane person. If that is what you are suggesting."

"It is." She tucked the note back into her pocket. "And you're going to help me find it."

"Oh, really?" he replied with a wry grin. "Why's that?"

"Because you promised to love me," she said in a dopey voice. "And, uh . . . honor me . . . and protect . . ."

He snickered. "Shut up, spaz."

Which led to more canoodling. In fact, the two remained so entwined and so oblivious for so long that by the time they let go, they had completely failed to notice Norwood and Heloise storming out of the house, Uncle Mort scaling the ladder, and the fact that he was now staring at them and had been for several minutes.

"Good grief," he said. "As if I didn't have enough to worry about."

Lex and Driggs jumped apart and wiped the spittle from their mouths. "What's up?" Driggs said in a terrible attempt at nonchalance.

"Hormone levels, obviously."

"What happened?" Lex pressed on. "Where are Norwood and Heloise?"

"Oh, they left hours ago," Uncle Mort joked. "Not that I'd expect you to notice, as busy as you were."

Lex smoothed out her hoodie. "Seriously, what's going on?"

"Nothing. We were just having a discussion."

"A discussion?"

"Okay, a heated discussion, but it didn't come to anything

more than that. Let's drop it for now, okay? It doesn't concern you."

"It *does* concern me!" Lex said. "I heard that meeting—half the stuff they were saying was about me! How did they find out I gave Zara the power to Damn?"

"Glad to see your piss and vinegar is back," Uncle Mort said with a smile.

"Yes. Your brilliant plan for me to visit Cordy in the Afterlife worked," Lex said flatly. "Your Nobel Prize is in the mail. Now answer my question."

"Well, that was my bad. I told Heloise about it, believing I could trust her to keep it to herself. I was wrong."

"You think?"

"We all make mistakes, Lex," he said pointedly.

She made a face. "Yeah, well, that doesn't explain why everyone keeps on insisting that I shouldn't be here."

"Lex, you're my niece. Charges of favoritism and special treatment are unavoidable. On top of that, you're a Junior. And judging by today's events, I think we can safely assume that that's another count against you."

"You're sure that's all?"

"That's all."

Lex studied him. "I think you're lying."

He stared back. "Prove it, kiddo."

This last statement hovered between them for a few moments, curdling the air.

"So," said Driggs, hoping to dissipate the tension, "how did you leave it with Norwood and Heloise?"

Uncle Mort looked at Lex for a second more, then turned to

Driggs. "I warned them not to do anything stupid. Though that hasn't stopped them so far."

"Can't you invalidate the results of their vote, since neither one of them is the mayor?"

"No," said Uncle Mort, sounding tired. "They did their homework — traditionally the major runs the induction vote, but there's nothing in the Terms that says it *has* to be done that way. They agreed to my two-month trial idea — begrudgingly — but until then, it looks like we're stuck." He rubbed his eyes. "And speaking of Terms, we need to set a few ground rules here with . . . this," he said, clearing his throat and gesturing at the two of them.

"With what?" Lex said.

"That," Uncle Mort replied, pointing to a suspicious-looking mark on her neck.

Lex's hand flew to her throat while Driggs shifted, uneasy. "Why?" he asked.

"Don't 'why?' me, Romeo. You know I trust you, but Lex is still my niece. In the absence of her father, it's up to me to do everything in my power to complicate and interfere with her budding love life."

Lex frowned. "Hey — "

"Now, you're still work partners, which means that a large portion of your time together will unfortunately be unsupervised. Complicating matters is the fact that you both live in the same house. So here's the deal: You will sleep in separate bedrooms. You will leave your doors open at all times. You will keep the public displays of affection to a minimum. You will not attempt to dismantle any of my surveillance equipment, which, I'll remind you, covers nearly every room of this house. And if I hear any article of clothing being unzipped, unstrapped, unhooked, or unbuckled, you will lose the body part that it corresponds to. Understand?"

Lex and Driggs looked at each other, then nodded, defeated.

"Good. Now, I'm off to chat with the rookies." Uncle Mort started down the ladder. "Oh, and your roof time has been limited to thirty minutes, max."

"Hey, unfair!" Driggs shouted. "Why?"

"I was a teenage boy once too, you know," Uncle Mort said, popping back up. "I know what your brain looks like. It's a three-ring circus in there." He looked at his watch. "Five more minutes," he said, disappearing once more.

Driggs groaned. Lex thought for a moment. "Maybe we can —"

"By the way," Uncle Mort shouted up at them on his way down, "you know what I love about my roof? How thin it is! Yessir, when it rains, I can hear each and every drop!"

Lex slumped, scowling. Driggs stared off into the distance, then turned to her with a sly look.

"We'll just have to get creative."

|||||||

With their roof time expired and Uncle Mort's cameras watching them like unblinking robo-hawks, Lex and Driggs had no choice but to flee the house. They made their way to Corpp's, where the mood was almost celebratory; the Seniors seemed pretty pleased with themselves for having made some headway against the Junior plague.

The atmosphere shifted, however, as Lex entered the pub. She could feel people's eyes on her, hear every mumbled comment as she and Driggs made their way to the bar.

"Sorry to crash the party," Driggs told Corpp.

"You hush your mouth. You know full well you're always welcome here." Corpp flashed Lex a wide grin and pushed forth two mugs shaped like skulls — Yoricks, Grims' favorite drink. "On the house, kids."

"Thanks, Corpp." Lex smiled back at the friendly bartender, his skin as brown and smooth as the thick liquid swirling within the mugs. She'd always felt safe in his presence, and tonight was no exception. His curly gray hair was comforting in the same way Pandora's gnarled hands were — these two had been here for decades. They'd seen everything, weathered every storm. If they said everything would turn out all right, who was she to argue with them?

"Where are Kloo and Ayjay?" Driggs asked.

Corpp frowned. "They had a couple of drinks, but I haven't seen them in a while. They looked rather uncomfortable."

"Shocking," said Driggs, glaring at the ogling Seniors. "I'll go find them."

Lex sat down on a stool as Driggs plunged into the crowd. "Glad to see you're feeling better," Corpp told her.

"Yeah, well, I got to see my sister, so — "

"So you feel whole again." He nodded as he wiped down the counter. "I can understand that, I suppose."

Something in his voice made Lex cock her head. "Is that not what you would have done?"

"Well, now, let me see," he said, throwing a dirty dishrag over his shoulder. "I'm not rightly sure what I would do. Don't get me wrong—I've seen plenty of folks pass on in my time, and sure, the temptation's always been there to head on up into the Bank and get one last look at them, but I suppose I just never thought it was my place to do so. Wouldn't want to keep reminding them, you know?"

Lex thought about all the stuff Cordy had said about missing life. Maybe he was right. "So if you died, you wouldn't want anyone to visit you?"

He let out a laugh. "Child, when I die, I'll be too busy painting up the Afterlife to give two shakes about what the living are doing." Lex glanced at the brush strokes on the walls, the color splashed across the counter. "Gotta get busy and set up a nice little place for me and the wife to spend eternity, now don't I?"

"What makes you so sure you'll die before Pandora?"

Corpp gave her a look. "The woman is a cockroach. She'll outlive every last one of us, mark my words." He tapped her mug. "Now, why don't you take a sip of the ole Yorick, and try to ignore all these blasted fools."

Lex thanked him again and took a gulp. The sweetness filled her mouth and warmed her gullet, the euphoric properties of the Elixir taking effect almost instantaneously. By the time Driggs returned to the bar, the collective stare fest around her had receded into the background of her mind like white noise.

"Come on," Driggs said, pulling her through the crowd. "They were hiding out in the bathroom, but I dragged them back in. We shouldn't have to cower like scared little mice."

Yet cowering was exactly what Kloo and Ayjay were doing, cramped into the back corner of the pub. The Seniors had given them a wide berth, as if a roll of invisible police tape had been set up around them.

"Hey, you're human again," Ayjay said to Lex before anyone could bring up the prickly subject of the vote.

Kloo elbowed him in the ribs, causing his hand to fly up and accidentally knock his eye patch askew. "It's called tact, Ayjay. Find some." She smiled sadly at Lex. "You doing okay, hon?"

Lex smirked and held up her mug. "I am now."

"Oops!" A cry rang out as something wet sloshed down Lex's back.

Lex whirled around to face Sofi, whose brown hair was swirled atop her head, its bleached stripes looking like they'd been drizzled on. "Sorry, Lex, toootally my bad," she said with a stiff smile, handing her a napkin. Though Sofi was the sole Ether Traffic Controller nerd among the Juniors, she still held the rather paradoxical reputation of being the ditziest of the bunch. "Welcome back."

"Thanks."

Lex didn't know what else to say. Ever since she and Driggs had become an item, Sofi had been treating them like war criminals. True, they had embarrassed her and gotten her in a heap of trouble, but Lex suspected her vexation had less to do with the job and more to do with the location of Driggs's arm, which was currently around Lex's waist.

"Well, toodles," Sofi said, wobbling away on a pair of skyscraping pink heels.

Lex watched her leave, as did Snodgrass, his eyes moving up and down with each bouncing step. "Ew," Lex said. "Bet they'd vote *her* in as a Senior in a heartbeat."

At the mention of the big *S* word, the group fell silent. Kloo and Ayjay stared into their mugs.

"Oh, crap," Lex said. "I'm sorry."

"It's okay," said Kloo. "It's just — God, this is so unfair."

"It is," Driggs said. "Which is why you have to work your asses off for the next two months. Show them how good you are, and by the time the next vote rolls around, they'll *have* to promote you."

"I don't know," said Kloo with a frown. Lex was unnerved; it was scary to see their calmest and most composed friend so upset. "Maybe we should just stay Juniors forever," Kloo said. "You guys are more fun."

"Oh yes," said Lex in a sullen voice. "Barrels of laughs, we are."

Kloo sighed. "I mean, we'll make the effort, but I'm not sure it'll work. They just seem so dead set against us. And who knows how much longer we're going to be here anyway."

"What?" Lex looked back and forth between them. "You're leaving?"

Kloo made a guilty face and snuggled closer to Ayjay. "Well, not for a few years. But yeah, eventually." They shared a smile. "We want to start a family."

"You can't do that here?"

"Children aren't allowed in the Grimsphere," Kloo said. "There aren't any schools, plus it's not the most ideal place to raise them."

"Because of all the death," Ayjay added unnecessarily.

Lex just stared at them, unable to fathom their stupidity. "You mean you'd give up all this — *and* wipe your memory clean — just to squirt out a couple of screaming brats?"

Kloo shrugged. "I want to go to med school, and Ayjay wants to open up his own gym. That's the plan, anyway. Although now I'm wondering if we should leave sooner rather than later."

She chanced a look at the menacing Seniors.

"It's starting to get a little too dangerous here."

5

Over the next couple of days Lex fell back into her old schedule so easily it began to feel as if she'd never left. None of her skills as a Killer had diminished — in fact, they seemed to have grown sharper, cleaner, more polished.

This did not go unnoticed by Driggs. "Were you practicing while you were gone?" he asked, pocketing his sapphire scythe as they approached an impaled truck driver. The Gamma, or soul, burst from the man's body as soon as Lex's finger graced his arm. The deathflash bathed them in a white light while the shock that accompanied all her Kills shot through her body like a lightning bolt. Driggs bent over the target, collecting the soul into his hands and guiding it into a Vessel. "Your speed is insane."

"Yeah, thanks," Lex muttered, polishing the pitch-black obsidian of her scythe. In simpler times she would have milked these compliments for all they were worth. But she wasn't sure anymore how proud she should be of her exceptional abilities, especially since they seemed to be the source of everything that had gone wrong in her life. As if having to lock herself in her room and Damn a pencil cup while Leonardo DiCaprio watched from the *Titanic* poster across from her bed wasn't embarrassing enough.

They next scythed to a police officer. An impossibly red, shimmering bullet hole sat in the middle of his chest. "And you're doing better with those, uh, urges," Driggs added.

"What?" Lex said distractedly, unable to tear her eyes away from the man holding the gun.

"I said you're doing a pretty good job of not tackling that guy and Damning the ever-loving shit out of him for shooting a cop," Driggs said more loudly. "I'm proud of you."

Lex scowled, taking care not to let him see her searing hands.

In terms of grumpiness, however, no one could match the sheer exasperation of Ferbus and Elysia, whose new partners were proving to be a lot harder to tolerate than they had anticipated.

"I. Give. Up." Ferbus yelled one afternoon to Driggs and Lex in the Juniors' circular red-leather booth at the Morgue, the town diner. "It took him two days — *two days* — to figure out how to scythe without dropping the damn thing. And now that we've *finally* made it out to the Field, everything is a question! 'Where are we now, Ferbus?' 'What happened to this guy, Ferbus?' 'Why are you banging your head against a wall, Ferbus?'"

"At least yours talks," Elysia said, irritably shoving a fry into her mouth. "Mine just stares. Like a cow. I try to engage, I try to take advantage of teachable moments, but how am I supposed to know if anything's even sinking in?"

Lex stifled a laugh. She loved Elysia, but the thought of the poor girl trapped for several hours with someone who wouldn't talk back to her was surely her idea of hell.

"Give them a chance," Driggs said. "Maybe you just need to get to know them better."

"Like you did with your partner?" said Ferbus, gesturing at Lex. "Good point. Maybe I should shove my tongue down Pip's throat and see what happens."

Moments later, Pip sat down at the table and started right in.

"What happens if someone dies underwater, Ferbus? Or underground?"

"I'll show you this afternoon!" Ferbus shouted. "Now stop asking! Just stop!"

"Pip," Driggs interjected in the hopes of avoiding an Incident, "why don't you tell us a little bit about yourself? What was life like before coming here? We all have really crappy backgrounds, so we'll understand."

Pip looked surprised, as if unable to comprehend being the one to answer questions rather than ask them. "Foster home. Too many kids, not enough parents."

Ferbus, a well-traveled former foster kid himself, softened a bit. "Amen to that," he muttered.

"What kind of stuff did you do once you turned delinquent?" Lex asked. "Don't be shy, we've all — "

"Robbed a Seven-Eleven," Pip said matter-of-factly, without a trace of embarrassment.

Ferbus dropped his onion ring. The other Juniors exchanged shocked glances. "Excuse me?" said Elysia.

Pip chomped at his fries. "Stole some licorice sticks, fashioned them into fake guns, and then threatened the clerk until he gave us some money," he replied. "Bang thought it would be a hoot."

"Interesting." Elysia glanced at Bang, still waiting for her food at the counter. "Why doesn't she talk?"

"I dunno. She never has." He shoved another handful of fries into his face and chewed as he talked. "Her family came over from India when she was three and who knows what happened to them after that. We both went into the foster system when we were six, and we've been shuffled around together ever since."

Elysia gave him a sad smile. "Is that why you're so protective?"

Pip shrugged. "She's my best friend. I watch her back, she watches mine."

Bang brought her tray to the table, cracked open her book, and started reading and eating. Ferbus nudged Pip. "She's cute too," he fake-whispered.

Bang stopped chewing and looked up, a string of cheddar stretching from her grilled cheese to her mouth.

Pip gave Ferbus a strange look. "I guess."

"Nice eyes."

Bang chewed once more, then stopped. Pip was still confused. ". . . Right."

Ferbus gave him a playful shove. "Come on, Pipster. You never thought about her that way?"

Bang sprayed her food across the table in a silent laugh. Pip looked horrified. "No! She's my sister! Ew!"

"Whoa, okay. Sorry."

"Besides, I'm not exactly interested."

Ferbus stared.

"In girls," Pip clarified, dunking another fry.

"Oh," Ferbus said automatically, then slowly grasped his meaning. "Ohhhh," he said again, his eyes widening, most likely in horror at his earlier comment regarding his tongue and Pip's throat.

Bang was still laughing to herself. Gradually, everyone else joined in. Including Ferbus, until he realized that he was the one they were laughing at.

"Oh, hey," said Lex. "I wanted to show you guys something I found in the library. In the Grotton section."

"What's a Grotton?" asked Pip.

"*Who's* Grotton." Elysia excitedly launched into one of her lectures, a "teachable moment opportunity!" neon sign practically lighting up over her head. "Only the most evil Grim of all time. Back in the fourteenth century, he found a Loophole — that's this little scroll that when placed in a jellyfish tank can give you the ability to Crash — which meant he could scythe off the grid whenever he wanted to. *Then* he figured out how to Crash with a specific destination in mind. *Plus* he was the only one ever born with the ability to Damn, which meant that he could kill people without removing their souls and instead curse them to an eternity of pain and torture. Add that all together, and you end up with a guy who terrorized both the Grimsphere and the real world, Damning hundreds of people. He's the worst of the worst."

Lex decided to jump in before anyone pointed out that Grotton wasn't the only one who had been born with the ability to Damn — Lex had, too. And she wasn't in the mood to discuss it, or her burny hands, or any of the other things that set her apart as having an innate streak of evil. Or whatever it was.

So she described what she'd seen in the library, all the Grotton books with WRONG BOOK scratched into them. Then she took out the note she'd found and flattened it on the table.

"'The key to the dead awaits overhead'?" Ferbus read. "What, like in a storage compartment?"

Elysia rolled her eyes. "Ferbus, you are the densest person on the planet."

"Well, do *you* know what it's talking about?"

"No, but — " She read it over once again, then shrugged. "No, not really."

"Just keep a lookout, okay?" Lex said. "For anything strange. Or overhead. Or keylike."

Just then a copy of *The Obituary* dropped onto the table. "Right there, front page," Ayjay said briskly as he and Kloo walked by. He looked exhausted. Lately the two of them had been putting in so many hours they often had to skip lunch.

"Atlanta this time," Kloo said out of the side of her mouth, pointing to the article and a picture of Zara. "She Damned the head of a dogfighting ring."

"Good," Lex said before she could stop herself. The other Juniors stared at her. Driggs looked especially disapproving.

"I mean — " She refrained from saying what she was thinking, that the world was probably better off, that Zara had done society a favor. Such unpopular opinions were what had gotten Lex into so much trouble in the first place. So she kept them to herself.

But she never stopped thinking them.

"How are you guys holding up?" Elysia asked Kloo and Ayjay. "And why are you talking all funny?"

Kloo grimaced. "We're not supposed to talk to you. It's stupid, I know, but Norwood will give us hell if he catches us. If we want to be Seniors, we have to act like Seniors," she said in a mocking tone.

Driggs almost growled. "Norwood is not in charge."

"I know," she said, her gaze fretfully flitting around the room. "But still, these longer shifts are hard enough. Maybe we can catch up sometime at Corpp's, okay?"

Ayjay sleepily grabbed a handful of fries as he left. "Doubtful."

Elysia watched them go. "Poor kids. Doesn't Norwood realize how crazy this is?"

"You know what's crazy?" said Pip. "Those things we put the souls in. Vessels, right? What are those things made out of? Looks like thread or something. Is it thread, Ferbus?"

"I'LL SHOW YOU LATER."

||||||

After lunch the Juniors headed to the Bank to get their scythes programmed for their afternoon shifts. While the rookies and their beleaguered partners were required to check in with Norwood and Heloise, Lex and Driggs could choose any available Etcetera in the hub. Each sat at his or her own cubicle, fingers flying across the keyboards of their Smacks, the computer-like devices connected to jellyfish that determined when and where a death was occurring.

"Sofi?" Driggs suggested, pointing. Sofi had skipped lunch as usual, dutifully pecking away at her Smack. "She's the only one who's free."

Lex groaned. They'd always checked in with Sofi over the summer, but lately Lex had done everything within her power to avoid the girl, choosing even the hostile Senior Etceteras over her. Especially now that Sofi's desk featured a new frolicking-fairy snow globe.

"Fine," Lex said. "Just don't be surprised if she tries to stab me with a nail file."

"Hi, Lex!" Sofi exclaimed, her honeyed voice dripping with false warmth. "Hi, Driggs!"

Lex was taken aback, but only slightly. Of *course* the little tramp would play nice in Driggs's presence.

Sure enough, Sofi gave him a playful shove. "Checking in?"

"Regrettably," Lex snipped under her breath, eyeing Sofi's roving hand.

"Omigod, I've *totally* missed you guys," Sofi said as she plugged their scythes into the Smack. "I guess we just keep missing each other, huh?"

Driggs smiled, ever the nice guy. "Something like that."

"I mean, I'm surprised they're still allowing you to do shifts at *all*," Sofi went on, almost frighteningly cheerful. "Because, like, I got suspended for two weeks after I got caught helping you."

Lex and Driggs exchanged glances. "Look, we're really sorry about that," Driggs said. "We didn't mean to get you in trouble."

"That's okay," Sofi said, leaning forward so that the neckline of her blouse dipped a little lower. "I'm sure you can figure out a way to make it up to me."

Driggs barely noticed the oncoming cleavage. A thoughtful look had come over his face. "Actually, I don't know why we *weren't* suspended."

"Maybe they want to keep you around so there are more chances for you to screw up," Sofi suggested, a slight edge to her voice.

"Or maybe they decided my sister getting killed was punishment enough," Lex snapped.

"Relax, spaz," Driggs muttered to her under his breath. He smiled at Sofi and pointed at her new snow globe. "So, where'd that come from?"

"Oh." Sofi's eyes fluttered. "It was a gift."

Something about her tone made Lex suspicious. "From?"

Sofi cleared her throat and started typing. "Um, Norwood and Heloise."

"What?" Lex exclaimed. "They hate the rest of us Juniors with the burning of a thousand suns and they're giving *you* presents?"

"Well, what was I supposed to do, say no?"

"Yes! Junior solidarity!"

Driggs folded his arms and glared at the directors. "Did they give you a reason, Sof?"

"Something about favors. I think they want me to keep tabs on the rest of you. But I'm not," she added quickly. She gave Lex a supersized smile. "Junior solidarity, totally."

On their way out of the Bank, Lex didn't know whether to laugh or punch her fist through a wall. "Norwood and Heloise are really barking up the wrong tree if they think they can turn that bimbo into a spy."

"True," said Driggs. "But we're not doing anything wrong, so really, we have nothing to worry about."

Lex huffed. "I don't get it. I mean, Zara killed Cordy — why in the world would anyone think I'm on the same side as her?"

"They don't know the whole story. They just see Juniors as one big threat, regardless of who killed who."

"But if they really think we're such threats, why *haven't* they kicked us out?"

"Because it would have to be over Mort's dead body. And Sofi's probably right about them waiting for you to screw up. They know what you're capable of, and they're going to twist it in a way that's to their advantage. You're their Exhibit A. Obviously, *we* know you're not going to lose your mind and go on a murderous Damning rampage, but the townspeople don't. The best way to get rid of the Juniors is to paint us as wild, out-of-control monsters, and that's exactly what Norwood and Heloise are doing."

"Unbelievable," Lex said as they arrived at the Ghost Gum. She stared at its smooth, chalky-white trunk, all the way up to the ghostly nest sitting atop its highest branches. Four months ago she didn't even know these people. Now they were plotting her demise.

For whatever reason, she thought of her mom. And dad. No matter how badly she'd misbehaved over the past couple of years, they'd always gone to bat for her — arguing with the principal to let her stay in school, meeting with the gym teacher to negotiate a way to replace all those punctured dodgeballs. They'd been such good parents. And yet she'd left them to come back to this bottomless fiasco.

It made her chest sting.

She ignored the pain, willed their faces out of her mind. "So now what?"

"We lie low, I guess. Maybe convince some of the more open-minded Croakers to come over to our side. We've already got Corpp and Pandora, and everyone loves them."

Lex sighed and readied her scythe. "Yeah, well, love doesn't always beat out fear."

"Sometimes it does," he replied with a smile, pecking her on the nose.

"Christ, Driggs. You're turning into a Lifetime movie."

"Your defense mechanisms are captivating, as always."

||||||

Lex's mechanisms, defense or otherwise, seemed to be tested at every turn over the next week. Norwood and Heloise's influence kept spreading through the town like a malicious fungus; Lex couldn't produce any evidence, but she was sure they were holding more secret meetings. It felt as if every one of her actions was being held under a microscope. As far as the Seniors were concerned, any misstep was evidence that Lex and the other Juniors were secretly plotting to bring down Croak, while their partner in crime, Zara, kept the fear alive everywhere else.

And throughout it all, Lex had to deal with the guilt of not spending every waking moment with her poor dead sister; in fact, she hadn't gone back since that first day. She told herself this was because she was too busy trying to solve the mystery of Bone's note, but she hadn't gotten anywhere with that either. Every time she jammed her hands into her pocket, she felt it there, taunting them, daring them to drop everything and lock themselves in a broom closet until they figured it out right down to the last letter.

Of course, they couldn't lock themselves in a broom closet. Or either of their rooms. Or anywhere in the house, for that matter. Uncle Mort wasn't kidding about constant surveillance. Anytime she and Driggs got within five feet of each other, he'd appear from nowhere and start chatting them up with thinly veiled weather-related metaphors.

"Hot today, huh?" he shouted one evening before dinner, popping his head into the living room as Lex and Driggs dove to opposite ends of the couch. "Better cool down soon." He grinned and made one of those two-fingered I'm-watching-you gestures.

Lex looked at her watch. Still a couple of hours before they had to leave for Corpp's; it was the rookies' one-week anniversary, which meant the Juniors would be meeting up to surprise them with a water balloon fight. "You're right, it's so nice out," she said loudly, dragging Driggs out of the house. "I think we'll go for a walk."

"I appreciate your commitment to fitness!"

When they were far enough down the road, Driggs plunged right back into her face, but Lex pushed him away. "I have a better idea," she said, marching toward the library. "We're going to figure out this note. Now."

"Oh." His face fell. "Yeah, that sounds fun too."

Once inside, she made a beeline for the Grotton section. "Here, look." They paged through the volumes on the shelves and studied each "wrong book" note, finally grabbing *Grotton: A Biography* and placing it on the large table.

"There." Lex flipped to the last page. "That's where I tore it out." She removed the note from her pocket, uncrumpled it, and fit it back into the page.

Driggs looked over the scratchy writing and bit his lip. "'The key to the dead awaits overhead.' But Croak is so flat. There aren't too many choices for things to be overhead."

"I know. The Bank is the only building with a second floor, and I doubt that whoever wrote this could sneak something in there." Lex briefly thought of the white figure that seemed to have been following her over the summer, then put it out of her mind and reached for the note once more. Here was something tangible, something real—not a blurry vision she wasn't even sure she had seen.

"Maybe it's not in Croak," Driggs suggested. "Could be in Necropolis—that's the capital, after all. Or what about DeMyse? On the other side of the country, all crazy and Hollywood-ish—pretty good place to hide something."

"Maybe," Lex said, switching her thinking up. "What about Bone? Maybe there's something in one of these books about him. Or her." Her eyes swept over the endless shelves of books, finally landing on the framed photos on the walls of Grims from years past, arranged in chronological order. "Maybe there's a picture."

"Lex, Bone could have been just some idiot kid with no respect for library property, with nothing to distinguish him or garner any mention in a book. It's probably not even his real name."

Lex frowned. "That's true."

"Plus, what makes him a bandit? And why is he sick?" He shook his head. "It's like he wrote the signature using Mad Libs. He may as well have signed it Spleen, the toasty orange tugboat."

"You're right," Lex said, slowly putting something together. "It doesn't make any sense!"

"You say that like it's a good thing."

"It is!" Goosebumps rippled up her arms as she grabbed a nearby pen and scrap of paper. "It's a code!"

"Or that. Sure."

Lex's hands were a blur as she wrote. "A simple substitution cipher? One letter for another? Or maybe it needs a keyword. Maybe Bone is the keyword. *Is Bone the keyword?*"

Driggs raised an eyebrow as she scribbled. "This is an interesting side of you I've never seen."

"My mom's a teacher," she said, staring at the paper without blinking. "Instead of cartoons and video games we got work sheets and word puzzles."

"I see." He reached in. "Maybe — "

"Don't touch!"

"Wow. Okay." He backed away, stifling a snicker. "I just think you're overthinking this."

She looked peeved. "Oh, am I, Sherlock?" She offered him the paper. "What do you think it is, just a simple anag —" Her eyes went wide.

Next thing Driggs knew, Lex was rummaging around in the closet. "Are you looking for your sanity?" he called after her. "Because I do believe it showed itself out a while ago."

She emerged with a Scrabble box in hand. "Silence," she said, dumping the tiles on the table. "Let me think."

Driggs sank into a seat next to her and put his feet up on the table as Lex spelled out BONE THE SICK SCYTHE BANDIT. Five minutes later she had rearranged them into several words, none of which made any sense.

"Nosy tennis?" she said. "No, wait. Sticky cabin? Shitty chicken?"

Driggs frowned. "Wait —"

"Shitty chicken? Really, Driggs?"

"No, no. Cabin." He thought for a moment. "Why does that sound familiar?" He switched CABIN with STICKY, removed the Y, and rearranged the remaining tiles to form a new phrase.

Lex read it aloud. "The cabin beyond the sticks." She turned to him. "Don't know what it means, but still! It's something!"

Driggs didn't reply. He just stared at the words, his eyes growing larger.

"Why am I the only one getting excited about this?" Lex said. "What's wrong?"

"I" — he blinked hard — "I think I just remembered something. I think I know what this means."

"Seriously? What? What are the sticks?"

"Sticks with a capital *S*. It's a name, Sticks River. And I can't — I'd have to show you — "

"Then show away," Lex said, excitedly pulling him out of his chair, all the way out of the library, and onto the street.

Driggs turned left, away from the town. "Where are you going?" Lex asked.

"Shhh." He looked back at the people on the street. "Keep walking."

When they reached Uncle Mort's house and then passed it, Lex raised an eyebrow. "I didn't think there was anything else down this way."

Driggs glanced up the road and donned a strange expression. "Mort brought me to this place only once, when I was fifteen. I had been a Grim for a year already — you know, since I came here earlier than everyone else, when I was fourteen — and I thought I knew every nook and cranny of Croak. Then one day Ayjay correctly pointed out that I didn't know what was past the Sticks River, and idiot that I was, I decided to find out. But Mort caught me before I even left the house and insisted on taking me himself, figuring that I would probably go and investigate on my own no matter how many times he stopped me."

"Little Driggs sounds a lot like me," said Lex.

"Please don't besmirch his memory." He glanced behind them, then faced forward again. "Anyway, one day after work he took me into the forest up there and turned off into a small, hidden path. It was fine at first. But once we took a few steps in, the air got chillier. My mind began to swim. I felt dizzy, disoriented — like thoughts were melting out of my head faster than I could think them. But Mort told me to keep going."

He rubbed his forehead, trying to remember. "Next came

these sharp, stabbing pains ripping through my stomach, then a sort of burn in my lungs, then a god-awful ache through my arms and legs. And once the searing headache set in, I think I sort of just fell over. Mort — who was holding up slightly better than me — eventually noticed that I had been reduced to a pile of quivering jelly, and he dragged me back to the entrance. And then, just like that, the pain was gone."

Lex exhaled noisily. "Weird."

"Yeah."

"And as usual, Uncle Mort didn't give you a single word of explanation."

"You're not going to believe this. He did." Driggs's eyes darkened. "He said that at the end of the path is an old, deserted cabin. And no one knows what's inside, not even Mort, because no one has ever been able to get anywhere near it. I think he's gotten the closest of anyone — he said that after the physical pain comes emotional torture, where your most terrible memories start flying through your head and start to drive you insane — but he couldn't take it, he had to come back."

"Wow," Lex said softly. Her uncle had demons, she had already known that — but were they really bad enough to physically stop him in his tracks? "Who else knows about this place?"

"Mort said he and I were the only ones. And now you." He let out a long breath. "He must have Amnesia'd me afterward, because I haven't remembered any of this in years, not until we spelled out those words. He must not have wanted me to go back and try again." He frowned and stopped walking.

"What's wrong?"

He swept his gaze across the landscape, then looked back at Lex. "Are you sure this is a good idea?"

"It's all we've got."

"Yeah, but doesn't this whole thing feel kind of off? Mort must be keeping that place secret for a reason." He scratched his head. "I don't know, maybe we should just burn that note and forget we ever found it in the first place."

"Are you crazy?" She held up the note. "You see this word right here? 'Redemption.' I want redemption, Driggs. I want to make things right. If there's even the slightest chance I can do that, no matter how ridiculous or far-fetched the words on this piece of paper are, I'm going to do it."

"Just like you did last time? Look how great that plan worked out — your sister got killed!"

Lex's mouth fell open. She felt like she had been slapped. A nasty comeback seemed to be the way to go, but nothing came to mind. Driggs, for his part, seemed to realize that he'd said something terribly wrong but hadn't the first clue how to fix it.

So, being the mature, reasonable individuals they were, they bolted. Driggs took off for Uncle Mort's house while Lex crammed the note into her pocket and stalked back toward town, pulling her hood up to hide her watering eyes. Yet the closer she got to the center, the more people stared, shaking their heads in disapproval.

"What?" she finally shouted at Trumbull.

"You should be ashamed of yourself," he said, wiping his butcher knife. "You kids act like this town is your own personal playground."

Lex bit her quivering lip and walked a bit faster. She'd been used to people hating her in high school, but this was different. These were people she supposedly belonged with. *Her* people.

The sorority girl Senior joined in, her hands on her hips. "Whatever happened between you and Zara — it affects us all." Her name was Riley, Lex had learned, and she was maybe in her late twenties. The gigantic sunglasses on her face made her look like a trendy housefly. "Other people's lives are at stake here too, you know!"

Lex ducked around her and ran up the porch stairs to the Bank. She blew past Kilda and headed up to the second-floor office, hoping to trick Snodgrass into letting her in. But another youngish Senior woman was there instead, looking at her with an intrigued expression.

"Hey, you're Lex, aren't you?" she asked. Lex wiped her eyes and prepared herself for another barrage of insults, but the Senior gave her a sympathetic look. "Were they harassing you again? Christ, this place is going to hell in a Norwood-and-Heloise-woven handbasket. Maybe if those two would shut their faces for five seconds, everyone else would wake up and remember how to think for themselves again."

This outpouring of independent thought caught Lex way off-guard. She didn't think Seniors were capable of it anymore.

The girl smiled, sending freckles everywhere. Her hair was black and cut short, with a long streak of red bangs sweeping across her forehead. "I'm Wicket." She leaned across the desk and held out her hand.

Lex shook it and looked around. "Where's Snodgrass?"

"He left for the day, saints be praised. I'm the graveyard shifter." She nudged Lex. "You want to go in and see your sister?"

"You're not going to give me a hard time about it?"

"Anything to piss off Snoddy," Wicket said, punching the code into the computer. "Plus it's common decency. She's your sister, for chrissakes. Go ahead, sweetie — and say hi to my better half."

Lex thanked her and stepped through the vault door, only to find that the atrium was empty once again. "Cordy?" Lex shouted at the Void.

"I'll get her," a miserable-sounding voice piped up. Edgar Allan Poe materialized from nowhere and flashed Lex the closest thing he could get to a smile.

"Ed!" She waved at him, then at Quoth, the raven sitting on his shoulder. She hadn't seen either of them since returning to Croak. Just their mere presence made her feel a million times better. "Where have you been all this time?"

"Martin Van Buren threw my favorite hat into a canyon," he snipped. "I was retrieving it."

Lex looked at his bare head. "Where is it, then?"

"A coyote ate it. Look, I don't have time for this," he said, stomping off to the Void.

At the desk sat a Senior with the exact opposite hairstyle of Wicket's — red and long, with black bangs. "Are you the better half?" Lex asked her.

The woman laughed. "Yes. I'm Roze." She greeted Lex with a pair of henna-stained hands, the intricate designs curling around her bony fingers. "And you're Lex, and I just want you to know — Wicket and I, we're big fans of yours. We've always been close with your uncle, and we know you're good people. Anyone who thinks otherwise clearly can't tell their head from their pooper."

Lex cracked a smile. "Thanks."

"Well, look who decided to swing by," Cordy said from be-hind her, on the heels of Poe.

Lex turned around guiltily. "I've been busy."

"Save it, Pants-On-Fire. I've heard it all before. Hell, I'm shocked you managed to squeeze my funeral into such a jam-packed schedule," she said in a haughty voice, though her eyes were light and joking. She bent her head to look under Lex's hood. "You okay?"

"Yeah," Lex said, sniffing and trying not to look as if she'd just escaped a lynching in the town square. "Just some . . . stuff. Going on. I'm fine. How are things in here?"

"Things are awesome," Cordy said. "I ate two entire pizzas yes-terday for no good reason, I built three more roller coasters — "

"Torture machines," muttered Poe.

"And I got myself a camel," Cordy finished with a smile.

Lex stared at her. "Why?"

"Duh, Lex, because I *can*. His name is Lumpy, he spits all the time, and he's freakin' adorable. We're going on a trip to Afterlife Egypt next week. I'm trying to convince Eddie here to come, but since he so disliked our jaunt to the Grand Canyon, I'm not sure he'd fare too well."

"I got sand in places where there should not be sand," he said testily. "Plus the vortex was quite unsettling. I did not enjoy that."

"Vortex?" Lex asked. "What do you mean?"

Cordy furrowed her brow. "You know, I'm not sure. I mean, I've only been here for a little while, but I haven't seen anything else like it. It wasn't too big — just a small area down in a corner somewhere — and it was this weird whirlpool of matter, or what-ever matter is in here. Just kind of draining everything around it into nothingness, like a swirly black hole."

Lex frowned. "That's weird." She turned to Roze. "You ever hear of anything like that?"

Roze nodded. "Yeah, the other day Lewis and Clark said they'd seen something similar in Yellowstone." She shrugged. "I'm sure someone's putting them there for fun. Like the time Eli Whitney erected those giant cotton gins all over the place to commemorate its anniversary. Some people just like attention."

As if on cue, a horseshoe pelted Poe right in the noggin. Quoth squawked and took off in a flurry of feathers. "Heads up!" Thomas Jefferson shouted between titters.

Poe huffed into his mustache. "Ingrate."

Lex stayed and chatted for a while longer, and by the time she said good night to Kilda and pounded down the Bank porch steps, she felt worlds better. Cordy wasn't mad at her for slacking on her visiting duties, Wicket and Roze had reaffirmed her faith that there were at least some people out there who didn't want to see her torn apart by feral wolves, and her fight with Driggs had faded into a distant memory. She didn't even feel mad at him anymore, not really. He was probably right. The note *was* a bit sketchy.

Other than the dull roar from the crowd inside Corpp's pub, Dead End was eerily silent. Lex squinted into the Field, its gaping, black volume broken only by the jagged angles of the Ghost Gum. As her eyes adjusted to the darkness, she happened to glance at the ground — and stop. An odd splatter of something stretched to her left while a series of long, drizzled drops extended from her feet all the way to the fountain. She took a few cautious steps forward, and that's when she heard it.

A faint, weak cough.

"Hello?" she said, breaking into a run toward the obelisk. She could have sworn the sound came from the center of the plaza, but no one was there. A sinking, horrible feeling began to creep into her stomach as she circled the fountain, still finding nothing. But it wasn't until she peered over the fountain's ledge, directly at the rapidly hemorrhaging gash across Driggs's chest, that she started to scream.

6

After that, the world fell silent. Half the town came pouring out of Corpp's to watch the scene unfold, Uncle Mort and Norwood pushing each other over to get to the fountain first, but Lex barely noticed. The townspeople's shouts of fear, Driggs's choked utterances of something that sounded like "She's here," Ferbus's cries for a doctor, Uncle Mort shouting at Lex to back away *right now* — all fell on deaf ears as Lex instinctively grabbed Driggs's arms, lifted him up with an adrenaline-fueled strength, and tore her scythe through the air.

When they emerged from the ether a few moments later, Lex thought she was dead. Blinding white light, like the atrium of the Afterlife, flooded her vision and nearly threw her off balance. But she held on tight to Driggs's shuddering body, summoning every last ounce of her strength to yell for help down the brightly lit, chaotic hallway.

|||||||

Lex was dreaming, but at least she was aware of it. She knew nothing was real — not the towering figure of Norwood, nor the tidal wave of blood á la *The Shining,* nor the biting stab wound in her rib cage —

Actually, the stabbing pain was very real; a hard plastic arm-rest had wedged itself into her side. With a jolt, Lex sat up and opened her eyes, only to find a middle-aged, heavyset woman clad all in blue staring back at her.

"Stay right there," the woman said, nervous. She reached over to adjust an IV tube, a confusing image for Lex until she realized that it was connected to Driggs's arm. They were in an emergency room. Driggs lay unconscious on the bed, a large white bandage across his chest, his jeans stained a dark red.

"Is he okay?" Lex asked.

"He lost a lot of blood, but he'll be fine," the woman said, backing toward the curtain. "Don't you move now. The officer just wants to ask you a few questions."

"What?" Lex jumped out of the chair. "What officer?"

The nurse let out a squeak. "Please don't hurt me!"

"I won't," Lex said, for the first time realizing how bad this must look. She patted her pocket. Her scythe was gone.

"Looking for this?" A tall cop waltzed through the curtain, nodding at the nurse as she sped away. He held up a Ziploc bag containing Lex's scythe.

"I didn't do this." Lex swallowed. "I need — I have to call — "

"Calm down," he said with a smile. "Your buddy's going to be just fine."

"We can't stay here. We have to go."

"Now, hold on a second, missy." His smile waned. "You materialize out of thin air with this poor boy all carved up, both of you covered in blood — no IDs, no cell phones, and no way to contact your parents — and you think I'm just going to let you go, no questions asked?"

Lex looked at her scythe in his hand, then at Driggs. She backed up against the wall. Now what? She was sure she could wriggle past the officer by herself, but there was no way she'd be able to escape with Driggs too. The more the impossibility of the situation weighed on her, the angrier she got. And the hard look on the police officer's face just added fuel to the flame in her chest and tingling hands. It would be so easy to take him down, so easy for her to Damn him right where he stood—

A commotion outside the curtain snapped Lex back to her senses. Smoke was now drifting in across the floor. "What the hell was that?" the officer said. He pointed at Lex. "Stay here."

As soon as he left, Lex closed the curtain back up, flung herself at the bed, and shook Driggs. "Wake up!" she half yelled, half whispered. "Driggs!"

His eyes fluttered. "Wha? Where are we?"

"Hospital." Lex started unplugging the tubes in his arm. "I summoned it into existence, or I opened up a wormhole, or maybe a giant goddamn eagle showed up to fly us here and save the day—I don't know! But we have to leave. Now."

Driggs looked down at his chest. "I've got like fifty stitches here."

"Your courage in the face of adversity is an inspiration to us all." She pulled at his shoulders. "Now GET UP."

The sound of hurried footsteps pounded through the smoke. Lex held her breath as the curtain swooshed open.

"She's right," Uncle Mort said to Driggs. "We gotta go."

Driggs nearly fell out of the bed as Lex dropped him to go hug her uncle. "Where have you been?" she asked him.

"Where have *I* been?" Uncle Mort looked incredulous. "You never cease to amaze, kiddo."

"Ow!" Driggs was doubled over. "Little help here?"

Lex ran back to his side. "Sorry." She grabbed his torn-up hoodie from the chair, put her shoulder under his arm, and looked at Uncle Mort. "Now what?"

He nodded toward the exit. "We leave."

"What about the police?" Lex said, lugging Driggs down the hall. "And the nurses and doctors and everyone under the sun who saw us get here?"

"Amnesia smoke bombs," he replied as they wove their way through the emergency room, dodging coughing patients and hospital staff. "Been itching to try them out for a while now. We're immune, but the Amnesia wipes everyone else's recent memory, allowing us to disappear in a puff of smoke like the ninjas that we are."

Lex squinted through the haze, her eyes unable to focus. Everything was loud and moving and chaotic, except for —

Through the smoke, leaning against a wall and staring directly at her, was a man in a white tuxedo.

She couldn't make out his face, but she felt his eyes on her all the same. He didn't move. He didn't seem to notice the smoke or the pandemonium surrounding it. He just stared at Lex, following her eyes as she made her way toward the door.

Out of nowhere, that same memory of the woods surfaced. Lex was back in Croak, at the beginning of the summer, inching through the darkened forest, following Driggs down to the lake in what was to be her water balloon fight initiation. Driggs had just disappeared from view, and the woods were swallowing her up in their shadows — until she registered that faint, white figure in the distance. It hadn't come any closer, but it had definitely been moving. Watching her, almost.

Watching her like the man in the tuxedo.

But then Uncle Mort made a sharp left and the man disappeared from view. Lex snapped back to the situation at hand, shifting Driggs's weight.

"At some point on the tour, I'd really love an explanation of all this," Driggs piped up.

"Only if you promise not to bleed all over my car," Uncle Mort said as he walked through the automatic doors to freedom, yanking Lex's scythe out of the distracted police officer's hand on the way.

Uncle Mort's yellow car glowed under the lights of the parking lot like a golden hunk of Velveeta. Lex laid Driggs across the back seat, then hopped into the front.

"You okay back there?" Uncle Mort asked Driggs once they were on the road.

Driggs made a thumbs-up with some effort, then dropped his hand to the floor and moaned. "Did you catch her?" he asked, his eyes squeezed shut in pain.

Lex turned around in her seat and looked at him. "Catch who?"

He opened one eye. "Didn't anyone see her? Zara!"

Uncle Mort stared at him in the rearview mirror. "Tell me what happened."

Driggs drew a heavy breath. "I was waiting for Lex to come home, but she never did, so I left to see if she was at Corpp's. When I passed the Bank, Zara grabbed me from behind and held her scythe to my throat. She whispered something — I couldn't hear it too well, but it sounded like, 'It's mine. Pass it on.' Then she slashed and pushed me in the fountain."

"'It's mine?'" Lex asked. "What was she talking about?"

"How should I know?"

Uncle Mort's gaze was going back and forth between the mirror and the road. "What color was her scythe?"

"Sadly, I wasn't able to take the time to appreciate its subtle hues as it tore through my skin." Driggs winced in pain. "Wasn't silver like her old one, though, I can tell you that much."

"What difference does the color make?" Lex asked.

"Could indicate who gave it to her," Uncle Mort said. "Only a few Grims on earth make replacement scythes. They're wildly illegal."

"But how did she Crash in without anyone noticing?" Lex asked.

Uncle Mort looked bitter. "Someone hacked into the security system and disabled it. Either Zara or someone she's hired."

Lex just blinked. "I don't get it. Why go through all that trouble just to slash him and leave? Why didn't she" — she couldn't say it — "do something worse?"

"Leverage, probably," Uncle Mort said. "She knows she can get you to do whatever she wants if she can use his life as a bargaining chip. Trust me, Driggs is worth way more to her alive than dead."

Driggs cleared his throat. "You know I can hear you, right?"

"Still, you're right, Lex," Uncle Mort said. "It's odd for her to just show up without a purpose. What did she say again, Driggs? 'It's mine'?"

"Yeah."

"*What's* hers? What was she looking for?"

Lex inhaled sharply, a sudden thought smacking into her brain. "The book!" she shouted. She looked at Driggs, then her uncle. "The Wrong Book!"

The car was silent for a few seconds as Lex dug into her hoodie pocket.

"Lex," Uncle Mort said, "would you like me to turn this car right around and bring you back to the psych ward?"

"Hang on," Driggs said as Lex pulled out Bone's note. "She might be right."

Lex gave him a look. "You don't have to sound so shocked about it."

"But it happens so rarely. Like an eclipse."

"Give me that," Uncle Mort said, snatching the scrap of paper from Lex's hand. He read it over, then looked at her. "Where did you find this?"

Lex hesitated. She hadn't yet told her uncle anything about Bone's note or what she'd discovered in the library after the attacks. She kept telling herself this was because she didn't want to bother him with silly fantasies —

But that was before Driggs had almost gotten gutted like a fish.

So she spilled everything. "*And* there was an empty space at the end of the shelf, where a book had been," she finished. "I bet Zara took it because there was another copy of this note in there! She's looking for the key to the dead and the Wrong Book too!"

Uncle Mort thought for a moment. "You might be right."

"Again with the shock. Thanks a lot, asshats."

"Ever hear anything about this stuff, Mort?" Driggs asked. "Bone, key to the dead, Wrong Book?"

"Bone, no," he replied. "Wrong Book? Yeah, every Grim has heard of that. Grotton's recipe collection of horrors."

"It disappeared centuries ago, though, right?" Driggs said.

Uncle Mort squinted down the road, then adjusted the side-view mirrors. "Hmm?"

Lex studied him. "Uncle Mort," she said, "is there something you're not telling us?"

He stared straight ahead and said nothing.

She leaned in closer. "Is the Wrong Book in Croak? In your basement? In the *trunk of this car?*"

"The Wrong Book is in a safe place," he said matter-of-factly. "That's all I can tell you."

"In the cabin beyond the Sticks?"

Uncle Mort jerked the wheel so sharply Lex had to grab the door handle to keep her head from hitting the window.

"Where did you hear that?" he shouted over Driggs's cries of pain from the back seat.

"Driggs told me," she quickly answered.

"Thanks, pumpkin," Driggs groaned. "Love you too."

Uncle Mort scowled. "What do you know about the cabin?"

"What do *you* know about the cabin?" Lex countered. "The signature on the note—it can be rearranged to spell out 'the cabin beyond the Sticks.' So it must mean something. Is that where the Wrong Book is?"

He gave up. "Yes. But," he added before Lex could start freaking out, "I don't know where the key is. No one does. And even if we did have the key, I don't know how to get past the protective shield. That was put into place long before I was a twinkle in my father's eye, and they didn't exactly leave a user's manual." When no one said anything, he rolled his eyes. "That's all I know, Officer. I swear."

"You've known this the whole time and you never told us?"

"I wasn't aware that you were in the market for forbidden atrocities of lore. Besides, it's my job to keep classified information classified. I'm the goddamned mayor, in case you've forgotten."

He had her there.

After a mile or two of silence Driggs asked, "How long was I out? I don't even remember the ride to the hospital."

"There was no ride," said Uncle Mort.

"Huh? Then how did I get there?"

"Yeah, I'd like to hear this myself," said Uncle Mort. "Care to share, Lex?"

Lex's throat went dry. "I don't know. I really don't. I — I saw him lying there all bloody, and without thinking, my hand just flew to my scythe and I tore us out of there. I swear, there wasn't a thought in my head other than keeping him alive — "

"You scythed at will?" Driggs said. "With direction? How in the hell — " He was overcome by a fit of coughing.

Lex looked at Uncle Mort. "I really don't know."

Uncle Mort sighed. "I guess when Zara Culled your power to Damn, you absorbed her ability to Crash. An even trade."

The Ziploc bag containing Lex's scythe sat on the dashboard. She picked it up and removed its contents, weighing her treasured weapon in her hand. It shone ominously in the lights of the highway, its darkness absolute. No wonder the townspeople feared her.

"But I didn't know what I was doing," she said. "Or where to go."

"We passed by the hospital on the way back from the rookie trip," Uncle Mort said. "It must have found its way into your subconscious."

"But how did you know where to find us?"

"As soon as you disappeared, I ran home and activated the CuffLink, a little project I've been working on ever since Zara kidnapped you. Can pinpoint and track the exact location of any Grim, as long as their Cuff is switched on."

Lex slumped in her seat. "I risked exposing us."

"It's a good thing you did," said Uncle Mort. "The cut wasn't too deep, but it was long, and he was losing a lot of blood. I'm not sure even our best medics would have been able to fix him in time."

"Uh, maybe we need better medics," said Driggs.

"Yeah, well, we've never needed them before. The Grimsphere hasn't seen violence like this in years. But you're right — we should stock up on more medical supplies, beef up security — "

"And next time we'll be ready for her," Lex said.

Uncle Mort let out a bitter laugh. "You better hope there's not a next time, kiddo. Half the town witnessed you Crashing out of there with a bloody, half-dead Driggs in your arms. What kind of a welcome-back party do you think you're going to get?"

There was nothing more to say after that. Driggs soon fell asleep, Uncle Mort fixed his eyes on the road, and Lex restlessly gazed out the window, seeing only her reflection in the glass as the black, limitless night blurred by.

||||||||

By the time they reached Dead End, it was nearly midnight. Uncle Mort tried to zip through town before anyone saw them, but the instant they got to the fountain, Norwood and Heloise barged out of Corpp's and stood in front of the car. A handful of townspeople trickled out behind them to watch.

"Get out, Mort."

Uncle Mort rolled down the window. "Hey, Woody. I'll have a quarter pounder with cheese, hold the mustard."

Heloise opened the passenger door and pulled Lex out of the car by her hood. "Here she is," she said with a triumphant smile, presenting Lex to the crowd as if she were a prizewinning trout. She glanced at the back seat. "The boy is in there too."

"And he's alive, I'd like to point out," Uncle Mort said as he exited the car. "Which, in the end, is all that matters."

"Oh, well, thank heavens," Norwood said in a mocking tone. "As long as he's alive, there's no need to ask what happened to him, or why he was attacked in the first place, or how in bloody hell *she* managed to Crash out of here on her own!"

"Look—"

"What's it going to take, Mort?" Norwood was seething. "How many more attacks need to happen before you admit that you can't protect us? Who stabbed you?" he yelled into the car. "Huh? Who was it, Driggs?"

Driggs shakily sat up and poked his head out the door. "Zara. But—"

"Zara!" Norwood turned to the crowd. "She was *here,* not ten feet away from the bar! I don't even want to think of how easy it would have been for her to barge in and Damn everyone in the place. We'd never even know what hit us!"

Uncle Mort looked amused. "And what would you have done to prevent this, Norwood?"

"A hell of a lot more than you have, that's for sure."

Uncle Mort's smile did not falter. "Could we have some specifics? Come on, let's hear your master plan."

A single bead of sweat appeared on Norwood's forehead. "Patrols around the perimeter — "

"Would be useless, since Zara is able to Crash inside to specific locations. The population monitoring system is our most effective security measure, fully capable of detecting people as they enter and exit Croak no matter where they're coming from — or it would be, if Zara hadn't hacked in and disabled it."

"What about a warning system?" Heloise said.

"The entire encounter lasted less than five seconds, Hel. I doubt that even with your admirable ability to sprint in heels, you would have been able to get there in time."

"Surveillance cameras!" a furious Norwood roared.

"Are already in place. In fact, *your* Etceteras are supposed to be monitoring them. How's that going, by the way?"

Norwood sputtered, but said nothing.

Uncle Mort turned to the confused crowd. "Folks, a threat of this nature hasn't terrorized the Grimsphere in centuries. That doesn't mean we can't protect ourselves, but we need to do it a little more creatively. We're not dealing with a cracked-out lunatic here — Zara is smart, focused, and willing to improvise and experiment with whatever will work to her advantage. This makes her unpredictable and extremely dangerous."

"That should be the Junior motto," Norwood snarled. "Because now *this* one can Crash, and yet you're still keeping her around. She can Damn too, can't she? That's great, Mort. A ticking time bomb right here in our own town, free to do whatever the hell she pleases despite the fact that this — all of this — was her fault to begin with!"

He turned to the crowd. "Isn't that nice, folks? He just let her right back in without even a slap on the wrist. She's probably even working with Zara. Hell, they probably *all* are! Doesn't seem fair, does it? Doesn't seem fair to the honest, hard-working citizens of this town to let these out-of-control brats play cowboys and Indians with our lives!"

Uncle Mort did not respond to this, but instead smiled calmly at the crowd. "We're doing everything we can to keep you safe. Trust me."

Norwood, now red, straightened his jacket and put his face close to Uncle Mort's. "You're a shitty mayor, Mort. And you're an even shittier liar." He grabbed Heloise's hand and started to walk away, turning back only to shout once more to the townspeople before disappearing into the night.

"He's going to get us all killed!"

||||||

The trio returned home exhausted. "That went well, huh?" Uncle Mort said. He held up an imaginary Yorick as he headed to the basement. "To the end of my reign."

"What?" Lex cried. "Come on, Uncle Mort, the people love you. They'd never —"

The door slammed.

Lex sat down on the couch, where Driggs had pulled up his shirt and was peeking under the bandage. "Oh, God," she whispered, getting a good look at his stitches for the first time. A lump tugged at her throat. "Does it hurt?"

"Not as much as the knowledge that you'll never let me forget you saved my life. I might rather be dead."

Lex tried to laugh, but it just came out as a weird gurgle.

Driggs replaced the bandage and gave her a crooked grin. "Seriously, though, thanks for doing what you did. Even if it was a little unorthodox."

Lex lightly ran her hand across the bandage, then across the scars that had been there for years. Driggs hadn't exactly grown up in the most loving home.

"And listen," he said, his face reddening. "I'm sorry about earlier, what I said about your sister. It was douchey."

"Yeah, but you weren't wrong. Things *are* getting dangerous. Clearly."

"Good thing chicks dig scars, right?"

"Oh yeah. The deader, the better."

"Necrophiliac."

She flipped him off. He grinned and ripped the bandage off his chest in retaliation.

"Ewww!" she shrieked, laughing as he put the bloody stitches closer to her face. "What is *wrong* with you?"

"What's the matter? Don't you want to see me naked?"

"*No,* I — well, yes." She smiled and put her hand on his chest. "Yes, I do."

She was just about to prove this to him when Uncle Mort pounded on the ceiling of the basement.

"I sense affection!" he yelled. "Knock it off, you two!"

Scowling at the camera, Lex retreated to the other end of the couch while Driggs pulled his shirt back down and gave her a disappointed look.

"Next time Crash us to a hotel room, okay?" he grumbled.

|||||

For the second time in the past twelve hours, Lex was awakened by uncomfortable furniture. She and Driggs had zonked out on opposite ends of the lumpy couch, and not all sorts of unclothed and on top of each other, as she would have preferred.

She rubbed her eyes. They'd fallen asleep with the lights on, but the sky was still dark. Her watch informed her it was 3:36 — plenty of time to get more sleep, but her brain wasn't really allowing that to happen. Besides, she was freezing.

She glanced at Driggs. His hoodie was practically a torn-up rag at this point, the ripped shards hanging loosely against his chest. He stirred in his sleep — maybe he was cold too. Lex grabbed the only nearby blanket and draped it over him, mentally writing an acceptance speech for her Girlfriend of the Year award.

Until the blanket caught on a scrap of paper sticking out of his jeans pocket. Frowning, Lex pulled it out and skimmed it —

"Driggs, wake up." She shook him. "Driggs!"

"Whaaat?" he groaned, squinting. "Why again? With the shaking?"

She held up the scrap. "I just found this in your pants."

Driggs raised an eyebrow. "What were you doing in my pants?"

She smacked him. "Focus! Read what it says."

"'If redemption is that which you prize —'" He bolted upright. "Another copy of Bone's note? Same handwriting, too?"

"Zara must have put it in your pocket!"

Driggs frowned. "She did put one hand around my waist. She could have easily snuck it in there. I was a bit preoccupied with, you know, not dying."

Lex grinned. "Which means Zara *is* after the key to the dead, the Wrong Book, the whole shebang. I was right!"

"Is that what she meant by 'pass it on'?" He examined the note more closely. "She wants us to find it and give it to her? Do we *look* like we run an ancient-book delivery service?"

"She must know we're looking for the same thing. She has to. Otherwise why insist that it's hers, when — "

She stopped. Driggs was looking at the back of the note. His face had gone pale.

"What?"

Wordlessly, he turned it around so she could see what had been written, in a hand different from Bone's. Zara's.

ONE PER DAY UNTIL IT'S MINE, LEX.

She looked at him, her blood ice. "One per day? One what per day?"

The next morning, Necropolis's newest rookie was found Damned in his bed, his body still smoldering.

7

The following week was excruciating.

True to her word, Zara kept on Damning — one per day, same as she had for the past few weeks.

Except her victims were no longer criminals.

"I feel vomity," Lex said one morning at the breakfast table, limply tossing aside *The Obituary*. A black-and-white photo of a smiling couple stared back at her, their honeymoon cut short after Zara had Damned the bride in her sleep. Lex counted on her fingers. "The nun in South Carolina. The Culler in Necropolis. That little boy — "

"Still can't believe that one," said Driggs. "Damning a kinder-gartner? She's sick."

"She's desperate," said Uncle Mort, prodding one of the sur-veillance gadgets he'd been tinkering with ever since the incident.

"But why? What's in the Wrong Book that she so badly needs?"

Uncle Mort looked up from his work to think. "Well, right now, Zara is small potatoes — going after criminals individually, one by one. Or she was, before she started killing innocents. My guess is that the Wrong Book contains some sort of method for extinguishing large numbers of people, say, an entire prisonful." He shrugged. "Either that or she's seeking a formula for immor-tality. Which would be, in a word, craptastic."

"Aren't both of those scenarios equally craptastic?" Lex said.

"Even if we did manage to get the Wrong Book, we could never afford to hand it over to her."

"Obviously. But it'll open up room for negotiations."

"Is there at least something in there *we* can use?"

"Lex. Seriously?" Uncle Mort said, looking about ready to disown her. "The Wrong Book's contents are poisonous, meant to destroy the world piece by piece until there's nothing left. It's been locked up and protected for centuries for that very reason. So I'm going to go with no."

"What makes her think we have it, anyway?" said Driggs. "Why does she think we're holding out on her?"

"She doesn't know whether we have it or not," said Uncle Mort. "But she also doesn't have the freedom to search Croak for it herself. It's a lot easier just to make you guys get it."

"Easier?" Lex said, rubbing her stomach. It had been a mess for days. "Damning innocents is the *easy* way?"

"It's working," he said. "Isn't it?"

It was. Ever since Lex saw Zara's scribbled words on that note, she had thought of little else other than finding the key. Every day that went by without progress, she felt the weight of another singed body on her conscience.

Driggs wanted to help in the search, but Uncle Mort had put him on strict bed rest and forbidden Lex to stay home with him all day. "No need to play nurse," he'd said. "We all know how that randy little scenario plays out." So the new plan was for Driggs to read over the books Lex grabbed for him from the library, while she would sniff out any clues she might find around town.

This plan, Lex quickly found out, sucked. The added pressure seemed to make things worse. She looked up every time she entered a building, but she saw no keys to anything, metaphorical or otherwise. Most days she just ended up at the Morgue around lunchtime, grumpy and defeated.

"What are you so pissed about?" Ferbus asked her. "*You* didn't get sliced and diced."

Lex's nostrils flared, but she held her tongue. She'd always found Ferbus's fierce loyalty to Driggs to be admirable, but after what happened, the rift that existed between her and Ferbus had widened considerably. Lex had a feeling she'd never hear the end of this.

Bang's nose was in a book, as usual, and Pip was reading *The Obituary*. He pointed at Zara's picture and the instructions underneath that explicitly stated she was not to be harmed when captured. "Why do they want to take her alive?"

Elysia put on a pained face. "Well, punishment in the Grimsphere is a little different than it is in the outside world. We Grims know that death means the Afterlife, and that's not so bad, is it? So in the eyes of the Grimsphere government, the best punishment is to keep criminals out of the Afterlife and alive for as long as possible, but under really terrible conditions."

Lex had never heard about this. "What, like torture?"

Elysia nodded. "The Hole," she said in a quiet voice. "Supposedly it's a deep, dark pit in Necropolis where you live out the rest of your natural life all alone, cold, and in the dark. If you stop eating, they force-feed you. If you try to commit suicide, they revive you. Most people lose their minds."

Ferbus let out a snort. "Sounds almost as much fun as watching your best friend bleed to death."

Lex shot him a smile so forced it hurt her cheeks. "Why don't you go hang out with him for the afternoon? I'll sub in for your shift."

Ferbus studied her, then nodded. "Okay. Maybe I can pick up some tips on how to stay alive in your presence, or . . ."

He trailed off. Three Seniors were looming over their booth.

"Hey, Damners," said Snodgrass with a menacing grin. "Doom anyone's soul to eternal torment today?"

"Like they're smart enough to plan anything without instructions from Zara," said Riley, still wearing those obnoxious sunglasses. She giggled and squeezed Lazlo, the punkish blond guy who guarded the Afterlife, whose arm was woven through hers.

Ferbus seemed to be fighting himself over whether to insult her or keep staring at her voluminous rack. "What do you want?"

"Just checking up on you guys," said Riley. "Make sure you're not plotting a terrorist attack or anything."

"In case your Neanderthal brain has already forgotten, Zara stabbed Driggs," Lex said, a flare of anger burning through her hands. "You think she'd do that if we were on her side?"

"Maybe, to throw off suspicion," said Riley. "Who knows why you kids do any of the crap you do?"

"And who knows why you guys are such assholes?" Lex countered, taking a sip of her soda. "Life is just full of little mysteries, isn't it?"

Snodgrass suddenly slapped the soda out of her hand, all joking gone from his face.

"Listen, you little shits," he snarled. "We don't appreciate our town being held hostage. It's not fair to the people who have been here for years, Grims who have to live in fear because some punk-ass degenerates decided they wanted to try their hands at playing

God." He leaned in. "So why don't you just get the hell out of Croak and go back to the miserable slums you crawled out of."

Ferbus and Lex simultaneously lunged at him. Ferbus seized his wrist and started to twist it, but Lex—

Lex's arm was being restrained with a firm, unyielding grip. She looked down into the jewel-like eyes of Bang, who shook her head and pulled Lex back into the seat. She didn't speak, obviously, but her message was clear: *Don't give them any more ammo.*

But the damage was done. Snodgrass wriggled out of Ferbus's grip and backed away from the table, drawing his scythe. The other two did the same. "Don't you *ever* touch me again," he growled, his eyes fiery with anger . . . and a hint of fear.

"What in the name of chicken fried steak is going on here?" a shrill voice rang out. Pandora hurried in from the kitchen, her face livid.

"Relax, Dora," Lazlo said, holding up a hand. "This doesn't concern you."

"Yeah," said Snodgrass. "Don't get your granny panties in a twist."

Dora's eyes widened as she spotted their scythes. "How dare you bully these kids around, especially in my establishment?" she hollered. "Last I checked, you were all adults. You better act like it or I'll throw you out, every last one of you!"

"But Dora, they attacked us," said Riley. "They're out of control! Everyone around here seems to realize that but you and your husband. And that idiot mayor of ours."

"Can it, tart," Dora snarled. "These kids have just as much of a right to be here as the rest of you. They work just as hard, they're just as committed, and I'll not have any of you disparaging them just because some puffed-up blowhard tells you to!"

"You're lucky you're senile, old bag," said Snodgrass. "Or you'd be a little more careful with what you say."

"I'll say whatever I damn well please," she countered. "You don't like it, find somewhere else to get lunch. There's the woods outside or the Dumpster out back, but I promise neither will have the triple-patty burgers you so love to stuff into that twit face of yours, Snoddy."

Snodgrass opened his mouth to say something more, then closed it. Without another word he led the others out the door.

"Yeah, that's what I thought," Dora said. "Pay them no mind, kids. This sure as hell won't be the last time you eat here at the Morgue."

But it was.

||||||

"What's happening to my hands?" Pip said.

"Hasn't Ferbus explained this to you already?"

"Ferbus stopped answering my questions days ago."

Lex sighed as she extended her finger toward a car crash victim. As if the scene at the Morgue hadn't rattled her enough, Pip was getting on her last nerve. No wonder Ferbus was in such a foul mood these days. She liked Pip, but his incessant questioning already had her wishing she could trade places with the targets.

"They get paler and thinner," she explained as she touched the target, careful not to let the shock shuddering through her body manifest itself in any obvious ways.

"Is that why Bang's hair is getting poofier too?"

"Yes."

"But why?"

"Exposure to the ether."

"But —"

"Let's have some quiet time for a while, shall we?"

Pip shut his mouth for all of two seconds as he positioned his hands around the Gamma, then opened it back up again. "What happens if I don't Cull the soul?"

Lex took a deep breath and tried not to picture herself stapling his lips together. "If a Culler allows a soul to escape before it is properly stored in a Vessel, the soul becomes a ghost."

"A ghost?" he said, his eyes wide as he Culled. "Like Casper?"

"Not remotely like Casper."

Once Pip finished placing the soul in the Vessel, he held up his scythe, a polished white marble with metallic flecks. Lex did the same with hers, and they swept them through the air simultaneously, then jumped through the rift. With barely a break of ether in between, the atmosphere switched to blazingly hot within mere seconds. Tall flames licked the walls, surrounding them both in a frozen, hellish trap.

"Then what?" he persisted. "Come on, tell me!"

Lex sighed as she reached down to the fireman's neck, gracing it ever so slightly. Of *course* Ferbus had weaseled out of explaining the creepy stuff. "A ghost isn't permitted entrance to the Afterlife," she told Pip as he Culled the soul, his eyes glued to hers. "So it just becomes a soul without a body, a consciousness that's trapped here on earth."

"What, like a floating mind?" said Pip. "That doesn't sound so bad."

"It does when you think about the fact that a ghost will be there to watch each and every one of its loved ones die, all the while knowing full well that it will never see any of them again — because they will move on to the Afterlife, where it can never follow. And once everyone it ever knew is dead and gone, the ghost is doomed to wander the earth for all eternity, unable to feel anything other than pain, anguish, and unfathomable sorrow."

Pip looked terrified. "You're kidding, right?" he said in a high voice.

"No. So hold on tight to those souls, okay?" she said gently, gesturing at his hands as he fumbled for the Vessel. "You don't want to be the one responsible for obliterating someone's right to an everlasting afterlife," she finished, repeating word for word what Uncle Mort had once told her.

"No way," he said with a shudder.

The shift only got bleaker from there. They'd just scythed out and landed in a classroom when Lex had to clap her hand over her mouth to keep from shrieking.

Half a dozen kids her own age lay strewn across the floor, the tiles sticky with blood. Their still-alive peers were frozen in various stages of panic — some running toward the door, a couple on their cell phones, a few tending to the wounded.

For the first time in a while on a shift, Lex felt well and truly sick. This was the part of the job she hated.

Pip looked about ready to pass out too. And no wonder; this was a terrible scene for his first multiple. "How could someone do this?" he asked, looking away as Lex touched the arm of a girl who bore an unsettling resemblance to Elysia.

"I don't know," Lex said. "Disturbed kids do disturbing things."

As her eyes fell upon a group of kids slumped over their desks, she swallowed. There it was — that enraged feeling again. That stinging at the bottom of her chest, rising. The one she had been trying so hard to suppress. Her hands grew hot —

Not here, she told herself, wincing. *Not now.*

They scythed again, landing in a hallway. Other Grim teams were farther down the hall, working on more targets. Lex bent down to touch her next target, a dark, good-looking boy crumpled next to his open locker, a chemistry book falling from his arms.

"Lex," she heard Pip breathe above her. He was staring down the hall. "The shooter — it's not a kid, it's a teacher!"

Lex followed his gaze down a trail of bloody footprints to a thin, bedraggled woman with her hands in the air, one of them clutching a gun. A group of police officers surrounded her.

"They got her," Lex said, relieved. "It's over."

Pip's face was pale as he Culled. "I bet Zara'll be paying *her* a visit."

Lex stared at the woman's face. There wasn't an ounce of remorse in it. It was fierce, frustrated; she was angry that she had gotten caught. She hadn't finished yet.

"I bet Zara will," muttered Lex, her hands still tingling with heat.

After that, they went for a while without talking, too deep in their own thoughts. It wasn't until they landed in the midst of a drug raid that Pip finally spoke again. "Can I ask one more thing?"

Lex tapped the target. "Okay."

"That!" Pip exclaimed, pointing at her quivering finger. "Those shocks you get when you Kill. What are they?"

"You noticed them?"

"How could I not?"

Stupefied, Lex just stood there, her outstretched finger frozen over the bullet-ridden body as Pip Culled. Once he finished with the Vessel, they both scythed and ended up back at the Ghost Gum. Their shift was over.

"Was I not supposed to notice?" Pip said, recoiling from the look on her face. "Okay, forget it. Bye!" He started to walk away.

"Hang on a sec," Lex said, yanking him back by the hood. "Let's have a little chat."

"No!" he cried, wrestling free of her grip. And before Lex's brain could catch up to her eyes, he jumped up to the first branch of the Ghost Gum, then swung up farther to the next and the next, until he was at least twenty feet up the tree.

"Hey!" Lex squinted up at him. "Come down! You're gonna get hurt!"

"No I won't. I can stay up here all day!" He perched precariously atop a thin branch, then fell backward until he was hanging upside down by his knees.

"OMIGOD!" Lex shrieked. "Get down!"

He folded his arms. "No way! You're going to yell at me!"

Lex heaved a knowing sigh. This wasn't the first time her congeniality had to be bargained for, and she doubted it would be the last. "I'm not going to yell at you. Please come down."

Pip studied her, then expertly pounced down, branch by branch, until he sat atop a low-hanging limb a few feet off the ground. He reached for Lex's hand and pulled her up next to him.

Agitated, she brushed off her hoodie. "God, Pip. You half monkey?"

"I climb stuff," he said, as if this weren't obvious. "Fire escapes, trees, parking garages, whatever I can find."

Lex was amazed. "I had no idea. Why didn't you tell anyone?"

"No one asked!"

"Not every bit of information has to be obtained through questioning, you know." She sighed and looked up through the branches to the weird little nest sitting atop them. "Okay, the deal with my shocks . . ."

She trailed off as she stared up at the tree.

"What?" said Pip.

Her mouth had gone dry. She turned to him. "Can you climb all the way up to that nest?"

"Yeah." He frowned. "Why?"

"The note, Pip."

"What, the key to the dead? You think it's up there?"

"I don't know," she said, grinning. "Let's find out."

"Okay!" Pip leaped up through the branches as if they were a flight of stairs. As he neared the top, where the limbs were thinner, the entire frame of the tree swayed, but he took no notice. Finally he reached the messy tangle of twigs and reached inside.

"Anything?" Lex demanded once he'd landed back on the ground.

He held out his hand. In it lay a flat white object carved from what looked like ivory. It was a rectangle, maybe three inches long and an inch wide, with a small protuberance sticking out of the middle, like a handle.

Lex's eyes could not have been any larger. "You think this is it?"

Pip looked confused. "I don't know. Doesn't look like a key."

"No, it doesn't. But it's *something*." She took the white thing from his hand and flashed him a big smile, her stomach settling for the first time in days. "Thanks, Pip."

"You're welcome." They began walking back to the Bank. "And about the shocks, you don't have to tell me if you don't —"

"Oh, they're no big deal," said Lex, waving her hand distractedly as she stared at the strange carving. "I just get them when I Kill. They come from a weird overdose of Killing power that I have for some reason."

"Because you're Mort's niece, right?"

"Huh?" She looked up. "What are you talking about?"

"Isn't that why the Seniors hate you? Because the Terms of Execution say that blood relations of Grims can't become Grims?"

She grabbed him, digging her nails into his arm. *"What?"*

"Ow!" He winced. "It mutates the powers or something, like inbreeding!"

"Who told you that?"

"I overheard some Seniors talking in the hub!"

Livid, Lex reached into her pockets and practically threw him the Vessels she had stored there. "Deposit these," she said, her hands shaking. "I have to go."

"Sorry! I didn't know it was a secret!"

Lex gritted her teeth as she stalked off in the direction of Uncle Mort's house. "Neither did I."

8

"How could you not tell me?"

Lex barged into the living room to find her uncle doing some routine maintenance on the jellyfish tank, Driggs eating Oreos and reading, and neither of them expecting the Category 5 hurricane that had just blown in through the front door.

"You lied to me!" she yelled, her hands growing hot for the umpteenth time that day. They were balled so tightly, her knuckles were cracking.

Uncle Mort took off the special lenses he used to inspect the tank. "You're going to have to be more specific. What did I lie to you about this time?"

"Why I'm not supposed to be here. That family members aren't allowed to be Grims."

"Ah." He looked away guiltily.

"I've asked you *billions* of times why people keep saying I never should have come to Croak. Every time, you've said the same thing: because I'm your niece, and that's all. Is that really all?"

"No."

Lex resisted the urge to give her uncle a healthy shove into the venomous jellyfish tank. "Then tell me why the townspeople hate me!"

He heaved a resigned sigh. "Because you and I are more closely related than any Grim has ever been to any other Grim."

Lex took a shallow breath. "How is that possible?"

He took off his gloves and sank into an armchair. "Well, remember, active Grims can't have children. Fertility is adversely affected by the proximity to the ether, to Elixir, and all sorts of other components — plus, the Grimsphere is no place to raise a family, even if women could conceive here."

Lex snuck a glance at Driggs, but Uncle Mort caught her. "That *doesn't* mean you get a free pass to ride the baloney pony whenever you want to. Got it?"

Lex looked away. Driggs buried his face back in his book, his ears purple.

Uncle Mort stared them both down, then continued. "Once a Grim woman retires and her memory is wiped, of course, she's free to procreate with as much vim and vigor as she pleases. But her offspring — and this is doubly true if the father is a Grim as well — are ineligible to become Grims, even if they exhibit the delinquent characteristics. The Terms just play it safe and take it one step further, prohibiting *any* blood relatives of Grims to become Grims themselves."

"Why?"

"The results would be too unpredictable to properly manage. It's widely believed that second-generation Grims would have more power, possess more innate Killing or Culling potential than regular Grims who have no connection to any Grims before them."

"That's precisely what *I* am!" Lex pointed to herself. "*I* have more power, *I* possess more potential, and *I'm* the one who sent the Grimsphere up shit creek without a paddle, all because *you* thought it might be a fun little science experiment to see what kind of Frankensteinian monster I might turn out to be!"

"Well, when you put it that way, of course it sounds terrible."

"So you knew all this would happen!" she shouted, throwing up her hands. "You knew I'd turn out to have too much power for my own good. You knew I would be able to Damn!" Her voice was getting screechy. "Hell, maybe you even knew that Zara would come after me and kill Cordy in the process!"

Uncle Mort glared at her. "Lex, if you think for a second that I meant for any harm to come to your sister, then you better get out of my sight before I do something I'll regret."

"Doesn't make a difference now, does it? She's dead!"

He took one glance at her overheating hands and pointed to her room. "Go discharge, Lex. Now."

Lex almost fought him on this, but he was right; she was about to erupt. So she fled to her room, the house shaking as she slammed the door.

Minutes later she emerged and tossed a singed pillow to the floor. "Happy?" she muttered, her eyes downcast.

Uncle Mort raised an eyebrow. "What took you so long?"

Her eyes stayed glued to the floor. "Nothing."

He studied her for a moment more, then sighed. "Look, you're right. I should have caught the warning signs with Zara. And trust me, I'll never forgive myself for failing Cordy like I did. But one thing I don't regret — and never will — is my decision to bring you here as a Grim."

Lex let out a breath, her anger melting. As whacked out as her uncle was, he loved her. He respected her, for some reason. And strangest of all, he believed in her — and not just in a schmaltzy Hallmark card way. The man legitimately believed that Lex would do great things.

But what were they supposed to be?

"I don't get it," she said finally, at a loss. "Why take the risk? Why violate the Terms like that, especially with everyone so opposed to it?"

He moved closer. "Because I saw potential in you," he said. "I've seen it for years, ever since you were young. And I thought that the Grim you could one day become outweighed any risks." He looked her in the eye. "I still do."

Lex slumped. "Even after all the horrible stuff I've done?"

"Especially after all the horrible stuff you've done."

That odd glint shone in his eye again, his scar even more pronounced in the orange light of the setting sun streaming through the windows.

"Something's up, isn't it?" Lex said quietly. "Me, Zara, Damning, Loopholes, Norwood — it can't just be a coincidence that all this is exploding at the same time after years of Grimsphere utopia. Something's happening. Or is about to happen. Isn't it?"

His smile gave nothing away. "Something is always about to happen, Lex."

She looked away, irritated that he was dodging her questions yet again. "Do you think I'm the Last?" she heard herself ask.

He gave her an odd look. "Huh?"

"That's what the townspeople said at the meeting."

Uncle Mort smirked. "The legendary Last, right under my nose. Wouldn't that be something?"

After a beat of silence, he headed toward the basement. "You two have fun catching up. Oh, and say hi to the camera!"

He waved at the small black bubble on the ceiling, then left. Lex just stared after him, still fuming.

"Um, sweetums?" Driggs piped up.

Lex blew a sweaty clump of hair off her forehead. "What did you just call me?"

He sank further under her glower. "I just — *ow!*" He reeled as Lex plunged into the couch.

"You never told me," she said through clenched teeth. "About any of this. And don't play the oblivious card," she said when he began to protest. "Because you knew — along with every other citizen in this town — who I was and that Uncle Mort breached every Term in the book when he brought me here."

"Yes, I knew!" he cried, checking his stitches to make sure they hadn't popped. "Christ, Lex! Why don't you just whip out the waterboard while you're at it?" He raised an eyebrow. "That is . . . if you're into that sort of thing?"

"Wow, Driggs. Wow."

"Okay, yes, we all knew. But you gotta understand, Mort swore us to secrecy. The Seniors were half in awe, half scared of you as it was, and the Juniors — well, to be honest, we were just curious about how it would play out. Plus, Mort didn't think it would be healthy, you know? Thought you might get a big head if you came in here thinking you were better than everyone." He grinned. "Too bad you did anyway."

She ignored this. "I still knew I was different."

"He was just trying to protect you."

"I think I've earned the right to be told these things. Especially since it's *my* life we're talking about here. You of all people should have been the first to enlighten me."

"I know, I know. I'm sorry. Let me make it up to you." He pulled a book out from beneath the couch cushion and pointed at a marked page. "Here. Took me all day to find it."

Lex took it from him and read:

> THE WRONG BOOK IS A STORIED TOME,
> YET NONE KNOW WHERE IT MAKES ITS HOME.
> FOOLS HAVE SOUGHT IT, MAD WITH LUST,
> ALL UPTURNING NAUGHT BUT DUST.

She looked at Driggs. "That's encouraging."
"Keep going."

> A THOUSAND PAGES THICK AT LEAST,
> ITS SCRIBE SIX HUNDRED YEARS DECEASED.
> SABLE LEATHER MAKES ITS SKIN;
> APT GARB FOR A WEALTH OF SIN.

> THE BEST OF GROTTON'S TRICKS INSIDE:
> PLOTS AND PLOYS AND SNARES PRESIDE,
> DARK DESIGNS OFT PUSHED ASIDE,
> ALL POWERS OF DEATH IN ONE COLLIDE.
> FOR IF YOUR GOAL BE RULE WORLDWIDE,
> THE WRONG BOOK'S SECRETS SHALL PROVIDE.

Driggs shoved an Oreo into his mouth. "Intense, huh?"

Lex nodded, then grinned. She'd almost forgotten. "I found something too."

Driggs's crumb-filled mouth fell open as she dropped the key onto the book. "You're *kidding* me."

She told him about the Ghost Gum, how the surprisingly agile Pip had bounded up to the nest to retrieve their prize. "Weird-looking thing, huh?" she said. "Ever seen anything like this?"

"Nope," he admitted, examining it. "We should show Mort, though. Maybe he — "

"I have a better idea," she said, yanking him up from the couch. "Field trip."

"Ow!" He clutched his chest as she shoved him toward the door. "You know, I never noticed how endearing you get when you torture people. The way your nostrils flare — it's just darling."

"Thank you."

They marched outside to the end of the driveway. "Cabin time," Lex said with a mischievous grin. "Let's open that sucker up."

"Don't the words 'force field of unimaginable pain' mean anything to you?" he asked as they walked.

"Decent band name, maybe."

"I'm just saying. What makes you think you can get through when Mort and I couldn't?"

"Well, I'm the closest thing there is to a second-generation Grim, right? I'm all special and superpowery — maybe I can get past."

"You can't see it, because I'm somewhat doubled over in pain, but I just rolled my eyes. Hard."

"Noted."

They walked for about fifteen minutes through a series of small hills and valleys until the paved street petered out into a dirt road. Soon they reached a small bridge spanning a bubbly stream.

"I never knew this was here," said Lex.

"It's not exactly a stop on the Croak trolley tour," Driggs replied. "This is the Sticks River."

The name even fit the bridge, which was made from thousands of little twigs all tied together to form its shape, as if it were built by an especially industrious colony of beavers. The wood crackled underfoot as Lex and Driggs crossed and arrived at the edge of the forest. The path extended into the trees by way of a small, dark opening.

Lex swallowed. She had not forgotten the fear that choked her throat when she'd spotted that white figure lurking in the woods. "We're going in there?"

"What, too creepy for you?"

"No." But the nails digging into his arm suggested otherwise.

They shuffled through the hole in the trees, the crunchy, fallen leaves on the ground loudly heralding their arrival, the setting sun growing dimmer as they walked. Lex glanced up at the dark, cobweblike limbs that seemed to be closing in on them. No animals stirred. Except for the two foolish teenagers who had stumbled within, the woods were silent.

The path began to narrow, becoming tighter and tighter, until Lex and Driggs were forced to walk single file, Lex somehow ending up in front. She was getting nervous. She didn't know where she was going or what to look for or —

Her foot rammed into a mossy log, knocking her off balance. Even in the fading light she could see that there was nothing up ahead but more forest. She looked at the ground. The path had disappeared.

"There's no road left," she said, panic in her voice. She whipped her head around to face Driggs. "So Dead End really is a dead end?"

He smirked at her. "What, you thought it was just a cute name?"

"Driggs," she said, trying to keep her tone steady, "show me the way to that cabin, or I swear to God I'll feed you to the first bear that inevitably shows up to eat us."

He started walking backwards, motioning for her to follow him. "Back up a little," he said. ". . . Seventeen, eighteen, nineteen — okay, stop."

He turned to his left and pushed aside some small branches. There, just off the path, was a tiny opening in the trees that Lex had passed right by without even noticing. It led to a narrow dirt lane that twisted through a mass of craggy shrubberies and ultimately disappeared in a patch of trees.

"Here we are," said Driggs in a chipper voice. "Off you go, special superpowery second-generation Grim."

Lex bit her lip and stared at the scary path. "Okay."

"Okay then."

"I'm going."

"Bon voyage."

He wasn't letting her back out of this one, not when she'd been so cocky. Tentatively, she tiptoed through the opening and into the trees, her sneakers kicking up leaves left and right.

One minute and seven seconds later she burst back out onto the path, panting and clutching her stomach.

"Ready to move in?" Driggs asked wryly.

Lex was so grateful he didn't say "I told you so," she fell in love with him all over again. "I don't think Ikea delivers to creepy enchanted forests," she choked out.

"Pity. I so love the neighborhood."

Lex straightened, her nerves all fired up. She hadn't quite *seen* the cabin, but she knew it was there. All she had to do was get inside and the needless carnage would stop. "We have to get through. The Wrong Book *has* to be in there." She was hopping around by now, her face flushed with excitement. "And who knows what else!"

He gave her a disapproving look, then started laughing as he headed back out toward the bridge.

"What?" she asked, following him and putting up her hood. It was starting to rain.

"What nothing. You're hilarious." His voice was skeptical, but Lex's excitement was infectious — even he couldn't hide the flicker of intrigue in his eyes. "Four months ago you refused to believe a place like Croak even existed, and now look at you. All jazzed up and concocting crackpot theories that probably involve a hidden flock of unicorns."

"Or dinosaurs," Lex said with a grin. "Let's not prematurely dismiss a *Jurassic Park* scenario."

It was getting almost too dark for them to see each other and the rain was really coming down, so they broke into a run, laughing all the way. By the time they got back to the house, they were soaked, muddy, and disgusting.

And horny.

"I call shower," they said at the same time.

Eyebrows were raised. A wacky idea took shape.

And by the time Uncle Mort figured out that the water had been running for far too long and that he had made the critical error of not installing cameras in the bathroom, it was too late.

They heard his heavy footsteps pounding up the basement stairs. "Did you lock the door?" Lex asked Driggs, panicked.

"I thought you did!"

"Shit! Quick, grab a towel —"

"I'm trying to — could you just — move —" The cramped conditions weren't doing them any favors, nor was the soapy tub, which caused Lex to slip and tear down the entire shower curtain. They quickly wrapped it around themselves, Driggs unfortunately yelling, "WHERE are my PANTS?" at the exact moment Uncle Mort burst in.

"Remember how I said I don't regret bringing you here, Lex?" Uncle Mort said, putting up his hand to block out the steamy, painfully inept scene before him. "I may have to revise my views on that."

Lex and Driggs, meanwhile, were trying so hard to put their clothes back on that it seemed as though they had forgotten how. Lex's shirt was on backwards, Driggs had his head through an armhole, and neither of them, still, could find their pants.

"I'm closing the door," Uncle Mort announced, aiming his gaze directly at the sink. "For precisely twenty seconds. When I open it again, you'll be dry, clothed, and . . . in control of your faculties."

Twenty seconds later Lex and Driggs piled out of the bathroom, their faces red. "We were just showering," Lex muttered.

"Of course," Uncle Mort said. "Everyone knows how impossible it is to get zestfully clean without assistance." He put a hand on each of their shoulders and marched them down the hall toward their rooms. "Grounded for a week, shall we say?"

"But Uncle Mort, we found the key to the cabin!"

"No Corpp's, no pay, no hanging around after your shifts. Straight back here and into your respective cells."

Driggs whispered to Lex out of the side of his mouth as they walked, "I never got grounded before you came here."

"You never touched a boob before I came here either."

"Touché." He flashed a goofy grin as Uncle Mort shoved him into his room and slammed the door. "Worth it!"

9

Later that night, Uncle Mort finally registered what Lex had said to him about the key, forced her to surrender it, and promptly took it down into his basement to run some tests.

"Bone," he said a few days later as he tossed it back into her room, where she'd been sequestered all week owing to the Incident That Must Not Be Named.

"Huh?" she said, picking it up where it had landed on the bed. "I thought we decided that wasn't his real name, just part of the code."

"No, I mean the key," he said. "It's made of bone."

Lex raised her eyebrow. "As in ivory?"

"As in human."

She let out a shriek and dropped it.

"Sweet dreams," he said with a smirk, closing the door.

Lex and the Juniors researched the key to within an inch of its life after that, but still found themselves drowning in a sea of failure. Which was unfortunate, since things were going from bad to worse, and then barreling straight on to catastrophic. Over the next month *The Obituary* kept rolling in with more reports of Zara's Damning attacks, each more disturbing than the last. While a few guilty parties were still peppered into the mix, the majority of her victims really did seem to be regular, innocent people — a respected veterinarian, an elderly lady in a nursing home, a well-liked Culler in Necropolis. Lex searched the Internet for any possible crimes they might have committed, fervently hoping that the vet had maybe built a kitten torture chamber in his basement, but nope — they were saints, every one of them.

Even the media in the outside world were starting to catch on, with laughable reports of "abnormal rises in the spontaneous combustion rate" popping up every few days or so. More teams had been dispatched from Necropolis to track Zara down, but without the ability to Crash, they were never fast enough, show-ing up at her last known location hours after she'd left. By the month's end, they were no closer to nabbing Zara, Lex still hadn't found the Wrong Book, and Ferbus had seemingly been replaced by a happy, upbeat doppelgänger.

"Happy Halloween, cats and kittens!" he said with a wide grin to the rest of the Juniors that day at Corpp's. "You ready?"

"For what?" asked Pip. "A costume party?"

Ferbus blinked. "What are you, ten?"

"It was a valid guess!"

Ferbus stifled a sneer. Even Pip couldn't bring him down to-day. "Grims in the Graveyard tomorrow," he said, rubbing his hands together. "Capture the Flag rules, Killers versus Cullers, all night long."

Bang worriedly looked up from her book, her increasingly pouffy bangs now growing out at a strange angle. She signed something to Pip. "That sounds intense," he translated.

"It's not," Elysia reassured them. "It's just a big game of hide-and-seek."

"Why isn't it tonight?" Pip asked.

A sad expression passed over Elysia's face. "Um, Halloween is too busy a night for Grims. Lots of kids get hit by cars." She forced a smile. "Which is why we do this the night after. To cheer us up."

Corpp hobbled over to them. "Can I get you kids anything else?"

Ever since the Morgue incident, the Juniors had decided that it was better to stay invisible than risk more conflicts with the Seniors, so they'd taken up a row of stools at the back of Corpp's bar for their lunch breaks and noshed on basketfuls of the fried food Pandora snuck in through the back door. Lex especially disliked the fact that they had to hide like frightened turtles, but she figured that since she was the cause of most of the Juniors' problems, it wasn't really her place to tell them where they could or could not scarf their corn dogs.

"We're good, Corpp, thanks," said Driggs. "You playing tomorrow night?"

"Defending the Culler base, as usual."

Dora entered with a basket of onion rings. "I'll be doing it for the Killer side, and you bet your sweet patootie I won't be quiet about it."

Corpp grinned and gave her a peck on the cheek. "When was the last time you were quiet about anything, dear?"

Lex watched them as they returned to the kitchen, thinking of her mom and dad. Were they keeping their spirits up too? Had they banded together in the wake of tragedy or fallen apart after Cordy died? She didn't even know. She hadn't stuck around long enough to find out.

She shifted in her seat. With all that was going on, she knew she should call her parents and make sure they were all right, but she just couldn't bring herself to do it. Locked in a stalemate with the telephone, she knew the the minute she heard her mother's weepy voice, the guilt would wash over her like molasses, too sticky and suffocating to scrape off.

Elysia spread out a copy of *The Obituary*. "Ah, crud," she said, pointing. "Look."

They followed her finger to a grainy photo of an expectant mother. Zara's latest victim.

"That is so. Messed. Up." Elysia made a face. "What is Zara *thinking?* How could she be so hypocritical? Damning all these innocent people completely goes against the whole vigilante-justice philosophy she worked so hard to establish in the first place."

"I'm sure that irony is not lost on her," Lex said thoughtfully, chewing the same french fry over and over. She'd been wondering about this stuff a lot lately, the motivations behind Zara's actions. They seemed erratic, yet somehow . . . not.

"But still," Elysia said. "I don't understand how she can do a one-eighty like that, just flip that switch."

"Well," said Driggs, "I think it's more that she sees it as a means to an end. If the Wrong Book contains a way to Damn vast amounts of criminals, then she feels justified in sacrificing a few innocents to get it."

"But she's still going after *some* criminals," said Pip. "She Damned that school shooter Lex and I saw." Indeed, a week after the shooting spree, *The Obituary* had confirmed the teacher's fiery demise. "We knew as soon as we got there that Zara would go after her. Right, Lex?"

"What?" Lex had flinched at the mention of the shooter. Now everyone was staring at her. "Yeah. Right."

Driggs gave her an odd look. "What's wrong?"

"Nothing. It's just — " She wiped her greasy hands with a napkin and wrung them in her lap. "Maybe it's not completely Zara's fault."

Ferbus choked on his onion ring.

"Okay, that's so not what I meant," Lex said as Elysia slapped his back. "I'm not defending her. She killed my sister and she's legitimately evil and I hate her. But — it's just that none of you know what it's like, the urge to Damn. It's like a drug."

Ferbus looked ready to say something highly unpleasant, but Elysia stopped him. "What do you mean, Lex?" she said gently.

Lex lowered her eyes. "When it flares up, it's like this . . . ache. You *have* to Damn someone — right now, as soon as possible, and it doesn't really matter who it is. Of course, it *does* matter, but — you know how sometimes you get so hungry you'll eat anything? That's what it's like."

"But you don't Damn people," said Driggs. "You just Damn office supplies and ugly housewares."

A bead of sweat formed on Lex's forehead. "I know," she muttered. "But it's not the same. It's like eating a Life Saver instead of a five-course dinner."

Pip's eyes were wide. "So it feels good to Damn?"

Lex sighed. "Yes." They looked horrified. "Look, I don't know why it does, and I wish it didn't. But I think that's why it's been so easy for Zara to Damn those innocent people. The Damning energy has to go somewhere, and maybe it no longer matters to her where. The whole slippery slope thing." She looked down. "That's my theory, anyway."

The group nodded, sullen. "Well," said Driggs, "good thing you've got more willpower than she does."

Lex thought of the school shooter, of how much she deserved the Damning that she got. "Yeah," she said bitterly. "Good thing."

||||||

Ferbus ended up having to wait just a little longer for his favorite night of the year. It was decided that since Zara knew that Grims in the Graveyard always took place the day after Halloween, it might be better to hold it the night after that and make her think it was canceled, in case she was planning anything.

So at seven o'clock the next evening, dozens of Grims assembled at the fountain. They chatted nervously, their usual fears ramped up even more now that they were out in the open, at night, in the dark.

Uncle Mort wasn't forcing anyone to play, of course. But he'd also been determined not to break tradition, going ahead with the plans despite the ever-present threat of attacks, hoping to put all those worries on hold for at least one night of — dare they think it — fun.

The Juniors were all for it, especially at the thought of getting a little revenge on the Seniors. They gathered together away from the crowds and handed out flashlights. "I wish we could be on the same team," Elysia said to Lex.

"You don't get to complain," Lex said. "You get Driggs, Pip, Kloo — "

"What Lex is trying to say," Driggs said, "is that Cullers are officially more awesome."

"You wish, D-bag." Ferbus backed away from the group. "Come on, Killers, let's talk tactics," he said, beckoning Lex, Bang, Sofi, and Ayjay to him. Once they were far enough away, he looked hesitantly at Bang. "Uh, how do I talk to this thing?" he shouted back to Elysia.

"She can hear!" said Pip. "How many times do I have to tell you that? Just talk!"

"Shut up, Pipsqueak! I wasn't asking you!" He turned back to Bang. "Think you can keep up with us?"

She signed something they didn't understand, but even Ferbus could tell it ended in a question mark. He let out a frustrated groan.

"Look, this is my first time too," Lex told her before he could jump in with something insensitive. "I don't know what I'm doing either."

Bang looked relieved. And luckily for her, Uncle Mort had jumped atop the fountain and begun demanding everyone's attention, bringing Ferbus's strategizing session to a premature halt.

"Happy post-Halloween, everyone!" he said, waving an air horn. "And welcome to the annual Grims in the Graveyard tournament. Rules are the same as years past, but for the rookies' sake — "

"Where's Norwood?" someone shouted. "And Heloise? Why aren't they here?"

The smile slid off Uncle Mort's face. "Norwood and Heloise were vehemently opposed to my idea of maintaining a sense of normalcy," he said in a quieter voice. "I'm told they are spending a quiet evening at home."

Rumblings of discord shot through the crowd. "Wait, they're not *here?*" Riley asked in a snotty voice. "You really think this is a good idea, Mort? What about security?"

Their outbursts weren't surprising. Zara's rampages had lately whipped the entire Grimsphere into an unprecedented frenzy of fear and paranoia. A few people had even left. The spidery proprietress of Ashes showed up on Uncle Mort's doorstep one day with suitcase in hand, begging to be Amnesia'd. He eventually talked her out of it, but she hadn't been the last.

Uncle Mort remained polite, but Lex could tell he was getting annoyed. "Countless measures are in place — cameras, alarms, the whole deal. If anyone scythes in, we'll know about it and take action. You're perfectly safe."

The townspeople looked at one another. They didn't seem convinced.

"All right?" Uncle Mort said. "Hoodies on, everyone. Roze, Wicket, start passing out the tags."

They got to the Juniors last. Roze handed Lex a sticky, fibrous blob. It looked like white cotton candy.

"Why aren't you guys working the graveyard shift?" Lex asked them.

"We took a personal day, got some subs to watch the vault," said Roze. "We've never missed a game."

"Okay, rules!" Uncle Mort had started yelling again. "Each side has a hidden base. The Killers' is somewhere on the north side of town, guarded by Pandora, and the Cullers' is in the south, guarded by Corpp. Your job is to seize the opposite team's base without getting tagged."

He held up one of the gooey blobs. "The tags you've received have been generously donated by our dear spider friends and treated so that they can't be removed for at least twenty-four hours. When you see a member of the opposing team, slap that sucker on them. If you get tagged, you are out of the game and must return back here to the starting point, the fountain. If you're still in play, you can return to the fountain to collect unused tags from your fallen comrades — but due to its high visibility, that may leave you vulnerable to attack."

Lex's skin began to tingle. This sounded awesome.

"First team to successfully seize the opposing team's base wins the game," Uncle Mort finished. "Any questions?"

The crowd was uncomfortably silent. The only people who looked excited were Wicket, Roze, and the Juniors.

Lex and Driggs gave each other a quick squeeze. "Hope you're okay with boyfriend-girlfriend-leniency rules not applying here," he told her.

"Hope you're okay with getting your ass kicked."

"When I give the first signal," Uncle Mort said, "your head start begins. Spread out, strategize, do your thing. When I give the second signal five minutes later, the game has officially begun. Stay within the limits of the town — no farther north than my house, no farther south than the Croak population sign, and no farther than the foot of the hills to the east and west. Got it?"

Everyone got it. And as soon as he blew his air horn, they were gone. Some paired up, some took off on their own, and a confused few crashed into one another as they scattered about. Lex followed the lead of those who had gone solo and ran by herself into the trees behind Corpp's. As soon as she found a good hiding place, the second air horn went off.

She instantly realized her mistake. A dozen other people had chosen the same patch of forest that she had, and half of those were on the other team. Cries of defeat and triumph soon rang out through the trees. Lex watched as several figures left the woods, their shoulders slumped in disappointment. Just as she was about to beat a quick retreat, a Senior Culler snuck up from behind. Luckily, a twig snapped beneath his foot, giving Lex the yoctosecond of warning she needed to duck away, whirl around, and slap the tag square on his chest.

"Agh!" he shouted. "Goddamn Juniors!"

She ran at full speed out of the forest, dodging another Senior on the way. At last she broke through the trees, only to be blind-sided by Elysia, of all people.

"Hi, Lex!" she chirped, tag in hand. "Are you having fun?"

Lex had to laugh. Only Elysia could strike up a friendly conversation in the middle of a bloodbath. "Yeah, I am. Why aren't you tagging me?"

Elysia looked torn. "I should, but . . . I really want to get Ferbus. He tagged me within the first two minutes last year. I had to spend the rest of the night at the fountain, Kilda gushing my ear off the whole time."

"So I get a free pass?"

"Yeah," Elysia said, smiling. "It's your first year, you should enjoy it. But I won't be so merciful next time," she warned, running away. "And tell Ferbus he's a dead man!"

Lex was tagless, so she decided to check out the fountain and see if anyone on her team who'd been tagged could give her some more. But to her surprise, there were almost no Killers. Instead, Kloo, Driggs, Roze, and Lazlo all sat atop the ledge, their faces bitter.

"You're out already?" she said as she approached, forgetting all about how vulnerable this would make her.

Driggs scowled. "She's like a ninja!"

"Who?"

"Bang!" said Kloo. "She's so quiet, no one can hear her coming!"

"Stocked up on tags early on, then started picking us off one by one," said Roze, a hint of awe in her voice. "You're lucky she's on your team."

"Why are you consorting with the enemy?" said Lazlo. He let out a whoop to his teammates in the woods, then flashed Lex a wicked grin. "Better run, sweetheart."

Lex did just that as a handful of Cullers emerged. She spied a gap in their lines and headed straight for it, finding refuge behind a shrub up against the library. She watched through its leaves, assessing the situation, until something started to feel strange. Someone crept to her left, watching her. The white figure from the woods flashed through her mind — but she was right in the middle of town; there was no way she'd be the only one to see it. She swallowed, turned her head, and nearly let out a scream.

Bang sat right beside her, staring with those gigantic greenish eyes.

"Christ, Bang, you scared me." Lex let out a nervous breath. "How were you able to get so many people?"

Bang shrugged and slunk away as usual, but Lex could have sworn she caught a smile.

"Hey." Ferbus was crawling toward her on his elbows, as if he were under heavy artillery fire. "Here's the situation. We're doing pretty well thanks to Silent Bob over there," he said, pointing at a skulking Bang, "but we're not in the clear yet. Word is that Sofi's gunning for you — "

Lex's mouth fell open. "But she's on our team!"

"Personal vendetta or something," he said, getting to his feet and leading Lex from bush to bush. "Like we Juniors need any traitors right now. The Seniors already want your head on a spike."

Lex grimaced. She was starting to wonder if they were just talking about the game.

She crawled behind him into another shrub. "You're screwed too," she said. "Elysia's gone rabid — agh!" A shadow darted across the branches of the tree above, the limbs bouncing and shaking off what few leaves were left. It swooped down and aimed for Ferbus, missing by inches.

"Dammit, Pip!" Ferbus cried. He grabbed Lex by the hoodie and sprinted toward the Bank. Pip followed above them, jumping effortlessly. "Talk about rabid," Ferbus said, gulping for air as they ran. "That little snot rag has been stalking me all night."

"I can't imagine why."

They searched the Bank's exterior for a place to hide. On the ground at the rear of the building was a slanted pair of doors leading to what Lex assumed was the basement. She kicked at the heavy steel, but nothing budged. She continued toward the front, her fingers desperately groping for asylum.

Miraculously, it came.

Her hand fell on an old wooden plank forming a sort of door in the side of the Bank. She pushed it. It bowed and creaked and finally swung open to reveal a pitch-black hiding place. "Get in!" she whispered, pulling Ferbus inside and shutting the little door behind them.

The room was only about four feet high, so they sat on the ground to catch their breath. "Well," said Ferbus, "I think it's safe to say I never envisioned this scenario."

"Let's pray it never happens again," said Lex, not relishing the thought of spending any amount of time in a confined space with Ferbus.

"Where are we?" he asked.

"Under the porch, I think." She looked around as her eyes adjusted to the dark. She was right; they could look out onto the town square through the thin slats of the wood that made up the stairs of the porch. If she squinted hard enough, she could make out Driggs sitting on the fountain, grumpily throwing rocks into the water.

A loud shriek sounded to the left of the fountain. Elysia had jumped onto Ayjay's back. "Where's Ferbus?" she demanded.

"I don't know!"

"Tell me or I'll shove this tag down your throat!"

Ferbus let out a low whistle. "Elysia the badass," he said with no small amount of admiration. "Who knew?"

With a final grunt Elysia tagged Ayjay anyway and scampered off. He threw up his hands and made his way in shame toward the fountain, where his fellow fallen players awaited to mock him.

"How long are we allowed to hide in here?" Lex asked Ferbus.

"As long as we want, but that won't help us win. We have to get to the base." In the small amount of light, she caught him sneering at her. "Too bad you can't just Crash us there."

Lex gritted her teeth and wondered how long she could go before ramming his face into the wall. Not long, she decided.

"Or maybe you only Crash in emergency situations," he went on. "Gotta save up for all of those. I'm sure we haven't seen the last of them, not with you around."

Lex threw her flashlight at him. He ducked out of the way and it clattered to the ground, switching on in the process. "Fungus, I'm only going to say this one more time. What happened to

Driggs was not my fault. If you've somehow got it into that oddly shaped head of yours that I *want* to see my friends get hurt, then you're even dumber than you . . ."

Ferbus looked at her surprised face. "What?"

She pointed. The flashlight had fallen into a corner, near the side that made up the foundation of the Bank. But instead of the light reflecting off the wall, it shone down a tunnel.

"Whoa," he said, backing up. "What the hell is that?"

She stuck the flashlight into the hollow. The dirt tunnel sloped down for a few feet before leveling out and leading onward, past where the light could reach.

Crouching, Lex stuck one foot in and looked back at Ferbus. "Well?"

He was aghast. "You're not really going in there, are you?"

"Why, are you scared?"

"No, I'm an intelligent human being who doesn't want to get devoured alive by a den of man-eating rats. Sorry."

"Not as sorry as you're going to be when I tell everyone you pissed your pants and cried like a baby." She inched farther into the tunnel. "I think Pip will be the first one I'll tell. He'll love that. Or even better, Elysia — "

"Fine!" he relented, giving her a dirty look. "But only if you stay in front."

She rolled her eyes. "My, what chivalry."

"To hell with chivalry. Your idea, you die first."

After a few twists and turns the path eventually straightened out into a smooth passage. Ferbus brightened as they walked, stooping under the low ceiling. "Hey, I think this is leading south," he said. "Maybe it'll lead us to the base!"

"Yeah! I bet Corpp dug it himself!"

"Shut up."

After several minutes they came to a steep incline. They climbed up, careful not to slip or fall backwards, as the dirt wasn't packed tightly enough for them to grasp a firm footing. Lex wondered when this had last been used. And for what.

Ferbus sniffed the air. "Feel that?" he said, pushing her along. "Wind. I think we're almost out."

He was right. A few more steps, and Lex's head poked out of the ground beside a gigantic gray boulder. She heaved herself up and wriggled through the opening.

"Holy crap," she said, brushing herself off. "Ferbus, you have to see this."

Below them stretched all of Croak, its streetlights shining with a soft yellow warmth. A few spots of flashlights twinkled within the trees while the fountain reflected the light of the moon, the figures gathered around it as small as bugs.

"This is Greycliff," Ferbus said in wonder, looking at the large rock, then back down at the town. "Man, I haven't been up here since I was a rookie."

"Best place to watch the sunset," Lex said, repeating what Uncle Mort had said when he'd brought her up here on her first day in Croak.

A crisp breeze swept across the cliff. Lex hugged herself and took a deep breath, the cool air bathing her lungs. It was so beautiful up here; she wondered why she never thought to visit. It'd be a nice place for her and Driggs to —

Next thing Lex knew, she and Ferbus were on the ground, digging their fingers into each other's arms and gaping at the source of the deafening *boom* that had knocked them over.

Where the fountain had been moments ago, a bright orange blaze now mushroomed above the square, followed by a thick plume of smoke. An acrid smell filled the air. Echoes of the explosion reverberated across the hillsides, then faded, giving way to the panicked cries of the people below. A wave of heat rushed up the cliff, bathing Lex and Ferbus in a fiery glow as they clung to each other, trembling, their faces white.

10

The tunnel felt downright oppressive on the way back — the way the walls seemed to close in, the suffocating dirt that got kicked up as they ran, the unending darkness. Lex hurried on, trying not to think about who may or may not be dead, instead telling herself that as soon as she burst through the little wooden plank door under the porch, she could take a gulp of fresh air.

But that wasn't the case at all.

The air around the fountain was thick with smoke, obscuring the people whose voices cried out from every direction. A loud whooshing noise sounded somewhere in front of them. Lex and Ferbus pulled the bottoms of their hoodies up to their noses to breathe easier, staying close as they felt their way around.

Lex's foot brushed up against something. She grabbed Ferbus.

He followed her gaze. "Is that an arm?"

She nodded and bent down to look at the hand. A flowery tattooed design flickered in the ambient light.

She stood back up, gagging. "It's Roze's."

A gust of wind swept through the square, finally clearing the air enough to see. There was another sharp burst of the whooshing sound, and as a white cloud erupted to their left, Lex realized that it was coming from a fire extinguisher. Its operator was yelling instructions to anyone who would listen.

"Get all the injured inside!" Uncle Mort shouted from the

fountain — or what was left of it. His face was covered with soot. "Into the Morgue, now!"

Lex ran to him. "What happened?"

"Lex!" He swept her into a violent hug. "Where the hell have you been? I thought you were — " He stopped talking but didn't let go.

"We were hiding. We just got here," she said, panic rising in her voice. "What's going on?"

He finally released her. "A bomb," he said, his face hard. "Must have been at the bottom of the fountain, too dark to see. Goddammit."

All Lex could think about was the last thing she had seen through the slats of the wood — all those people sitting around the fountain — Driggs one of them —

She grabbed at her uncle's hoodie. "Where is everyone?"

"Either hurt or tending to those who are hurt. Too soon to tell which is which." He pointed at a couple of people on the ground. "Go help them. Help whoever you can find."

Lex and Ferbus ran to the figures. Lex held her breath as she reached for them, but both were Seniors she didn't know.

"Ayjay!" she cried, spotting him as he walked past. "Help us!"

Ayjay stared blankly, as if he didn't even recognize them. "Kloo?" he asked.

"No, it's me and Lex," Ferbus said. "What's wrong? You can't find her?"

He ignored them and kept walking, his eye glazed over.

The Morgue had never looked more like its namesake. Dozens of moaning people stretched across the tables, the chairs, every available surface. The already dingy floor was made even fouler by pools of blood seeping across its tiles. Those who weren't injured ran hurriedly around the room, tossing bandages and medical supplies. Lex spotted Sofi, Lazlo, and Snodgrass among them.

A team of strong hands took the victims from Lex's and Ferbus's arms and carried them away, leaving Lex to switch into full-blown panic mode as she scanned the restaurant. "I don't see him!"

Ferbus swallowed. "I don't see any of them."

Lex choked back a sob, fears screaming through her. Was this all it took? One little explosion to wipe out the only things she'd ever cared about?

She eyed something with a sheet over it. Blood seeped out onto the floor from the lumpy figure underneath. Lex bent down.

Ferbus grabbed her arm. "Lex, don't —"

She tore off the sheet. Roze's glassy eyes stared up at her, the bloody stump of her shoulder oozing a black fluid. Lex reached out to touch her face when she was grabbed around the waist from behind, a messy strand of brown hair poking into view.

Lex struggled for breath as she hugged Driggs, her ribs nearly cracking. Ferbus piled on top of both of them. "You're okay," she whispered.

"Yeah," Driggs breathed, shaking his head, "but I shouldn't be. I was at the fountain all night, then I leave for two seconds to take a piss, and . . ." He pulled himself away from them and looked down. "I shouldn't be."

"You got lucky," said Lex. "That's not your fault."

"Still." His eyes were troubled. "Where have you been?"

"We'll explain later," said Ferbus, anxious. "Where's Elysia? Kloo? The rookies?"

"Elysia's over there," he said, pointing to the corner. "Burned arm, but otherwise okay. I don't know where the rookies are, or Kloo. Or Ayjay."

"Ayjay's outside, looking for — " The words were barely out of Lex's mouth when Ayjay ran in through the door, Kloo limp in his arms. Her eyes were fluttering.

"Clear a table!" he shouted.

Riley, who'd been directing traffic and holding a piece of gauze on her forehead, looked around the room. "There aren't any left. Maybe the space on the floor over there — "

"No, take mine!" A blond head poked up from the corner. Elysia hopped out of her booth, wincing at the pain in her bandaged arm. She walked toward the rest of the Juniors, fine for a moment until she began to stagger. Ferbus lunged forward and caught her.

Ayjay raced to the table and held Kloo's hand as the Seniors assessed her. She was trying to give them medical instructions, but it seemed that she couldn't quite form the words.

"You kids, out," Trumbull told the Juniors. He grabbed a handful of bandages and other supplies and threw them into their hands. "Go back outside, see if anyone else needs help. It's getting too crowded in here."

"But Kloo — "

"Out!"

Reluctantly, Lex, Driggs, Elysia, and Ferbus wove their way through the hemorrhaging sea of humanity and piled out the door. The air had cleared, affording them a full view of the aftermath. The obelisk had been blown clean off the fountain — yet remarkably, it was still largely intact, lying on its side near the door of Corpp's. A few small fires still smoldered, but Uncle

Mort was putting them out. Not many people were left on the ground — what few remained seemed to be only slightly injured — but some had been laid out on the porch of the Bank, Wicket working furiously among them. Her eyes were red and wet — she'd undoubtedly learned of Roze's fate, but was still going. Norwood and Heloise, on the other hand, stood idly among the victims, wearing coats over their pajamas and doing more gawking than helping.

The Juniors hurried to the porch and began to distribute the supplies. Norwood sneered at them. "Where have *you* been?"

"We were in the Morgue," Driggs said, bandaging a woman's knee. "Enjoying your night off?"

"We told him," said Heloise, a haughty tone in her voice. "We told Mort not to do this, that it was only an invitation to chaos. There we were, spending a quiet evening at home, and boom!"

Lex glared at her, noting how much shorter she was without her spiky stilettos. She didn't look nearly as threatening in slippers. "Well, thanks for taking some time out of your lounging to help," Lex said, pressing a piece of gauze over a man's gaping head wound. "Could you hold this for a minute while I grab some tape?"

Heloise hesitated and made a face. She tapped Norwood's shoulder to get him to help, but after one quick look at the cut, his lip curled as well.

Lex's eyes narrowed as she got up to get the tape herself. "I see. Wouldn't want to get any blood on our hands, would we?"

Uncle Mort let out a shout from the square. "Everybody out of the Bank!" He waved his hands and pointed at something above them. "There's another one!"

Lex jumped off the porch and looked up. Under the eaves of the Bank roof, a small red light blinked back at her. She took out her flashlight and shone it at the boxlike object. Colorful wires stuck out of it in all directions.

Her breath caught in her throat. "Get them out!" She echoed her uncle's words and gestured hard to the others. "Wicket, we gotta go!"

Wicket's face fell. "We can try, but — " Her eyes looked desperate as the Juniors began to grab the victims. "There's not enough of us," she said more quietly.

Norwood and Heloise fled the porch. "Get back here and help!" Wicket shouted after them, but they stormed over to Uncle Mort.

"Do something!" Norwood told him.

"Do what?" Uncle Mort's face was furious. "Fly up there and get it? You bring your broomstick, Hel?"

"This is no time for jokes, Mort," she countered.

"The real joke is that you two cowards bothered to show up at all." Uncle Mort took off for the porch, leaving the couple to fume for a few seconds before running into the Morgue.

"You guys should go," Wicket whispered to the Juniors on the porch. "It's too late."

"No!" said Driggs. "All these people — and what about you?"

She looked at them, miserable. "I don't care."

"*Wait!*" A strident voice cut straight through the panic. Pip was a blur as he dropped down from the trees, ran across the square, and began to scale the Bank.

The Juniors jumped off the porch to watch him climb. "What are you doing?" Ferbus yelled. "Get down, idiot!"

Pip ignored him and went even quicker. When at last he reached the top, he grabbed the bomb from under the roof's peak and tucked it under his arm.

"What's he doing?" Driggs asked as Pip descended.

"I don't know," Elysia said, "but he's only bringing that thing closer to us."

A whistle came from the trees. Bang bounded out of the woods and ran up to the Bank, where Pip had landed on the roof of the porch. She whistled again. He nodded and tossed her the bomb.

The Juniors cringed as it soared through the air, but Bang gingerly caught it in her outstretched hands. She flitted to the fountain and set the contraption on the ledge. Crinkling her nose in concentration, she got to work, poking at the wires and removing components from the device. The entire square was silent; even the injured had stopped moaning to watch.

Time seemed to slow down. The seconds crept by, each more agonizing than the last. Finally, with one last yank, Bang straightened up and tossed the bomb to the ground, where it landed with a crunch.

The red light was off.

A few people let out a cheer, but most simply stood around with their mouths hanging open. A second later, half a dozen Seniors came out of the Morgue and scurried to the porch to provide Wicket with some much-needed backup, wholly unaware of the situation that had just unfolded in the square. Uncle Mort grabbed a few of them on the way, directing them to sweep the other buildings and make sure there weren't any more explosives waiting to detonate.

The Juniors just gaped at Bang. "How did you do that?" Elysia asked.

Bang let slip a shy smile and signed something that no one understood. "She went through an electronics phase last year," said Pip, swinging down from the roof of the porch. "For our science fair she built a working solar-powered lawn mower and a robotic —"

"And you!" Ferbus yanked Pip into an affectionate headlock. "SpiderPip!"

Driggs gave his head an appreciative shake. "You sure know how to pick 'em, Mort."

Uncle Mort was staring at the rookies, his expression stunned yet impressed. "Guess so."

"What in tarnation is going on?" Pandora hobbled onto the street from the direction of the Field. Her eyes swept across the destruction of the square. "Mercy . . ."

Corpp appeared a few minutes later and hugged Dora close as they conferred with Uncle Mort. "You think Zara planted the bombs when she attacked Driggs?" he asked.

Pandora shook her head. "I scrubbed that fountain top to bottom getting that boy's blood out of it. I didn't see any bombs."

"Then how do you figure she slipped past your sensors tonight?" Corpp quietly asked Uncle Mort. "I thought alarms were in place."

Uncle Mort looked troubled. "They are."

"Then what happened?"

"I'm not sure." He gave Corpp and Dora a knowing look. "But if I were to take a wild guess —"

They flinched at the sound of a loud bang behind them. Ayjay had kicked open the door of the Morgue and was now walking calmly across the square.

"Ayjay?" Lex called out. His face looked funny. "You okay?"

"Too much," he muttered to himself as he walked, tearing off his eye patch and hurling it to the ground. "Too much."

The Seniors' expressions changed in an instant; they knew something was wrong. Uncle Mort broke into a run after him. "Ayjay!" he called out, frantically gesturing at the Juniors to help in the chase. "Stop him!"

Ayjay took one look back at Uncle Mort, then began sprinting toward the Bank. Wicket said something to him as he bounded up the stairs of the porch, but he blew right past her, jumping over a prone body and heading into the foyer.

The Juniors started after him, but no one was fast enough — not even Pip. Lex pushed through the crowd and caught up to her uncle as he pounded up the stairs to the second floor. "What's going on?"

"Kloo's dead."

"What? You don't know that!"

"Trust me. She is."

"But — " Lex sputtered, remembering what she had gone through when Cordy died. "Even if she is, Ayjay knows she'd be too confused to see him this soon in the Afterlife! Why would he go in there?"

"He's not."

"Then why are we chasing him?"

Uncle Mort slowed as they stepped into the office. The sole Senior working the graveyard shift watched them, dumbfounded. The door to the Lair was wide open, the security keypad ripped out of the wall and hanging by a wire.

Uncle Mort's shoulders sank. "We're too late."

Ayjay sat curled up in a corner, clutching an empty bottle of Amnesia and staring groggily at the crowd of people gathered around him.

He blinked once.

"Who are you?"

11

Lex emerged from the woods, hugging herself. She let out a breath and watched the cloud of vapor drift away as she walked toward the center of town. Clouds blanketed the sunless sky, turning the morning into a gray, stagnant realm of crapitude. Ferbus and Elysia sat atop the remnants of the fountain reading *The Obituary*. Driggs pounded his feet on the ground and blew into his hands to keep them warm.

Work had been called off for the day; Necropolis had agreed to take on Croak's targets while Uncle Mort and the town dealt with the aftermath. Most of the victims had been stabilized and were recuperating, and those who hadn't been as lucky were laid out in the alley behind Corpp's — seven in all. They'd be buried the next day.

"Hey," Driggs said as Lex reached the fountain. "All done?"

Lex nodded and pulled her sleeves over her trembling hands. The pillar of fiery anger in her chest had been surging like a sun storm ever since the explosion, and it had just come to a head, sending her into the forest to discharge. "Sorry. I just — there's been a lot to rage about."

"I know." He glanced back at the woods. "What did you Damn?"

"I don't know," Lex said, distracted. "Dirt or something."

Driggs raised an eyebrow. "You can Damn dirt?"

"I can Damn whatever I want," she snapped.

"Whoa, okay," he said, holding up his hands. "I just — hey, how'd it go?" he said to someone behind her.

"Fine," Uncle Mort said, walking briskly. "He didn't put up a fight or anything."

Not only had everyone stayed up all night tending to the victims, but the Juniors also had to pack up Ayjay's entire room, making sure to discard anything that had to do with Croak. Meanwhile, Uncle Mort had taken Ayjay into isolation and begun the delicate process of dissolving his career as a Grim. This involved a lot of sedation combined with something that was almost like hypnosis — Lex wasn't sure. Whatever it was, it had convinced Ayjay that he'd spent the past five years in college, but had gotten into a car accident and injured his eye as well as the part of his brain that affected his memory. Lex thought this sounded ridiculous, but Ayjay bought it — and why wouldn't he? What other explanation was there?

After that, all that was left to do was stick Ayjay on a Greyhound bus with nothing but a forged college degree, a couple forms of identification, and five thousand dollars to his name. It felt cruel — it *was* cruel, but there were no other options. That gigantic whiff of Amnesia had erased all memories Ayjay had ever had of Croak, including Kloo.

Which, after all, was the point.

Lex rubbed her eyes and tried not to picture Ayjay sitting alone on that bus seat, his eye futilely searching for answers as to who he was, where he was going, why he was on a bus, and who on earth had put him there. "What about the population monitoring system?" she asked Uncle Mort.

"Seems like it's working," he said. "The sign clicked to two less when we passed out of the town limits, then plus one when I came back, just like it's supposed to. And I checked the logs from last night — it was working just fine, no glitches."

"Then how did Zara get in without us noticing?"

Uncle Mort lowered his voice. "I don't think she did."

"'The bomb went off at eight fourteen p.m.'" Elysia was reading from the newspaper, her speech peppered with little squeaks of pain as Ferbus changed her bandage. "'Rumors of a second, undetonated bomb have surfaced, but such claims have yet to be confirmed. Seven are dead, and many more are injured.' Ow!"

"Sorry!" Ferbus cried, flapping the bandage. "Too much pus!"

Elysia gave him a sour look mixed with a hint of a smile, then continued. "'Authorities say that Zara was able to breach the protective safeguards in effect, but details as to how she accomplished this are still unclear. One thing is for certain: No detection devices were triggered, despite Croak's authorities' claims that the town was prepared for any type of intrusion.'"

"They don't like you, Mort," said Driggs.

Uncle Mort snorted. "What else is new?" He flashed them a hollow smile. "Won't be long now."

Driggs frowned. "What's that supposed to mean?"

"I have a call to make," Uncle Mort said, heading for Corpp's. "You kids stay together. I'll be right back."

Driggs sat down on the ledge with a sigh. "Where are our little rookie saviors?" he asked Elysia.

"Back at the Crypt, sleeping."

Lex kept pacing, her body not allowing her to calm down. She was too busy thinking about Zara. And the bodies rotting not thirty feet away from them.

None of this made any sense. Up until now, Zara had carefully targeted her victims, whether they were criminal or innocent. Blanket destruction just wasn't her style.

Lex stopped short in front of Corrp's, where the obelisk had fallen. The point caught her eye — she'd never really looked at it before, it had been so high up. She crouched down to examine it, then drew back, surprised. Etched into the stone was a series of symbols:

"Driggs," she called. "Look at this."

He walked over and crouched next to her. "What's that?"

"I don't know. Have you ever seen these symbols before?"

"No."

"Not in any of those books you read while researching Croak, the Wrong Book, Grotton?"

"No, nothing."

Lex thought for a moment. Then, in a flash of revelation, she grabbed a nearby shred of paper debris and a charred piece of wood and began to make a crude rubbing.

"What are you doing?" he asked.

"Saving our asses."

"Naturally. How?"

"Not sure yet," she said, sweeping the paper into the air with a flutter and taking off toward the library. "Give me five minutes!"

He started to follow her. "What —"

"Alone!"

||||||

Lex could feel the resistance. She strained against it, pushed as hard as she could, but the resulting pain got to be too much. She tried to fight through it, gritted her teeth until she thought for sure her body would break apart, and then *bam* — she'd relent and it'd throw her right back to where she started.

Once the allotted five minutes had passed, Driggs walked into the library. "You okay?"

"Yeah," she said breezily, brushing off her hoodie.

He sat on the table and stared at her. When she said nothing, he crossed his arms.

"What?" she asked.

"You going to tell me what you were doing?"

She blinked.

"Lex," he said patiently, "you know how you love that thing I can do with my teeth? Consider it off the table until you tell me what's going on."

Lex held firm for a moment but ultimately caved. She did love that thing. "I was trying to get into the cabin, okay?" she said, lowering her voice. "I thought that maybe the symbols on the obelisk had something to do with it, that if I had them in my head, I could somehow get past the shield —"

Driggs grew angry, as she knew he would. "By Crashing? Are

you nuts? You don't know how to control it — and even if you did, are you remotely prepared for whatever's waiting for you inside? Why take the risk?"

"Because seven more people are dead!" She took a step forward. "Dozens more are injured, Ayjay fried his own goddamn brain, and now that Zara's tested the waters, she knows precisely how vulnerable we are for next time. So I want to get to the Wrong Book first, before Zara does. Because if it falls into her hands, if she gains one more advantage over us, that's it. We're toast."

Driggs looked as if he was thinking this over and was almost about to agree when a yell came from the town square.

"Something's up," Lex said, looking out the window.

"We'll fight more about this later." Driggs opened the door. "Come on."

Heloise had shooed Ferbus and Elysia away and taken a position atop the fountain's ledge. The frumpiness of the previous night was gone; she was back in fine form, with bright red shoes to match her lipstick.

The citizens of Croak — those who could walk, at least — poured out of the Morgue and gathered around her. More filtered in from the Bank, and some even came from the direction of their homes, as if they'd known to meet at a specified time. Lex looked at her watch. Noon, on the dot.

The Juniors gathered in the back, near Pandora and Corpp. "Not good," Elysia muttered to Lex.

"Thank you for coming," Heloise announced. "We have a lot to talk about." She began to walk back and forth atop the fountain, her heels clicking across the stone. "As we all know quite well by now, the Grimsphere is under attack. And when people are under attack, the one thing they must never display, under any circumstances, is weakness — not in their defenses, not in their willingness to fight, and most assuredly not in their leadership."

Uncle Mort poked his head out of Corpp's. Heloise cleared her throat and stared at him, causing everyone to turn around and do the same. "Show's starting, I see," he said, stepping outside and leaning against the building. "Break a leg, Hel."

"Up until a few months ago," she continued in a honeyed voice, "Mort was an exemplary mayor. No one is disputing that. But times have changed, and Mort has not changed with them. He doesn't seem to see the danger we're in, to realize that we cannot continue to live our lives in the carefree way we once could. What's more, he has relied on old tried-and-true defenses — defenses that are not only obsolete but detrimental to the cause of protecting our fair citizens. We need look no further than the pile of bodies behind the Morgue to affirm that changes must be made."

The door to the Morgue clanged open. Norwood stood in its frame for a beat, then swaggered toward the fountain. He climbed up next to Heloise and opened his arms to the citizens.

"The events of last night were tragic, horrific, and, above all, avoidable," he boomed. "With the proper precautions in place, we could have caught Zara and stopped her from perpetrating this unnecessary attack, this heartbreaking loss of life. Sadly, we cannot turn back the clock — but what we *can* do is prevent it from ever happening again."

Heloise faced Uncle Mort. "Will you join us up here, Mort?"

"No," he calmly replied, just loud enough for them to hear. "Whatever you have to say to me, you can yell it from there. It's never stopped you before."

Heloise bristled and began to protest, but Norwood held up his hand. "Very well," she said in a prickly voice. "Go on, darling."

Norwood drew a deep breath. "I propose a recall election. Vote here and now on whether the citizens of Croak believe that you are fit to continue governing this town, or if a suitable replacement should be installed as mayor, in which case I humbly submit my name for approval."

A few people, mostly the Juniors, cried out in protest, but Norwood ignored them. "Mort?" he said. "Sound fair?"

"Not really." Uncle Mort did not show any emotion other than that of mild amusement. "But by all means, proceed with your little election."

As Norwood and Heloise quietly conferred with each other, the Juniors rushed up to Uncle Mort. "Norwood really gets off on this voting thing, huh?" said Ferbus.

"Can he do this?" an angry Driggs asked Uncle Mort. "Legally?"

"Yes," said Uncle Mort. "Though it hasn't been done in decades."

Lex was seething too. "You mean he doesn't even need presidential approval?"

"No. By the people, for the people, or something like that. The president of the Grimsphere will accept whatever the citizens decide."

"Even if the citizens are idiots?" Lex shouted, but Norwood was speaking again.

"No need for a secret ballot," he said, quietly adding, "I think we're all of the same mind here anyway." He raised his chin and spoke in a clear, ringing voice. "All those in favor of removing Mort from the office of mayor and henceforth installing me as his replacement, please raise your hands."

A sea of hands shot up into the air with no hesitation. A clear majority, even with those absent due to injuries.

"Well, that's that," Norwood said with a simple smile. "From this day forth, Mort, you are relieved of your position as mayor, as well as that office's rights and responsibilities. Immediately following this meeting, Snodgrass and Lazlo will escort you to your home to retrieve all pertinent items and information. You will immediately surrender all privileges, confidential information, and security clearances to myself and Heloise, and you will be stripped of all authority over any citizens or groups of citizens in Croak." He smiled. "Including the Juniors."

Uncle Mort's eyes were hard. "And if I refuse?"

"You'll be dealt with accordingly."

Snodgrass and Lazlo stepped up next to Norwood and cracked their knuckles.

Uncle Mort let out a snort as he pushed himself off the wall. "Hired goons?" he said as he walked through the square. "Someone's been studying up on their Mob movies."

Norwood kept addressing the crowd. "Heloise will be my second-in-command. You will treat us both with the respect that the office demands and come straight to us with any problems, questions, or reports of dissent."

"Reports of dissent, huh?" Uncle Mort said wryly. "That's confidence, right there."

"Shut your smart-ass mouth, Mort!" a man toward the front butted in. "My partner is dead, all because your security system turned out to be worthless. We've given you second chance after second chance, and now we're paying for our stupidity. So I'd knock off the sarcasm if I were you."

The Juniors started to jump to Uncle Mort's defense, but Pandora outyelled them all. "This is pure codswallop!" She marched toward the fountain, her hands balled into fists. "Mort's a phenomenal mayor! We can't blame him for the fact that we're being terrorized by a sociopath! It's not his fault!"

No, Lex thought, her chest tightening. *It's mine.*

"A *Junior* sociopath," Heloise gently reminded her. "And we all know who encouraged that sort of free thinking in the first place."

"If it weren't for Juniors, half of you would be dead!" Ferbus shouted. "Pip and Bang dismantled that second bomb!"

"Rumors," said Heloise, brushing her hand through the air. "No one saw that but you kids — "

"It's true!" Pandora screeched.

" — and a couple of feeble-minded geezers," Heloise sneered back at her. "How are we to believe a word any of you say?"

"*You* saw it!" Driggs shouted.

Heloise clucked her tongue. "I saw nothing."

"*I* saw it!" Pandora was livid. "What's wrong with you people? You're really going to hand our town over to these slimeball *creeps?*"

Uncle Mort spoke at last. "Calm down, Dora. Better to go quietly, I think. Don't want to ruffle anyone's nose hairs." He offered Norwood and Heloise a little salute. "Godspeed, you two. I'll hand over whatever you need, and I'll be happy to assist with the transition in any way I can."

"That won't be necessary," said Norwood with a gigantic smile. "We've got everything under control. Heloise will be taking over as head of security, so your services in that capacity will no longer be needed. You may, however, go back to your previous position as a Killer, if you so choose."

"Oh, I so do," he said. "Targets will be a nice change from the stiffs I currently work with."

Norwood ignored this and turned back to the crowd. "Now, for a few new ground rules. A curfew will be in effect, starting tonight. No one may be out of their house after ten, not even to indulge in inebriations."

Corpp let out a sigh. "There goes the business. Again."

"Second," Norwood continued, "Croak is now officially on lockdown. No leaving the town for any reason, except for your shifts. Cancel any vacation plans you may have made, including those for the upcoming holidays. If you absolutely need to leave, come to us and we will discuss the possibility."

"Discuss, meaning refuse," said Dora.

"Third, there are to be no more visits to the Afterlife for anyone, with the exception of those whose positions allow." He looked at the Juniors, then at Wicket. "This rule has been disregarded in the past, but will be enforced with the utmost rigidity from now on. No entry whatsoever."

Wicket looked at Lex and gave her a helpless shrug.

"And fourth, and most important, is the method by which we will be enforcing these new rules," said Norwood, a vicious look in his eye. "Mort will hand over the Cuff tracker he's developed, and starting tonight, each and every one of your locations will be tracked until further notice."

The crowd, which until this point had been relatively accepting of the new changes, broke into a chorus of complaints. Uncle Mort simply shook his head.

"That way," Norwood continued over them, "we will know where you are at all times. If Zara enters the town limits again, she will register in the security system as an unauthorized intruder and will be that much easier to catch as long as everyone else is already being monitored."

"Unreal," Driggs said.

"Needless to say, the wearing of Cuffs is now mandatory," Norwood went on. "Immediately following this meeting, you will form two lines, and Heloise and I will lock your Cuffs in place. Keep in mind that Cuffs are tamper-resistant once locked, and anyone caught attempting to remove theirs will be punished severely, as will anyone who tries to leave the Croak city limits without authorization."

"So now Croak is a prison," said Lex through gritted teeth, wishing she hadn't just discharged, wanting to feel the heat surging through her hands.

Norwood was making a sympathetic, calming gesture. "I know this may seem harsh now, but trust me," he said with a smile. "This is for the good of the town. I promise."

Some townspeople still didn't look happy about this latest development, but the more Norwood talked, the more they seemed to accept it. As long as it was for the good of the town.

"That will be all for today," Heloise offered as a conclusion. "Thank you for your confidence and support. We promise to do whatever we can to keep you safe, capture Zara, and return Croak to its once-peaceful state." She turned to Snodgrass and Lazlo and gave them a nod. They nodded back and began to prod Uncle Mort down the street in the direction of his house.

"Oh, and one more thing," said Norwood, loud enough for Uncle Mort to hear. "From this point forward, all Junior Grims are indefinitely suspended from their positions."

Lex's stomach sank.

"What?" Driggs yelled first, with Lex, Ferbus, Dora, and Corpp joining in at a frightening crescendo. The Seniors looked at the shouting Juniors as if they were feral animals, as if here was the evidence that these uncontrollable hooligans should have been exiled years ago.

Hot tears came to Lex's face as she yelled, even though she tried to blink them back. Killing was the one thing she had been put on this earth to do — what was she if she couldn't do it anymore?

Norwood smiled at the Juniors and continued talking over them. "No shifts, no scything, no Killing, no Culling. Juniors shall instead attend to duties that either Heloise or I assign to them, the types of duties that more accurately befit those in subordinate positions."

Uncle Mort broke free of his escorts and ran back to the fountain. "You son of a bitch!" he yelled at Norwood. The measured calmness was gone; Lex had never seen him so mad. The entire crowd — even the Juniors — fell silent. "You don't have the authority to do that, and you know it!"

"It would seem I just gave myself the authority," Norwood answered. "You really think the president would object?"

Uncle Mort didn't answer that. "The Field is the safest place for the Juniors to be," he replied instead, practically growling.

"The random transmitting nature of the ether makes it harder for Zara to find them. Forcing them to remain in Croak all day is too dangerous!"

"That is a risk we are willing to take," Heloise said, narrowing her eyes at him. "The vast majority of our recent problems can be traced back to the Juniors. They simply can't be trusted. We'd like to keep a close eye on them in the hopes of avoiding any further . . . incidents."

Satisfied with her explanation, she gave her hands a clap. "Now! Everyone line up so we can get those Cuffs locked."

The people started to form themselves into lines while Uncle Mort just stood there, looking defeated.

Then he pulled something from his pocket.

Norwood stopped directing people and studied him. "What are you doing?"

"I said I'd go quietly," Uncle Mort said, holding up a handful of Amnesia smoke bombs and smirking up at Norwood. "I never said I'd make it easy for you."

The square instantly burst into a cloud of mist and chaos. Though the townspeople were immune to the Amnesia, the smoke was thick enough to blind them, and blind them it did. Furious, Norwood and Heloise jumped off the ledge and waved their arms around, trying to see through the fog.

"Dora!" Heloise yelled above the roars. "Where's the fire extinguisher?"

Pandora slapped on the most innocent face she could muster. "Well, gee, Heloise, I don't think my feeble-minded brain can remember."

Heloise clenched her fists and turned to Snodgrass and Lazlo, wherever they were. "Find it!" Seething, she and Norwood groped for Uncle Mort — but he'd already disappeared into the fleeing crowd.

Lex felt a strong hand grab her shoulder. "Gather up the other Juniors as fast as you can," Uncle Mort said. "I'll meet you all back at the house. Go."

Lex passed the message on to Ferbus and Elysia, who took off for the Crypt to get Pip and Bang. Lex and Driggs stayed behind to search for Sofi, ultimately finding her with several others inside Corpp's, coughing.

Driggs sidled up next to her and tried not to look too conspicuous. "Come with us."

"What?" she said with a hack. "Why?"

"Mort wants to see all the Juniors."

"Right now? Are you wackadoodle?"

Lex jumped in. "Sofi, come *on*."

"No way. I don't want to do whatever it is Mort has planned, or miss getting my Cuff locked. *Some* people around here actually get in trouble when they do something wrong," she said, giving Lex a look.

"So you're just going to blindly obey Norwood like all these other lackeys?"

"No," Sofi insisted. "Norwood's a jerkface. I'm not his lackey."

"Then aren't you angry?" said Driggs. "You're a Junior — he put you out of work too!"

Sofi still looked hesitant. "I just don't want to get kicked out."

"Forget it," Lex said, pulling Driggs away. "She's not coming. Let's go."

Driggs shrugged her off. "Sofi, *please*. Come with us."

"Driggs!" Lex shouted, exasperated. The bar was filling up; soon they wouldn't be able to sneak out without everyone seeing them. "Let's go!"

Watching Lex, a flash of anger shot across Sofi's face. She grabbed Driggs's arm. "Don't listen to her, Driggs," she said. "She doesn't deserve you. She's crazypants, she's only going to get you exiled. Besides, Norwood's going to find you anyway. Just do what he says and you won't get in trouble!"

Driggs looked at her for a second, then shook his head and pulled away.

"Driggs!" Sofi shrieked.

He ignored her and kept walking toward the back of the bar. He and Lex snuck into the alley, hurried straight past the dead bodies without looking, and flat-out sprinted back to the house. Ferbus, Elysia, Pip, and Bang were inside, waiting for them, all out of breath from running and looking very worried. Uncle Mort stood next to the jellyfish tank.

"Sofi's not coming," Driggs told him, panting. "Too scared of getting in trouble." He watched as Uncle Mort pulled on a pair of heavy work gloves. "What's going on?"

Uncle Mort swallowed. He looked hesitant to speak. Finally, he sighed. "I thought they'd have their little fun, play at being mayor, maybe make up a rule or two, and that's it. But with the bombs, and now the suspension of you kids, I — " He chewed at his lips. "The truth is, I can no longer guarantee your safety."

The Juniors exchanged nervous glances.

"What I *can* do," he continued, "is give you a chance to escape. Not today — Norwood'll be here any second, and we won't have enough time to put a plan together. But at least this way we can be ready when things go from bad to worse. And I promise you, they will." He took a step toward the tank. "Now, I don't expect you to be experts right off the bat — it's something you'll have to practice. But it worked for Zara, and Lex should be able to give you some pointers along the way."

"Pointers for what?" Pip asked, taking Bang's hand. Their eyes were huge. "What are you doing?"

The older Juniors sat with their mouths open as Uncle Mort reached into his pocket and pulled out a white scroll woven from spider silk, its surface dotted with instructional diagrams.

"You've got to be kidding me," said Ferbus.

Lex's brain snapped. "This — that's impossible," she stuttered. "There aren't any Loopholes left. Zara found the last one!"

Uncle Mort smirked and held the Loophole over the tank. "Then it's a good thing I found the second-to-last."

He dropped it in. The water instantly began to bubble and fizz. Before long, it had turned into a churning cauldron, its contents shuddering, splashing water to the floor.

"Roll up your sleeves," Uncle Mort instructed. "And line up. We don't have much time."

Driggs stepped in close and spoke in a low voice. "Mort. Are you seriously giving us the ability to Crash?"

Uncle Mort's face was somber. "Might want to grab a pillow to yell into," he said, firmly grasping Driggs's arm and guiding it toward the water. "These sting like hell."

12

Three weeks later Lex found herself poised at the door of the Bank, out way past curfew, tracked both by cameras and by the CuffLink, and ready to storm the lobby in a most unauthorized fashion.

There was no point in being coy. She held her head high, turned the knob, and walked through the door.

▏▏▏▏▏▏▏

Despite its eventual excitement, that evening had started out much the same as all evenings had in the weeks since the attack: über-lamely.

Life in Croak had become intolerable. Minutes after Uncle Mort had stung the Juniors with the Loophole-infused jellyfish venom, Norwood and Heloise had burst into the living room, locked all their Cuffs, and confiscated Uncle Mort's CuffLink, which meant that all the Juniors' movements — and Uncle Mort's — were now being painstakingly tracked. This left them with no way to practice or even learn how to use their new abilities, as Crashing from one location to another — even if it was only a few feet away, to the other side of a room — would set off all sorts of alarm bells, bringing Norwood and Heloise down on them faster than anyone wanted to imagine.

Morale was at an all-time low. Efforts to decode the obelisk's symbols had gotten nowhere. Norwood had made good on his promise to relegate the Juniors to the most menial tasks his malicious mind could think up: fetching coffee for the Etceteras, cleaning the windows of the Bank, raking leaves, and, as fall turned into winter, shoveling snow. They didn't get paid anymore, as "real interns work for free," Heloise often chimed. And even if they had received any compensation, there was nothing to spend it on: the curfew meant no Corpp's, and no Corpp's meant no way to drown their sorrows in the sweet bliss of Yoricks.

Really, it was only a matter of time before Ferbus snapped.

"Screw this!" he cried on their thirteenth straight night of Ferbusopoly, heaving the collection of game boards and tokens into the trash. "Screw Colonel Mustard, screw Queen Frostine, and screw that godforsaken thimble! I'm done!"

The next night, Lex and Driggs arrived to find him sitting on the floor amid a pile of wires and electronics. "He's lost it," Elysia told them. "He bought a used TV and a bunch of extra controllers for the Nintendo —"

"Xbox!" Ferbus said without looking up.

" —and now he's setting it up for this game where we're all supposed to shoot each other. Or team up and fight aliens. Or robots. It's unclear to me at this point."

She got the hang of it soon enough, though, as did the rest of the Juniors. In fact, they turned out to be pretty good at obliterating one another — perhaps unsurprisingly, given their chosen careers and the fact that it was the perfect catharsis for their pent-up frustration. Especially Elysia, who clearly had a lot of unresolved anger issues.

"DIE!" she screamed as she mashed the controller that evening, exploding some poor pixilated being into a glob of blood and guts. "DIE, ENEMY SCUM!"

"Damn, Lys," said Driggs, his tongue sticking out of his mouth in concentration. "You could really give Zara a run for her money in the whole decimating-our-population department."

He was kidding, of course; Zara's totals couldn't be matched. In addition to the daily slaughter of innocents, she was now picking off Grims with increasing regularity. Most were from Necropolis, and although she oddly seemed to be leaving DeMyse alone, she'd managed to sneak in and Damn two Croakers despite Norwood's promises of increased security. But the new mayor had an explanation for everything, simply declaring that the victims must have been working for Zara all along. Those who cooperated and remained loyal to the Grimsphere had nothing to worry about, he'd say, always with a smile.

Elysia threw a grenade at Driggs, Pip, and Ferbus, whose characters disintegrated behind a pile of rubble. "I win! Again!"

"Whatever," said Ferbus, irritably grabbing her controller away. "That was a practice round anyway."

"Then why are you so pissed?" Bang signed.

"Shut up, MacGyver."

Bang gave him the finger, but she was smiling. Ever since she'd dismantled that bomb, everyone had started paying a little more attention to the previously shy, mute girl. They'd even begun to pick up some of her signs. As it turned out, she was just as capable of intelligent conversation as the rest of them.

Ferbus gritted his teeth and reloaded the game as Elysia got up to do a victory dance around him, one that involved a lot of thrusting. "I! Win! Again! — Oh, hey, Sofi," she said. "Want to play?"

Sofi had been trying to sneak through the hallway to her room, but she paused briefly in the hallway now that everyone was staring at her. "No thanks," she said, tucking her laptop under her arm. "Have fun, though."

Elysia stared at the empty doorway once she'd left. "Maybe we should tell her. About — you know." She gestured at the jellyfish scars on her forearm.

"No," Lex said quickly. "She's never asked, and if we told her, she'd probably pout so hard her lips would fall off anyway. Let's just keep quiet and not make things worse."

"Yeah, what does she care?" Ferbus said, starting a new game. "Hellspawn always gives her the easiest jobs anyway. Skanks, the both of them. Stupid skanks!"

Lex agreed with Ferbus's astute observation, but she didn't say anything more. Sofi was still friendly with everyone, but a definite rift existed now, and Lex had a strong suspicion it was because of what had happened between her and Driggs at Corpp's. Sofi never quite met his eye anymore or flirted with him the way she used to.

Lex, meanwhile, found that she couldn't stop doing either of those things. Other than video games, the whole Wrong Book debacle, and the fact that Zara could drop in and slaughter them at any moment, Driggs was Lex's main distraction these days. In fact, his inventiveness in finding new ways to be alone together had reached a series of sexy new heights. They'd locked lips behind the paint aisle of the hardware store, in the walk-in refrigerator at the Morgue (much to Pandora's simultaneous disgust and delight), and, of course, all over the roof of their house. Once, they even fooled around in the Bank, brazenly making out right there on the couch of the foyer as Norwood walked in on his way to the hub.

"You suspended our working privileges," Driggs coolly told him after receiving a lengthy scolding. "Not our God-given right to eat each other's faces. Deal with it."

Lex tried to focus on the game, but she was pretty solidly losing, judging by the amount of blood spurting from her character's neck. "This is what comes of growing up with only roller coaster simulation games," she said, blindly mashing the controller. "Stupid Cordy."

"How's she doing these days?" asked Pip.

"I wouldn't know." Lex scowled. "Wicket said she went deep into the Void a few weeks ago on an excursion to Afterlife Egypt."

"Don't worry, Lex," Elysia said tenderly, decapitating Lex's character with a bayonet. "She'll come back eventually."

Lex tossed the controller aside with a sigh and watched the map at the bottom of the screen, following the little icons as they scurried around the terrain. "Well, she's already dead. Doesn't seem like a fate much worse could befall her."

"But Kloo hasn't shown up either," said Pip. "Right?"

"Oh, that happens sometimes," Elysia said. "Grim souls don't always want to see us or be reminded of their old life."

Lex had stopped listening. She stared harder at the map. Something was itching at her brain, but —

"Does anyone have a map of Croak?" she asked.

"Closet," said Ferbus.

Lex sprang from the couch and dug around the closet until

she found it — crumpled and stained, but readable. Next she grabbed her bag — after administering the Loophole, Uncle Mort had insisted that each Junior pack some essentials and carry them at all times in case they had to make a quick getaway. Among Lex's essentials was the rubbing she'd made from the obelisk, which she smoothed out in front of her.

Lex traced a line across the features of the map, then an identical line across the symbols:

Every one of her hairs stood up on end. "The symbols are a map," she said. Everyone except Ferbus looked at her. She held up the rubbing. "If the single line at the bottom represents the obelisk, then the two crossed lines are the Bank. The next one is the Ghost Gum, where we found the key, and the last one is the cabin in the woods — it all fits!" She pointed at the cross symbol. "The only thing left is something hidden at the Bank!"

"Like what?" said Driggs.

"Probably a way to get past the cabin's shield! Like a neutralizer! What if — "

"Ha!" yelled Ferbus, the only one still playing. "Just stole Elysia's rocket launcher!"

Elysia grabbed her controller. "You *what?*"

At that point almost everyone lost interest in the symbols and started blowing one another's heads off again. But Lex's mind was still buzzing with possibilities. Back when she'd been looking for the key, she'd dismissed the Bank as being too busy and visible for someone — the white figure, or whoever — to sneak something in. But maybe not.

"I'm going to go look around in the Bank," she announced, grabbing her hoodie.

Driggs, Ferbus, and Elysia were too riveted to the game to protest. "But it's almost ten," said Pip. "And we're not allowed in the Bank anymore."

"What more can Norwood do to me? Throw me in jail?"

"He could take away your scythe," Bang signed. "Or make you clean his basement. Again."

"Yeah," said Pip. "How are you going to sneak in?"

Lex shouldered her bag and grinned. "I'm not." She bent over Driggs to kiss him, slipping Bone's key into his pocket for safekeeping in case she ran into trouble. "See you later."

"Okay, muffin," he said robotically, his eyes glued to the screen as he smooched the air. "Be safe and so forth."

||||||

Norwood and Heloise were waiting for her, scythes drawn as she stepped into the Bank. Kilda watched from behind the counter, her eyes as large as her flowery brooch. The poor woman hadn't had much to do since the tourist season ended, but Norwood and Heloise still made her stay at work until curfew.

"Hi, everyone," Lex said to them in a steady voice. Confidence was key. She reached into her bag. "I just came to — "

"Hold it right there!" Heloise yelled.

Lex slowly raised her hand, revealing a can of cranberry sauce she had bought for tomorrow's Thanksgiving dinner. "Just dropping this off for Kilda," she lied. "It's from Uncle Mort."

Norwood scowled. "I don't care if it's from the goddamned Pilgrims. You're not supposed to be here."

Lex snuck a glance at Kilda, who gave her a small wink. Kilda had always had a soft spot for the Juniors, who hadn't been there long enough to develop the deep-seated irritation that most other citizens of Croak had built up toward her. Plus, she had a big crush on Uncle Mort.

"I told her to come!" Kilda said, her jolly voice not faltering for a second as she grabbed a gigantic bowl of potpourri and dragged it across the counter until it was directly beneath Norwood and Heloise. "I'm *so* sorry, I don't know what I was thinking! I must be — ha!" She crushed a handful of Amnesia-soaked rose petals into their noses. A glassy look settled over both their faces. "Go sit on the couch!" she instructed them. They did.

Kilda looked at Lex. "How can I help?"

"You just did," Lex said, thoroughly impressed at her foresight. Those things must have been highly concentrated for them to have an effect on Grims. "But I also need to take a look around. Is that all right?"

"For now!" Kilda wrung her hands. "They won't remember a thing, but it won't last long, so you'll have to hurry!"

Lex briefly assessed the foyer, looking under the couches and skimming the brochures in the rack. From there she jumped behind the counter and pawed through Kilda's desk, but all she found was a bunch of papers, files, bowls of sticky candy, and a fancy letter opener shaped like a sword — which, for all she knew, *was* the neutralizer. How was she supposed to know when she'd found what she was looking for if she had no idea what it was?

"Kilda, have you ever heard of something hidden inside the Bank?" she asked. "Something important?"

Kilda stroked her chin. "There's the tunnel under the porch, but it's just a passageway! There's nothing in there!"

Lex assessed her remaining options. The hub was full of working graveyard shifters; she couldn't go in there without getting tackled by a team of Senior Etceteras, so she decided to forgo it for now. Instead she made her way toward the flight of stairs that led up to the Afterlife and lightly knocked on the door.

Wicket answered a few moments later. "Whoa!" she said. "How did you get here?"

"Lies and trickery. Can I come in?"

"Sure. I knew you'd make it sooner or later." She made a rude gesture at the floor, in the direction of the hub. "Suck it, bastards!"

Wicket's pain and outrage over Roze's death had morphed into a fervent desire to overthrow Norwood and Heloise. She'd decided — along with a little encouragement from Roze herself, now in the Afterlife — that the best way to do it was to become a double agent, to gain Norwood's trust and use it to elicit classified information. Which she happily passed on to Uncle Mort.

Lex told her what happened, relaxing now that she was in friendly territory. "I'm looking for something," she said. "Ever see anything weird up here? Something that doesn't belong?"

Wicket considered this. "Not that I can think of."

Lex ducked into the Lair to snoop around, but she emerged empty-handed. She leaned against the wall, thinking quickly. "I have it on good authority that there's something hidden in the Bank that could be . . . beneficial. To our cause." She picked a leaf off the potted plant and shredded it nervously. "But it couldn't be in the hub — too many people around. There's the basement, which I've never seen — "

"Just used for storage," Wicket said. "That's what I've heard."

"And I didn't see anything out of the ordinary in the foyer, so all that's left is . . ." She trailed off and dropped the leaf shards as her eyes landed on the vault. "Oh, crap on a spatula."

Wicket's eyes widened. "You think it's in the Afterlife?"

Lex sighed. "It's gotta be. That's the best hiding place there is. But it's so huge in there! And it's not like I can touch anything. How in the hell am I supposed to find it?"

"I don't know," Wicket said, swinging the vault door open. "Go find out."

Lex was surprised. "You sure? It's against Norwood's rules."

Wicket folded her arms. "You think I give a rat's ass about Norwood's rules? Besides, if he's passed out downstairs, he won't find out until much later. I'll tell him the rotten Junior punk hit me. He'll love that."

Lex gave her a thankful smile, plunged inside —

And immediately forgot about the hidden whatever-it-was as Cordy tackled her. Or tried to. In actuality, they just repelled each other and landed on their butts in the fluff. "Happy Thanksgiving, Sis!"

"Cordy!" Lex stood up and looked around. "Edgar! And — oh my God, Kloo! Where have you guys been?"

They shot Lex a trio of tired smiles. "Traveling, hon!" said Kloo. She looked happy, Lex was glad to see. "We just got back."

"I ran into her on my way out of town," Cordy said, "and it seemed like the only polite thing to do was ask her to come along." She gave Edgar a peevish look. "Wish someone had given *me* the grand tour when I first got here."

"I *would* have," he said, "but my walking stick was misplaced at the time. Would you have me traverse the unending realms of the eternal universe without my walking stick?"

"Next time, I'm going to shove that walking stick where the Void don't shine," said Cordy under her breath, who had far less patience for the dead poet than Lex did. "But Lex, guess what! I've got a surprise for you."

"I'm sure you'll love it," said Edgar in a voice suggesting that he positively loathed it.

"Hang on," Lex said. This was getting weird. Everyone was far too cheerful, especially given the aftermath of the bombing and what Ayjay had done to himself. "Kloo — are you okay?"

"Fine," she said with a smile. "Takes a little getting used to, but I like it here. So many different ways people have died! Very interesting, from a medical perspective."

Lex raised an eyebrow. "I mean, about Ayjay," she said. "We tried to stop him, but — "

Cordy erupted into a loud and obviously fake coughing fit. Edgar began hauling Kloo toward the Void, dramatically itching his body. "Chickenpox is back," he moaned. "Time for more cala-mine."

Kloo let out a sigh but let him lead her away. "We've been through this, Ed. You can't get chickenpox more than once. Or, you know, when you're already dead."

"I don't know what to tell you," he snipped. "I'm a miracle of modern science."

Lex watched them go. "What was that all about?"

Cordy gave her a pained look. "She doesn't remember Ayjay."

"Huh?"

"Doesn't make any sense, I know. *He's* the one who Amnesia'd himself, right? That's what Wicket told me. But when she got here, she had no memory of him at all. Croak, yes. All the other Juniors, Uncle Mort, even the failed initiation vote. But not Ayjay. It's like someone just X-acto–knifed him out of her brain."

This disturbed Lex on a level she didn't even understand. "Has anything like that ever happened before?"

"I don't think so." Cordy frowned. "I've been asking around, but everyone's stumped. It's this weird little anomaly that no one can explain — not even Grims, not even people who have been here for centuries."

Lex shuddered. What was going on with the Afterlife these days? First the vortexes, now this?

"Anyway," said Cordy, "we try not to talk about him around her. Besides, maybe it's all for the best. Maybe it'll be easier for her to move on, find someone new." She grinned. "Like I did."

"You what?"

"I told you, I have a surprise." Cordy whistled. A figure materialized at the edge of the Void, then grew larger until it was standing in front of Lex, golden and bejeweled and nearly naked.

He was about the same age as they were, but his eyes shone with an ancient wisdom. His feet were bare, as well as his chest, which was adorned with a huge golden necklace the likes of which Lex had never seen back on earth. The sheen coming from his caramel-colored skin made it seem as if he was glowing. Lex studied his face. His teeth were so blindingly white that she half expected an audible *ding* to sound when he smiled. She was pretty sure she'd never met any godlike, rock-hard Egyptian guys before, but she couldn't shake the feeling that he looked sort of familiar . . .

"Lex, this is Tut," said Cordy. "My boyfriend."

Lex's eyes bulged. "As in *King* Tut?"

"The one and only," the boy said, his voice deep and sonorous. He looked quite pleased with himself.

"Isn't he hot?" Cordy whispered.

Lex looked at him again. He was holding up his shiny gold necklace and checking out his reflection.

"He's . . . something else," said Lex. "Where did you find him?"

"The Pyramids, where else? Poe was off dying of sunstroke or whatever, leaving me to dismount from Lumpy all by my-self — which is *not* easy to do, I'll have you know — and I almost fell to the ground, when someone caught me. Can I help it that that someone just so happened to be the most famous Pharaoh in all of history? Can I help it that he dropped dead at the oh-so-sexy age of eighteen? And can I help it that I got lost in his eyes? His hot, hot eyes?"

"I can bench-press a camel," Tut added.

"And he can bench-press a camel," said Cordy, nodding and patting his chiseled abs. "He lifted Lumpy. It was very impres-sive."

"So let me get this straight," Lex said to Tut. "You came all the way across thousands of miles and millennia just to hang out with some random commoner girl you just met?"

"Lex!" Cordy scolded her. "This is the first real shot I've ever had at a relationship. Just let me have this. Need I remind you again of the hotness?"

Lex stifled a snicker as Tut swept a hand through his perfectly coifed hair. "No. I think I got it."

Cordy lovingly gazed at him for another minute or so, then turned to Lex. "So how are Mom and Dad?"

Lex's gaze fluttered to the ground. "I'm . . . sure they're fine."

"What?" Cordy shouted. "Jesus, Lex, you haven't talked to them? What kind of monster are you?"

"I just — I didn't think — " Lex sputtered, but she couldn't come up with a decent answer. She should have called them by now, she knew that. But leaving them had been hard enough; she'd barely been able to look them in the eye. What more was there to say?

She *did* miss them, though. It had been nearly three months since she'd last seen her mother and father, and while her usual out-of-sight, out-of-mind tactics had been working, deep down it felt as if a part of her had shriveled up like a dried flower.

Cordy was still yelling. "I'd give up my favorite novelty pyramid-shaped hat to see them again for a single second, and you haven't spoken a word to them since you left?"

"I sent them an anniversary card," Lex said weakly.

Cordy looked ready to wring her neck. "You better call them tomorrow for Thanksgiving, Lex. I mean it." She shook her head in disgust. "They lost both their daughters. You owe them at least a few minutes of your precious time."

"Fine! You're right. I'll call."

They stood in grumpy silence. Lex threw one last glance around the Afterlife, not finding her neutralizer, not even caring anymore. She'd look for it later. For now, she just wanted to get out of there.

"I better go," she said, heading for the vault door. "See you later."

Cordy just glared and remained silent. But Tut gave her a jaunty wave and another dashing smile.

"Farewell, peasant!"

13

The next day Lex sank back onto Driggs's bed and glanced out the window at the falling snow, admiring its beauty, its purity, the way it erased everything with a total disregard for all the woes of the world. She would have admired its silence as well, if Driggs weren't blowing out her eardrums with a blistering drum solo.

She yawned. She'd lain awake into the wee hours the night before, obsessing over Cordy and her guilt crusade, the neutralizer that she'd neglected to dig up, and Kloo's weird memory lapse.

But she resolved to shove all that to the back burner of her brain, at least for the next few hours. The other Juniors, Corpp, and Pandora were coming over for a feast Uncle Mort had insisted upon hosting, despite the fact that he'd never done such a thing before and that the entire enterprise was sure to fail in a most spectacular manner. Lex couldn't wait.

What was to happen after that was another story.

"WHAT'S WRONG?" Driggs yelled over a cymbal crash upon catching Lex's troubled face. "Sorry. What's wrong?"

"Nothing." Lex fiddled with his pillow, visions of Cordy's stern face pounding through her head. "My parents are going to strangle me over the phone today, that's all."

Driggs gave her a sympathetic look. "They are not."

"Of course they are," she said. "I haven't called in forever. Plus there's the whole skipping-town-after-my-sister-got-killed thing. Probably won't be thrilled about that either."

"Cheer up, emo kid. Focus on the legendary deep-fried Turkeyzilla."

At the mention of Pandora's promised entrée, Lex cracked a smile. "What is it about turkey that makes people lose their minds?" she asked. "One year Mom lost her engagement ring while stuffing it and forced us to keep eating until we found the damn thing." She smiled at the memory of her laughing parents taking a picture of their daughters covered in giblets. "And breaking the wishbone — remember that?"

"Can't say that I do," Driggs muttered.

The smile slid off Lex's face as she remembered who she was talking to: the poster child for abysmal childhoods. "Crap. I'm sorry."

He shot her a dry grin. "Relax, spaz. Lest you forget, I'm not a fragile little snowflake."

"I'm still sorry. Holidays sucked, I take it?"

He shrugged. "I got a bike for Christmas once."

"That's cool."

"I think it had been stolen."

"Ah."

He twirled a drumstick. "My parents didn't have any money. Or seemingly any desire to see their kid happy. So I spent most Thanksgivings eating greasy KFC and most Christmases outside in the snow, building the presents I wished I had gotten."

Lex stared at him. "That is the saddest thing I have ever heard."

"And yet I get no six-figure book deals. Where's the justice in this world?"

Lex laughed and grabbed his hand. She traced her finger across his palm and wrist, up his arm, and across the chest that she knew was dotted with scars. Her focus jumped back and forth between his mismatched eyes. Now wasn't really the time to ask — but really, would there ever be a good time?

"What happened to them?" she said. "Your parents."

He looked down at his beat-up Chucks. "They're dead."

Lex nodded. She'd been suspecting that for a long time. "How?"

He opened his mouth, then closed it and glanced out the window. "Not today, okay?"

Lex felt a pang of something — hurt, maybe? That he didn't trust her enough to tell her? But as she watched how he sank back into his drumming rhythm, pounding at each drum as if it had personally insulted him, she knew that wasn't it. He just didn't want to reopen those scars.

Lex lay back down on his bed and watched him play for a while. The way his lean muscles bulged underneath his T-shirt, the furious blur of his hands, the tiny beads of sweat gathering on his brow and spiking his hair, the way his tongue stuck out of his mouth in concentration — it was enough to make her forget all about her parents, his parents, Cordy, the neutralizer, everything but the fact that that tongue hadn't yet graced the back of her throat today —

Driggs stopped mid-beat, as if he could hear her thoughts. "Mort ran out to the grocery store, right?"

"Yeah. To get biscuits."

"The lines are probably pretty long. He could be there for a while," he said with sudden mischief in his eyes, wiping a line of sweat from his forehead. He pulled out a key and dangled it in front of her face. "What say you?"

Lex grinned. "Attic?"

Early retirement had suited Uncle Mort well; when he wasn't out on shifts, he spent most of his time in the basement, working, placing furtive phone calls, even making Sparks for all the Juniors. Such distractions had afforded Lex and Driggs the perfect opportunity to perform an exhaustive audit of his home surveillance system until one day they finally, gloriously, found a blind spot: the small staircase that led to the attic.

Once safely up there, they immediately got down to their face-slobbering business, stopping only to sneeze or brush a cobweb away. "Just keep listening for his bike," Lex said between snogs. "If we get caught, he might lock us up here forever."

"He didn't take the bike," Driggs said, going in for another.

Lex pushed him back. "What?"

Driggs just sat there with his tongue hanging out. He put it back in. "He took the car."

"Why? He only drives the car when he needs the space for passengers." She looked out the small, dusty window. As if on cue, the cheddar yellow Gremlin rounded onto Dead End, popping out against the whiteness of the snow like a misplaced taxicab. "Crap, there he is!"

Driggs peered through the grime as the car stopped next to the Bank. "What's he doing?"

"I don't know. But someone's yelling at him." She squinted. "Is it Norwood?"

"Of course it's Norwood." Driggs thought for a moment. "I have an idea. Come on."

Lex followed him back down the narrow staircase to a large gadget sticking out of the living room window. "How is a satellite dish going to help?" she asked as he aimed it at the car.

"Not a satellite dish. A parabolic microphone."

"A what now?"

He donned some headphones, then tossed her a pair. "Put these on."

The voices came through the earpieces as clearly as if they were in the next room. "Whoa. How — "

"It's a long-range listening device. Shh."

Lex closed her mouth and watched as Norwood leaned into the driver's-side window.

" — out of your mind?" he was shouting. "What is *wrong* with you, Mort?"

"Lighten up, Grinch," said Uncle Mort. "It's the holidays."

"I don't care if it's the goddamn Apocalypse! No visitors allowed! And for Chrissakes, *them?*"

"If you have a problem, take it up with Necropolis. The president is well aware of the situation."

"The — what? You went over my head?"

"It wasn't easy, I assure you," said Uncle Mort, shifting the car into gear. "That thing gets bigger every day."

He stepped on the gas and sped off down the road, leaving Norwood in a cloud of exhaust and fussiness.

Lex and Driggs tore off the headphones and stared at each other. "Okay, wait," Lex said. "Who's coming over for dinner that we know of?"

Driggs counted on his fingers. "Corpp and Pandora, all the Juniors, Wicket — "

"No, Wicket's not coming," Lex said. "Norwood would get suspicious."

"Right." Driggs frowned. "Then that's it. I don't know who else it could be."

They kept watching as the car wound its way up the hill and came to a stop in the driveway. Uncle Mort got out and stretched, then opened the door to the back seat.

A familiar pair of boots crunched down onto the snow-covered driveway. The hand that grabbed Uncle Mort's wore a distinctive ring, a ring that had once been lost in the stuffing of a Thanksgiving turkey.

"Oh my God," Lex rasped. "Mom."

||||||

Thirty minutes later Lex, her parents, Uncle Mort, Corpp, Pandora, and the rest of the Juniors all sat in folding chairs around the kitchen table that Uncle Mort had elongated by adding a couple of plywood boards from the garage. A plastic tablecloth featuring spritely Pilgrims spanned its surface.

The menu: legendary deep-fried Turkeyzilla, gravy, stuffing, mashed potatoes, cranberry sauce, and green beans.

The theme: dysfunction.

"So," Elysia said to Lex's parents with her ever-friendly grin, "how are you?"

"How do you think they are?" Ferbus whispered.

She kicked him under the table. "I mean — um — what do you do? For a living?"

Lex's mother, who hadn't said much, continued to stare down the table at the sea of black hoodies while picking at her potatoes.

Lex's father cleared his throat. "I'm a contractor," he said. "And she's a teacher."

"Omigod! *I* wanted to be a teacher!" Elysia turned to Mrs. Bartleby. "Do you love it?"

"Hmm?" She snapped back to attention and smiled vacantly at Elysia. "Oh, yes. I do. The kids are a nice distraction."

"From what?" Pip asked.

Bang smacked her forehead. Lex squeezed Driggs's hand even tighter, causing him to choke on his stuffing. He coughed and hacked until the offending morsel flew out of his mouth, landing in Sofi's glass of water.

"Ewww!" she squealed.

"Drink around it," Pandora scolded. "So! I hear New York City is lovely this time of year."

"Well, it looks nice, I guess," Mr. Bartleby said. "But shoveling out the driveway is a pain in the neck. The girls used to help, but now . . ."

Sensing the impending awkwardness, Corpp jumped in. "Well, Lex has been a wonderful addition to our community. She's smart, friendly, a joy to be around —"

"And don't you worry about the boyfriend," Ferbus said, pointing to Driggs. "I keep him in line."

Mrs. Bartleby's eyes widened, looking at Lex and then Driggs. "You have a —" she sputtered. "He's your —"

Ferbus went white. "They didn't know?"

"Oops!" said Uncle Mort in a theatrical voice, getting up from the table. "Almost forgot the biscuits!"

"Let me help you with those," Lex said through clenched teeth, following him to the counter. A series of pained hugs and greetings had ensued when her parents arrived — but the rest of the guests showed up so soon thereafter that Lex hadn't gotten a chance to talk to them, much to her relief. Still, she hadn't stopped seething. "What were you *thinking?*"

Uncle Mort gave her a reproachful look. "I was thinking that your parents were probably going to feel more lonely and depressed this Thanksgiving than they've ever felt in their lives, and that maybe we could help alleviate some of that by hosting a dinner featuring the one and only daughter they have left."

"A dinner of *horrors?* You know my track record with family gatherings!"

He ignored her. "Here we are!" he said, turning back to the table with a giant platter. "Biscuits aplenty!"

Lex grunted and took her seat. "I'm not sure how much longer I can do this," she whispered to Driggs.

"Me neither," he replied. "I think my hand is broken in three places."

"Sorry."

"And your dad seems to be shooting me some sort of a death stare."

Lex glanced at her father. "That's bad."

"Think he brought the shotgun?"

"It's entirely possible."

"All I'm saying," Ferbus went on, trying to redeem himself and failing, "is that we all look out for one another here." Mr. Bartleby looked at him. Ferbus began to sweat. "Because, you know. We all need somebody. Uh, to lean on."

"Stop talking," Bang signed.

Elysia gave Lex's parents a sympathetic grin. "I think what my idiot partner is trying to say — through the magic of corny song lyrics, for some reason — is that you don't need to worry about

Lex. She's like a sister to me." She realized her poor choice of words as a pained look came to Mrs. Bartleby's face. "Or an especially close cousin." She shut her mouth and stared at her potatoes. "Frig."

Lex was now crushing Driggs's hand into a fine paste. Other than the folding chairs creaking and Pip obliviously scraping the last bits of food off his plate, the table was silent.

"Good beans!" Pip threw in.

||||||

After dinner Uncle Mort made a big deal out of getting everyone to help bring the plywood boards back to the garage — everyone except Lex and her parents, whom he forced to stay put and relax. So there they sat in the living room, Lex sandwiched between them on her uncle's ratty sofa, cursing him to the deepest circles of hell for trapping her like this. Yet again.

"Interesting crowd you're running with," her father said.

Lex so wanted to scream that *he* was the one who sent her here, but instead she bit her tongue and picked at the couch cushion.

Her mother took a shaky breath. "Perhaps we should have thought things through a little more carefully," she said. "If we'd known how you would turn out, if we'd known how much you'd change . . ." She looked out the window. "We thought we were doing the right thing."

Lex softened. "You were, Mom," she said. "I'm happy here. I finally have friends, and they're really important to me."

Her mother let out an uncharacteristic snort. "More important than your own family?" she shot back with an edge in her voice. "All this time we thought we were providing a good life for you, when in reality all you've ever wanted was to run away at the first chance you got. And no wonder, with this — this boyfriend of yours — "

"It's not like that, Mom."

"Then what is it like?" Her mother pursed her lips. "You're still a child, Lex. You're still our responsibility. You can't just cut us out of your life!"

"I'm not!" Lex felt a lump in her throat. "I thought this was what you wanted, for me to knock off all that delinquent stuff and grow up!"

"Oh, you've grown up all right. Too fast, if you ask me. Dropping out of school, bolting right back up here to do God knows what."

"I *had* to come back — "

"Dammit, Lex! Don't lie to me!"

Lex gaped at her. This was a woman who'd kept a swear jar in the kitchen for as long as Lex could remember, so strong was her distaste for vile language. Lex had never heard her swear, not once in her whole life.

Tears were forming in her mother's eyes. "Had to come back — to find your sister's killer, right?" she said in a sarcastic voice. "How *dare* you use that as an excuse?"

Mr. Bartleby gently squeezed his wife's arm. "Hon — "

"How could you abandon us like that?" she went on. "Leaving us to pick up the pieces, to try to figure out how to get out of bed every morning with the knowledge that one daughter is dead and the other doesn't love you anymore!"

Lex could feel her face crumpling. "Mom — that's not — "

"And all along, you're having a grand old time up here with your friends, acting like you never even had a sister, like you don't even have parents, like you don't even care!"

"I *do* care!"

"Then act like it!" With that, her mom jumped up from the couch and bolted to the bathroom.

Lex's hands were shaking uncontrollably. She shoved them under her arms, not knowing whether to cry or apologize. Or run off into the woods, never to be seen again.

Her father sighed. "She's had a rough time," he said. "I mean, we all have, but she's taken it especially hard. Feels like she failed Cordy. As a mother."

"But it wasn't her fault," said Lex. "She couldn't have done anything about it."

"I know. But still, parents are supposed to protect their kids, no matter what."

Her father rubbed his shiny bald head, then took a deep breath. "I don't know what it is Mort's got you doing up here," he said in a steady tone, "and I don't want to know. It's not farming, that's obvious. But I trust him, and you. So do me a favor, will you?" He looked at her. "Be safe. Please. Your mother and I love you so much — I know she seems mad now, but it's only because she worries, and misses you. Both of you."

Outside, it began to snow. He glanced out the window. "She spends hours in your room looking at all those pictures, torturing herself. Wondering how it happened, if Cordy felt any pain, whether she's in a better place now. If anything happened to you, too — " He shook his head. "It'd kill her."

Lex stared at her sneakers. Everything was so unfair. What

had her parents ever done to deserve this? Why couldn't they
have the nice, normal family they'd earned after sixteen years of
devoted parenting?

She looked at her father. "Dad," she said, "if I told you I knew
for a fact that Cordy was okay, would you believe me?"

His eyes met hers.

"Yes."

Just then, everyone plowed back into the house. As they
shook the snow off their boots and drenched the kitchen floor,
Uncle Mort poked his head into the living room. "We were
thinking of getting a little post-dinner Pictionary game going,"
he said. "What do you think?"

Lex quickly wiped her eyes and gave him a forced smile. "Sure.
Whatever."

They piled into the living room and sat wherever space allowed, while Corpp stayed behind in the kitchen to mop up the
mess they'd made. Driggs plopped down on the floor in front of
Lex. "You okay?" he mouthed. Lex just grabbed his hand again.

"Where's your mom?" Uncle Mort asked, removing an easel
from the closet.

Lex and her father exchanged glances. "Just . . . freshening up."

They divided into teams and began playing without her. But
ten minutes later — amid cries of "Broccoli spaceship! Broccoli
SPACESHIP!" — Lex started to worry. Her mom hadn't returned.

"Maybe I should go check on her," she whispered to her father.

Ferbus hurled the marker to the ground when the timer ran
out. "It's a *forest fire!*" he cried. "God, are you people blind? Can't
you — "

A bloodcurdling scream ripped through the house.

Everything that came next seemed to happen in slow motion. Ferbus dove to the floor, the easel collapsing on top of him. Uncle Mort drew his scythe and lunged into a protective stance in front of the rest of the Juniors, who had huddled together in the arms of Pandora.

And Lex and her father slowly rose from the couch, their eyes locked in horror on Zara and the scythe she was holding to Mrs. Bartleby's throat.

14

"Where is it, Lex?"

Zara's face was all business, as if she didn't even register the other people in the room. She stared straight at Lex, her eyes hard.

Lex swallowed. Not Mom. Not Mom too. "Don't hurt her," she said, watching her mother's eyes bulge in fear. "Please."

"If you don't give it to me right now, I will," Zara rasped. The spaces around her eyes were dark and hollow, the whites of her eyes bloodshot. The sheen in her once-luminous silver hair was gone. She'd also lost a lot of weight; she looked sick and sweaty and pale, like a drug addict. "I swear to God, I'll slit her throat. You don't want to be responsible for the death of *another* loved one, do you? Before you know it, you're going to get your whole family killed!"

"What's going on?" Mr. Bartleby said, his voice quivering. "Who is that?"

"No one," Uncle Mort said, never taking his eyes off Zara. "Just stay calm."

The Juniors were desperately tapping at their Cuffs to call for help, but the Cuffs had gone dead. "We have to go get Norwood!" Sofi shrieked, jumping to her feet.

"*Sit down!*" Zara shouted. Sofi froze and stared at her with wide eyes, then slowly sank back down to the floor.

"Give me the Wrong Book, Lex." Zara's new scythe was

smaller and made out of what appeared to be plain old glass. Her strung-out state made it seem as though she should be shaking, but her hand was steady as she pressed the scythe tighter to Mrs. Bartleby's throat, drawing a spot of blood. "Have I not provided enough incentive by now? How are all those innocents feeling on your conscience? How would you feel about adding one more?" she said, yanking Mrs. Bartleby's arm.

"I don't have it!" Lex shrieked, helpless. "I swear. We don't have it. We don't know where it is."

"You're *lying!*" Zara exploded. "God, Lex, you love to make things difficult, don't you? Leaving me high and dry in California, stealing my scythe, snatching up the key to the dead for yourself — *my* key, *my* rightful property." She narrowed her eyes. "And the whole time, acting like you're above it all and want nothing to do with all this nasty Damning business. But you're not so perfect after all, are you?"

Lex stole a glance at the others. "I don't know what you mean."

Zara grinned. "Sure you do. Haven't you told them? About your little extra credit project? By now you must be up to — "

"Stop!" Lex yelled. A spark of rage shuddered through her chest, her hands growing hotter by the second. "What *happened* to you, Zara? Damning all those innocent people, bribing me into giving you information that I don't even have?"

"Liar. You know *some*thing." She shifted her hand, digging the scythe deeper into Mrs. Bartleby's skin.

"Okay, okay!" Lex tried to think. How much could she tell her without giving everything away? "The book is in a cabin in the woods. But there's some sort of protection around it. We can't get in. No one can."

Zara thought about this for a moment, then scowled. "Sorry, Lex. That's not good enough."

"The key!" Driggs butted in, desperate.

Lex's stomach plunged. "Driggs, no."

"Yes. We don't know how to use it anyway. It's not worth your mom's life." He got to his feet and dug around in his pocket. "Here," he said, slamming his hand into Zara's. "Take it."

Zara looked impressed. "Thanks, Slash. Good thing you survived after all." She pushed him to the floor, followed by Mrs. Bartleby. She turned back to Lex with a taunting smile, almost as if she couldn't help herself. "Too bad the same couldn't be said for your sister."

That did it.

With an animal-like howl, Lex rushed at Zara, her scalding hot hands outstretched. There was no uncertainty this time. This time she really was going to Damn her.

But when her hand touched Zara's skin, nothing happened. No fire. No darkness. Not even a flicker.

Zara's face opened into a wide grin, infuriating Lex even more. She lunged again, but this time Zara ducked out of the way, revealing a heretofore forgotten Corpp standing behind her and holding a shovel above her head, ready to knock her out.

But it was Lex he met instead.

It all happened so quickly — Lex was moving too fast to stop herself, too blinded by rage to realize what was happening. That the person she'd tackled to the ground — the person whose soul her hands were incinerating — was not her mortal enemy, but rather the friendly old barkeep who'd been kind to her since day one.

Lex yanked her hands away, but it was too late.

The room plunged into darkness.

The screams from the others were bone chilling. Even Bang's mouth hung open, frozen in a silent shout as the blackness amassed over Corpp's crumpled form, then plunged inside, causing it to burst into flame. Lex watched, too stunned to move. The Juniors hugged one another, some looking away and crying, some unable to tear their eyes from the sight of Corpp's sizzling body. Sofi let out a piercing scream, jumped up, and ran right out of the house. Lex's parents remained huddled on the floor, their eyes shut tight. Uncle Mort grabbed Pandora and held her head to his chest, forbidding her to watch.

Only Driggs jumped into action. He broke away from the Juniors and knelt over Corpp, his face glowing in the light of the small fires popping up along the old man's brown skin. Almost instinctively he held his hands over the body, steady and confident, as if he were Culling Corpp's soul.

And all at once the flames disappeared.

Or rather, they arose from Corpp's skin and floated up into Driggs's waiting hands, where they lingered for a moment before vanishing in a puff of smoke. The room was silent, every person in it looking at Driggs, then at Corpp's chest, which had begun to rise.

But once — only once. With his last breath fading, Corpp opened his eyes, looked at Driggs, and said in a wondrous, almost sad voice, "It's gone."

With that, he died.

Pandora fell onto his body, clutching him so tightly it seemed as though her gnarled hands would break. No one else knew what to do or where to look, dividing their attention between Corpp, Zara, and especially Driggs, who was sitting on the floor, dazed.

Even Zara couldn't stop staring at him. "What the hell was *that?*"

As soon as she spoke, the spell was broken. Uncle Mort started toward her, but Zara barely noticed. She kept her eyes on Driggs and pointed at him. "You're next," she said, her voice quivering with fury.

"Get her!" Uncle Mort yelled — but he wasn't quick enough. He grabbed only air as Zara hacked her glass scythe through the air and disappeared, leaving behind nothing but the chaos she had wrought.

Lex sat on the floor, paralyzed. Her hands didn't hurt, but she wished they did. She wished they had burned right off at the wrists.

And her parents — God, her parents. "Mom," she said, her voice cracking. "Are you okay?"

"She's fine," her father said, smearing a spot of blood from her neck. "Just a scratch."

Mrs. Bartleby's eyes were huge. "Lex, what happened? Who was that?"

Uncle Mort jumped in before she could respond. "You two," he said, pointing to her parents. "Come with me."

"What?" Mrs. Bartleby said. Her husband helped her up from the floor. "Why?"

"Don't you want to see Lex's room?" Uncle Mort said. "She cleaned it, just for you."

"Lex? Cleaned her room?"

As Uncle Mort led them away, Lex assessed the damage. Driggs was still kneeling on the floor, staring at Corpp's charred body, while Pandora hugged her dead husband and sobbed. Lex forced herself to her side. "Dora," she said, the words barely audible. "I'm so sorry."

"Don't waste your breath, girl," Pandora said, finally lifting her head from Corpp's chest. Lex's heart caught in her throat, until Pandora's face broke into a mournful smile. "I'll slap you silly if you start wagging your tongue with apologies. It was an accident. You were just trying to protect us." She turned to Driggs, a look of wonder in her eyes. "And you," she breathed. "You unDamned him."

Driggs's brain was still stalling. All color had drained from his face. "No," he said in a shaky voice. "No, I don't think — "

"You did." Her eyes were wet as she grabbed his hand. "Thank you, thank you . . ."

Uncle Mort returned from Lex's bedroom. "We gotta go," he said, drawing the curtains. "Sofi saw everything, she must have sounded the alert by now. Norwood and Heloise and half the town will probably be here in a few minutes to arrest us."

"Us?" Ferbus pointed at Lex. "But *she* did it!"

"She didn't mean to!" Elysia shot back. "Besides, you know they're just going to blame all of us anyway, no matter what we say!"

"Exactly," said Uncle Mort. "So here's the plan: Juniors, you'll go first. The Cuffs are dead for the moment, so at least they won't be able to track us. I'll stay behind and deal with Lex's parents, then catch up to you. Pandora" — he squeezed her shoulders — "you know we have to go. I'm sorry."

"I know," she said, nodding. "Go. I'll handle the brute squad."

Uncle Mort peeked through the curtains. "They're coming," he said. "We don't have much time. You've all got your stuff, right? Scythes, bags?"

The Juniors nodded and grabbed their bags. Lex snuck a glance into hers and did a mental checklist. Scythe, Lifeglass, Cordy's Spark, some clothes, the plastic skull-and-crossbones lighter, Captain Wiggles . . .

"But we can't go out the front door, they'll see us!" said Elysia. "And we can't go out the back door; they'll find our tracks in the snow!"

"Right. Which is why we're not leaving through any doors at all." Uncle Mort hastily assembled his own bag, then took out his scythe.

The Juniors finally caught on. "You want us to Crash out of here?" said Ferbus. "With *direction?*"

"It's our only option."

"But we've never done it before! There's no way!"

"You guys are full of surprises. Haven't we learned that today?" He threw a sideways glance at Driggs, who went even paler.

"What about Sofi?" Elysia asked.

"I guess — " Uncle Mort looked pained. "I guess we leave her."

"But where do we Crash *to?*" Bang signed.

Uncle Mort took something out of his pocket. "Here."

It was a photograph of a desert. The yellow ground was dry and cracked, its surface shimmering in the hot midday sun. Bright blue sky, no clouds in sight. And sitting in the middle of it all, unfurled majestically across the ground and having no business being in the middle of an uninhabited desert, was a spotless red carpet that vanished into the horizon.

Driggs slowly raised his head. "You want us to Crash to De-Myse?"

"But that's on the other side of the country!" said Ferbus. "We can't Crash that far!"

Uncle Mort patted his bag. "Don't worry, I've got all your Sparks. If any of you die, I'll know about it."

"Well, that's comforting."

"But — " Elysia started. "How do you know Zara won't follow us there?"

"She's never attacked DeMyse, not once. They must have better security measures than we do. Plus, I have other . . . business to attend to there." He held up the photo again. "Concentrate on this image as hard as you can. Memorize every inch. Then scythe, all at the same time." He looked out the window again. "They're almost here. You have to leave."

"Wait," Lex said. She looked in the direction of her room. "What's going to happen to Mom and Dad?"

Uncle Mort hesitated, then pulled a vial of Amnesia out of his pocket.

"No," said Lex, her heart sinking. "Don't."

"I have to," he said. He looked tired. "They've seen more than anyone on the outside should see, and they won't understand it. Why worry them like that?"

Lex thought of how upset her mom had been since Cordy died. "Right."

"I promise all they'll remember is that they saw you for Thanksgiving and it was a pleasant, stress-free visit. All right?"

Lex nodded. "Yeah. Okay."

"Now go."

The Juniors hurriedly took out their scythes, but all they

could do was stare back at him. A loud pounding came from the door.

"Mort!" Norwood's muffled voice rang out. "Open up!"

"*Go!*" Uncle Mort yelled.

The Juniors held their partners' hands, closed their eyes, and scythed.

15

A vulture circled overhead.

Lex looked down. Hard, solid ground crunched beneath her sneakers. Cracks in its surface cobwebbed across the expanse, forming a sea of natural cobblestones. Just as in the photograph, a red carpet sat to her left, leading straight into the distance. The horizon looked wet, the mirage shimmering furiously in the heat of the midday sun. Elysia lay on the ground a few yards away. Behind her, a moaning Ferbus rolled onto his back, sending a cloud of dust into the air.

Driggs was looking at the distant hills, but Lex knew his brain was elsewhere. How had he known how to stop the Damning? How had he been able to — she didn't even know what to call it — to Cull the evil out of Corpp's body? It sounded so ridiculous, but —

But it happened. Everyone saw it.

Lex finally squeezed his hand and whispered, "You okay?"

Driggs looked at her, his eyes wide. "I don't think 'okay' is allowed to be in our vocabulary anymore."

"Hey." Ferbus had gotten up and was heading straight for Driggs. "Dude, what the hell was *that*?"

Driggs let go of Lex's hand and swallowed. "I don't know."

"Bullshit! Your stupid girlfriend Damns the ever-loving crap out of our collective grandfather, and you just so happen to be able to fix it? And you expect me to believe that you didn't *know* you could do it? Why didn't you tell me?" Ferbus was so mad, flecks of spit were flying out of his mouth and falling to the ground, where they sizzled on the hot sand. "I'm your best friend! Or I was, until this *freak* came along—"

Driggs clocked him. Right in the nose.

Blood exploded out of Ferbus's face as Driggs grabbed him by the collar. "You *are* my best friend, you selfish bastard," Driggs said in a disturbingly quiet voice. "Even when you say dumbass things like that." Ferbus snuffled and opened his mouth, but Driggs wasn't done. "And I know you're not stupid enough to believe that Lex Damned Corpp on purpose. She was obviously trying to stop Zara, which is the same thing you would have done if she had a scythe to my throat, or to Mort's throat, or to *anyone's* throat."

Ferbus tried to talk again, but Driggs grabbed his hoodie even tighter. "And no, I *didn't* know what I was doing. Don't you think that if I knew I had the power to reverse Damning, I'd have been doing it all along to all those innocent people? You think I'd just keep it to myself and let those people suffer? I was *just* as surprised as you were to see that fire disappearing from his body, so what I *really* need right now is for you to have my back like the friend you're claiming to be, because I'm confused and scared and totally freaking out about this, okay?"

Ferbus, sporting the mother of all bewildered looks, finally broke free from Driggs's grip. He looked at the ground as he wiped the blood from his face, then squinted back up at Driggs. "Sorry, dude," he said sheepishly. "I just thought—shit, I don't know what I thought."

Driggs said nothing — just stared at his bloody knuckles, his face twisting in horror as if he'd only just realized what he'd done.

"Thoughts are not your strong point, Ferb," Elysia said testily. She looked at Lex. "Are you all right?" She reached toward her, then flinched back.

Lex looked away, thoroughly humiliated. "I'm not contagious," she said in a small voice.

A faint whoosh sounded behind them. Uncle Mort had landed right on target at the end of the red carpet. "See? Told you you'd make it!" He looked at the blood-soaked Ferbus, now lying back on the ground with his eyes closed and his nose pinched. "What happened to him?"

"Family squabbles," said Elysia.

"Ferb? You all right?"

Ferbus raised a thumbs-up. "It's broken for sure."

"Can only be an improvement." Uncle Mort glanced around. "Where are Pip and Bang?"

No one answered.

A little bit of the color went out of Uncle Mort's face. "Crap. Uh — " He looked around again, as if expecting them to materialize any second. But the valley produced only silence, a tiny gust of wind scattering the dust across their faces.

He opened his bag. The Juniors peered inside. Seven Sparks, one for each of them, plus Uncle Mort. All of them were flickering — none shone bright, like a flashlight. "They're still alive, at least."

"But where are they?" said Elysia.

"I don't know." He swallowed. "Let's get moving."

"Without them?"

"You want to stay here and wait?"

Even in their thermoregulated hoodies, the sun was broiling. The arid air had already parched their throats. The sand stung at their eyes.

Elysia looked around nervously. "No, but — agh!"

Pip landed on top of her, followed immediately by Bang, in a mess of tangled limbs, scythes, and, oddly enough, snow.

"We got lost in the Rockies!" Pip yelped. "I saw a mountain goat!"

"Thank God," Ferbus said, scrambling toward him. Pip opened his arms for a hug, but Ferbus ducked out of the way to scoop up a handful of snow. "Ahhhh," he sighed, holding it to his mangled nose.

Lex pulled Uncle Mort aside. "Are Mom and Dad okay?"

"Other than a pair of splitting headaches, they're fine. Pandora will make sure they get home."

Lex winced. "You sure she's up for that?"

"Lex, we're talking about the woman who single-handedly administered the deaths of Martin Luther King, Jr., John Lennon, and half the victims of Pearl Harbor. I think she can handle getting your parents onto a bus."

"But what if Zara comes after them again?"

"I don't think she will, at least not anytime soon. Not when she can still use them — "

"As leverage," Lex finished bitterly. "Right."

"Though now that she's got the key, there isn't much left for her to squeeze out of you."

Driggs, overhearing them, dug into his pocket. "You sure about that?"

"What?" Lex shrieked, grabbing the bone key from him. "But — you gave something to her, I saw it!"

Driggs turned to Uncle Mort. "Zara is now in the possession of a highly coveted key to your attic," he told him. "Sorry."

"That's okay. I'm sure it was of more use to you two than it ever was to me."

Lex looked at her uncle's unfazed face and frowned. "You knew?"

"I know everything, kiddo."

Lex scrutinized him. "Something's going on here, isn't it?" she said, lowering her voice. "Something bigger than just Zara."

With one final, cryptic glance at the both of them, Uncle Mort turned around and began walking down the red carpet.

"Where are you going?" Lex shouted after him, looking at the spot where the carpet faded into the horizon, leading nowhere.

With a small smile, he gestured for the rest to follow. "DeMyse awaits."

‖‖‖‖

An hour later, crankiness had reached a maximum. Feet were shuffling, hoods had been pulled up, and heads were pointed down at the never-ending red carpet, Ferbus's nose honking all the way.

"I'm tired," said Lex.

"I'm thirsty," whined Pip.

"I've lost at least sixty percent of my bodily fluids," wheezed Ferbus, a wad of bloody Kleenex in his nose dancing as he spoke.

Elysia, holding him upright, let out a grunt. "How much farther?" she asked Uncle Mort.

"Not far." Their fearless leader's voice was calm, but even he was starting to look frazzled. His hair was sticking out in a lot more odd places than usual.

Lex hung back, letting the others walk ahead so she could talk to him. "Is Corpp going to be okay?" she asked in a quiet voice. "You think he got to the Afterlife?"

He ran a hand through his hair. "I honestly don't know. He looked all right at the end. Whatever Driggs did seemed to have reversed the effects of the Damning."

At the sound of his name, Driggs slowed down and joined them at the rear. "Mort, seriously. *Any* idea what in the hell I just did back there?"

Uncle Mort shook his head. "Beats me. All I know is that if any of that happens again — if Lex loses control and Damns someone again — then you'd better be right there next to her to fix it." He sighed. "As if you two needed another excuse to be attached at the hip."

"Don't worry, Mort," said Driggs. "I'll be dead soon anyway."

Lex shoved him. "That's not funny."

"What? Zara's made it her life's work to Damn people, and I can undo it. You heard what she said: I'm next." He lowered his voice. "My chances of survival just plummeted to zero."

Lex did not want to think about that. "What happened with Norwood?" she asked Uncle Mort, changing the subject.

"Well, he sounded pretty grouchy when he took an ax to my kitchen door. I'm guessing Sofi told him the whole thing."

"Bitch."

"Give her a break," Uncle Mort said. "She just didn't want to get in any more trouble."

"Yeah, right. What she wanted was for me to get thrown in the Hole."

Uncle Mort wiped some sweat from his face. "At least she left before you did whatever it was you did, Driggs, so there's no chance of that little nugget getting out."

"Yeah, but what about Lex?"

"Lex," he said with a hint of intrigue as he took off for the front of the group, "is now public enemy number one."

Lex tried not to let this terrify her as much as it did, but it was only a drop in the bucket at this point. There were way too many things to be terrified of right now.

Seeing the unsettled look on her face, Driggs handed her a couple of Oreos, having apparently packed them as one of his essential items. She was silent as she chewed, the dry crumbs choking her already parched throat. She was grateful that no one had asked her about Zara's "extra credit" comment, but she couldn't be sure that would last. Better to keep them focused on one of the many other worries of the moment.

"What do you think Corpp meant?" she asked Driggs.

"About what?"

"When he said 'It's gone'?"

His eyes were pained. "I don't know."

Lex decided to say it out loud. They were both thinking it anyway. "Do you think he meant his soul?"

Driggs licked his chapped lips. "I don't think so. I mean, he was still alive for a second or two more. How could his soul have disappeared *before* he died?"

"Because I think that's how Damning works. It rots the soul while the person is still alive — that's why the jellyfish can't pick up on the death and why the Gamma doesn't get to the Afterlife." She swallowed. Her throat was getting drier and drier. "I took his soul away."

"But I — I put it *back*." Driggs sighed. "I don't know how I know it, but I do. And after I did, Corpp died just the same as anyone else. Time froze, a Senior Grim team showed up right after to Kill and Cull his soul, and now he's in the Afterlife. I'm sure of it. Look, we can check the Afterlife here in DeMyse. We'll put out the word, get him to come see us."

Lex shook her head, remembering her conversation with Corpp. "No, he's a hider. He won't come out of the Void, not even to see Pandora. He told me."

"Then we'll ask around. Maybe someone has seen him." He gave her a desperate look. "He's got to be in there."

She stared back. "And if he's not?"

A commotion toward the front of the group brought their conversation to a halt. Bang was standing stock-still in the middle of the carpet, staring intently into the distance and signing too frantically for anyone to understand her.

"What's she saying?" asked Elysia.

"She can see something," translated Pip. "Up ahead. Buildings!"

Ferbus lifted his head from Elysia's shoulder. "This could just be the massive blood loss talking," he said in a slurred voice, "but I see it too."

A moment of silence ensued as they squinted. "There's nothing out there," said Elysia, a hint of hysteria creeping into her voice. "Nothing but desert. And more desert. We're going to die out here and the vultures are going to eat our skin off and our skulls are going to be made into Yorick mugs and it's all your fault!" she yelled, pointing accusingly at a cactus.

A beat passed.

"Well," Uncle Mort said, "looks like the crazies have arrived. Much earlier than usual, it would seem. We must be getting close."

Lex jogged up to her uncle. "Why are we heading for DeMyse if they're just going to arrest us the minute we get there?"

"They won't. The mayor and I go way back. Trust me, you'll be safe."

"I have trusted you implicitly ever since I came to Croak, and look where it's gotten me."

"Strolling through Death Valley on Thanksgiving," he said with a wink. "Don't say I never show you a good time."

The shimmering mirage on the horizon was forming into a bunch of odd shapes. The shapes grew larger as they walked, eventually starting to resemble buildings. And palm trees. Soon the sunlight began to reflect off moving things — cars, possibly. The Juniors broke into a sort of limping run, the prospect of water and shade and an Arctic-grade air conditioner looming large in their minds as the buildings rose higher in the empty blue sky. Yet even when they got up close — or as close as they dared — it still sat behind a wavy filter, as if they were viewing it all through a giant pane of distorted funhouse glass.

"It's just a mirage," Driggs said, disappointed.

"Could a mirage do this?" a deep, sonorous voice boomed. A figure stepped out from the waviness and became clear.

"Great," said Elysia, throwing her hands up in exasperation. "Now Willy Wonka's here."

Lex stared. "Whoa."

Elysia's grabbed Lex's arm. "You can see him too?"

They all could, and Elysia's description wasn't far off. The man was, in fact, dressed very similarly to Willy Wonka in the old movie — in a velvet purple suit and orange fedora, wielding a shiny cane. But that's where the similarities ended. This man was black and bald, and he wore a tight, shiny shirt underneath the jacket, plus a zebra-print belt and a pair of ridiculously expensive-looking sunglasses. His goatee was shaped into a point, and a single gold tooth sparkled when he smiled. He looked like a stereotypical seventies-era Halloween-costumed pimp.

"Are you a pimp?" asked Pip.

Uncle Mort sighed. "We need to work on your first impressions, kid."

The man acted as if he hadn't even heard. "Greetings, weary travelers!" he thundered, speaking with the confidence and volume one would use to address a nation, rather than a thirsty, bedraggled group of teenagers.

Uncle Mort pushed through to the front of the pack and shook his hand. "Hey, man, good to see you again. Kids, this is Leroy — "

"LeRoy," the man corrected him, placing a heavy, fancy accent on the second syllable. He smiled widely, his gold tooth blinding. He looked directly at Lex but made no indication that he feared her, wanted to arrest her, or even recognized her. Instead he swept his cane in a wide arc and pointed the way into town. "Enter!"

The Juniors walked to the end of the red carpet, took one last look at one another's sweaty faces, and stepped through the waviness.

16

Lex had never been to Las Vegas, but even she knew that this place was Las Vegas times ten. On crack. It was as if the town had been placed in a blender with a giant disco ball, shaken with a Mardi Gras parade, and then had vomited a pile of glitter and tinsel all over itself. Hundreds of shiny surfaces caught the sunlight, scattering broken reflections in every direction. Sleek, expensive cars sped past, their surfaces also polished to a dazzling gleam. Each building was painted a bright color, and the road itself was made from the dried sand of the ground, shaped into rectangles and resembling the Yellow Brick Road. Lex didn't have to follow it to know that it covered a city that was much, much larger than Croak.

"Oh. My. Lord." Elysia gaped. "Are we dead?"

"I don't think so," said Lex, watching a pair of women walk by on heels that no human should have been able to balance on. "I don't remember the Afterlife being this . . . flamboyant."

"Welcome to DeMyse!" LeRoy said, yet again sweeping his cane through the sky. "The crown jewel of the Grimsphere. Anything you need, DeMyse has it. Hats? Down the street. Avocados? Garden's on the left. Yoga studio? We've got thirteen, take your pick. Champagne?" Magically he produced a tray of flutes. The Juniors took them and sipped, still in shock. "Rolex? Botox? Painkillers?" He held up a pill bottle.

"I'll take those," honked Ferbus, popping off the cap and downing two at a time.

"Anything you need, we are at your disposal." LeRoy smiled. "Now come!" He clapped twice and strode off down the street, gesturing for them to follow.

Lex didn't know what to make of any of this. She felt safe, sort of, but this place was . . . weird. Driggs seemed to sense it too; his eyes were troubled as they took in the glittering street.

But the rest of the Juniors were in awe, their heads whipping around every time some new, shiny thing grabbed their attention.

"Palm trees!" said Pip. "Porsches!"

"Truffle pizza!" Ferbus exclaimed.

Lex frowned. "Croak has pizza."

"Look! A pool!" Elysia squealed.

"We have a pond," Driggs pointed out.

"You mean that disgusting muddy puddle? I'll take chlorine, thank you very much."

"Yeah, well, I'll take a nice tall glass of the Bank's lemonade," Driggs countered. "I'm thirsty as hell, I don't want champagne." He chucked the contents of his flute into a nearby bush.

"Hey, who shit in your Oreos?" said Ferbus in a loud voice, the combination of alcohol and drugs manifesting rather promptly. "What's so wrong with living the high life?"

"Nothing, it's just — " Driggs lowered his voice. "Don't you think this place is a little strange?"

"A little?" Bang signed sarcastically.

"Well, maybe," said Elysia. "But isn't that the whole point of traveling, to see new and interesting places?"

"No, he's right," said Lex. She glanced back at the high-heeled women, who were laughing hysterically as they juggled their bulging shopping bags. "Something's off."

Elysia shrugged. "Well, until you figure out what it is, I say we relax and enjoy the moment. After the day we've had . . ." She trailed off at the memory of the death and destruction they'd witnessed less than two hours before, looking ashamed for having gotten excited about any of this. "We could use a change of scenery, is all I'm saying."

"Listen to Elysia," Uncle Mort said, coming from behind them on his way up to LeRoy. "She knows what she's talking about."

Lex gave him a dubious look. "Ten minutes ago she was professing her love to a gecko."

"Ugh," said Elysia. "Was I really?"

"Don't worry," Uncle Mort told her. "The sanest member of the party is always the first one to lose it. That's how you know you're on the right track."

"I'm not the sanest?" said Driggs.

"*I'm* not the sanest?" asked Lex.

Uncle Mort rolled his eyes and kept walking.

|||||||

LeRoy led them to a garish pastel pink hotel with a giant flamingo on its sign.

"Extra towels? Second floor," LeRoy said as they walked into the foyer. "Parking? Ample. Ice machines? Five. *Five* ice machines."

"Wow," Pip said, glancing up at the stained glass ceiling as Le-Roy sauntered to the check-in desk. "Croak doesn't even have a hotel!"

"Who'd want to visit a crummy little town in the middle of the Adirondacks?" said Ferbus.

"Who'd want to visit a gaudy pile of crap in the middle of Death Valley?" Lex shot back.

"Other Grims," said Driggs. "They think this place is cool. Kilda came once, brought back the brochures. Talked about it for weeks."

"Kilda talks about new flavors of gum for weeks," Lex said, but she had to admit — as splashy and overwrought as DeMyse was, the place had a certain draw.

LeRoy had insisted that each Junior get his or her own suite, complete with heart-shaped, quadruple-jet hydrotherapy Jacuzzis, but Mort decided that shared rooms would make it easier for them to keep track of each other — Lex with Elysia, Driggs with Ferbus, and Pip with Bang. So LeRoy returned with three keycards and handed them out, then clapped twice again and led them up the grand staircase.

"What room are you in?" Driggs asked Lex.

She snickered. "Platinum. You?"

"Caviar," he said, reading his card. "Ew."

When they reached the top of the stairs, LeRoy snatched Bang's keycard out of her hand and dipped it into the slot of a door labeled GUCCI. "Meeting time!" he declared, ushering them inside.

They took seats all over the room — some on the bed, a couple on the cushiony sofa. Uncle Mort sank into a large armchair. Lex opted to stand by the balcony door overlooking the pool.

"Let me begin by saying we're simply *thrilled* to have you here as our guests," LeRoy said, once again in that political-rally voice. "Grims from all over the planet flock to our fair city for its world-class TLC — tranquillity, luxury, and cognac, cognac, cognac!"

"We're not here on vacation," Driggs said.

LeRoy folded his hands into a triangle under his chin. "Of course you are," he said, the smallest twinge of tightness creeping into his voice. His smile grew wider, falser. "And now that you're here, you'll want to take advantage of everything we have to offer. Daily facials! Bountiful gym equipment!" He began doing squats. "Pilates every hour on the hour, except on weekends, when it bumps up to every half — "

"Wait a minute." Lex tore her gaze away from the smiling, relaxed sunbathers she'd been watching. "I know what's so messed up about this place. You people are too happy!"

LeRoy froze mid-squat. "Of course we're happy. With seven different tanning salons to choose from, who *wouldn't* be?"

"That's not what I mean," said Lex. "I mean that the Grimsphere is being terrorized by a raging lunatic and you're just carrying on as if it's nothing!"

LeRoy regarded her coolly. "It *is* nothing. It's none of our concern."

"None of your concern?" Driggs rose from the couch. "There's a war going on out there! *You* should know — Zara killed your Etcetera director!"

LeRoy held up his cane and pointed it at Driggs, barring him from coming any closer. Uncle Mort watched warily from the armchair but didn't move. "That was months ago," LeRoy said. "And Zara hasn't attacked us since. That's more than your town can say, or even the capital. Trust me, our security is impregnable. You'll be safe here."

"But she's still tearing up the rest of the country! Doesn't that bother you?"

"As I said," LeRoy said in a firm voice, "those troubles are none of our concern. What brought *you* here is *also* none of our concern."

Driggs swallowed, then looked at Lex, who had shrunk. "You know who I am?" she asked.

"I know exactly who you are," said LeRoy. The smile stayed on his face, but his eyes narrowed microscopically. "And your presence here is all the more reason for you to keep quiet."

"I think what ole LeRoy is trying to say," said Uncle Mort in a patient voice, finally getting up from the armchair, "is that he is being more than generous by providing a place to stay in our time of need. The type of discretion this man can provide — " He clapped his hands on LeRoy's shoulders and squeezed them a little too tightly. "Trust me, no one can keep a secret like LeRoy."

LeRoy gave him a pained smile, then turned to the Juniors once more. "And in return, I ask only that you relax, enjoy yourselves, and keep the unpleasantness to a minimum."

"How?" said Lex. "Won't people recognize me?"

"Unlikely," LeRoy said cheerfully. "Politics, current events, all that ugly news — none of it reaches us here in DeMyse. Entertainment, though . . . let's just say that our gossip magazine offerings rival those of the juiciest — "

"Wait. You mean you don't let anyone know what's happening on the outside?"

"Princess, I do what is necessary to keep order in my town. My only job is to protect my citizens. I do that by providing a luxuri-ous, carefree lifestyle, and that is what my people have come to expect." One of LeRoy's nostrils flared. "If you upset that delicate balance, you will no longer be welcome here."

He finished with an expression that reminded Lex of a snake. She looked at him, then at the rest of the wide-eyed Juniors, then at Uncle Mort. "Really? We're just going to go along with this?"

Uncle Mort folded his arms and nodded. "His city, his rules."

"But —"

Bang made a cut-it-out motion across her throat. Against every bit of her better judgment, Lex trained her eyes to the floor and shut her mouth.

"Wonderful!" LeRoy shouted, the consummate host once again. "I'll leave you to get acquainted with your rooms. Care to take in some refreshments this evening? Six tearooms, nineteen nightclubs, and one all-you-can-sip Courvoisier trough! But don't stay out too late. Limo tour in the a.m.! Be ready at eight o'clock sharp!" And with a flourish, he vanished out the door.

The room was silent for a moment. "I have a headache," Fer-bus finally said, patting his tender face and sinking into the bed.

"Hey, go bleed on your own pillow," Bang signed, yanking hers away.

Elysia inspected his nose. "It's really starting to swell."

"Maybe you should go get some ice from one of the *five* ice machines," said Driggs.

"Or consult one of the *dozen* plastic surgeons," Lex said. "Seri-ously, what planet is that guy from?" she asked Uncle Mort. "And why does this place look like a really bad drug trip?"

"That's just part of its defenses," Uncle Mort said. "If any

Death Valley hikers get lost or disoriented, they see this place all bedazzled to hell and think it's just a mirage. That usually scares them off, but if they get any closer and enter the city limits, it's so outrageous they'll never believe it was real. Add a few drops of Amnesia, and the whole thing becomes nothing but a fevered hallucination."

"But this can't just all be for show," Driggs said. "Those people out there look like they've bought into the glitz and glamour with every last dollar they've got."

"Well, that was an unintended consequence," Uncle Mort said with a shrug. "It started off as a façade, but as time went on, people got used to the lavish lifestyle. You can only coo over so many teacup poodles before you start to believe they're absolutely essential to life."

"But why don't they care about what's going on in the Grimsphere?" Lex asked. "How can they be so shallow?"

"Well, LeRoy didn't exactly fall off the turnip truck — underneath all that zebra print, he's a pretty smart guy. He goes to great lengths to maintain the illusion that DeMyse is a paradise, and the people go along with it, either because they want to or because they don't know any better. Same idea as the mirage: they see what they want to see." He scratched at his stubble. "That's not to say he isn't up to something. That's half the reason I wanted to come here, to make sure he's really on our side."

Lex studied him. "And the other half?"

He walked to the door. "Better rest up if you plan on going out tonight. And clean yourselves up, would you? You look like you just dragged yourselves through a desert, for Chrissakes."

||||||

That evening, Lex lay on her bed and stared across the room at the naked wall. Never had she thought she'd miss her much-maligned *Titanic* poster, but at that moment all she wanted was a little glimpse of Leonardo's perfectly sculpted eyebrows.

She took out her Lifeglass and gave it a swirl. She rarely looked at the thing — too many bad memories were stored inside — but it seemed somehow important, in the wake of all that had happened that day, to get a good look at the things that she might never see again, the things she truly missed.

An image of her parents floated to the surface of the glass, making her chest burn. Even though their time together that afternoon had been short and hostile, she was glad she'd gotten to see them. She hated that she couldn't fix their pain, couldn't be the daughter they so desperately needed her to be.

She missed Croak, too. She already hated DeMyse. Whereas Croak was homey and comfortable, this place was too fake, too vulgar. The people looked plastic and pointy. Even the bed was hard.

And then there was Corpp.

She tried to tell herself she was being ridiculous, that she couldn't miss someone who'd only been gone for a few hours . . . but she did. A deep, dull ache had settled into her stomach the moment her hands had touched him, and it hadn't gone away. He'd always been so nice to her, even after what happened with Zara and Cordy, even when the rest of the town had turned on her and the Juniors. He and Pandora stuck by them, never forgetting what it was like to be young and scared and —

And stupid. Stupid enough to Damn the wrong person.

He was an old man, she told herself. Old and happy. Even in the Lifeglass he was content, repainting his bar into an ever-changing masterpiece. He'd been married to his soulmate for decades and had the pleasure of serving his friends night after night. He'd led a long, full life.

But these thoughts were the kind that might help someone with grief, and that's not quite what Lex was feeling. Grief itself wasn't even so bad anymore — it was an emotion for people for whom death was a mystery, for people who knew nothing of what lay beyond the grave. Grims knew for a fact that death was just a transition to a better place.

No, Lex was grappling with her old friend guilt, that searing stab of knowledge that she had been the one to turn the last few minutes of Corpp's life into total agony.

Tears welled up in the corners of her eyes and ran down the sides of her face. A box of Kleenex sat atop the nightstand, but she didn't make any attempt to grab it. The warm liquid felt good seeping into her pillow, wetting her neck, making a clammy mess.

Now what? she thought. *Now what, now what?*

Now what came in the form of Elysia, who was kicking at the door. "Let me in!" she shouted. "I come bearing cute shoes and tight pants!" Elysia had left the room right after showering — to go exploring, she told Lex, though Lex suspected she had just wanted to give her new roommate some time alone.

Well, Lex had gotten it. She shoved the Lifeglass back into her bag, wiped her face, and dragged herself to the door. She opened it to find an Elysia-shaped pile of shopping bags and shoeboxes.

"I just came from the boys' room, spiffied them up a bit. They look — oh dear," she said upon seeing Lex's blotchy face. "You need a hug." She dropped everything and swept Lex up into one of her patented suffocation embraces. As usual, Lex relished every moment of it. The girl had a gift.

"What's with all the stuff?" Lex said after she'd let go.

Elysia dragged the bags to the bed and plopped herself down in the middle of them. "Remember what LeRoy said about going out tonight? Well, I've been asking around, and it turns out that it's like a religion around here."

"So?" Lex said, sitting next to her. "How is that different from Croak? We go to the bar every night too. Or we used to. I don't know what'll happen now that Corpp's — "

"No, no, it's different here," Elysia said, expertly steering Lex away from the bleakness. "At home we just hang out and play drinking games, and it's all real casual. Here they take it to a whole new level."

"Aren't you still freaked out about Zara, though? What if she finds us?"

"You heard LeRoy — she never comes to DeMyse. Besides, what are we supposed to do, shut ourselves in this hotel and never come out again? We can't let our lives be dictated by fear, Lex."

Lex raised her eyebrow. "How much of that did Uncle Mort tell you to say?"

Elysia coughed and looked guilty. "Um, percentage-wise?"

Lex sighed. "Lys, I wiped out Croak's most beloved citizen today. You really expect me to go out and party it up tonight like nothing happened?"

Elysia took Lex's hand. "Don't you think sitting around here feeling terrible about it will be worse?"

"I don't know." Lex looked into Elysia's eyes. "You're not scared of me, are you?"

Elysia let out a gentle laugh. "Come on, Lex. You're the best friend I've ever had. I'll never be scared of you."

"Promise?" Lex said. "Even if I do awful things like this, if

I" — she let out a long breath — "if I keep hurting people, even if it's by accident? You'll still stick around?"

"Of course I will." Elysia squeezed her hand. "I'm exceptionally sticky. Haven't you noticed?"

At this, Lex finally smiled. "Thanks, Lys."

"Now!" Elysia reached into the shopping bag. "I got something for everyone, and you're last but certainly not least. We're going to have a good time tonight if it kills us." She pulled out a shimmery blue top made from about a square foot of fabric and held it up to Lex with a mischievous look in her eye and a scarily large grin on her face. "We're going clubbing."

17

Lex wobbled out into the hall on a pair of the very high heels she'd seen on those two women that afternoon, but she wasn't pulling them off with nearly as much dignity.

"I feel ridiculous," she hissed at Elysia, who had come out of her own transformation looking even cuter than usual in a sassy silver top, extra-dangly earrings, and perky lip gloss. The self-proclaimed clubbing guru hadn't shut up for one second about how much she missed the scene and how fiercely she was going to tear up the dance floor.

"You look slammin'," Elysia told Lex. "That shirt is gorgeous on you."

"This is not a shirt. This is a napkin with armholes."

"It's flirty!"

"It's gross."

"Well, it matches your eye shadow," she said, blowing on Lex's eyelid.

"Which I also hate." She'd fought hard on that one, flinging gobs of eyeliner and mascara and blush all over the bathroom, but Elysia had won out in the end. "I told you, it's too heavy."

"It's *supposed* to be heavy," Elysia insisted. "You look sophisticated."

"I look like a clown whore."

"There are the guys!" Elysia said, dragging Lex down the hall. Driggs and Ferbus were stumbling out of their room, trying to make a quick getaway without being seen. But Elysia was too quick for them. She smiled with pride, reveling in the results of her makeover. Lex, on the other hand, just stood there with her glossy mouth wide open.

Both boys wore designer jeans, buttoned-up Armani shirts, and shiny black shoes. Ferbus's orange mop was brushed, for once, and Driggs's hair was styled into spikes with what looked like five gallons of gel.

Lex almost peed from trying not to laugh.

"Aren't they handsome?" Elysia said, straightening Ferbus's collar.

"Indeed they are." Lex pricked a finger on one of Driggs's spikes and gave him a randy grin. As silly as he looked, the sexy couldn't be denied.

Driggs, too, regarded her with a distinct horniness. "Wow. You look —"

"Like a clown whore. I know."

"I was going to say hot," he said, squeezing her bum. "Slutty hot, but hot."

"These PANTS are too TIGHT!" Ferbus pulled at his crotch. "You can't tell me these are meant for human attire, Lys. The boys need to breathe!"

Elysia yanked the waist of his pants back up. "They're *supposed* to be tight. Plus, they take the focus off your face," she said with a wince at his nose, which had gotten even uglier.

Pip and Bang then piled out of their own room, looking much like the others. Bang looked particularly transformed, her hair teased up into a voluptuous coif, her gangliness augmented by the heels, her lined eyes even more piercing.

"Put that away," Elysia said, grabbing Bang's book from her hand and tossing it back into their room.

"These shoes are pinchy!" Pip cried.

"My bra strap keeps showing," Bang signed.

"It's *supposed* to show!" Elysia said, exasperated. "Amateurs!"

They left the hotel and ventured onto the sidewalk, looking like a sideshow of circus freaks as they wound their way through the bustle of nightlife. Though the sun had set, the brightness of the town had barely diminished, dazzling lights and neon signs flooding the streets with an artificial glow. Drunken carousers shouted from one balcony to another, music poured out from the doors of nightclubs and bars, and a distinctive, fruity smell wafted through the crisp desert night air.

They soon arrived at a pair of glass doors labeled ETERNITY. "This is supposed to be the best club in town," Elysia said as they got in line between a pair of red velvet ropes.

Lex held on to Driggs for balance atop her heels. "According to?"

Elysia glanced down the line. "Someone I met."

"Whoa, wait," Ferbus said. "Who?

She put on an innocent face. "Just some Junior. He said this is where they all come, and I thought it would be a nice way for us to start, you know, mingling. Get into their good graces."

"And by good graces, I assume you mean this guy's pants," said Ferbus with a grimace. Elysia said nothing, but looked up and down the line again.

"This is stupid," Lex said. "We should be home."

Driggs nodded. "Or back at the hotel."

"Doing what?" said Ferbus. "Damning and unDamning the

monogrammed towels? Look, I don't like the prospect of dancing with a bunch of rich douchebags any more than you do, but Elysia's right, you can't just sit around in a fort made of extra hotel pillows and torture yourselves over things you can't change."

"No," said Driggs, "but we *could* at least keep working on a way to get to the cabin. There's got to be a library here. Maybe it has different books, ones we don't have in Croak."

"And what if Zara comes back?" Lex added. "She could Crash in at any minute, and here we'll be, sitting ducks in tight pants and high heels that I can't even run in."

"Would you guys knock it off?" Elysia said. "This is our first chance at fun in *weeks*. Mort insisted that we come out and enjoy ourselves, and I for one am inclined to listen to him. So just stop talking. You're embarrassing me in front of all the cool people."

"Are you saying we're not cool?" Ferbus said.

Elysia looked at the three of them, then turned back to the doors, saying nothing.

Lex sighed, resigning herself to the night. She turned to the boys. "Did you really make a pillow fort?"

They stared back at her, confused. "Of course we did."

By the time they reached the front of the line, Elysia was so excited she practically cattle-prodded them all into the club. A thick fog pervaded the room, allowing the various lights and lasers to take tangible forms as they whipped across the dance floor, which was packed with dozens of writhing, sweaty bodies and pounded with a steady techno beat. The crowd was made up of Seniors, but no one looked older than thirty. A balcony wrapped around the dance floor, giving it the impression of a gladiatorial pit.

Lex nearly lost tiny Elysia in the tall crowd, but soon spotted her scurrying toward the bar. "Over here!" she was yelling.

The music was slightly quieter near the bar, though the fruity smell had grown stronger. "What do you think?" Elysia said as they gathered around. "Friggin' awesome, huh?"

"It's loud," Ferbus complained. "Corpp's was never this loud."

"And way too chaotic," said Driggs. "This would be the perfect place for Zara to attack."

Elysia shot them both annoyed looks. "Okay, what you guys need are some drinks." She turned to the bartender, a tall, drippy-looking guy with sideburns. "Hi, we'd like some Yoricks, please."

He nodded and grabbed a shaker. "Five?"

"What? No, six —" She did a double take. "Where's Bang?"

They looked back at the dance floor, where Bang was grinding up against a man at least ten years her senior.

"Daaaamn," Elysia said as the Juniors stared in shock. "Girl can *move*."

"Ewww!" Pip cried, covering his eyes.

Elysia had already moved on to something else. "There are the Juniors!" she said, pointing.

Walking toward them in a pack were at least two dozen teenagers. Some sported the odd hair changes of the ether, some were clad in unspeakably pricey clothing, and all of them wore facial expressions that suggested they owned not only the club but each and every inch of DeMyse.

"Wow," said Lex with a gulp. "That's a lot of Juniors."

Even Elysia had gone a little pale. "DeMyse is bigger — so there are more of them," she said, though her voice had lost some of its confidence.

Two who were dressed more lavishly than the others stepped out in front of the group: one, a girl with a pug nose, diamond earrings in each ear, and a shimmery, swanky dress; and the other, a boy with beady, weasel-like eyes. His hair was slicked back with half an oil rig, and he wore a three-piece suit, complete with tie.

"Well, look what the sticks threw up," the girl said.

The boy snickered. "I've heard Croakers were hillbillies, but I expected at least a modicum of class." He shook his head and gave them a piteous look. "Silly me."

The pair continued on their way, exchanging wicked smiles as their Juniors followed behind. One, a hulking Asian girl, seemed to be glaring especially hard at Lex.

"I don't think they like us," Pip observed.

"What's not to like?" Lex said dryly. "We offer convenient Damning and unDamning services, we bring mayhem wherever we go, and — lest anyone forget — we're hardcore fugitives!"

"Keep your voice down," Driggs warned. "LeRoy might restrict the information flow into this city, but he can't keep people from gossiping. If anyone finds out who we are and why we're here —"

"I know why you are here," a voice piped up.

Lex felt her heart skip a beat. Slowly, they turned around to find a boy grinning at them.

"For our world-famous Yorick cosmopolitans, of course!" he said.

"Oh, thank God." Elysia put her hand over her chest. "Hello again!" she said to the boy, her voice fluttering into a higher octave.

Ferbus grabbed Driggs's shirt, panicked. "Did he say cosmopolitans?"

The boy smiled at Elysia. "*Hola, bonita.* What do you think?"

"Oh, it's amazing," Elysia gushed, turning back to her friends. "Guys, this is Riqo."

"Pleased to make your acquaintance," he said with a Spanish accent. A pair of sunglasses sat atop his curly dark hair, and his tanned brown skin shone so smoothly that Lex doubted the kid even had pores. "Do not worry about the rest," he said, nodding back at the DeMyse Juniors fading into the crowd. "They are . . . resistant. To newcomers."

Elysia let out a high-pitched laugh. Bang, having finished her dance, swished over to the bar, took one look at Riqo, and broke into a dopey grin.

"I will be back in a little while," he said, dancing into the crowd. "Have fun — and do not be afraid to dance!"

Bang turned to Elysia and made a face like a panting dog. Elysia collapsed into laughter. "I know, right?"

"Good Lord," said Ferbus. "I need a drink."

"Six Yoricks," the bartender announced, setting them down atop the bar. Each was a different neon color, all served in martini glasses. The stems contained glow sticks, and sticking out of the rim of each glass, stabbed through with a plastic sword with a skull on top, were bright red maraschino cherries.

Ferbus stared in horror at the desecration of his beloved Yorick. "What. The hell. Is that?"

||||||

An hour later the Juniors were smashed.

After downing their fruity drinks, Elysia and Bang had hit the dance floor and not stopped since. Lex and Driggs begrudgingly joined them, making sure to stay far enough away to avoid getting hit in the face by Bang's rapidly expanding hair. Pip was there too, bouncing and weaving through the clubgoers like a field mouse.

Ferbus was the only one still at the bar. Decrying the "girlification" of the Yoricks while greedily inhaling them nonetheless, he leaned against the bar and made eyes at the endless parade of girls walking by.

"Lllladies," he purred, grinning at a gaggle of them. They took one look at his bruised, purpling nose and hurried away in disgust. "They'll be back," he told his Yorick.

"So what do you think?" Driggs said to Lex, his arms wrapped around her waist. "Weirdest Thanksgiving ever?"

"Well," said Lex, "now that you mention it, I suppose that Damning a good friend, fleeing to the middle of a desert, and topping off the evening with a bouncy little rave *is* an odd way to kick off the holiday season." She was trying to be funny, but it only made her feel worse. Her gaze fell to the floor.

He looked at her sadly, his one blue eye popping out in the flashing lights of the club. "Seriously, what is *wrong* with us?"

Lex hugged him tighter. "I don't know."

They clung like that for a long time, savoring the heat of each other's skin as the crowd pressed them closer together, the bass pounding so hard they could feel the vibrations resonating through their bodies.

Yet when Lex leaned in for a kiss, Driggs flinched away.

Her chest twisted with that irrational fear yet again — that he'd finally come to his senses and realized he was dating a hobgoblin. "What's wrong?"

He looked at her worried expression and let out a small, apologetic laugh. "Oh, no, nothing. It's just — " He sounded embarrassed. "Your lips are really goopy. And wet. Like a glazed ham."

Lex exhaled, relieved. True, her boyfriend had just compared her to a pork product, but it was a lot better than the alternative. "I know, it's disgusting." She wiped her mouth with her hand, then licked her lips until the glop was gone. "Good?"

Driggs, his eyes never leaving her tongue, leaned in closer. "So good."

The strobe lights kicked in next, transforming their entwined forms into a flickering column. A beach ball soared over the top of the crowd, inching its way across in a jerky, slow-motion arc with each flash. Lex followed it through the air until something just behind it caught her eye. Way up in the balcony, someone stood at the railing, watching her.

A man in a white tuxedo.

It was the same man Lex had seen at the hospital the night Zara attacked Driggs. The air was too foggy for her to make out the details of his face, but somehow she knew it was him.

She wrenched away from Driggs.

"What?" he asked, the residue of her lip gloss smeared across his cheek.

Not allowing her face to register any confusion, she gave him a quick smile and broke away. "Bathroom break. I'll be right back."

She pushed her way through the crowd to the stairs, taking only a few wobbly steps of terror before yanking off the high heels and tossing them to the floor. Once at the top, she hurried on in her bare feet, struggling to see past the people in her way, until at last she reached the spot where the man had been standing.

He was no longer there.

She whipped her gaze around the balcony. Small, cozy tables were scattered throughout, accommodating dozens of gorgeous people, all talking and drinking and laughing. Some were making out. Some seemed to be doing even more than that.

But the man was gone, as if he had vaporized. Disheartened, she looked back out over the crowd below, resting her arms on the railing.

She immediately jerked them back. The railing was freezing.

But freezing wasn't the right word. It wasn't physically cold so much as the *idea* of cold — like it had never been warm, had never known what warm was. It felt alone and empty, as much as a railing could have feelings. It felt like nothingness.

"What are *you* doing here?"

She turned around. The DeMyse Juniors sat at a table in a darkened corner, sipping their Yoricks and looking at her as though they'd just caught her rolling around in a trash heap.

Under most circumstances Lex would never have put up with this much attitude, but she had enough sense to realize that this was neither the time nor the place to start hurling snobby, entitled assholes off balconies. She was hiding out. She had to be careful.

"Nothing," she muttered. "Leaving."

On her way back to the bar she spotted Elysia and Bang, who had converged into a Riqo sandwich. "Shameless, aren't they?" said Ferbus, on his third and final Yorick and, with the way he was holding his martini glass, looking like he'd just stepped off the set of *Sex and the City*. Driggs stood beside him, uncomfortable and tugging at his pants. His spikes had started to droop.

"Ready to go?" Lex asked him.

"Yeah." He let out a loud whistle and motioned for the girls and Pip to return to the bar.

"*Adiós, bonitos!*" Riqo said as they left, dancing back into the fray.

"We should take off," Driggs told them, in the responsible voice of the eldest Junior. "We have a limo tour in the morning."

Elysia let out a disappointed huff. "Fine," she said. "But I am so coming back. This place is amazing. The music, the fog, the drinks ... the eye candy ..." She and Bang swapped devilish grins.

"I don't know what you're so excited about," Ferbus slurred, downing the last of his Yorick. "Speedy Gonzalez was gawking at Pip a lot more than either of you."

Pip's eyes grew huge. "Really?" He spun back around, searching for Riqo in the crowd.

Elysia looked as if she had swallowed a bug. "Let's get out of here," she said in an annoyed voice, leading the group toward the door. She threw an angry glance back at Lex. "*Where* are your *shoes?*"

"Keep it down, Lys," Ferbus said with a smirk. "You're embarrassing yourself in front of all the cool people."

18

"To your right is Pelts, featuring fur coats made from every mammal in the Northern Hemisphere!" LeRoy announced. "And to your left is Pelts II, featuring fur coats made from every animal in the Southern Hemisphere!"

A bleary-eyed Lex looked up from the limousine window and glanced at Driggs, who woke when as his head banged against the glass. Ferbus and Elysia were fast asleep, and Pip and Bang were yawning. Uncle Mort sat up front with LeRoy, who didn't seem to notice that half his audience had fallen into comas.

Lex felt like crap. And not just because they'd stayed up late or because of what had happened with Corpp. It was all that, plus a strange, uneasy feeling pinballing around her stomach, a restless dread that insisted they had been too reckless, that something terrible was going to happen now that they'd allowed themselves a little bit of fun. The man in the white tuxedo, the constant threat of Zara — there were too many dangerous variables in the mix, yet everyone had let their guard down. It couldn't happen again.

"Up the street is the Mayor's Mansion, home to yours truly," LeRoy went on. "And to your left is our luxury mall, the Mausoleum, famous throughout the Grimsphere for having everything. Simply everything. Designer clothing? Yes. Electronics? Yes. Fine jewelry? Yes."

"Oh. My. God," Lex whispered. "How much longer could it be?"

"Maybe we can stop him," said Driggs. "Pip, pretend you're about to throw up."

"I *am* about to throw up!"

" — Chaise longues? Yes. Garden sculptures? Yes. Volcanic — "

"We have to do *something*," said Lex.

Bang helpfully held up her book, which was filled with doodles of unspeakable things being done to LeRoy.

"I don't think we're allowed to dismember the mayor," said Driggs in a regrettable voice. "Nice detail on the machete, though."

"And now! The grand finale!" LeRoy boomed.

The limo jerked to a sudden stop, flinging the Juniors into a pile on the car floor. LeRoy turned around in his seat and smiled at them. "Exit!"

Clawing at the doors, they scrambled out of the limo and lined up on the sidewalk. Lex looked down.

A skull looked back up at her.

Just an outline, though, one of dozens that spread down the sidewalk in both directions. The engravings of the skulls were stamped into the concrete itself, with pairs of handprints forming the eyes and names forming the mouth — names of notable Grims, she guessed.

The Juniors now stood in a wide, beautiful plaza. At the center sat a fountain with a tall obelisk, just like the one in Croak. And straight ahead was a huge building — a gilded, ornate pagoda obviously styled after that Chinese Theatre in Hollywood that Lex had always seen on the Oscars.

LeRoy opened the trunk of the limo, pulled out a metallic briefcase — the kind that in movies always contains money or guns — and led the Juniors across the plaza to the entrance of the building. They stepped through a pair of heavy doors into a high-ceilinged room. LeRoy came to a stop, clicked his heels, and spun around to face them. "The Bank!"

Like the hub back in Croak, there were desks with Smacks and a tank of jellyfish, but that was where the similarities ended. Where Croak's hub was sleek, dark, and futuristic-looking, De-Myse's was airy and bright, owing to the wall-to-wall windows surrounding the space and the multitude of skylights set into the ceiling far above. The jellyfish tank measured at least five times longer than Croak's. The Smacks were white and lustrous, and many of the Etceteras sat atop large beanbags or inflatable gym balls rather than desk chairs.

The Juniors gawked. Never had they thought a hub could be a *fun* place to work. With the duo of Norwood and Heloise constantly running Croak's with an iron fist, it had always felt like more of a penitentiary.

"Enter further!" LeRoy boomed.

Their footsteps clacked atop the polished marble floors as he led them to the middle of the room, where a girl stood at her desk seemingly barking orders at herself. As they got closer, however, it became clear that she was wearing a wireless headset. And that she was obviously the director of Ether Traffic Control.

And that she was the enormous Junior girl who had stared so intently at Lex at the club the evening before.

It was impossible not to recognize her. The girl was more than six feet tall and built like a lumberjack. She gave the Juniors a fleeting glance but never stopped talking, not for a second, her

voice choppily jumping from one word to another in an Australian accent.

"The director of Ether Traffic Control is a *Junior?*" Lex said to
Driggs. "How did that happen?"

He shrugged, still staring. "Looks like she knows what she's
doing. And I'm guessing that if anyone told her she couldn't have
the job, she would have snapped them in half."

The girl made a "come on" motion at Pip and Bang, then im-
patiently pointed at the scythe slot in the Smack.

Pip looked up at Uncle Mort. "We're checking in? For a
shift?"

Uncle Mort looked conflicted. "I'd rather you didn't, but like
I said, the ether is the safest place for you to be. Harder for Zara
to find you."

Lex broke into a huge grin, as did the rest of the Juniors. "So
we can work again?"

Uncle Mort looked up at the skylights. "I don't see Norwood
or Heloise SWAT-teaming in here to stop you."

Lex joyously grabbed her uncle around the waist. LeRoy, not
to be outdone, cleared his throat and gave each of them a handful
of Vessels. "Yes, in exchange for free room and board here in *fabu-
lous* DeMyse, you will work just as if you were one of our Juniors.
One five-hour shift per day."

"Five?" Lex said. "How come we have to do ten hours back
home?"

Uncle Mort looked back at her blankly. "Because I tell you to."

Lex made an outraged face, but her brain was already spinning. More free hours in the day meant more time to figure out
what to do about Zara.

Bang signed something at Uncle Mort, her hands a blur.

"Sure," he said. "I think you and the Pipster are trained up enough to be partners now. If it's okay with Ferbus and Elysia, that is."

Elysia looked at Ferbus. He flashed her an obnoxious grin, then honked. "Ugh," she said, disgusted.

Pip and Bang did an elaborate celebratory handshake, then eagerly handed over their scythes to the girl. "Wait," Lex said, stopping them. She looked at Uncle Mort. "If we check in, Norwood and Heloise will see our scythes show up on their Smacks. They'll know where we are."

LeRoy laughed. "Worry not, young Grims. DeMyse shall provide." He opened the metallic briefcase.

Lex swallowed a gasp. Lining the case were six gleaming, razor-sharp glass scythes, each identical to the one Zara possessed.

The other Juniors realized it too. Lex could feel their anxiety, their desire to protest, but the harsh look on Uncle Mort's face silenced them all. Driggs, who could read Uncle Mort better than anyone, gave him a slight nod.

"Thank you, LeRoy," Uncle Mort said in an overly polite voice. "Go ahead, kids. Take them."

Pip and Bang picked scythes out of the case and handed them to the director. She stuck them into the Smack, still talking into her headset as she checked them in. She did the same for Ferbus and Elysia, then Driggs and Lex, glancing at Lex for just a second longer than the others.

Once they were all checked in, LeRoy ushered them back out to the plaza. He clapped twice. "Work begins now!"

Unsure, the Juniors clutched their strange glass scythes and stared at one another, then at Uncle Mort.

"You heard the man!" he shouted in an uncharacteristically

jubilant voice. "Go reap some souls — you know you want to! Group hug!"

He gathered them up into a tight, almost crushing embrace. "Not a word out loud about this until I say so," he hissed. "Or I will Damn you myself."

He let them go and waved. "Have fun, champs!"

||||||

The deaths in DeMyse's jurisdiction weren't all that different from the ones back in Croak. Granted, some were a little odder — like the stuntman who died in a freak accident on a movie set or the woman shot down after stealing a few million dollars' worth of casino chips from Caesars Palace — but all in all, it was just another routine Field shift.

Except that it involved illegal glass scythes.

Fearing Uncle Mort's wrath, the Juniors said nothing about it, not even when they met up again in the Bank after their shifts. After unloading their Vessels into the tunnel, they stood back and took in the vault door, a metallic behemoth that was at least twice as large as Croak's.

Lex's stomach turned. Time to find out if Corpp still had a soul.

Driggs must have been thinking the same thing. "Moment of truth," he said. He took a step toward the vault. "If he's in there — "

"Whoa, whoa, whoa," said a small, snippy man jumping in front of them. "No tourists."

Driggs put on a friendly smile. "Actually, we're not tourists. We're visiting Juniors from — "

"I don't care who you are. DeMysian Seniors only. Off you go."

So off they went, grumbling the whole way. The director of Ether Traffic Control still stood at her desk, still yelling into her headset. The Juniors watched her as they passed, Lex catching her eye once again.

"What's the matter?" Driggs asked her once they'd exited the Bank into the plaza. "You've got the weirdest look on your face."

"I could be wrong," Lex said, "but I could have sworn that somewhere in that girl's string of instructions I heard her say 'Meet me at the Dungeon, Lex, seven tonight.'"

|||||||

"Now *this* is more like it," said Ferbus.

The Juniors stepped down a narrow flight of stairs hewn from cold gray stone. It spat them out into a dark tavern filled with what were clearly the more unsavory denizens of DeMyse. In a small corner booth a man with one eye sat sharpening his scythe. At another table, two mostly toothless women took turns gulping down a cup of brackish liquid. Various other degenerates sat at the bar, which was made from a single gigantic wooden log that had started to rot.

"We're going to die here," said Elysia.

"The skeleton was cool, at least," Driggs said, referring to the figure that sat guarding the entrance like a long-deceased bouncer. They'd pulled on its arm, and the door had opened.

"Which is more than we can say for my rotten uncle," Lex added. She was dying to hear more about the glass scythes, but Uncle Mort hadn't been at the hotel when they'd returned from work, and they hadn't been able to find him before they left for the Dungeon.

A loud cry rang out. None of the patrons seemed to notice or care, but the Juniors stirred and looked for its source. Standing next to a grungy booth was the director of Ether Traffic Control herself, who gestured for them to come closer.

"G'day!" she yelled, sweeping them all into the booth with her trunklike arms. "Sorry about earlier, mates. Couldn't risk talking to you directly — too many wandering ears about."

"Huh?" said Lex.

"The name's Broomie." The girl smiled. "As in, brew me!" she shouted at the bartender, who threw her a bottle of something. She yanked the cap off with her teeth, then spit it onto the floor and took a long swig. "Don't worry, yours'll be along shortly," she said, noticing the shocked looks on their faces.

As Broomie continued to chug, Driggs turned to Lex. "What is happening right now?"

"Couldn't tell you," said Lex, equally confused.

"*I'll* tell you what's happening," Broomie said, slamming her bottle down on the table. "That rotten-ass bastard LeRoy and his blind-ass puppets running this town like a stupid-ass carnival, that's what."

She looked at the Juniors as if she expected them to have the capacity to respond. But there they sat, like a pile of open-mouthed dead fish.

"I'm sorry," Driggs said politely, folding his hands up under his chin, "but I'm going to have to ask you to rewind a little here."

"Rewind? Sure. Twenty years ago, China. Middle of a monsoon. My mother's water had just broken, and my massive noggin showed no signs of slowing — "

"Okay, fast forward," Driggs jumped in. Pip looked ill.

"Orphaned and shipped off to Australia?" Broomie suggested, as if offering chapter options from her autobiography. "Arrested after stealing half a million dollars' worth of pearls? Freed by LeRoy and brought to DeMyse? Promoted to the second-highest office in the city?"

"Okay, right there," said Driggs. "Go."

She gave him a wide grin. "A couple of months ago, when that Zara bitch knocked off our director, there opened up a talent vacuum in the Etcetera department. I've always been a bit advanced, and even though I was still a Junior, I was the best candidate for the job. At least that's what I told LeRoy. Idiot bought it."

She finished off her drink in one huge gulp as they stared. "I know what you're thinking," she said, chucking the empty bottle back at the bartender. "Drunk Australian, real shocker. But keep in mind, I'm a six-foot-five Asian who can hold my liquor, so I'm already doing my part to shatter stereotypes, right?"

A large tray of bottled Yoricks danced its way toward their table. Riqo popped his head out from behind the drinks. *"Hola,"* he sang, handing them out and taking a seat next to Broomie.

"Wait, wait, wait," Elysia said to him, flustered. "I thought you were part of that uppity Junior clique. You too," she said to Broomie. "We saw you with them at the club."

Broomie wrapped a massive hand around another bottle and rolled her eyes. "I know," she said. "Riqo and I only hang out with those vapids so that no one'll get suspicious. Truth is, we've been against LeRoy's policies for years." She took a gulp. "All the censorship and isolation bullshit — it's not right. I think deep down he's a decent man and is just trying to protect us, but he's doing it all wrong. This city has become nothing but a brainless playground for the Grimsphere's elite, and we're sick of it."

"But you're the director of Ether Traffic Control," said Lex, now even more surprised. "You're one of those elite."

"Makes it easier to keep an eye on the guy," she replied. "I've learned a hell of a lot about the intricacies of DeMyse's government, and that's worth having to put up with all his rubbish."

Driggs stole a glance at Lex, then looked back at Broomie. "What does any of this have to do with us?"

Broomie let out a hearty laugh. "You don't have to be cagey with me, mate. I know who you guys are. Especially you, Queen of the Damned."

Lex bristled. "Whatever you've heard about me — "

"Is true," said Broomie. "Listen, it's fine. We're on your side, and Mort's. We've been following all this since the beginning — underground channels, obviously — and we hate the way you blokes are being treated over there with that Norwood wanker in charge."

"We know there are bad things going on," said Riqo. "And we do not want to be in the dark any longer."

"We want to help," said Broomie. "We want to matter."

Lex broke into a smile. She couldn't help it. The Seniors in Croak had been so hostile to her for so long now, she hadn't thought that anyone might still be on her side. She could have kissed them.

Instead, in her elated stupor, she knocked her drink over.

"You'll have to excuse my partner," said Driggs. "She loses a few brain cells every time someone pays her a compliment. Fortunately, it doesn't happen too often." He reached across the table to shake Broomie's hand. "I think what she would say, if she weren't in shock, is thank you. And welcome aboard the crazy train."

"Yeah, yeah, happy to have you," said Ferbus, grabbing a drink. "Now, on to more important matters — what is *up* with these bottled Yoricks?"

|||||||

They stayed out late, even later than the night before. The Juniors filled Broomie and Riqo in on what had gone down in Croak, what Norwood and Heloise were up to, and the latest developments with Zara. The mysteries surrounding the Wrong Book, the key, and the symbols on the obelisk were of particular fascination; both Broomie and Riqo were eager to help figure out how to get past the protective field, excitedly insisting on a trip to the DeMyse library.

Pip and Bang left sometime around midnight, while Ferbus and Elysia lasted until three, leaving with Riqo as he showed them some photos from his hometown in Mexico. But for Lex and Driggs, the evening stretched on to the staggering hour of six in the morning. Broomie and her alphabet-belching abilities were just too much fun, and their gabfest had continued until long after they'd reached their three-Yorick maximum.

"Maybe you can help us out with something else," Lex heard herself say at one point.

"Mort's gonna kill you," Driggs reminded her under his breath.

Lex ignored him. "Those glass scythes that LeRoy gave us — where did they come from?"

Broomie frowned. "Don't know, I just thought they were substitutes. Never seen them before. Why, are they special?"

"Not special, exactly," said Lex. "It's just that Zara has the same kind."

"You're kidding," Broomie said, her eyes widening. She thought for a moment. "Nope, don't know where they might have come from. LeRoy's never mentioned anything to me." She frowned. "Which is odd."

They traded theories for a little while longer, until they realized that the sun was rising. "Bugh," Lex moaned as they stumbled outside. "This was probably a bad idea."

"Get used to it, mate," said Broomie. "DeMyse is all about the nightlife."

"Yes, I'm becoming increasingly aware of its — hey!" She pointed across the street. "There's Uncle Mort!"

The deposed mayor was indeed walking down the sidewalk, and at a very hurried pace. In fact, he was almost running. And glancing over his shoulder to make sure he wasn't being followed.

"Let's follow him," said Lex.

"Can't," Broomie said, looking disappointed. "I've gotta be at the Bank or people will get suspicious. But you guys go. Fill me in later."

Lex and Driggs said goodbye and snuck across the street, making sure to stay out of Uncle Mort's field of vision as they tailed him. He wound through narrow streets and hidden alleys, hurrying all the way to the outskirts of town before disappearing around a corner.

Lex and Driggs looked up. They'd stopped in front of a pair of gilded gates, behind which sat a long driveway leading to a gigantic white estate. "That's the Mayor's Mansion," said Driggs.

"Yes, I gathered that," said Lex, pointing at the large golden sign above the gate that read MAYOR'S MANSION.

Driggs gave her a Look.

"What are you doing here?"

They whipped around to find Uncle Mort standing behind them. He looked mildly panicked.

"How did you do that?" Lex sputtered.

"Catlike stealth. I repeat, what are you doing here?"

Driggs tried to appear squirrelly. "We . . . could ask you the very same question."

Uncle Mort rolled his eyes. "Nice try, Mr. Bond." He glared at Lex. "I bet you've been gabbing about the glass scythes, too." When Lex made a guilty face, he sighed. "I swear, it's like talking to a wall."

"Are you here to see LeRoy?" Lex asked. "Can we come with you?"

"No. Go back to the hotel and don't leave until I — "

"Hello?" a voice crackled. "Mort?"

Uncle Mort walked up to the gate and punched a button on its intercom. "Yeah, it's me."

"And you've brought your Juniors! Excellent! Enter!"

The gate clicked open. Uncle Mort glared at the camera above his head, then at Lex's and Driggs's grinning faces. "Get in," he said gruffly, pushing them through. "I should really put some bells on you two."

They approached the front door, its gold-plated surface blinding in the rising sun. LeRoy opened it to greet them. "Welcome!"

he shouted at a volume not suitable for the early hours of the morning. "Come in, come in. Can I get you some fresh-brewed Indonesian kopi luwak? Most expensive coffee in the world — made from beans that have passed through the digestive tract of a monkey! Or perhaps some oolong tea, straight from the Chinese province of—"

He never finished, as Uncle Mort's forearm had flown up and pinned his neck to the polished mahogany wall.

19

"Driggs, Lex, don't move," Uncle Mort barked.

They weren't planning on it. They just stood and watched him, their faces incredulous.

"Why'd you do it?" Uncle Mort demanded.

LeRoy's eyes were bulging. "I don't know what you're — "

Uncle Mort pushed harder on his windpipe. LeRoy was starting to make little choking noises. "Tell me what happened," Uncle Mort said, his voice not wavering. "Or better yet, show me. Show me everything, or I'm going to the press."

LeRoy broke free from his grasp. "All right," he rasped, his bravado gone. "This way."

Looking like a cowed puppy, he led them to a widened atrium. At its center sat a large nude sculpture of LeRoy in the pose of *The Thinker*.

"Tasteful," Uncle Mort deadpanned.

"Thank you," LeRoy said sincerely, missing the slight. He grasped the head of the sculpture and tilted it back on a hinge to reveal a small button within. When he pushed it, a previously invisible door opened up in the wall behind them.

"After you," Uncle Mort told him.

LeRoy nodded timidly and disappeared into the darkness. Uncle Mort followed, then turned back to face Lex and Driggs. "You'd better stay here."

Lex stared at him. "You're kidding, right?"

He gave her an exasperated look. "Apparently, I am."

Exchanging nervous glances, Lex and Driggs followed him through the door and emerged into a poorly lit low-ceilinged room.

A room full of weapons.

Guns of every size and shape dotted the far wall. All manner of knives, swords, grenades, crossbows, and other horrific devices gleamed threateningly to their left. And on the right, lined up in a bulletproof case, were dozens of glass scythes.

Uncle Mort scanned the wall and spoke quietly. "Dammit, LeRoy."

"She threatened to burn my city to the ground! She said if I didn't give her one, she'd Damn me and find someone else on the black market who would!"

"Which we both know is a lie. She wouldn't dream of Damning you — you're the only one in North America who could have given her what she needed. With no scythe, no identification, and no way of flying overseas, you were her only option."

LeRoy set his jaw. "I had no choice."

Uncle Mort looked as though he didn't believe that. "Did she come straight here after Damning her stepfather?"

"Yes. Apparently someone had advised her to do so, said I'd be a pushover." He cleared his throat in distaste. "She hitchhiked to the edge of the valley, then hiked through the desert on foot. Walked right up to my front door and demanded a replacement. The nerve of that girl!" He made a bitter face. "So, yes, I cut a deal with her. She'd leave DeMyse alone, as long as I gave her the scythe and kept quiet about it."

Uncle Mort glared at him. "While still giving her free reign to Damn the rest of the country."

LeRoy straightened up a little. "I'm not proud of what I did. But it *has* kept my city safe. I'd already lost one good man, I wasn't prepared to lose any more." He almost looked sad. "I wish there had been another way, Mort. You know that."

Uncle Mort turned away from him. "Was the scythe all she took?"

"Yes," LeRoy said, eager to please. "Once I gave it to her, she Crashed out and that was the last I ever saw of her. I swear." He glanced at Lex and Driggs. "Though now that I've provided safe haven for you and your Juniors . . . I don't know. If Zara finds out, our deal will almost certainly become null and void."

For the first time, LeRoy appeared truly worried.

"Destroy the scythes. All of them." Uncle Mort headed for the door, then turned back. "I won't go to the press. But now you owe me. Remember that."

He stalked out of the room. Not knowing what else to do, Lex and Driggs followed, leaving LeRoy alone with his weapons and doubts.

〣〣〣

"Well, I'm a right bloody idiot," said Broomie, smacking herself in the head that night at the Dungeon. "How could I not have figured that out?"

Broomie had thoroughly ignored the Juniors when they showed up for work at the Bank earlier that day, but it was all part of the plan. At night, they'd meet in secret at the Dungeon, all the while keeping up the charade that Broomie was just another conceited Junior and Lex and the gang were the weird, shabby outcasts.

"I knew something felt wrong," she said. "Our security system is mediocre at best—I should have known that that alone couldn't stop Zara. Hell, if your techie genius uncle couldn't keep her out, what made me think that our prancing ninny mayor could? He practically rolled out a second red carpet for the bitch."

"But he really didn't have a choice," said Elysia.

"Sure he did," said Pip. "Zara was scytheless—how hard could it have been to lock her up and alert the authorities?"

"Maybe she had a crossbow!" an inebriated Ferbus shot back, spraying Pip with Yorick.

Broomie gently pulled Ferbus's bottle out of his hands. "Go easy on these, mate," she said. "They're a little more potent than the ones you're used to."

"Poppycock!"

"What I want to know," said Driggs, restraining Ferbus, "is who tipped off Zara to come to DeMyse in the first place. LeRoy mentioned that someone had told her that he'd be a pushover, which makes sense — she wouldn't have known that on her own. None of us Juniors had ever met him before."

Broomie frowned. "That's true. But who could it be? Who'd have enough knowledge of the Grimsphere to be able to steer her like that?"

Lex coughed on her Yorick. After a few moments of hacking, she looked up at the Juniors with watering eyes. "Bone."

"But there is no Bone," said Driggs. "The name was just part of the clue."

"Whoever wrote the note, then! Think about it," she said, her voice phlegmy. "Don't you think it's weird that Zara knew exactly how to steal my Damning ability? She never could have thought of that on her own. She must have had outside help."

The Juniors' eyes grew wider as they thought this over.

Driggs turned to Lex. "What was that thing she said to you when you asked how she knew it would work?"

Ice ran up Lex's spine as she recalled Zara's face that day in her stepfather's basement. "She said, 'I have my sources.'" Lex looked around the table. "That's it. That's how she found the Loophole. That's how she knew about Damning. Remember when Uncle Mort said that only a handful of Grims had ever heard of it?"

Driggs nodded. "Whoever wrote the note must have gotten to her early on, taken advantage of how much she hated her stepfather." He met Juniors' shocked faces. "They've been coaching her this whole time."

It took a moment for that to sink in.

"Which means we can never hand over the key," said Lex. "Or the symbols, or the Wrong Book, if we ever find it. It would be dangerous enough in the hands of Zara, but if she's teamed up with someone even worse . . ."

A flash of white streaked through her mind. The figure in the woods. The man in the tuxedo —

The voices of her friends snapped her back. "There must be something we can do," said Riqo.

Driggs was thinking. "The neutralizer," he said. "The thing that can get us past the cabin's shield. If it's in the Afterlife in Croak, it could also be in the Afterlife here, and that means we have a chance of grabbing it before Zara does. We have to get into that vault."

"How?" said Elysia. "There's no Wicket here to sneak us in."

"And Vern's a dill," Broomie said. "Takes his job way too seriously. I've got no clout with him."

"Guys, chill!" said Ferbus, his glassy eyes suggesting that he was already quite chilled. He flung an arm over Lex's shoulder. "Lex will think of something. ALWAYS finagling her way into tricksy situations, this one! She's the bee's knees, amiright?" he slurred before passing out on the table.

The Juniors stared at the puddle of drool forming under his cheek. "Bottled Yoricks aren't for everyone," Broomie said.

||||||

Ferbus, though drunk as a skunk, wasn't wrong. Lex *was* the bee's knees, and she *did* think of something. The solution finally came to her one afternoon while she, Elysia, and Pip were helping Riqo in the community garden.

"Nothing in this one, either," Elysia said with a sigh, throwing another heavy book to the ground. They'd brought research with them from the Grotton section of the DeMyse library to look for information about the protective field, but they still hadn't found anything.

"Watch the blueberries!" A bare-chested Riqo turned to Pip. "You know, they have always been my favorite," he said, sweating and digging into the earth with a spade. "I think I will enjoy them even more, now that I see how much they match your eyes."

Pip's blueberry-like eyes widened. Which was quite a feat, seeing as how they'd already stretched to their limit when Riqo took off his shirt. "Thank you!"

Elysia shot them both a dirty look.

Lex's eyes, however, were fixed on something else. "What's this?" she asked, pointing at a drawing in Riqo's gardening guide.

Riqo took the book from her and smiled. "Ah, that is the famed *Ficus compos mentis,* also known as the Lucidity Plant. Ingest one leaf, and your head will become as clear as a drop of fresh morning dew."

Lex stared at it a little harder. "I've seen it somewhere before."

Riqo laughed and shook his head. "That is quite impossible," he said. "It has been extinct for many, many years."

"Are you questioning my mad botany skills?" Lex joked. "Because I'll have you know I studied with the finest — What the hell is that?"

A translucent blob was drifting down the street. It held a vaguely humanoid shape, but no distinctive features could be made out in the blur. It was as if a part of the wavy mirage illusion that surrounded the city of DeMyse had broken off and decided to take an afternoon stroll.

"Oh, nothing," said Riqo, grabbing a roll of paper towels and cleaning off his hands. "It is only Morgana."

"Huh?"

"I do not know if that is her real name, but it is what we call her." Riqo wiped some sweat from his brow. "She is a ghost who has wandered through the desert for centuries. We do not know who made her, or why, or who she was in life, only that she chooses not to interact with us. So we let her be."

Elysia sighed. "Must be awful to be a ghost," she said, shaking her head. "Family dead, friends dead, stuck all alone for eternity on this miserable rock with no way to eat or feel or take part in the life that everyone else shoves in your face all day." She yanked out a weed. "I'd strand myself in the middle of the desert, too."

"Yet even ghosts cannot resist the *fab*ulousness of DeMyse," said Lex, opening a packet of seeds. "With its dazzling lights and heated pools and endless supply of plastic surg — "

She froze midsentence, dropping the seeds.

"That is not where the turnips go," said Riqo, but Lex didn't hear him. She'd already grabbed the roll of paper towels and taken off for the Bank.

|||||

Lex situated herself in the line to the vault, poofing out her hair and ignoring the half of her brain that was telling her how risky and stupid and potentially mortifying this was. She dutifully sucked on the lollipop she'd grabbed from one of the Etceteras' desks, making sure to smear the cherry red coloring around her lips.

When she got to the front of the line, the snippy Vault Post guy was there as usual. He took one look at Lex and put his hands on his hips. "I thought I told you, no Juniors allowed in the — "

"How DARE you, Vern?" Lex screeched in a high, haughty voice that even she found terrifying. "Don't you recognize me?"

"I — what?" Vern's face crinkled up in confusion. "Who — "

"HONestly, Vern," she said with a huff. "I thought we were close, you and I."

He squinted, then opened his eyes up wide, then squinted again. "Is that you, Jacqueleen?"

"Of COURSE it is," Lex said, who'd never met anyone named Jacqueleen in her life. "Who else would I be?"

"It's just — you look so different, I — "

"You like it?" Lex fluffed her hair and prayed that the paper towels she'd stuffed down her shirt were doing their job. "I had a little work done."

"Ohh," said Vern in a relieved voice, as if this sort of misunderstanding happened all the time in DeMyse. Lex puffed her fake knockers out even farther and gave the lollipop a naughty little lick. Vern, staring intently, reached for the vault door, missed, then reached again and waved her through. "I see. Yes, you look fantastic. Very youthful."

"THAT was the POINT," Lex sang as she sashayed through the door. "Ta!"

The Afterlife in DeMyse looked the same as it did in Croak — bright, fluffy white stuff everywhere — but instead of presidents, inventors, and other historical figures, the atrium was full of Hollywood icons. John Wayne took the hands of the targets and led them toward the Void while Marilyn Monroe flipped up her dress for the hooting crowds.

"Crap," Lex said aloud to no one, her heart deflating. It was way too busy in there to get any decent information. What was she going to do, just walk up to James Dean and ask him to search the Afterlife for some mysterious item she couldn't even describe?

"Hey, turdface!"

Lex's jaw fell open. "You've *got* to be kidding me."

Cordy rode atop her camel with Tut sitting behind her, Kloo biking alongside them, and Poe bringing up the rear, walking with a limp. "There she is, the little fugitive," Cordy said with a droll grin. "Screwed yourself pretty good this time, huh, Sis?"

"What are you doing? How did you get here?"

"I think the bigger question is, where did those new sweater kittens of yours come from?"

Lex yanked the paper towels out of her hoodie with an impatient grunt. "*Why* are you *here?*"

"Excellent question," Poe snipped with a frown, massaging his feet.

"We decided to take another little road trip through the Afterlife," Cordy said. "As soon as Corpp told us what happened — "

"*Corpp?* You saw him?"

"Concord," Tut said in a bored voice, smoothing his eyebrows, "tell the peasant not to shout so."

Kloo rolled her eyes and gave Lex a reassuring smile. "Yeah, we saw him. He came through the atrium, went into the Void, and hasn't been seen since. We hear he's settled down somewhere in the Afterlife version of the Horsehead Nebula, painting up a storm."

Lex felt as if five tons of weight had instantly lifted from her shoulders. "So his soul isn't gone."

"Nope," said Cordy. "Looked pretty happy, from where I was sitting. Which was on a freakin' camel!" She gave it a big, smacking kiss. "Lex, meet Lumpy."

Lex regarded the disenchanted-looking beast. "Hi."

Lumpy spit in her face.

"He likes you!" Cordy cried.

Lex irritably wiped the mucus from her cheek and turned back to Kloo, the only sane member of the party. "How's the mood back home?"

Kloo smiled in the way people smile when they're trying to hide bad news. "Well, it's not great. Norwood and Heloise think you're the devil incarnate. They've made it their mission to convince the whole town of it, and from what Wicket tells us, it's working. The rest of the Grimsphere is starting to buy it too. Except for DeMyse, of course." She let out a whistle. "You guys are lucky to be here."

"Oh, yes," Poe said to Quoth, who looked ruffled from the trip. "We're all *so* lucky to be here."

"We wouldn't have to be, if Sofi hadn't ratted us out," Lex said, scowling. "Is she enjoying the Crypt now that she has it all to herself?"

"Ah, her," Kloo said with a chuckle. "Well, Wicket said that at first she was pretty bummed that you left her behind. But since she was such a big help in alerting Norwood and Heloise to what you'd done, they — you're not going to like this — they gave her her job back."

"Ugh, of *course* they did," Lex said, not even surprised anymore. "And" — her stomach clenched, but she pushed on — "how's Dora doing?"

"Better than you'd think," said Kloo. "She keeps trying to persuade the town that Zara is the bad guy and not you. She constantly yells at Norwood and Heloise, calls them all sorts of names — she's the only one they'll back down from. Honestly, I think Corpp's death has only made her feistier, if such a thing is possible."

"Good." Lex let out a breath. "Good."

"Wicket also said — " Cordy started. "She told me that Mom and Dad visited." She was trying to hide it, but her eyes were pained. "How are they?"

Lex swallowed. "They're . . . okay."

Cordy folded her arms. "Lex. Don't lie to me."

Lex didn't know why she ever tried. "Dad's hanging in there. And Mom is . . ."

She trailed off. Cordy stared for a moment more, then nodded.

Lex's stomach twisted once again. As if she weren't crammed up to her eyeballs in guilt as it was, Cordy always made her feel worse. She sighed and looked into the Void, wishing there were some way to fix everything she'd done, or at least to stop Zara. They still hadn't found anything in DeMyse's books on the neutralizer, or the Wrong Book, or Grotton —

Wait a minute.

She squinted even harder into the Void. Why hadn't she thought of this before?

Luckily, no one was paying attention to her. "I grow weary of this talk," announced Tut, digging around in a bag attached to the camel. "Where are my figs?"

Kloo let out a sigh. "That boy and his figs."

"I know," Cordy said dreamily, staring at his six-pack. "What a tasty slice."

Lex had to get out of there, but she didn't want to panic anyone. "Remind me again why he's still with you?" she said, inching away from them.

Cordy glared at her. "Because we are an item," she said testily. "And I'll thank you to keep your jealousy to yourself. I'm sorry that you ended up with a weird-eyed freak while I got the leader of the ancient world, but that's just how the camel spits." She dug her heels into Lumpy and waved. "We'll see you around, okay?"

"We're leaving?" Poe said, incredulous and bitter. "So soon?"

"Silence, Mustache," Tut yelled down to him. "You irk me."

Poe scowled and started muttering to himself. "I shall shove him into a vortex, I shall. The one at Mount Rushmore, right up Jefferson's nose . . ."

Lex would have comforted him, but she was already halfway to the vault door. Once they'd turned their backs, she bolted. She had to find Uncle Mort.

||||||

Luckily, she knew where to look. She threw a casual hello to the girl at the hotel's front desk, flitted up the stairs, and pulled out the keycard Uncle Mort had given her in case of an emergency.

This was close enough.

She fit the card into the slot and turned the handle, only to find that the room was a complete mess. Ever since the incident at the Mayor's Mansion, Uncle Mort had spent the majority of his time in DeMyse holed up in this very room, hacking through firewalls and blocked television channels. He, unlike everyone else in DeMyse, wanted to know what was going on in the outside world. He'd managed to get through to a few media outlets and had even persuaded some poor swiper to smuggle in daily copies of *The Obituary*.

Lex stared at the stacks of newspapers as she entered the room. TERROR IN CROAK, one read. NEW MAYOR DEMANDS JUSTICE, screamed another, with a picture of Norwood looking dashing and heroic. Lex tried to ignore the biggest headline — MANHUNT FOR CRAZED JUNIOR CONTINUES — alongside a small blurred photo of herself, but she knew it would still haunt her dreams for approximately forever.

Uncle Mort wasn't there. She stuck her head into the bathroom, but he wasn't there either. She was just about to leave when a gust of wind billowed out the curtain that had been drawn in front of the balcony.

Lex crept up to the sliding glass door. It was open, just a crack. Two muffled voices came from the balcony.

"—but it's happening," said Uncle Mort. "I promise you that."

"You're sure?" LeRoy replied.

Lex frowned. They'd made up already? It had been only a week since that nuclear meltdown at LeRoy's mansion.

"Positive," Uncle Mort replied. "A year, maybe less."

"Jesus." LeRoy let out a long breath. "So soon."

They were silent for a moment.

"How can you be so sure?" LeRoy asked. "You haven't seen it yourself."

"One of our dead lost a memory. And I've heard other reports. It's getting bad."

"Maybe they're mistaken. Maybe *you're* mistaken."

"Roy, I've been at this for years. You really think I'd mess up the calculations? Forget to carry a three?"

"Well, no. You're the expert, always have been. It's just—"

"What?" There was an uncomfortable, accusatory pause. "You're not gonna wimp out on me, are you?"

"Mort. Of course not."

"Because when the time comes, you can't hesitate. Not for a second."

"Don't you think I know that? I just think—" LeRoy made a sucking noise through his teeth. "Let's say we do everything right, follow the plan to the letter. What if it doesn't work? There are no more chances."

"It will work."

"Yeah, but we're getting into some déjà vu territory, man," said LeRoy. "You said the same thing years ago — "

"I know what I said. I was wrong then. I'm right now."

LeRoy let out a grunt, then said nothing for so long that Lex thought he had fallen asleep.

"You really think they're the ones, huh?"

"Yes."

The confidence in Uncle Mort's voice made Lex shiver.

"Well, then," said LeRoy, sighing in a way that suggested he was getting up from a chair. "We'd better do what we can to protect them."

"That's all I'm saying. Never let your guard down." Uncle Mort tore the curtain open. "Right, Lex?"

20

Lex jumped back from the door with a yelp. Uncle Mort gave her a sly look. "Admiring the window treatments?"

"I was just —"

"The Deluxe Suite!" LeRoy vaulted into the room and spread his arms out wide, back to his old bombastic self. "King-size bed featuring Egyptian cotton linens. Thread count? Fifteen hundred!"

"Knock it off, Roy," Uncle Mort said, pushing him toward the door. "I need to reteach my niece how privacy works. I'll catch up with you later."

LeRoy stepped out into the hall, twirled around, and gave them both a deep bow, but not before Uncle Mort had started to slam the door shut. "Exhausting," he said with a sigh. He sat on the bed and studied Lex. "So, out with it. How much of that did you hear?"

"Enough for me to be thoroughly confused yet irreversibly intrigued."

"Excellent. That'll make my silence on the matter all the more torturous."

Lex rolled her eyes. She hadn't expected him to tell her anything, but his evasiveness still pissed her off just as much as it always did. "I thought you two hated each other."

He shook his head. "Like I said, LeRoy and I go way back.

You of all people should know that it's the people we're closest to whose heads we most want to rip off." He folded his arms. "Speaking of which, what are you doing here?"

Lex remembered the reason she'd torn out of the Afterlife like a crazed bat. "I got past the vault today, and I — "

"Against the rules, obviously. Continue."

"I ran into Cordy and Kloo, and they said that Corpp made it to the Afterlife — which is great, but it got me thinking. Whatever happened to Grotton?"

"Huh?"

Lex sat down on the bed. "Maybe we've been going about all this research in the wrong way. Maybe we've spent so much time focusing on what's *in* the books that we haven't noticed what's *not*." She leaned in. "In all the books about Grotton, both in Croak and DeMyse, not one of them says anything about his death."

"So?"

"What if he got to be so powerful, he — I don't know, became immortal or something?"

Uncle Mort kept a straight face, though Lex thought she saw him swallow a snicker. "Grotton was tracked down and murdered, kiddo."

"Oh." Lex slumped. She glanced at her picture in the newspaper. "How? Grimsphere-wide manhunt?"

"Not exactly." He looked reluctant. "Grotton was lynched by regular people, not Grims."

Her eyes widened. "Seriously?"

"Yeah. Witch-hunts were all the rage at the time, and he was at the top of their list. Some farmer got him in the end, I believe. That's why it's not in our history books, because it's a bit of an embarrassment to the Grimsphere that they never succeeded in bringing him to justice."

Lex was disappointed. "Kind of a lame death for such a powerful guy."

Uncle Mort gave her a disapproving look; he had always hated the way she admired Grotton. "He got off way too easy. If the Grims had caught him, they'd have thrown him in the Hole to rot."

"And I'm guessing no one's ever seen him in the Afterlife?"

"Nah. He's probably so far into the Void he'd take centuries to find."

Lex sighed. So much for her earthshattering revelation. "Well, *some*one's carrying on his work." She told him about the Juniors' theory, that whoever scribbled all the notes in the library had been training Zara from the start.

He nodded. "I've been thinking that too. There's no way she could have orchestrated all this on her own, without any help."

"And —" Lex hesitated, then continued. "I never told you this, but over the summer I saw a weird white figure in the woods. It didn't seem like such a big deal, but then I've also seen this other guy in a white tuxedo, he was at the —"

"Why am I just hearing about this now?"

Lex blinked. "It didn't seem important. Do you know what it is?"

He twisted his mouth, thinking. "No."

He was lying, and Lex knew it. "Why won't you tell me what you and LeRoy were talking about?" she demanded.

"Because that," he said, "was a private conversation."

"About the thing that ties all this together, right? The big gobsmacking secret?"

After a moment he nodded.

"I knew it," Lex said quietly. "All this time. I keep asking and asking, and you always deny it. Now you admit it, and you still won't tell me what's going on?"

"Soon."

Lex paused. That one little word was more than she'd ever gotten out of him. "Soon?"

He looked her in the eye and dropped his voice. "Lex, what's going down here is big — very big — and there are a lot of moving pieces to deal with. You being one of them." He drew closer. "Think of this as one big game. I need to be able to bluff, trick, and even cheat, all without worrying that I've offended my niece by keeping her in the dark. You need to accept that sometimes you're on a need-to-know basis *for your own safety*. There are certain bits of information that, if divulged by the wrong person or at the wrong time, can be deadlier than any weapon, set off more explosions than any bomb. So, yes. Soon." He shook his head. "But not right now."

Lex took a shallow breath, as if inhaling too loudly would cause him to change his mind.

But her gratitude soon turned to suspicion. "Hang on. Did you know that Corpp was in the Afterlife?"

"Of course I knew. You think I don't talk to Pandora and Wicket? Cuffs aren't the only method of communication, you know."

Lex smacked his arm. "Why didn't you tell me? You know how I've been worried sick about his soul, and so has Driggs!"

"I was hoping to teach you a bit of a lesson," he said, serious. "Get you so worked up over the possibility of Damning Corpp's soul that you'd learn to be a little more careful next time. Especially now that Driggs can — well, whatever it is that he can do, this unDamning thing. I don't want you getting into the mindset that you can be reckless and do whatever you want because he can simply correct your mistakes."

"I told you, it was an accident! Why are you *so* — "

"When's the last time you discharged, Lex?" he interrupted, warily staring at her hands. When she didn't answer, he pointed at the bathroom. "Go."

Lex stalked into the bathroom and slammed the door.

After a few minutes Uncle Mort put his ear to the door and knocked. "Everything okay in there?"

Lex emerged with her eyes narrowed. The shower curtain lay in the bathtub, crumpling in flames.

Frowning, he pushed past her and turned on the water. "Why is it still burning?"

Lex didn't answer. Instead, she stalked to the door to the hallway, absent-mindedly flicking her pirate lighter on the way.

"I know what you're doing, Lex."

She stopped in her tracks. Uncle Mort finished dousing the fire and leaned on the bathroom doorway, staring at her. Her mouth went dry.

He took a couple of steps closer. "I've known all along. And I haven't stopped you, even though it goes against every fiber of my moral code to let it continue, because I know that the alternative could get very messy." He opened the door to let her out. "I don't like it, but all things considered, you're doing the right thing."

Lex was hardly breathing. "I am?"

"Yes." He nudged her out into the hall. "Just don't let it get out of hand."

The door closed.

|||||||

"I could be doing something about this!" Driggs exploded angrily at lunch one day. The Juniors had been scouring one of Uncle Mort's bootlegged newspapers and had discovered that one of the Croakers, the spidery proprietress of Ashes, had been Zara's latest victim. "If I really can reverse the effects of Damning, I could be saving those people from all that torture!"

"Too right," Broomie said, "but you're in hiding. And you don't even know for sure what it is you can do. Maybe you'd make it worse."

"I guess," Driggs said, not satisfied. "I just feel so pathetic. So far, our time here has been an epic fail. Haven't found any more info in the library, haven't found the neutralizer in the Afterlife —"

"And," Lex said, "I think Vern is starting to have a thing for Jacqueleen. I really need a better exit strategy, because yesterday he pinched my ass before I could —"

"That's it!" Elysia cried. "That's what we should do!"

"Pinch her ass?" Ferbus said.

"No, you moron," Elysia said, smacking him over the head with *The Obituary*. Ever since they'd gotten to DeMyse and become partners again, their incessant squabbling had grown worse. "I mean that if we want to feel useful, we should draw up an exit strategy in case Zara attacks! She's going to find out sooner or

later that LeRoy is harboring us, and we all know it's not going to
be pretty when she does."

"Can't we just Crash out of the city?" Ferbus said.

"Yeah, but they can't," Pip said, pointing at Broomie and Riqo.
"Whatever we do should keep *all* of us safe."

So over the next couple of weeks a plan was constructed. Unfortunately, it came with a rather pernicious side effect: all the
new talk of crisis management majorly amped up the Juniors'
paranoia. Before long they'd been reduced to a pack of jittery,
sleep-deprived zombies who left the hotel only to work or drink
themselves stupid at the Dungeon.

By the time New Year's Eve rolled around, Uncle Mort had
had enough. "Have some fun, for Pete's sake," he told them after
informing the manager of the Dungeon that no Juniors were permitted to enter the bar that night. "Go somewhere different, so-
cialize, talk about things that don't involve our imminent deaths.
You're starting to look like mole people."

So. Fun it was.

"Well, don't we look spiffy this evening," said Ferbus, lounging by the hotel pool, his pasty white skin visible from space as he
sipped a Yorick cosmopolitan. "Fun" apparently meant something different to everyone.

"Shut up, Ferbus," Lex said, tugging at her dress.

Elysia, in the pool, surfaced with a splash. "The shoes look
fab, Lex!" Since Lex had disposed of her last heels, Elysia had
taken it upon herself to provide a replacement pair.

"Where are you going?" Pip asked Lex. "Somewhere ro-
maaaantic?"

"None of your business, Blueberry Eyes."

A smarmy grin spread out from beneath Ferbus's now hideously crooked nose. "Just so you know, my plans for tonight involve planting my ass in my room and watching the *Jurassic Park* movies until my eyes bleed, so you and Driggs better find someplace else to bump uglies."

"Ooh, you can use our room!" Elysia said. "I'm going over to Pip and Bang's to watch *Love Actually*. Because *some* people around here actually possess human needs and emotions." She glared at Ferbus.

"I have human needs," Ferbus replied. "I need to watch people get ripped apart by dinosaurs in the bloodiest fashion possible."

"Okay, ew to all of you," said Lex, wobbling toward the exit gate. "And rest assured, if any uglies are going to be bumped, it will be far, far away from any of you, preferably on a moon base."

Lex couldn't help but smile at the prospect as she made her way onto the street. With Uncle Mort distracted by the secret meetings he was always holding with LeRoy, she'd thought that some quality alone time with Driggs would have been a given. But things hadn't worked out that way. There were roommates to deal with now, and with all the scheming they'd been doing, Lex and Driggs were often too exhausted with worry to summon up any viable hormones.

So Lex was psyched. She made her way into the restaurant, Lights Out, and spotted Driggs toward the back. He was once again wearing Uncle Mort's ill-fitting old suit, and once again, he looked ridiculous.

But still hot. Driggs could wear a tap-dancing walrus costume and still look hot.

He did a spit-take as she approached. "Holy shitballs," he said, scanning her up and down. "You look gorgeous."

Lex laughed. "Thanks."

"You're wearing a dress," he informed her.

"And yet I haven't burst into flames. I'm just as surprised as you are."

"Well, warn me next time so my heart doesn't explode." He got up to pull out her chair.

She snickered. "Pretending to be a gentleman, are we?"

"Gotta try at least once a year, or I'll lose my license." He ran a hand up her leg and grinned. "Nice gams."

She leaned in to kiss him, sniffing at the tart scent of his aftershave. "Nice face."

After a fairly lengthy smooch that the other patrons didn't seem to fully appreciate, Driggs sat back down and gestured at their surroundings. "Isn't this place nuts? Look, that violinist over there is serenading people. There are mints in the bathrooms. And look how many forks we get!"

Lex glanced at the plentiful silverware on the table and scrunched up her face. "Are you sure you can afford this?"

"I already told you, yes. I'm very fancy."

"Come on, let me chip in a little."

Driggs looked offended. "Lex, stop. I think I can handle buying my girlfriend an eight — " His face paled as he read the menu. He swallowed. "An eighty-dollar steak."

Lex was equally horrified. "I'll just get a salad," she said, nearly vomiting on the words.

"No way," said Driggs, sitting up a little taller. "You are my date. As such, you are going to sit here and enjoy our romantic dinner — and *not* talk about how we're all in constant mortal peril — and eat a cow that, according to these figures, was descended from royalty. Got it?"

Lex smiled. "Got it."

The following two hours were the nicest Lex could recall having had in quite some time. They chatted, they laughed, they flirted, they devoured their delicious royal cows, and not one word was mentioned about Zara, Norwood, Damning, un-Damning, or the fact that the Grimsphere was derailing before their very eyes.

For one night, they felt almost normal.

"So," Driggs said to Lex after the waiter had cleared their plates, "how badly do you want to sweep all the candles off this table and get down to it right here on top of these priceless linens?"

"Seeing as how I've pictured little else in my mind for the past hour, I'd say pretty badly," Lex replied, sipping her water in what she hoped was a devastatingly sexy manner. "Although I do have a key for Uncle Mort's suite — the one with the hot tub — "

Driggs grabbed the waiter's sleeve. "Check, please."

Lex grinned. This dress had paid for itself.

But her face changed in an instant, screwing up into a scowl as she stared at something behind Driggs. "Oh God."

"What?"

She pointed at the large window facing the street. Uncle Mort was banging loudly on the pane and yelling something incomprehensible.

"Jesus." Lex cupped her hands around her face, humiliated. "He's worse than my *dad*."

Seeing that he wasn't getting any response, Uncle Mort barged into the restaurant, blew past the maître d', and grabbed Lex's arm. "Come on, we're leaving."

"What is *wrong* with you?" she said. People were staring. "You *told* us to get out and have some fun! Am I not allowed to have dinner with my boyfriend?"

"Not tonight."

"Why?"

The window shattered.

Like everyone else, Lex dove to the ground. Yet Uncle Mort promptly yanked her back up to her feet, then pointed through the screaming patrons and broken glass to the chaos unfolding outside. "That's why."

Standing in the midst of it all, grinning, was Zara.

|||||||

Luckily, she hadn't spotted them yet. "We have to get to the Dungeon," Lex told Uncle Mort in a hushed voice as they raced through the kitchen and out the back door. Her heart pounded as they ran, her mind trying to concentrate on the emergency plan rather than the sickening possibilities of what might be happening. People could be dead. The other Juniors could be dead. Or Damned. Why had she *left* them?

She grabbed Driggs's hand and didn't let go.

"No," Uncle Mort told her. "You're not going to the Dungeon. You're going back to the hotel."

"But we've planned for this! The Juniors know to go there. Broomie said there's a back room where we can hide, and if Zara finds us, I'll — " She glanced down at her hands. She'd tried to Damn Zara last time, but it hadn't worked. "I'll think of something."

"Sorry. This is nonnegotiable, Lex."

Lex swallowed a lump in her throat. Uncle Mort hijacking the plans had not been one of their contingencies.

"Go straight to the hotel," Uncle Mort instructed. "Change, grab your stuff, then go to my room and do not leave, no matter what happens." He stopped running to stare at Lex. "And don't you dare jump in and try to fight her."

"But—"

"No buts. You stay in that room and don't go near the door. Now, give me your scythes. Your real scythes, not the glass ones."

"What? Why?"

"Are you really going to make me ask you twice?"

Lex glared at him, then dug around in her purse and slapped her scythe into his hand. Driggs reached into his pocket and did the same.

"Good. Now run." Uncle Mort bolted again, this time in the opposite direction from the hotel.

"Where are you going?" Driggs shouted after him.

"Cashing in on a favor! I'll be back as soon as I can!"

Lex and Driggs squeezed each other's hands a little tighter and took off for the hotel, Lex kicking off her shoes on the way. The girl just wasn't built for heels.

"How did she *find* us?" she huffed as they ran.

"Don't know," Driggs said, panting. "Maybe someone in Croak tipped her off. Maybe they tortured it out of Pandora or Wicket."

Lex grimaced and tried to clear that image from her head. "This screws everything up! What about the other Juniors? What about Broomie?"

"I'm sure they're fine," he said, though his voice was uncertain.

"We'll all be fine." He pulled her hand up to his mouth and kissed her knuckles.

Lex's throat tightened. "So much for a perfect evening."

"At least I didn't have to pay for the steak."

They jumped over a body lying in the neon-lit street. Driggs gave it a longing stare as they passed; Lex knew he wanted to go back and try out his unDamning powers, but there was no time. The growing din echoed off the walls of the buildings, peppered with shouts, screams, and more breaking windows. They'd managed to slip by Zara, but they could still hear her yelling, demanding to know where something or someone was.

The lobby of the hotel was empty. Lex and Driggs quietly inched up the stairs and headed to Lex's room. She grabbed her stuff and changed into regular clothes and her hoodie, all the while telling herself that Elysia's stuff was missing because she was somewhere safe, not because Zara had already gotten to her.

Over in Driggs's room, Ferbus's things were gone too. After Driggs had changed and stuffed everything else into his bag, he looked forlornly at the suit, in a sad heap on the bed.

"Just leave it," Lex said. "Put it out of its misery."

They crept down the hall to Uncle Mort's suite. Lex slid the key into the door and pushed it open.

Broomie had her arm raised, ready to hit Lex with the butt of her scythe. "Christ Almighty, it's you," she said, lowering it.

"Shhh," said Lex, relief washing over her as she stepped into the room. The rest of the Juniors sat on the king-size bed, all hugging their bags and looking terrified. Riqo stood at the window and was peering through the curtains at the street beyond the pool.

"About a dozen bodies, as far as we can tell," Broomie filled them in. "LeRoy, bless his heart — he's opened up the Mayor's Mansion and barricaded nearly everyone else in there."

"Why aren't you with them?" Driggs asked.

Broomie looked at him as if he were a moron. "And let her catch all of you?"

"I *told* Uncle Mort that we had a plan," Lex said, "but he wouldn't listen — "

"Shh!" Riqo hissed nervously from the window. "I see her."

"She's not coming here," Broomie said, her voice shaky.

"Sure she is," said Ferbus. "We all know who she's after." He glared pointedly at Lex.

"Shut up, Ferb," said Elysia. "If she wants Lex, she's going to have to get through all of us first."

Lex's throat got tight. "Thanks, Lys."

"You're welcome." She frowned. "Did you lose your shoes *again?*"

"Coming closer," said Riqo, still looking out the window. "She is — " He gave them a helpless look. "She has entered the hotel."

Lex tried to get angry, angry enough to be able to Damn, but her hands weren't growing any hotter. She was too scared.

Driggs swallowed and put his arms around her. They sat down on the bed with the others.

And waited.

Waited.

Someone shuffled outside the door.

Pip looked up at Broomie. "What do we do?"

Elysia whimpered. "We don't even have our scythes."

"Well, I do," Broomie said, reaching into her hoodie pocket. She raised it and slowly approached the door.

"Broomie, no," said Lex. "Uncle Mort said not to go near — "

The door swung open. A figure carrying a bag darted in, then wheeled around to face them, dodging Broomie's scythe mid-thrust.

" — the door," Uncle Mort finished Lex's sentence. "Guess you really do listen to me every once in a while, huh, Lex?"

He hurried to the bed. "She'll be here any second. Take these." He emptied the bag onto the bed, scattering a bunch of scythes across the mattress. Lex recognized the emerald of Bang's, the purple amethyst of Elysia's, the orange agate of Ferbus's.

"What did you do to them?" Driggs asked, reaching for his sapphire.

"Not me. LeRoy."

"Huh?"

"Turn your Cuffs on," Uncle Mort instructed. "They should be working now."

"But that'll give away our location!" Lex said. "Norwood will know where we are!"

A loud *boom* shuddered at the door. Zara was trying to kick it down. "Lex!" she screamed, kicking again.

"Turn the goddamn Cuffs on!" Uncle Mort repeated. The Juniors reluctantly obeyed as he flung his bag over his shoulder and shook Broomie's hand. "Thank you both," he said, reaching for Riqo's as well. "We'll be in touch."

"What?" Lex exclaimed. "They're not coming with us?"

"But we can't just leave them here!" Pip said.

"Don't you worry about us, mate," Broomie said. "We'll head her off. The important thing is that you get out, go somewhere safe."

"No!" Lex yelled. "This was not part of the plan!"

Broomie gave them a guilty smile as she backed up into the bathroom. "Not part of *your* plan. It's been *our* plan all along."

Riqo followed her. "Good luck, *amigos*. Oh, and Pipito? Here." He tossed a sack to Pip, then gave them all a little wave and shut the door.

"Scythe. Now," Uncle Mort instructed the Juniors.

The door was splitting. *"LEX!!"*

"Scythe where?" yelled Driggs, squeezing Lex's hand.

"Doesn't matter."

"Doesn't *matter?*"

A terrifying *crack* filled the room as the door splintered apart.

A stare-down ensued. Zara stood there, breathing heavily. She was gaunt, even skinnier than she had been all those weeks before. She looked as though she hadn't slept in months, the skin on her haggard face nearly translucent. Loathing filled her eyes as her gaze swept across the Juniors. They stared back, barely blinking.

The bathroom door swung open. Broomie and Riqo exploded out of it with a shout, scythes drawn for a fight they couldn't possibly win. Yet for the slightest of seconds Zara was distracted. She swung her scythe without caring where it landed, finding it a home in Riqo's chest. Blood spurted out of his mouth, staining the white carpet — the Juniors screamed —

"Go!" Uncle Mort yelled over them.

They scythed and were gone.

21

They landed in a dark room, their flailing bodies crashing to the floor in a heap.

"Cuffs off!" Uncle Mort shouted. This time they complied instantly.

Bang was the first to extract herself from the mess. She felt along the wall for a light switch, but instead found a hanging cord. When she yanked it, a set of curtains swept aside to reveal a wide floor-to-ceiling window.

Outside sat a gigantic mountain, its snowy pathways dotted and bathed with light. Every few seconds a figure came racing down the trails. Chairlifts swayed as they climbed up the slope, as did dangling skis and snowboards.

"Oh my Lord," said Elysia. "We're in Aspen."

Ferbus finally found a light and snapped it on. They were in yet another deluxe hotel suite, this one complete with fireplace. "Whoa," he said as everyone staggered to their feet. "Upgrade."

Lex wasn't paying attention; she was too busy trying to strangle her uncle. "We left them!" she cried, grabbing him by the neck of his hoodie. *"Why?"*

He broke away from her grip. "They wanted to stay and defend their town."

"But Zara's going to kill them! She stabbed Riqo!"

"Doesn't mean he won't make it. He's a strong kid. And if

not — " Uncle Mort's eyes lowered. "He'll go to the Afterlife. At least she didn't Damn him."

"How optimistic of you," Lex spat.

They glared at each other.

"Hang on," said Ferbus. "How do you know we're in Aspen, Lys? And more important," he said, looking at Uncle Mort, "*why* are we in Aspen?"

Uncle Mort sat on the arm of the couch and took a weathered atlas out of his bag. "Don't look at me," he said, skimming it and nodding at Elysia. "It was her idea."

Elysia looked more confused than any of them. "I — when we scythed, it just popped into my head. My parents came here for their honeymoon, and I remember looking through their photo albums. I think this was their room! It looks just like the pictures..." She stopped and looked at the others, who were gaping at her.

Elysia looked ready to cry. "I thought we were gonna die," she said in a quieter voice. "My parents were the last thing I thought of, and then we were here. I didn't mean to."

"Don't worry, Lys," Uncle Mort said. "You did splendidly."

The rest of the Juniors patiently waited for an explanation, but Uncle Mort didn't immediately deliver — either because he was trying to formulate one or he was a lot more worried about Broomie and Riqo than he was letting on.

Eventually he rubbed his eyes and stood up. "Okay. The reason we're in Aspen is because this time around, you're the ones deciding where we Crash to."

He took a deep breath. "When I took your scythes, I brought them to LeRoy — he owed me a favor, if you'll recall — and had him link up all our scythes to all our Cuffs, so that where one of us wants to Crash, the others instantaneously follow. The downside is that we'll be back on the grid and show up on the Cuff-Link, so whoever has been helping Zara will no doubt be able to hack back into that system and pass on our location to her. But there is a slight delay, which means that if we keep our destinations fairly random and unpredictable it'll be harder for her to track us."

"Destinations?" Elysia asked. "As in more than one?"

"Well, now that our Cuffs are connected, our maximum distance is limited to just over six hundred miles. It's going to take a few Crashes to get across the country and back to Croak."

"Wait, why are we going back to Croak?" Ferbus said. "Norwood and Heloise still want to chop us up and use us for firewood!"

"And don't you think Zara will follow us there?" Elysia said. "We'll be putting everyone in danger again!"

"Not as much danger as they'll be in if we don't," Uncle Mort said. "We need to figure out how to get the Wrong Book out of that cabin before Zara does."

"That's what we've been *trying* to do," said Driggs.

"Besides," Uncle Mort went on, "certain things in the Grimsphere are swiftly deteriorating. Things that you kids need not worry your little heads about, but suffice it to say that if Norwood and Heloise keep getting in the way of situations they know nothing about, things will end badly for all of us. I need to get back before they screw the pooch any more than they already have."

He stood up. "So here's the plan. We'll squat here for the

night — should be safe, since I don't think Zara anticipated us leaving, and she couldn't have traced us that quickly. Do not, under any circumstances, turn on your Cuffs. We'll leave in the morning."

Everyone nodded except for Lex, who let out a snort.

Uncle Mort looked at her. "Is there a problem, kiddo?"

"Yes. This is ridiculous." She got to her feet, feeling angrier than she had in a long time. "Why are we running from her? We fled like cowards yet again, just abandoned all those innocent people! They don't know what to do! They don't even know what's going on!"

"Zara was looking for *us*," Uncle Mort said. "Now that we're gone, she won't stick around for long."

"People are still dead! And here we are, selfish as always, escaping with our tails between our legs and leaving Broomie and Riqo behind to finish the mess we started, if they even survive! Why can't we *fight* her?"

"Because we'd *lose!*"

For the next few seconds the only noise was the skiers swooshing down the slopes outside.

"Zara can be defeated," Uncle Mort continued in a measured voice, watching Lex. "In fact, I'm counting on it. But the losses we'd sustain if we fought her at this *very moment* are losses I am not willing to suffer. I've no doubt that you could take her, Lex, but we all know by now that Zara doesn't play nice. She won't go after you first. She'll Damn Elysia, then me, then everyone in this room, then Driggs. And after that, she'll finally come for you, and then, yes, I believe you could beat her. But by then, what would be the point?"

Lex was too angry to speak, her hands scorching. For one

quick, sick moment, something inside her longed to lunge at her uncle, to feel the heat of his skin sizzling and melting under the power of hers. It would be so easy, such a simple way to quell the chronic, insatiable hunger. Why hadn't she thought of Damning any of these idiots before? They were practically defenseless, trusted her completely, would never see it coming—

With a horrified gasp Lex wrenched herself out of the kitchen. She ran out onto the frigid balcony, where a deck chair instantly met its fiery end.

As the flames died down, she hugged herself and propped her arms up on the balcony railing. For a few minutes she just stood there watching the mountain, until the door opened behind her.

"Moved on to lawn furniture, I see," Uncle Mort said. "I'll alert the area Home Depots."

Lex said nothing.

"It's getting worse, isn't it?" he said.

She just kept looking at the slopes, knowing that if she looked at him, she'd break down. "That wasn't me in there," she rasped. "It really *is* a disease. I can see why it's been so easy for Zara to go after innocents, to throw away all those moral convictions in a heartbeat."

Lex closed her eyes. When she spoke again, it was in a small voice.

"I've tried so hard to be good."

Uncle Mort walked up next to her and rested his arms on the railing so that his shoulder touched hers.

"You are good, kiddo."

Neither said anything for the next few minutes. They stared straight ahead, watching the carefree skiers, their breath puffing and fading into the cold night.

"I'm sorry for blowing up in there," Lex muttered. "I just feel so stupidly helpless."

"I know," he said. "It's hard to sit by and watch others fight your battles for you. But Zara has nothing to lose. You have everything. Do you really want to make that gamble?"

She looked up at the stars. "No."

Another silence.

"But she killed my sister, Uncle Mort. Sooner or later I'm *going* to fight her. I won't be able to help it. You know that."

"I do. All I'm saying is, wait until you have the advantage. Back there in DeMyse, trapped in a hotel room full of your friends—wrong time, wrong place, wrong everything." He sighed. "Part of being a good strategist is knowing when you're licked. Believe me, I'd have loved to swoop in and save every one of those DeMysians. But my number one priority is the safety of you kids, and that meant getting you all out of the city, even as it burned. So that's what I did. And I'd do it again. And again. Every time."

Lex swallowed over the lump in her throat. "I guess I should say thank you."

"Don't strain yourself. Go back in there and calm everyone down, and we'll call it even."

Lex gave him a small smile and headed back inside. The Juniors watched her. "Sorry, guys," she said. "Just my daily freakout. Don't mind me."

"It's okay, Lex," Elysia said with a weary smile. "We'll be sleeping in the same room where my parents spent their first nights as newlyweds. I'm right there in Crazytown with you."

Ferbus got up and headed toward the kitchen. "I'm starving," he said. "Anyone have any food?"

The Juniors dug around in their bags and shook their heads. All but Pip, who frowned, took out the sack that Riqo had tossed him, and opened it.

"I do." He looked up with a sad little smile. "Blueberries."

||||||

No one slept well that night. Partly because they were still shaken up and worried about Broomie and Riqo, partly because Elysia kept complaining about the "yuck factor," but mostly because the couple who'd originally booked the suite wouldn't stop banging on the door. They were soon joined by the hotel staff, none of whom could break in, not even with the master keys. Then again, it's fairly difficult, even with a key, to open a door that's been blocked by a wardrobe.

"You guys ready to go?" Uncle Mort said the next morning over a breakfast of coffee, a few leftover blueberries, and a packet of peanuts split seven ways.

"Yeah," Driggs said dryly. "I think we've had enough of the high life."

They stood in a circle and took out their scythes. "Who's next?" Bang signed.

"I'll go," Ferbus said, grinning.

Uncle Mort raised an eyebrow. "Okay," he said warily. "You're not thinking of a casino, are you?"

"Nope!"

"Or a strip club?"

"Not . . . anymore."

"You know what? Just empty your brain completely. Shouldn't take long." Uncle Mort looked around the circle. "Remember, guys — simultaneously. When I say go, turn on your Cuffs and leave them on; we'll be doing these jumps in quick succession, and we won't have time to switch them on and off. I'm guessing Zara will be caught off-guard by this first Crash, but after that, she'll know we're on the move, so be ready for her. Got it?"

They nodded nervously.

"Cuffs on. Ferbus, whatever pops into your head. Scythe!"

〰〰〰

They landed in a field with a light dusting of snow.

"Middle of nowhere?" Elysia said, looking around. "Interesting choice."

"No *waaaay!*" Thrilled, Ferbus broke from the group and started running toward a series of objects on the horizon.

Driggs snickered. "This should be fun."

As they got closer to Ferbus's shouts of glee, the forms that had made no sense at a distance began to take shape into something that made even less sense: stacks of old automobiles, seemingly dropped from space but arranged in an undeniable pattern.

"Carhenge!" Ferbus jubilantly danced through the pillars, taking it all in. "Man, you hear about it, you dream about the day you might get to see it, but it's even better than I imagined!"

Elysia blinked. "What is Carhenge?"

"Don't you get it?" said Ferbus, the grin still on his face. "It's like Stonehenge." He pointed. "But with cars."

The Juniors stared at him. Bang coughed.

"Well," said Uncle Mort after a moment, "as riveting as" — he consulted his atlas — "rural Nebraska is, it's probably best that we keep moving."

Ferbus's face fell. "But the gift shop."

Uncle Mort rubbed his temples. "Tell you what, next time we're being chased by a murderous criminal, I'll try to schedule in a little more time for sightseeing." He formed the Juniors back into a circle. "Let's not assign a designated driver this time. We'll scythe, and whoever thinks of something first, somewhere farther east — that's where we'll go. Ready?"

||||||

This time around they were greeted by the stoic faces of George Washington, Thomas Jefferson, Theodore Roosevelt, and Abraham Lincoln, all wearing caps of snow. "Ooh, Mount Rushmore," Ferbus said bitterly. "Because dead presidents are *so* much more fascinating than the subtle, delicate art of automotive sculpture."

"East!" Uncle Mort said, exasperated. "Not north!"

"Uh, guys?" Pip said, pulling on Uncle Mort's sleeve. "People are looking at us."

Looking and yelling. The gang had scythed into the middle of a crowded observation platform and, having materialized out of nowhere, were now the ones being observed. One mother grabbed her children and held them tight. Another kid burst into tears. A security guard muttered something into his radio, then started toward them.

"Um — " Uncle Mort stuttered. "Run."

The Juniors obeyed, sprinting for the exit. "Away from the crowds, so they don't see us leave!" Uncle Mort yelled as they ran. "Whose bright idea was this?"

"Mine!" Lex shouted back. "I wanted to see if anything was wrong with Mount Rushmore!"

Uncle Mort stopped so fast that all the other Juniors ran past him, but he grabbed Lex before she could get very far. "Why would anything be wrong with it?"

"Edgar said that the one in the Afterlife is being sucked into a vortex or something."

Lex couldn't be sure, but she thought she saw her uncle flinch.

But they had no time to stand around and discuss it any further; the security guard had almost caught up with them. "No more public places, even if you're familiar with them!" Uncle Mort shouted at the Juniors up ahead. "And no — "

Zara materialized in front of them, her face twisted in fury. She reached out for Bang, missing by inches.

"SCYTHE!" Uncle Mort yelled.

|||||||

The world went quiet.

They'd landed in the middle of a narrow forest road. The other locations they'd scythed to that day had gotten just a little bit of snow, but this place was drowning in nearly three feet of it. The flakes still fell, blanketing the trees in a soft fuzz, screaming the kind of muted silence that only a blizzard can produce.

"Now where are we?" Lex asked.

Uncle Mort let out a long, irritated breath. "Beats me. Somewhere even farther north. We could be in Canada, for all I know. What part of 'east' don't you kids you understand?"

"Give us a break, Mort," said Ferbus. "We're new at this."

"I don't even want to know who thought up this one," Uncle Mort replied. "Let's just get out of here."

Lex nodded and looked around at the big white lumps that were her companions. She counted six, including herself.

"Wait." A sliver of ice ran down her back. "Where's Driggs?"

The others looked around.

"Driggs," she called out, her voice becoming higher and more panicked. "Driggs!"

The whiteness turned into a blur as she waded and dug through the snow, her hands freezing. Zara got him, she knew it. And she'd hold him hostage this time, especially now that she knew what he could do. She'd torture him, turn Lex into her slave, and then Damn him as soon as he had served his purpose as leverage.

Lex's eyes melted into a mess of tears, both from the stinging cold and the unthinkable possibilities running through her mind. Her throat was raw from yelling, her voice becoming raspier and more desperate. *"Driggs!"*

And then she saw a hand.

The hand was connected to an arm. And the arm was connected to the rest of him, sitting in the ditch next to the road and silently waving.

Relief turned to anger. Very quickly. "Are you *kidding* me?" she exploded, stumbling toward him. "Why didn't you answer? Was that supposed to be *funny?* I thought you were —"

"Sorry," he said, holding up something white and furry. "I landed on a rabbit."

Well, that cinched it. A wet-haired Driggs sitting in a snowdrift and petting a bunny was officially the most adorable thing Lex had ever seen.

She grabbed his head and gave him a kiss, then smacked

him, causing the bunny to hop off. "Don't you *ever* do that again."

"Hey, lovebirds!" They heard a panicked Uncle Mort yell. They glanced back just in time to see him and the other Juniors running toward them, away from the snowdrift that had just cushioned Zara's fall. "Care to join us?"

|||||||

They skidded onto a polished floor, their shoes leaving streak marks of snow and slush.

"Where —" Ferbus started before realizing how loud his voice sounded bouncing around the stark, thankfully empty room. He blinked in disbelief at the dozens of priceless works of art adorning the walls. "Holy Picasso, Batman."

"I thought I said no more public places, no matter how familiar they are, even if they're closed for the holiday," Uncle Mort said, glaring at Pip and Bang. "You guys are *terrible* at this."

But their faces were glowing. "The Art Institute of Chicago!" Pip said. Bang signed something to him. Grinning, he faced the group. "We used to come here every few months for school field trips. We both thought of the same place!"

"Art *and* junk cars," said Elysia, shooting Ferbus a sarcastic look. "What a cultured group we are."

"At least it's warm and indoors," said Pip.

"And oh so easy to find," a voice dripped from the next room. Zara stepped into the doorway and lunged at Pip, trying to Damn him but only succeeding in grabbing his scythe out of his hands.

An alarm went off somewhere. *"Run!"* Uncle Mort yelled. He

and the Juniors took off down the dark, screeching hall. "Bang, grab Pip's hand and Crash through with him!"

But Bang ignored him, opting instead to break off from the group and take a sharp right turn into another gallery. Lex glanced in terror at Driggs, then back at Zara, whose face was crazed as she tore through the hallways, gaining on them —

Until, suddenly, she was in the air.

A lanky leg had poked out from one of the side galleries, tripping Zara and sending her flying. Both Zara's and Pip's scythes soared through the hallway in a wide arc and landed in the nimble hands of Bang, who tossed Pip his and joined the group again.

Pip grinned up at Uncle Mort. "Good thing we scythed to such a familiar place, huh, Mort?"

"Don't even start with me, kid." Uncle Mort grabbed Zara's scythe out of Bang's hand and took one glance back at Zara, who was struggling to her feet, her frustrated howls mixing with those of the screeching alarm. "I'm picking the place this time, guys. Go."

||||||

All seven of them landed in a cramped, dingy restroom. Lex recognized it as belonging to that truck stop somewhere in Ohio where Uncle Mort had bought her the plastic pirate lighter.

"See?" said Uncle Mort. "Nonpublic places. Nonpublic." He tried to sound mad, but they could tell he was relieved.

"But Zara can't follow us anymore — we have her scythe!" said Elysia. "She's stuck in Chicago!"

"True, but that doesn't mean we're in the clear yet. We've still got Norwood to deal with." He tucked the glass scythe into his bag and checked his atlas. "We should be close enough now to get back to Croak. Scythe to the population sign just outside the town limits so we won't show up on the grid. I think we can visualize that well enough without being linked together, so go ahead and turn your Cuffs off. That way our location can't be tracked when we get there." He paused to catch his breath. "Still, be prepared for anything. I don't know what kinds of patrols Norwood has set up. Just go with the flow and everything will turn out okay."

"And if it doesn't?" Lex asked.

He shot her a look. "Then we'll throw a hell of a party in the Afterlife."

The road to Croak was deserted.

After a thorough check of the surroundings Uncle Mort deemed it an acceptable place for them to hide out until night-fall, when they'd attempt to sneak in and meet up with Pandora. So the Juniors hiked into the woods and settled in for the long wait, hugging each other for warmth.

"I'm going to take a leak," Uncle Mort said. "Don't move from this spot."

He turned back to them. "And maybe grab a nap while you can. If all goes according to plan, we'll be spending the night at Pandora's, but . . ." He gave a tired shrug. "You never know."

||||||

Sometime later Lex awoke, baffled that she'd been able to fall asleep in the first place, as cold as she was. She must have been more tired than she thought. Living in constant fear was exhaust-ing.

The last thing she remembered was snuggling up next to Driggs in a large, hollow stump that had formed a sort of love seat, her hands in his pockets, as if they were a typical pair of teenagers on a romantic trek in the woods, with all the time in the world to be young and smitten. She couldn't quite remember what they'd been talking about — the jumps around the country, maybe? Something about his parents? Either way, she'd started to fall asleep midsentence and Driggs had left her alone to rest.

The thermoregulated hoodie had kept her warm for the most part, although her nose and ears had grown numb. A piece of bark was poking into her back, but she didn't sit up just yet. She kept her eyes closed and strained to hear Uncle Mort, who was talking in a hushed tone.

" — don't know. The girl continues to defy all laws of what's supposed to be possible. Just when I think I have her figured out, she goes and changes the rules again."

"But why?" That was Driggs. "Why is she able to do these things?"

There was a pause. "Because she's special."

Something tingled down Lex's spine.

"Because of the bloodline thing? Because she's your niece?"

". . . Sure."

"That's not really an answer."

"No, I suppose not."

Neither spoke for a moment.

"Is that why she can Damn?" Driggs eventually asked.

"That's a good question."

"Well, what about me? I'm no one's nephew, how come I can unDamn?"

Lex opened her eyes, just a slit. Enough to see Uncle Mort leaning forward, a spark in his eye.

"That's an even better question."

Leaving it at that, he got up and walked away.

Still keeping her eyes slightly open, Lex shifted her view. Bang and Pip had fallen asleep propped up against a tree, their heads drooping together. But Ferbus and Elysia were wide awake and hugging each other for warmth.

Elysia looked upset. "What if they're really hurt?" she said. "I mean, you saw Riqo . . . all that blood . . ."

"They're fine," Ferbus said, squeezing her closer. "Look, if anything, we should be worrying about ourselves. What's Broomie going to say when she finds out we got to spend all day in the freezing cold Adirondacks? Her jealous rage will be terrible to behold."

Elysia giggled. She sniffed and nervously fiddled with her earring. "I just feel like such a terrible friend."

"Lys, if one were to look up the word 'friend' in the dictionary, I'm pretty sure there'd be a giant pop-out, confetti-spewing, musical illustration of you."

Another small smile. Elysia looked up at him. "Why are you being so nice to me all of a sudden?"

Ferbus just smiled back, then brushed a piece of hair out of her face and whispered something in her ear. A look of surprise spread across her face. She sat up and looked at Ferbus straight-on. They both swallowed at the same time, then began to move their heads in at an awkward angle.

But that was as far as they got. A loud crack sounded somewhere within the woods, the sound of a branch snapping. Everyone, including Lex, jumped to their feet, back on high alert. Uncle Mort scanned the trees, waiting for another noise, but the forest remained silent.

Elysia heaved a nervous sigh. "I don't know how long I can keep doing this."

"I wish we could start a fire," Pip said. "I'm freezing."

"And I'm still starving," said Ferbus. "Isn't there anything we can eat out here? Pinecones? Frozen berries?"

Lex watched as he dug his shoe into the ground, kicking up some dead leaves —

Her brain short-circuited.

All this time she'd been looking for the neutralizer in the Afterlife. But she'd been wrong.

"What's the matter?" Elysia asked her.

"That's it," she whispered, digging into her pocket for her scythe.

"That's what?"

"The neutral — "

Lex's answer was drowned out by a loud battle cry. A mob of people exploded from the woods, Norwood and Heloise at the forefront. Lex watched in horror as her friends went down one by one, knocked out by the butts of the Seniors' scythes like some terrible, nightmarish version of Whac-a-Mole. Meanwhile, Uncle Mort had seized Norwood and was trying, from the looks of it, to physically rip his head off.

Lex backed up against the big hollow stump, staring at an unconscious Pip, hating herself beyond measure for the decision she was about to make.

"Lex!" Driggs turned to grab her, but he found himself staring at nothing.

She'd disappeared.

||||||

The force of Lex's landing spun her like a top. Even when she stopped, the room kept going, spiraling across her vision. A loud voice only added to the confusion.

"Ho-ly shiiiit."

She shook her head until the walls of the office on the second floor of the Bank came into focus. Unfortunately, that didn't leave much time for dealing peacefully with Snodgrass, who'd jumped out from behind his desk and was carefully creeping toward her, as if one wrong move would cause her to shatter.

"Unreal," he was saying, his eyes huge. "All this time we've been looking for you, and here you are, dropped right into my lap." He grinned. "If this doesn't net me serious Brownie points with the mayor, nothing will."

"Stay back, Snodgrass," Lex said, almost growling. She was *not* in the mood. She hadn't traveled clear across the country, deserted her friends, and taken a gigantic risk based on a mere hunch just to have it all screwed up by this asshat.

"Give me the scythe, kid." He got closer. "Come on, don't make this any harder than it has to be," he said, grabbing her arm.

"Let me go!" She tried to break free, but Snodgrass was stronger than he looked. She struggled harder, slashing his leg with her scythe.

"You little bitch!" He snatched the scythe out of her hand and restrained her from behind, his hot breath on her neck. "No wonder you're such a hot commodity. You've got quite a bit of fight in you, huh?" He put his mouth close to her ear. "I like that."

Lex fought back a wave of nausea. "Don't."

He turned her around to face him. "Relax, kid."

"Get off me!"

With adrenaline-fueled strength, she pushed him away as

hard as she could. He fell backwards and hit the desk, his head smashing into the corner with a sickening crunch.

He slid to the floor. Lex didn't know if he was alive or dead.

But she didn't have time to find out. She took her scythe from his limp hand, hastily turned around to grab a handful of what she'd come for, and scythed out of the room, shaking the whole time.

||||||

Lex took a few calming breaths with her head between her legs, staring at the sticks beneath her feet. Her arms felt bruised from where Snodgrass had clutched them, and her heart stuck in her throat when she recalled how she'd abandoned her friends, abandoned Driggs . . .

But she forced herself to focus. The Seniors weren't killing the Juniors, just knocking them out. They'd be okay.

In theory.

She straightened up. The Sticks River looked the same as it had a few months before, but snowier. She'd landed right in the middle of the bridge. The sticks crackled beneath her feet as she made her way down the side that led to the woods.

The sky was clouded over and gray; that plus all the ether-surfing and time zone differences made it impossible to tell what time it was. She proceeded just as Driggs had when he'd brought her here, through the small opening and down the darkened, narrow path, watching the left side until she spotted it: a small break in the trees.

She opened her hand and stared at the few leaves of *Ficus com-*

pos mentis that she'd plucked from the small potted plant in the office, a plant she'd looked at a billion times and never given a second thought. She *knew* she'd seen it somewhere before when Riqo had showed her the picture in his gardening book. It had been there the whole time, just waiting for someone to figure it out.

Thankfully, that someone hadn't been Zara.

Lex stuffed a couple of leaves into her mouth and began chewing. They tasted . . . well, leafy. A slight tingle sizzled through her tongue and stung her throat. She waited, but nothing changed. She thought maybe her vision had become a little bit sharper, but she could have been imagining that.

No point in turning back now. She brushed aside the branch and stepped onto the path, all the while bracing herself for the excruciating pain . . .

But it never came.

She passed a fallen log that she had seen her first time down this path, remembering that by the time she had gotten to it, she'd been ready to vomit. This time she grinned, and even started walking faster, with a bit of a spring in her step. The forest smelled wonderful, the air so crisp and light.

Driggs had said that after the physical pain came mental pain, but Lex felt nothing. At this point she must have gotten farther than Uncle Mort ever had. It was then that she knew, beyond a doubt, that she was really doing it. She had succeeded where everyone else had failed. One more turn in the path —

And there it was. The cabin.

A shower of goosebumps rippled across her skin. Trembling, she took two more steps toward the structure and stopped.

She'd been expecting something along the lines of a large, dilapidated log cabin, but she couldn't have been more off. It was small — a single room, no more than ten by ten feet, only about eight feet high, with a sloping roof. The walls were white — not the gleaming, pure white of new-fallen snow, but rather the dirty, speckled mess of week-old snowdrifts — and made of an odd, vaguely familiar material. But not even the walls could distract Lex from the strangest thing of all: the cabin had no door.

Keeping her distance, she circled the cabin, but she still couldn't find a door. What was the point of having a house with no way to get in?

She had to move closer. Coming back around to the side facing the path, she edged up to the cabin — then jumped back, a shriek catching in her throat.

The walls were made of bone.

Petrified bone, but bone all the same, its unmistakable curves, shapes, and textures all fused together into a solid structure. The darker areas that Lex had earlier mistaken for smudges of dirt were in fact small gaps where the pieces didn't quite fit together or had broken off.

Lex wiped her sweaty hands on her hoodie and swallowed. Maybe she should leave. This was beyond creepy. She thought for a moment, listening to the eerie silence of the trees, sniffing at the woody smell, watching the vapor from her breath puff out into the air and sink to the ground.

She frowned. That was odd.

She blew out another cloud of vapor, and again it went down, not up, seeping into the bottom left corner of the cabin. Crouching down, Lex moved her fingers along a flat opening that seemed larger than the others, about three inches long. Its edges weren't raw and jagged like the rest of the gaps, but smooth. Shaped, even, as if it were built specifically to accommodate . . . a key.

Her heart racing, Lex yanked the bone key out of her pocket and stuck it into the slot. She wiggled it around, pushed it in a bit harder, then finally pulled it down like a lever.

A loud click came from within the wall. Lex jumped back and watched in astonishment as a corner of the building opened up, the wall unfolding to reveal a dark hole just large enough to admit one determined, curious, terrified teenage girl.

She wriggled through on her stomach, pulling at the dirt floor. When she stood up, all she saw was darkness. She blinked a few times, her eyes adjusting to the small amounts of light coming in through the gaps in the bone. Soon she could make out a wooden table upon which sat a thick yellowed book bound in black leather.

She couldn't believe it. The Wrong Book. Just sitting there, waiting for her to pick it up.

So she did. And she was just about to crack it open when she heard the sound of a match being struck. A small lick of flame danced to life, then settled on a candle.

Lex stopped cold.

"It's you," she whispered.

"It is."

"Bone?"

"Not quite."

"Then who?"

The man in the white tuxedo began to laugh. The cackles grew exponentially louder, bouncing and echoing around the small cabin until they almost seemed to be coming from the walls themselves. He leaned forward until he was inches from Lex's nose, flashing a hellish, terrifying grin that turned every last drop of blood in her veins to ice.

"I'm Grotton."

He blew out the candle, and the room went white.

23

Lex pounded across the Sticks River bridge, the twigs crunching beneath her feet just as they had fifteen minutes before. A light snow was falling, but she barely noticed. She felt stoned. Her mind was a nuclear war zone, blasted away by a shock wave of unprecedented *What-in-holy-hell-just-happened-to-me?*

Minutes later she was standing under the Ghost Gum tree. Its branches reached into the sky, the skeletal fingers cradling the nest that had once concealed the key to the cabin — the key, Lex now realized, to the future. Because what she'd seen in that cabin —

It changed everything.

"There she is!"

As a sign of just how out of it she was, Lex did something she'd never done before: she dropped her scythe. The sound of the voice had sent her into a full panic. She whirled around. Riley and Trumbull were racing toward the tree.

She scanned the snow for her scythe, but couldn't find it; it had sunk straight through to the ground, taking her Crashing ability with it. She plunged her hands into the whiteness, desperately pawing through the freezing powder but coming up with nothing. And with the Seniors fast approaching, she was out of time.

She broke into a run. The snow made it hard to go quickly, but she trudged through as fast as she could, coughing as she struggled for air. She could hear Riley panting as she closed in, only a few feet away now. Hot tears sprang to Lex's eyes as she pumped her legs, but it was no use. A strong shove from behind and it was all over.

Lex fell hard. Her knees crashed all the way through the snow to the ground beneath, skidding across mud and grass. Riley grabbed her with a pair of gloved hands and turned her face-up. "Gotcha," she said with contempt, securing Lex's wrists with a hard plastic band.

Lex let out a cry. She couldn't help it. Staring up at their cruel faces, she didn't feel like the powerful, invincible Lex anymore. She felt like what she really was — a small, scared kid in a shitload of trouble.

"The Juniors," she stammered as they pulled her to her feet and began dragging her toward the Bank. "Are they okay?"

They ignored her. "Find her scythe," Riley told Trumbull. "Norwood'll want it for evidence. After we're done with her, we can head back up to the office for the body."

"The body?" Lex was confused for a second, then felt sick. "Snodgrass is dead?"

"Don't play dumb, kid," Riley growled, no doubt upset over the fate of her friend. "It won't help your chances."

Lex was shaking uncontrollably by the time they reached the Bank. It had been an accident, she wanted to tell them — but they'd never believe her. After all, she was a fugitive. She'd already murdered Corpp, and now she'd killed again.

She thought the Seniors would bring her into the Bank to see Norwood and Heloise, but instead they walked around to the rear and opened the locked cellar door. They escorted her down some steps into a narrow hallway. Several steel doors lined the concrete walls, doors with thin hinged slits toward the bottom, heavy padlocks on top, and no windows. A lump formed in Lex's throat as she realized what they were.

Prison cells.

Her breathing became shallower. "Since when does the Bank have a jail?"

"Since always, missy," said Trumbull, opening one of the eight-inch-thick doors. "Norwood's just the first mayor in years with enough sense to use it."

Now literally kicking and screaming, Lex clawed at the door with her tethered hands, grabbing the frame and pulling her head back into the hallway — but the Seniors were too strong, over-powering her once again.

But in that one brief moment she saw the Juniors. Guards were pushing them down through the cellar door — Ferbus and Elysia, Pip and Bang, all worse for the wear but generally okay. Then Uncle Mort, his face a bloody mess. Then — then —

Then Riley clubbed her over the head, and everything went dark.

‖‖‖‖‖

Lex lost track of time after that. The buzzing fluorescent bulb in her cell stayed on all the time, a dim, grayish light that made her sleepy. Yet sleep rarely came.

It could have been three days, it could have been ten. It could have been a month. Her head throbbed constantly. The plastic band around her wrists had been cut, but it didn't really matter; she no longer felt the need to Damn, to discharge. Every once in a while she'd pound on the concrete walls and yell at the top of her lungs, but the thick soundproof walls all but guaranteed that no one heard her. She certainly couldn't hear anyone else.

Food slid through the narrow slot in the door a couple of times a day, but even that was a joke. A slice of bread, some oatmeal, a thin soup. After a while double portions began to trickle in, but they were still meager at best. Lex tried not to think about that eighty-dollar steak, or how she should have ordered five more to hold her over.

Since there was no bed, she sat on the floor with her head on her knees, picking at the grass-stained hole in her jeans, replaying the last few months in her mind. How many mistakes had she made? She counted dozens. Especially that last part, those precious few seconds she'd spent in the cabin. All she'd had to do was grab that book and run, and things could have turned out very differently.

On the rare occasions when Lex did fall asleep, nightmares woke her right back up again. Terrible, agonizing images of her friends being tortured, of a body falling from a tall building, of Zara stabbing Riqo in the chest again and again and again.

And the bomb. For some reason, the explosion that had devastated Croak was on a loop in her brain. She saw it from different angles, in heightened detail, slow motion, sped up, zooming in on the victims as they died. Lex found this odd; the destruction of that night had been harrowing, to be sure, but Zara's invasion of DeMyse was more recent, its horrors fresher in her mind. But still she dreamed only of the fountain's blast, and even after she'd thrashed herself awake, the images wouldn't go away.

Adding to the growing dread was the knowledge that Zara had never attacked, never followed the Juniors back to Croak. They'd taken her scythe and bought some time, but by now she surely could have hopped on a bus or hitched a ride from Chicago. What was she waiting for?

One day — or night — the slot flicked open. Lex, expecting food, dragged herself to the door to silently accept the tray from whoever shoved it through. She'd given up on talking to them long ago.

But this time a pair of eyes looked back at her, covered by a familiar strand of bleached-blond hair.

"Lazlo?" she rasped, her voice hoarse from yelling.

"Prepare yourself," he whispered, pushing the tray through.

Lex shoved it aside, spilling a few gray blobs from the two bowls. "Prepare myself? For what?"

He looked her right in the eye. "The trial."

The slot snapped shut.

||||||

Lex couldn't extrapolate a single thought from her mind for the rest of the day — or night. They all jumbled together, tangling themselves into an unsolvable maze, none making sense. She slept fitfully, dreaming again about the bomb and waking with a scream. Then more hours of restless, futile contemplation, until finally the door opened.

Lazlo was standing there. He tossed a pair of gloves into the cell, presumably to keep her from Damning anyone. Once she put them on, he grabbed her elbow. "Let's go."

He led her down the hallway and up out of the cellar. The winter air felt electric on her skin. Lex's eyes reflexively shut tight; she hadn't seen sunlight in so long, and it was extra bright as it reflected off the snow. She turned her head toward the sun and let it warm her face. It was around noon, from the looks of it. Lazlo said nothing as they crunched over the snow toward the library.

"Why didn't you handcuff me?" she asked.

"Because I know you're not going to try anything," he said, tightening his grip on her arm.

He was right about that. It wasn't as if she could escape; she wouldn't get far without her scythe. And what would Damning anyone else accomplish at this point?

"I'm sorry about Snodgrass," she said.

Lazlo let out a snort. "That makes one of you."

"Huh?"

"The guy may have been my partner, but he was still a douche-bag."

He said nothing more, but the brief exchange was enough to make Lex wonder. Lazlo hated Snodgrass? Who else did he hate?

She was the last one to arrive. Norwood, Heloise, and several other Seniors sat at a table at the front of the library, with the townspeople sitting in rows facing them. Wicket and Kilda were right up front, but Pandora was nowhere to be seen. Ferbus, Elysia, Pip, and Bang stood lined up on the right side of the room, looking pale and frightened. "We're okay," Bang signed to Lex. "Could use a shower, though."

Uncle Mort stood at the front, next to the table. And to his left —

"Driggs," Lex breathed. Lazlo placed her between the two of them, then walked to the back of the room, where he stood with his arms crossed like a bouncer.

More than anything, Lex wanted to tackle Driggs to the floor and spend the next decade or so huddled in his arms. But she didn't want to give Norwood and Heloise the satisfaction of knowing how much they'd tortured her by separating them. Neither did Driggs, from the look of it. So he merely hooked his pinky in hers and glanced at her with darkened, hollow eyes.

"You're so skinny," she said quietly, her voice breaking. Everyone was thinner, but Driggs looked as if he'd literally been starved.

His voice was hoarse too. "I told them to give my food to you."

Lex nearly gagged, thinking of all those double portions. She didn't know whether to burst into tears or clock him for being such an idiot.

"Let's begin," Norwood said. "We're here today for the sentencing of—"

"Whoa, whoa, whoa," Uncle Mort said. "I thought this was a trial."

Heloise flashed her trademark nasty smile. "Oh, we already held the trial. You were found guilty." She feigned surprise. "Did no one tell you?"

A flare of heat shot down through Lex's hands. She ripped the gloves off and tried to calm herself down, to cool off. Wrong place, wrong time. Wouldn't accomplish anything.

Uncle Mort glared at Heloise. "Well played," he said quietly. "From one guilty party to another."

A strange expression clouded Norwood's face. "I beg your pardon?"

"Oh, nothing. Forget it." Uncle Mort looked straight at him. "Wouldn't want to say anything too explosive."

Lex's breath caught. What did he mean by that?

"As I was saying," Norwood boomed, his confidence return-ing, "the prisoners' guilt has been proven beyond a reasonable doubt, due to the overwhelming evidence presented by our eye-witness." He pointed at Sofi, who was staring straight at the seat in front of her, avoiding the eyes of the Juniors. "These are dan-gerous, deadly felons who have not only murdered in cold blood but also fled from the authorities, thereby endangering countless innocent lives. Their unspeakable — "

"Wrap it up, Woody," Uncle Mort interrupted again. "No point in dragging out this farce any longer than it has to be."

Norwood looked furious at having his thunder stolen, though his sneer soon morphed into a smile. "Very well," he said, stand-ing up. "I'll skip straight to the sentence."

The room went absolutely still. Norwood looked each one of the Juniors in the eye, then Uncle Mort, then finally Lex as he opened his mouth to speak.

"Life in the Hole. For all of you."

Pandemonium.

The crowd jumped to their feet, cheering — except for Wicket and Kilda, who were doing their best to fake it, and Sofi, who stayed in her seat, staring at the ground. The mayor and his wife sat down and leaned back in their chairs, taking it all in with un-abashed delight. Uncle Mort's smile was gone, his eyes darting frantically around the room. The Juniors on the other side looked utterly lost, too shocked to even cry. Driggs was staring down at the floor, breathing heavily.

Lex threw up. Vomited right onto a nearby pile of books. *She* was the one responsible for giving Zara her power, for Corpp's death, for the Juniors having to flee Croak, for everything. And now her friends were going to rot deep within the earth for the rest of their lives, all because of her.

She couldn't even hear the shouts of the crowd over the frantic, terrified beating of her own heart. She couldn't feel her body anymore; she'd gone numb. And she couldn't see straight — the room was spinning, the lights transforming into a kaleidoscope of color, Lazlo a blur as he grabbed the four Juniors from the other side of the room, shoved them toward the door, and pushed them out onto the street . . .

It took a minute for Lex to realize what he was doing.

"Run!" Lazlo shouted at them. "Go, now!"

She stumbled to a window and watched the Juniors trip over themselves, trying to figure out what was happening. As Lazlo's words sank in, they took one anguished look back at the library, directly at Lex. She put her hand on the glass, locked eyes with Ferbus, and pointed to the Bank. He gave her a solemn, grateful nod, then grabbed the others and led them to the secret opening underneath the porch. Seconds later, they were gone.

The window disintegrated under Lex's hand. Uncle Mort had thrown a chair through the glass and was now clambering out onto the sidewalk, reaching for her and Driggs. "Come on!"

Lex stretched her hands toward him, but before they could make contact, a hairy pair of arms grabbed her around the waist. Trumbull.

"Take them back to their cells!" Heloise shouted, furious.

Trumbull and another Senior shoved Lex and Driggs out the door, stomping on Lazlo's crumpled form as they left. "Thank you," Lex whispered to the heap, but got no reply.

Uncle Mort had vanished. Driggs never let go of Lex's hand as they were escorted back to the cellar; they'd been gone for no more than ten minutes. They were still glued together when they reached his cell. The Seniors tried to separate them, but Lex clutched his hand even tighter, as if it were the last time she'd ever hold it. For all she knew, it was.

They kissed, even as the Seniors kept pulling them apart — a messy, hurried, violent kiss, their teeth knocking against their lips and causing them to split and bleed. It's not how Lex would have wanted it to end, but when was the last time anything had worked out the way she had wanted it to?

With one final tug the Seniors tore them apart, Lex's fingers still grasping at the empty space where Driggs's had been. The next thing she saw was her cell and its buzzing fluorescent light, followed by the door slamming shut behind her.

All at once, the fury came. The heat sparked deep within her chest, then rippled down her arms and into her hands. The only thing in the room was the tray that her breakfast had come on, but it was enough. Letting out an unearthly cry, she slammed her hands down on top of it, setting it on fire.

And that's when the light went out.

||||||

More days passed, this time in total darkness. Even less food came. Lex felt like a tiny, insignificant speck floating through the deepest voids of outer space. A few days after that, she felt like something even smaller — a mere particle, a lonely electron.

A few days after that, she felt like she no longer existed at all.

||||||

Until the night the door opened.

Lex squinted into the light from the hallway. "Come on," a female voice said.

Lex got to her feet and approached the door. "Heloise?"

"Not even close."

With an angry snarl, Zara yanked her out of the cell.

24

"Don't struggle," Zara said, pulling Lex down the hallway. She was dressed in dark clothes and carried a bag on her shoulder. "We can't Damn each other, but don't try anything else either. Trust me when I say that it would be very bad, and not just for you."

Lex's hands started to shake. For who?

She glanced at the door to Driggs's cell; the lights had been turned off in his, too. She thought about shouting, but he'd already suffered enough on her account — starved himself, even. Why freak him out even more?

Zara dragged Lex over the unconscious guards and outside into a heavy snow. Thick, fluffy flakes fell from the night sky, making it difficult to see through the white haze. When they reached the front of the Bank, Lex stopped and gaped.

The town was empty. No lights, no people. Only the falling snow.

"Where is everyone?" she asked.

"I rented out the town for the evening," Zara answered, her face looking even paler in the white reflections. "Struck up a nice deal with Norwood and Heloise."

For a split second Lex had a terrible thought. "They've been working for you this whole time?"

Zara let out a laugh. "Give me a little more credit than that,

Lex. I'd have to lose my mind to ever want to associate with those clowns." She yanked on Lex's wrist again. "Come on."

"Where are we going?"

"To the Bank," Zara said, narrowing her bloodshot eyes. "We're gonna work a shift, you and I."

||||||

The Bank was deserted too, and dark. Lex was stunned. This meant that Croak was completely offline, with no working Etceteras, no one guarding the Afterlife, no one out in the Field. Even Kilda was gone.

Only one light was on, in the hub, and it belonged to Sofi.

"Hi, Lex!" she said in a chipper voice. "Checking in?"

The sudden comprehension stabbed Lex like a rusty needle. Who better to disable the security systems for Zara than her tech-savvy former partner? "You *bitch!*" Lex yelled. "How could you do this to all of us? You're a Junior, too!"

"Puh-leeze, Lex. You guys always hated me, especially you."

"We didn't hate you! We hated that you sided with Norwood!"

"I never sided with Norwood. I told you, he's a total jerkface." Sofi typed something on the keyboard, then flipped over one of her snow globes and watched as the flakes drifted through the water. "I sided with Zara. And why not? She's the only one who ever cared about me."

"She doesn't care about you! She's *using* you! You think you'd be worth anything to her if you couldn't get her past the security systems?"

"Quiet," said Zara, giving Lex a dirty look. She handed Sofi her glass scythe along with Lex's own obsidian scythe.

Lex stared. "Where did you get those?"

"I raided Norwood's treasure-trove of confiscated items. Got all your buddies' scythes too." She patted the bag — Uncle Mort's bag, Lex now realized. "Check us in, Sofi."

Sofi dutifully inserted the scythes into the Smack and began tapping at the keyboard. Lex gave her a pleading look. "Don't do this, Sofi. Help *me,* not her."

"Why should I?" Sofi inspected her cotton candy–colored nails. "You're just going to go running back to your dreamy little boo anyway."

"Jesus, Sofi, is this about Driggs? You've got to be kidding me!"

"You *knew* I liked him."

"Oh my Lord — "

"But no, it's not just about Driggs. It's about survival. I help Zara, I stay safe."

"You seriously believe that? Sofi, Zara is a *liar.* She made the same promises to the mayor of DeMyse, and he and everyone in his city are probably Damned by now!"

"Because *he* broke her rules. I won't do that."

Zara removed the scythes from the Smack and pulled on Lex's arm. "Let's go."

Lex took one last look at Sofi, who gave her another little wave. "Traitor," Lex muttered.

Zara steered her into the Field, boldly plunging through the whiteness as if she owned the place. Which, technically, she did.

Yet as they reached the Ghost Gum, two blurry figures jumped out from behind the tree, scythes drawn. "Whatever you're planning to do, stop!"

Lex's jaw dropped. Norwood and Heloise were trying to save her?

Zara looked at them irritably. "I thought I already dealt with you two."

"Give Lex back," Heloise said to Zara, keeping her distance but clearly willing to throw her scythe if Zara tried anything. She was bundled up in a fur coat, the snow quivering on her hat. Lex felt a surge of gratitude, one that faded as soon as Heloise added, "She's ours. We'll lose our sway with the people if we let her slip through our fingers now. We'll look like fools!"

"You *are* fools," said Zara.

"Please, she's the only one we have left — "

"Sorry," Zara said. "We made a deal. You gave me the town, I gave you the evidence against her. I never said you could have her back."

"Evidence?" Lex asked, a funny feeling in her stomach.

"Oh, come on, Lex," Zara said with a wry smile. "It was masterfully done, might as well own up to it. Even if you *did* steal some of my thunder. I mean, your work with that teacher who blew her students' brains out — just beautiful."

Lex's gaze darted from Zara to Norwood, then Heloise, then back to Norwood, who let out a short, biting laugh and removed something from his coat.

Lex nearly passed out.

He had her Lifeglass. Her memories.

He held it up, images of charred bodies swirling to its surface. The schoolteacher's determined face as she was arrested, followed by her Damned corpse on the floor of her prison cell. "You've been doing it for months, haven't you?" he said to Lex with a triumphant grin. "Damning those criminals all over the country, hiding behind Zara's shadow so no one would suspect you?"

Lex swallowed. "That's not —"

"I suspected it all along," he continued, relishing every moment. He tapped the glass again and two new figures floated by, along with a dog cage and a small boy. "I'm not stupid, Lex. Two kidnappers Damned in Chicago the same week Mort's got you picking up those rookie brats? In Chicago?" He rolled his eyes. "Doesn't take a genius."

Lex couldn't reply. She'd been so careful, too — going off on her own, quickly Crashing to criminals and Damning them, then Crashing back and setting some object on fire with her plastic lighter as false evidence before anyone could tell what she was doing.

"Why didn't you rat me out?" she finally managed in a hollow voice.

"Couldn't prove anything." He tapped the Lifeglass. "Until now."

She looked at Zara. "And you?"

Zara shrugged. "You couldn't very well get me what I needed if you were in the Hole."

"The Hole," Norwood butted in, "is more than either of you deserves. I swear, when the president hears about this —"

"Shut up," Zara snapped at him, her eyes flashing. "Don't you dare get all high and mighty, Norwood. You of all people know what it takes to advance in the world, to seize power. To give your people the illusion of safety and gain their trust, all while turning them into frightened sheep who'll do whatever you tell them to."

A smile crept onto her lips. "I have to give you bonus points for that little feat, at least. Though I'm somewhat insulted that everyone so readily believed that *I* would resort to something as crude and mundane as pyrotechnics."

It hit Lex all at once. The dreams, the lack of a security breach alarm that night, Uncle Mort's cryptic comment at the trial . . .

"You did it," Lex said, gaping at Norwood and Heloise. "You set off the bomb and made everyone think Uncle Mort's security had failed. You killed your own citizens just to incite a mutiny!"

Norwood narrowed his eyes. "We sure did," he whispered, his lip curling. "And it worked like a goddamn charm."

Lex's hands surged with heat. "You're murderers, too," she said. "You're no better than Zara!"

"And no worse than you," Norwood countered. "I should probably be thanking you, Lex. That trial was pure theater, a rousing success." He smiled. "Those people *hate* you. Imagine what they'll think once they see this!" He held up the Lifeglass.

Lex was breathless. "At least I go after the sort of people who deserve to be Damned! Zara killed *children!* And *you* slaughtered your own citizens in cold blood!"

"We did what had to be done!" Heloise burst in. "That buffoon uncle of yours was running this town into the ground. Thinking he could bring an abomination like *you* here — I mean, really! The man was a danger to our society, and those people just needed a good solid push in the right direction. We merely gave it to them."

"At the expense of innocent people's lives!"

"Collateral damage," Heloise said with a distasteful sniff. "We regret the loss."

Lex could barely see straight. "I'll expose you," she said. "I'll tell the town what you did, and *you'll* rot away in the Hole for the rest of your lives too!"

Norwood snickered. "Good luck with that. You don't have a shred of proof."

Lex opened her mouth to protest, but no words came. He was right.

"Besides, you should count yourself lucky," he went on. "If we'd stuck to my original plan and just thrown the damn bomb into the Crypt, this Junior problem would have been over and done with long ago." He sighed. "Still, progress was made. That's all that matters."

"*Progress?*" Lex yelled. "You killed Roze, and Kloo, and practically Ayjay — "

"Exactly." Heloise brushed her hands together and gave her husband a nasty smile. "Rebels, every one of them, gone and out of the way."

Norwood grinned right back at her. "Good riddance, right?"

Lex couldn't take it anymore. Her hands were on fire.

That little voice whispered in her head: *Do it.*

And this time she listened.

She sprang at the couple with outstretched, scalding hands. Her left smacked Heloise across the face while her right landed in Norwood's palm, both making contact — and Damning — at the same time.

Shadows from the resulting fire shot up the Ghost Gum's branches, blooming like a mushroom cloud. Norwood dropped the Lifeglass, staggered a few feet back, and fell deep into the snow, no longer visible in the blinding blizzard. Heloise, on the other hand, dropped right where she stood, her body erupting in flames, her tortured cries rising into an inhuman wail.

Lex didn't watch. Instead, she looked up. The heat was melting the snow on the branches; drops of cold water fell on her face, pinpricks stinging her skin like embers. She'd felt good after Damnings before, but they were nothing compared with this.

Zara spoke up once the wails had died out. "Well done," she said simply, as if complimenting Lex on a hard-won chess match. "Come on, we have a shift to do." She held out Lex's scythe.

Lex didn't take it. "I'm not going anywhere."

Zara snickered. "Classic Lex, always in need of a little persuasion." She took the bag from her shoulder and opened it. "Your friends' scythes weren't the only things I found."

Lex's mouth went totally dry as she looked inside, every emotion disappearing from her brain but fear.

Seven Sparks.

Six flickering.

One blazing white.

Zara held out Lex's scythe. "Just one target. Let's go. Or I'll make them all shine, every last one of them."

Lex numbly took her scythe from Zara's skeletal hand. "Who?" she demanded, the bottom dropping out of her stomach. "*Who?*"

|||||||

They scythed simultaneously and landed at Greycliff, the big boulder overlooking Croak. Frozen in time, the suspended snow hung around them like icy, twinkling stars. The silence of the world was absolute.

Zara promptly grabbed Lex's scythe out of her hand and put it in her own pocket. "Not going to make that little mistake again."

Lex barely noticed. She'd scythed into the ether without thinking. Her entire being was in a state of full-blown panic, her mind swimming with the possibilities of who the target could be—

Then she spotted the body.

It was covered by a few inches of snow. He must have been out there for hours, shivering in the cold, curling himself up into a ball for warmth. Hands and feet bound, hood pulled over his head, Chuck Taylors dirty and soaked through. Face white. Lips blue.

No breath.

No pulse.

No life.

|||||||

"That empty, snowy road with the bunny—that was yours, wasn't it?" Lex had asked Driggs as they nestled in the hollow tree stump the day they'd scythed across the country and back to Croak. "Why did you pick that place?"

"I didn't. Not really." He rubbed her fingers, both of their hands stuffed into his pocket. "I just pictured a place that was calm and quiet. Where nothing could hurt us. Just like the woods I used to run away to when I was little, when my dad got mad. Far away from danger, from Zara, from adults who should be mature

and reasonable but instead want to kill us, from all of" — he
kicked at his scythe — "this."

Lex smiled and looked up at him. "It was beautiful."

He smiled back and kissed the top of her head. "It was for
you."

|||||||

Lex stopped. That was the only word for it. Her whole body,
every thought running through her head, everything that made
up the quivering mess of a human that was Lexington Bartleby — all of it came to a screeching halt. Likewise, the stalled
snow hung in the air, watching her, the world fixed in a reverent
silence.

Somehow her body lurched forward, but Zara stopped her.
"Don't move," Zara said, positioning her fingers above Driggs's
head.

Lex didn't move.

"He's dead," said Zara. "But he hasn't been Killed yet. His soul
is still in there. Which means — "

"He can still be Damned," Lex finished.

"Bingo." Zara's hand still hovered steadily above his body.
"This can go one of two ways, Lex. You answer my questions honestly, do what I say, and I'll let you Kill him. I'll Cull him, he'll go
to the Afterlife, and you can see each other again. Refuse, and I
Damn him. Sound fair?"

Fair had been left in the dust long ago. But Lex gave a shaky
nod.

"Do you have the key?" Zara asked. "The real key?"

"Yes."

"Give it to me. No — " she said when Lex took a step forward. "Toss it."

Lex did. Zara caught the shard of bone with one hand and shoved it into her pocket.

"What does it open?" she asked next.

"A cabin. In the woods, past the Sticks River."

Zara nodded. She knew that part was true. "How do you get past the shield?"

"There's a plant — you eat it, you can walk right through. It's on the second floor of the Bank."

Zara let out a small puff of a laugh, as if she thought this was clever.

"Is the Wrong Book in that cabin?"

"Yes."

"Have you been in there? You've seen it?"

"Yes."

"Did you take the book?"

"No."

Zara narrowed her eyes and brought her hand closer to Driggs. "I said be honest, Lex."

Lex hesitated. A drop of cold sweat ran down her back.

"One more chance. Do you have the Wrong Book?"

"Yes," Lex lied.

"Give it to me."

"I don't have it. Not on me."

Zara inched her hand closer to Driggs.

"I'll get it for you!" Lex shouted, desperate.

Zara stopped.

Lex took a deep breath and tried to speak evenly. "It's hidden in the woods. Let me Kill him, and I'll take you to it."

Zara considered this for a moment, then slowly stood up and kicked at Driggs's body as if it were roadkill. "Do it. And then straight to the Book, or I'll Damn them all."

Lex dropped to her knees and pushed Driggs's hood back. His hair was half wet, half frozen. His face was so, so pale, like a marble statue. His eyelids were closed, snowflakes accumulating in the lashes, cloaking the one brown eye and one blue eye that had made him her own special, amazing weirdo.

She began to cry, sort of. It didn't feel like crying. More like convulsing, her muscles locking and unlocking in a weird seizure that probably looked every bit as ugly as their last kiss had. It was fitting, in a way.

Every atom in Lex's body ached in protest, but she knew what she had to do. Without a word she closed her eyes and kissed his bloodless, frozen lips, the deathflash blazing as his soul burst from his body. The usual shock exploded through Lex's face, down her neck, and into her torso, ricocheting through her body like a spray of bullets. The pain roiled and seethed until finally coming to a slow, trembling stop, her lips tingling just as they had when he'd first kissed her that night on the roof.

"I'm sorry about this, Lex," Zara said.

At that, Lex immediately stopped crying. She stood up and pulled her hood over her head.

Zara squatted down and started to guide Driggs's blue, wispy soul into her hands. "But you just didn't seem to be grasping the urgency of my situation," she continued. "I made it perfectly clear what it was I wanted from you, and yet you wouldn't give in. So I had to resort to something drastic."

She rocked her head from side to side, cracking the bones in her impossibly skinny neck. "You understand why Driggs, of course. He could reverse the effects of Damning. He would have ruined everything."

In that moment Lex could see just how far gone Zara really was. Whether she was controlling her Damnings or her Damnings were controlling her, it made no difference. That line had blurred into nonexistence.

"He was an obstacle," Zara went on, still collecting the soul, taking her sweet time with it. "He was dangerous. And most of all, he was expendable. You should be thankful I let him die so peacefully. The prospect of stabbing his guts out sure had its charms, but I decided to be merciful and go with hypothermia. So you kind of owe me."

Lex's voice was barely audible. "I owe you *nothing*."

"Oh, but you do." Zara stood up mid-Cull, causing some of the blue mist to drift back into Driggs's body. The whites of her eyes were nearly gone, they were so red. "You owe me that book. It was never supposed to be yours, Lex. *I* was meant to find it. All those notes, those instructions written in code — they were left for *me*." Her voice was growing louder. "He picked me from the start, when I first came to Croak. He showed *me* how to find the Loophole, taught *me* how to Crash with direction, told *me* how to steal your power to Damn. *I* put in all the work! That book is mine!"

Lex narrowed her eyes. "And Driggs was *mine*."

With that, she tackled Zara to the ground and wrapped her hands around her throat.

Zara's eyes bulged. She clutched at Lex's hands, trying to tear them from her neck, but that only made Lex squeeze harder.

Lex could feel Zara's windpipe moving beneath her skin, the

veins in her emaciated neck throbbing against her fingers. Zara's eyes were at once both wonderful and terrible to behold, all confusion and popping blood vessels. Her legs kicked spastically, her tangled silver hair creeping across the snow like a spider web.

And then something odd happened.

Zara's face crumpled.

She was crying. Her eyes swam with tears, panic, and regret. The years of chronic rage melted away, right in front of Lex's eyes. It was as if a younger, more innocent version of Zara had fluttered up to the surface after being shoved down for too long, one that had never meant for any of this to happen.

But Lex didn't stop squeezing.

Not when a new emotion started to register in Zara's gaze, a frenzied horror that heightened as the swirling blue light flowed out from her fingertips, danced through the dots of stationary snow, and rose up into the sky. Not when Zara stared straight at Lex, her fingernails digging into her hands, trying to warn her. Not even when her lips silently mouthed, "Ghost."

Only once Zara was dead did Lex relax her grip.

And that's when the panic set in.

Lex yanked her hands from Zara's neck and looked up. The bluish mist floated away over the town, its light reflecting off the white specks like a glowing wintery aurora.

Driggs.

What had she done?

She took a deep, shuddering breath as the mist faded and the bitter cold finally caught up to her, making her feel more than ever like an insignificant molecule on some forgotten, dead planet.

She had to get out of there. And she'd have to take Zara's body; if she could prove to the townspeople that she'd killed her, maybe a small part of this nightmare would finally be over.

Picking through Zara's pocket, she grabbed her scythe and the bone key, shouldered Uncle Mort's bag, and looked back to steal one last glimpse at Driggs.

But when she turned around, her heart clenched.

His body had disappeared.

25

Lex dropped Zara's body under the Ghost Gum with a thump, next to the sizzling remains of Heloise.

She could barely breathe. Driggs's face swam across her memory, making her retch. It felt as if her bones were shredding themselves into tiny pieces and poking up out of her skin like jagged little splinters.

"Lex?" Uncle Mort stepped out from behind the tree. "Wicket saw the fire and called me — the Juniors are at a hotel — what happened?"

She shook her head but couldn't speak. She started crying again as he took her into his arms.

"Lex? What's wrong?"

She took a few breaths and tried to form the words. It hurt even more to say it out loud. "Zara killed Driggs."

Every muscle in Uncle Mort's body tensed, just as Lex's had. A shuddering breath escaped his lips, as if he'd been punched in the gut. He said nothing, only swallowed a few times and kept stroking her head with trembling hands. "How?" His voice was heavy, as if he were trying not to cry.

"She must have scythed into his cell long before she came for me," she said in a halting voice. "Tied him up, brought him to Greycliff, and just — just left him there in the cold. For I don't know how long." She squeezed her eyes shut. "Then she came back to check me in for a shift — "

"What? How?"

"Sofi. She's the one who's been hacking into our defenses. And then Zara made me scythe, and Driggs was there, and I had to — to Kill — "

Uncle Mort broke away from her, furious. Lex glanced across the Field. A sea of dark shadows was moving across the snow from the direction of the Bank. The townspeople.

Uncle Mort stared at the tree for a long time, then looked down. "And this?" he asked, kicking Zara's body.

Lex stared out from beneath her hood. "I strangled her," she said in an oddly detached voice.

Uncle Mort stared back, breathing heavily. "Good job, kiddo."

A loud hacking noise interrupted them. Lex and Uncle Mort squinted into the darkness, where a figure stumbled toward them through the snow, tripping every couple of feet before falling to the ground.

"No," Lex said, her voice shaking in horror. "*No!* I Damned you!"

Norwood stared at his hand, dazed. "I felt it at first . . ." He cautiously wiggled his fingers. "But I caught your hand, and I . . ."

An all-too-familiar feeling of dread landed hard in Lex's gut. The same one she had felt a few months earlier, when Zara had Culled Lex's power to Damn.

Norwood looked up at her, pure terror in his eyes. "What did you *do* to me?"

Lex shook her head. She didn't want to acknowledge the possibility, didn't even want to *think* that something as insane as that could happen on top of everything else that had gone wrong that night . . .

Norwood finally spotted his wife's grisly remains and began to moan over them, gently stroking her charred form. Uncle Mort reclaimed his bag and dug through it until he found his scythe, just in time to face the townspeople.

They materialized out of the murky snow like an army of ghosts. Some had flashlights. Others had weapons.

All gaped at the bodies of Heloise and Zara yet kept their distance. Norwood staggered to his feet and smoothed his clothes, still staring mournfully at his wife. He looked lost.

"People of Croak," he started, his voice uneven. He cleared his throat and gestured weakly at the bodies. "As you can see, Zara's dead. Lex —"

He broke off and turned around to face Lex, clearly dreading the announcement of her victory. His eyes were desperate, wrecked, as if he had nothing left to live for.

And then — they changed. All at once they blazed with the same wild, crazed hunger that had overtaken Zara.

"Oh, no," Lex whispered.

Norwood turned back to the people. *"I killed Zara."*

The resulting roar of the crowd was terrifying. Riley and Trumbull looked particularly rabid in their approval; Trumbull even waved his butcher's knife.

Lex grabbed Uncle Mort. "He can Damn," she said in a croaking voice. That corrupted look in his eye had confirmed it.

"What?" Uncle Mort hissed. "How?"

"I tried to Damn them both, but he must have Culled my —"

"Lex Damned my wife!" Norwood went on, his voice now strong and loud, cutting through the snow like a blade. "She, Mort, and the other Juniors have been working with Zara all along! They're trying to destroy the Grimsphere, to eradicate our way of life! Are we going to let them?"

"No!" they cried.

"No," Norwood said in a quieter voice, turning back to Lex and Uncle Mort with a wicked smile. "No, we're not."

Uncle Mort took a step back, pulling Lex with him. "We have to run," he whispered, his face ashen. "Crash to the cabin, as close as you can get."

Lex watched the townspeople, who stood in stunned silence for a moment before exploding across the Field toward them, Norwood at the head. "But what about the others?" she panted, kicking up snow as she staggered backwards. "Pandora, Wicket, Lazlo, everyone on our side — we don't know if they're safe!"

"We have to leave them," Uncle Mort said breathlessly, gripping his scythe. "We have to grab the Juniors and get the hell out of here."

Lex reluctantly raised her scythe, a sob shoving its way up out of her throat. *"Why?"*

Uncle Mort shot her one last glance before the two of them disappeared into the ether, his eyes more panicked and alive than she'd ever seen them.

"Because I think you just started a war."

||||||

They landed on the Sticks River bridge.

The world soon reduced itself to a white, fuzzy blur. Lex could hear nothing but the pounding of her feet on the ground and the beating of her own heart as they ran into the forest.

She closed her eyes. Each pulse throbbed through her head like the ticking of a clock. Her whole body ached, a massive bruise. And the panic that had risen in her chest was becoming unbearable.

Not to mention the grief.

"Lex."

She opened her eyes.

Uncle Mort had stopped running. His forehead was shiny with sweat, his normally spiky hair matted down and wet. "You all right, kiddo?" he asked, his eyes crinkling in exhaustion.

Lex said nothing as she tried to catch her breath, worlds and galaxies and universes away from all right. She swept a frozen hand across her face, smearing tears, snot, and snow into a slushy goo on her sleeve.

"He'll be fine, you know," Uncle Mort said.

Lex squinted at him. In the faint light of the moon he looked just as wrecked as she did. Driggs had been like a son to him — they'd lived together, worked together, teamed up to relentlessly mock Lex together. No doubt he'd envisioned great things for his adopted kid, wanted to see him grow up and become the man that he was already so well on his way to becoming.

His grief would be just as strong, and Lex could already see it in his face. Something had gone out in his eyes, something not even she could replace.

"No, he won't," she said.

"You said she killed him, right? Not Damned him?"

"Right, but I —" Her voice was hardly above a whisper. "I think I ghosted him."

Lex could almost hear the blood draining from his face. "What?"

"Zara was Culling his soul when I jumped her, and she let it go. I saw it float away over the town. It never got into the Vessel."

Uncle Mort swallowed, then rubbed the stubble on his chin, then engaged in the usual other tics that happen to people when they're trying not to cry. "Are you sure?"

"Well, his body disappeared . . ."

"What?" He blinked. "Ghosted bodies don't disappear. They decompose just like any other—"

A shout rang out in the distance. Lex, glad to escape any discussion involving the decomposition of Driggs's body, broke into a sprint alongside Uncle Mort. "They found us already?"

"They know we haven't left the town limits," he panted, "and Norwood probably had them scour every inch of the place. It was only a matter of time before they found our tracks in the snow."

They pressed on through the trees, finally arriving at the path to the cabin. "We're going to have to push past the shield," Uncle Mort said between breaths. "It'll hurt, but—"

"No," Lex said, reaching into her pocket and pulling out some leaves. "Eat this. It'll let you through."

Lex truly did feel like shit, but the way her uncle's eyes bulged in shock almost made her feel a little better.

"You got in?" he said. "When did you figure that out?"

"The day we all scythed back to Croak, when I split from the rest of you. But—wait, why are we going to the cabin?" The word alone made her squeeze her scythe even tighter, her hands instantly beginning to sweat. "To get the Wrong Book?"

He gave her a guilty look, the kind he always flashed when owning up to something he'd known about all along.

"To get Grotton."

||||||

Lex did her best to stifle the scream rising in her throat as she followed Uncle Mort through the narrow opening. The last time she'd been in this cabin, she'd never felt so scared in her life. She'd panicked and run, forgetting to take the Wrong Book, forgetting everything but the fear pounding through her head, a terror that had lasted long after she escaped into the snow.

The interior of the cabin glowed a sickly yellow color, the candle on the dusty wooden table throwing strange shadows across the bones that made up the walls. The Wrong Book sat beside it. And behind that, sitting in a chair, was Grotton.

"Hello," he said.

Lex studied the strange man, really got a good look at him this time. He had gray hair but didn't appear to be too ancient — in his sixties, maybe. He no longer wore a white tuxedo, but rather a drab, shapeless ensemble of rags. A knowing grin played on his lips and stood out against his long, sunken face, which was the color of eggshells. His eyes were also gray, but incredibly penetrating, as if he could see right through to the deepest, most humiliating pieces of one's soul.

"Long time no see, Mort," he said, his voice like rustling paper. "Twenty years now?"

"Just about." Uncle Mort practically growled, never breaking eye contact. Lex could see the disgust rippling through his face. These two clearly had a history together.

At least it seemed that way, judging by the way Uncle Mort was rubbing his scar.

"I suppose you're here to kidnap me," said Grotton.

"You going to put up a fight?"

"And ruin the fun before it begins? I wouldn't dream of it."

They were interrupted by a faint rustle coming from the corner of the cabin. Both Lex and Uncle Mort whipped their heads around to face its source, but nothing was there.

Lex looked back at Grotton and grabbed her uncle's arm. Her mind felt like a jigsaw puzzle that had been dumped on the floor. "You told me he was dead," she whispered to Uncle Mort.

"To be fair, he *is* dead."

"Please," Grotton said. "Biologically challenged."

"You told me he was in the Afterlife," Lex said. "Not that he was an undead demon living right in our own backyard!"

"Again with the slander," Grotton said. "A simple 'ghost' would suffice."

That same rustling noise sounded from behind them again, growing louder. This time Lex felt an odd tickle along the base of her neck.

Something was off. True, she'd spent only about thirty seconds with Grotton the last time she'd been here, but in that short time she hadn't felt anything approaching this sensation: a feather running up and down the inside of her spine, sending each of her nerve endings into a blast of chilly prickles.

She turned around once more, expecting to face a blank wall. But this time a figure stood there, flustered and confused and whipping his gaze around the room. His eyes were wide with shock—so wide, in fact, that it was easy to see their color.

One brown, one blue.

Lex stood absolutely still, as if the mere act of breathing would cause him to disappear. She didn't know what her body was doing, but she was pretty sure it wasn't anatomically possible. Her insides were melting, seeping out of her feet.

Finally Driggs's eyes landed on Lex.

He broke into a grin.

And in the space of a yoctosecond, their bodies melded so tightly together they practically threw off sparks. Lex ran her hands through his hair, ignoring the fact that it was still half wet, half frozen.

"You're here," she said, holding his face in her hands, her voice a gooselike mix of confused gasps and joyous screeches. "You're—"

She almost stumbled to the floor, her hands groping at empty space.

"Driggs?"

He popped back into existence on the other side of the cabin. This time, however, he was nothing more than a shimmering outline.

Uncle Mort tentatively reached out to touch Driggs's chest, but his hand passed right through. Driggs showed no indication that he had felt anything. Neither did Uncle Mort, except for the look of horror on his face.

"Okay," Driggs said with an expression that suggested he was trying very hard not to lose it. "That's new."

A sob escaped Lex's throat, the tears forming on her face ones of both joy and heartbreak. "What's going on?"

"I think—" His voice sounded the same, but different some-how—far away. He was flickering now, going from opaque to transparent like a staticky television station. "I'm dead?"

Uncle Mort's eyes were enormous. "Lex said you were ghosted."

"But only part of you!" Lex remembered now. Zara hadn't fin-ished Culling—some of his soul had made it into her hands, and some hadn't. "So you're—what, half ghost and half alive?"

Uncle Mort shook his head. "That isn't possible."

"Of course it is," said Grotton. "He's a Hybrid."

Uncle Mort glared at him. "I've never heard of that before."

"That," said Grotton, "is because I just made it up."

"Hang on," Driggs said. "Does this have anything to do with the fact that I can reverse the effects of Damning?"

"Yes," said Grotton. "You are a Damning Effect Reverser."

They stared at him.

"I made that up as well."

Uncle Mort took a deep, patience-restoring breath and turned back to Driggs. "How did you know where to find us?"

"I didn't." Driggs looked at Grotton. "You brought me here, didn't you? I felt you pulling me."

"We ghosts need to stick together," Grotton said. "Wallowing in eternal torment is much more bearable as a group activity."

Driggs looked sick.

"Don't listen to him," Uncle Mort told Driggs. "You're not a ghost, you're—" He shook his head. "I don't know yet. But we need to leave. Norwood is going to find the head of the path any second now, and I'm not sure how well the shield will hold up against that many people."

Lex was only half listening. She couldn't take her eyes off

Driggs, who was now staring at the candle's flame. Through the palm of his hand.

She went to his side. "I'm so sorry. I'll fix you, I swear. This is all my fault. If I hadn't attacked Zara — "

"Less sorrys," Uncle Mort interrupted, shouldering his bag. "More leaving."

Lex nodded. She'd basically be apologizing to Driggs for this for the rest of her life. It could wait a few hours. "Okay," she told Uncle Mort. "What's the plan?"

"First we grab the other Juniors out of the hotel. Then we make a break for it."

"And go where?"

He paused, seemingly for dramatic effect. "Necropolis."

Lex's eyes bulged. "Seriously?"

"We need to get to the president before Norwood does. If what you told me is true, Lex — if he really can Damn now — then he's a far greater threat than Zara ever was."

"Because he's in a position of influence."

"Right."

"Wait," said Driggs. "Norwood can Damn now?"

"Yeah," Lex said. "Oh, and I started a war. A lot happened in the time it took you to float on over here."

"And none of which we have time to discuss," said Uncle Mort, sticking a foot into the tunnel. "Let's go."

"No."

Driggs was shaking his head. "I'm not going anywhere until you tell us why," he said, the solidness of his body coming and going in waves. "Why for months we've been operating under this secret agenda that you can never seem to talk about. Why you had that Loophole all ready to go for us. Why you dragged us back here to Croak only to get us arrested and tortured. Why we're in this cabin. Why we're in a war. And why starting it was worth my *life*."

Uncle Mort slowly turned around. He looked in the direction of the growing din of the townspeople, then at Lex, then Driggs, his eyes red and downcast. When he spoke, his voice was quiet.

"Simply put, the Afterlife is eroding," he said. "All this human intervention — the Damning, the Loopholes, the Crashing — it's taking a toll on the fabric that holds the Afterlife together. The signs have become more pronounced in just the past few months alone — those vortexes popping up all over the place, and memory deletions, like what happened with Kloo."

"The past few months," Lex said. "You mean, once I got here?"

Uncle Mort neither confirmed nor denied this. "Grims were supposed to be middlemen," he went on. "They were never meant to change the rules or tinker with the constants of the universe. But they have, and they've been doing it for centuries." He shot a pointed look at Grotton. "It's finally come to a head, and if we don't do something about it soon, the Afterlife will — in a word — die."

They were silent. Lex instantly thought of Cordy. What would happen to her? And Edgar and Kloo, and all those billions of souls. Would they just . . . disappear?

"Of course, things never would have gotten this bad if not for that nonsense you pulled with Zara," Uncle Mort shot at Grotton. "Since when are you in the business of training protégées?"

Grotton let out a proper British sniff. "I got bored. Sue me."

"Bored?" Lex butted in, angry. "You taught Zara how to Crash, how to murder people, how to steal my Damning power — you got my sister *killed* — because you were *bored?*"

Grotton gave her an innocent look. "You try being cooped up for centuries in a little box of a room. One gets a bit punchy."

"Punchy, my ass," said Uncle Mort. "You were trying to finish it off. If you can't have an afterlife, then no one can."

Grotton's face darkened. He spoke after a moment in a low, calculating voice. "Why should they? No one truly deserves it."

Uncle Mort clenched his hands into fists, then shook his head and turned away. "Grab the Wrong Book, Lex. He's bound to it; wherever it goes, he goes."

Lex just stood there, her brain reeling with all the people who had suffered because of this man. This *thing.* "He's really coming with us? You trust him?"

"Of course not. But we need him."

"Why?"

Uncle Mort sighed. "Because the only way to fix this mess is to destroy the one who made it in the first place."

Lex glanced at Grotton, who didn't even look fazed by this statement. Almost as if he'd been expecting it.

Or hoping for it.

"How do we destroy him?" she asked.

"Not we," Uncle Mort said, his voice low. "You."

Lex swallowed, once again getting that strange feeling of expanding, of growing out into something much larger than herself. This time it seemed astronomical.

Grotton gave Lex a devious smile, his teeth cracked and yellow. "Looks like you're stuck with me, love."

A yell rang out from somewhere outside the cabin. "They're almost here," Uncle Mort said. "Seriously, we have to leave. Now." He dropped to the floor and started crawling through the narrow tunnel.

Driggs walked directly through a wall, then stuck his head back in. "Well, that's a perk."

"Enjoy it while you can," Grotton said. "It gets old rather quickly."

Driggs came back into the cabin and eyed him. "Do you know why I can unDamn?"

"I do."

"And what about me?" said Lex. "Am I the Last?"

Grotton looked between the two of them, then let out a nasty, mischievous chuckle. "What fun we're all going to have together," he said, passing through the wall to the outside. "What fun!"

That left Lex and Driggs alone in the small room. The candle was about to run out of wick and the light had diminished considerably; darker shadows flung themselves up the walls, trying to escape.

Driggs looked at Lex. "This is fucked up."

"To put it mildly."

"We're in a war."

"I know."

"Then why," he asked, "are you smiling?"

Because Uncle Mort had her back, and always would. Because Grotton was real, and would soon pay for his crimes. Because Driggs was broken, but she was going to fix him. She was going to fix everything.

Lex grabbed the Wrong Book with one hand, her scythe with the other, and stepped toward the tunnel, still grinning.

"Because we're going to win it."

Gina Damico grew up under four feet of snow in Syracuse, New York. She received a degree in theater and sociology from Boston College, where she was active with the Committee for Creative Enactments, a murder mystery improv comedy troupe that may or may not have sparked an interest in wildly improbable bloodshed. She has since worked as a tour guide, transcriptionist, theater house manager, scenic artist, movie extra, office troll, retail monkey, yarn hawker, and breadmonger. Her first novel was *Croak*. She lives outside of Boston with her husband, two cats, and a closet full of black hoodies.

www.ginadami.co